PRAISE FOR
THE LITTLE THINGS *that* KILL

"A compassionate exploration of friendship and betrayal wrapped up in a true page-turning mystery. In Fox's YA mystery, a teenager must piece together the truth behind her apparent suicide—and the events leading up to it—from beyond the grave . . . Fox's captivating mystery explores adolescent friendships, betrayals, and suicide with cleverness and an abundance of compassion. The characters are well developed, distinctive, and compelling. (Nicole, a gifted singer-songwriter, guitar player, and actor, is sympathetic and relatable; she's also judgmental and a bit conniving.) Readers will enjoy the author's imaginative worldbuilding and exploration of the supernatural and will be especially enthralled by the dizzying twists and turns as the circumstances surrounding Nicole's death are revealed."
— KIRKUS REVIEWS (STARRED REVIEW)

"Fox (author of *Leeta Simtar*) explores teen angst, the power of friendship, and the spirit world in this redemptive supernatural drama."
— BOOKLIFE BY PUBLISHER'S WEEKLY

"Using humour and pathos, Annie Fox leads her audience through the last tragic hours of the life of sixteen-year-old Nicole Sondra Benson to a fitting conclusion."
— JULIE HAISELDEN, WHISPERING STORIES

". . . a really great book . . . [I] would recommend it to anyone that loves YA, witchy, self-discovery books."
— LISA, GOODREADS

"Annie got me in ALL my feelings with this story! I am completely blown away . . . it reached me on a very emotional level and REALLY hit home for me!"
— VIXEN, GOODREADS

"I absolutely love this story made me cry a few times . . .
I highly recommend it . . .
and can't wait to read more by this author."
— @CHERYLLINSIMMS

"The author really understands teens, their emotions, and their angst. If you enjoyed *Before I Fall* or *If I Stay*, you will definitely enjoy this book!"
— @NYXIE.READS

"Wow. The last young adult book I read I felt as if I rolled my eyes the entire time, but Annie Fox brought young adult novels to a whole new level. As a 30-year-old I could not put this book down. I would recommend, as well as read again!"
— @BASIC_BOOK_GIRL

"This book has me all up in my emotions. The amount of tears I shed reading this book is insane . . . made my heart ache. I really look forward to reading more by Annie."
— KRISTINA, GOODREADS

"I absolutely loved this book. I devoured [it] in 24 hours . . .
full of emotion, friendship, guilt, grief, betrayal,
and so much more."
— AUDREY COULOMBE, GOODREADS

". . . authentic portrayal of female friendships . . . a must-read for paranormal enthusiasts looking for an engrossing and thought-provoking story."
— @BIBYLIKESTIKTOK

". . . a unique paranormal story that keeps you hooked from the very first pages . . . a standout in its genre."
— CARMEN, GOODREADS

". . . a wonderful story about taking responsibility for your actions, especially when they hurt other people."
— JILLY BEAN, GOODREADS

THE LITTLE THINGS that KILL

LIBRARY
Restricted Area: Mentors Only
Reflection Center
ORientation
SANCTUARY
SUBSTATION 15
Meditation Center

Evaluation Hall
Memory Projection
Meeting Area
Dormitories
Advanced Tutorials
Dream Tour
Amphitheater

Other Books by Annie Fox

- *The Teen Survival Guide to Dating and Relating*
- *Too Stressed to Think? A Teen Guide to Staying Sane When Life Makes You Crazy (with Ruth Kirschner)*
- *Middle School Confidential Book 1: Be Confident in Who You Are*
- *Middle School Confidential Book 2: Real Friends vs. the Other Kind*
- *Middle School Confidential Book 3: What's Up with My Family?*
- *Are You My Friend? A Raymond and Sheila Story*
- *Are We Lost? A Raymond and Sheila Story*
- *People Are Like Lollipops*
- *Teaching Kids to Be Good People: Progressive Parenting for the 21st Century*
- *The Girls Q&A Book on Friendship: 50 Ways to Fix a Friendship Without the DRAMA*

More at books.AnnieFox.com

The Little Things that KILL

A Teen Friendship Afterlife Apology Tour

BY ANNIE FOX

Electric Eggplant

ElectricEggplant.com

Cover illustration by Liz Amini-Holmes

ISBN-13: 978-1-943649-08-2

Visit us at TheLittleThingsThatKill.com

*For David, you make everything possible,
even the impossible.*

EMILY. Do any human beings ever realize
    life, while they live it? — every, every mi-
    nute?

STAGE MANAGER. No.

    —Thornton Wilder, *Our Town* (3)

Nicole

A SHRILL BUZZER splits my brain in two.

My hand searches for my phone, but it's nowhere. If I have to open my eyes to find my phone to stop the damn alarm, I'll never get back to sleep. I must have left it in the pocket of my jacket, which is . . . somewhere. BUZZ. BUZZ. BUZZ. Shut up, phone. Dad will hear and walk right in with his way-too-cheerful-for-this-time-of-day "Rise and shine, curly girl" routine. I'm not ready to rise, and I sure don't feel like shining. I just want to sleep.

Thank God, the buzzing stopped.

I try to fall back to sleep, but a copper light seeps under my eyelids. What now? Did I forget to close the shades? I must have been out of it when I came in last night. Where was I? Can't remember. Just go to sleep. Yeah, right. Not with that light in my face. Geez, can't a girl go out and have fun without an insanely early wakeup call from Mr. Sunshine?

All right. All right. You win. I'm up.

A spotlight blinds me. I shield my eyes, but there's no escaping the brightness. A shadowy figure appears up ahead.

"Dad?"

The figure is there and gone before I can make out who it was. I blink hard and the light splinters into a thousand tiny rainbows shooting in all directions. In the remaining soft glow, a crowded room comes into focus, only it's not my room. I'm standing on a large round platform rimmed by a sleek, transparent, shoulder-high barrier. I might have been here before, but I can't remember when. There have to be at least twenty kids standing around. Most look around sixteen like me, but a few are super young. What is this place? It's not actually a place at all. There are no walls, no ceiling or sky, only this floating platform in the middle of nowhere. Why does it feel familiar? I don't know any of these people. I want to go home. I'm calling Dad to come pick me up. *Where's my phone?*

I touch the sleeve of the dark-haired guy in front of me. "Hey, where are we?"

He turns. Blood covers his face and hands. A gunshot must have blown that hole in his gut. I'm going to puke. The guy stares at the right side of my head and looks like *he's* going to puke.

"What are you looking at?" I ask.

He turns away, like he's seriously grossed out. This has to be some sick joke, but now I'm worried. I pretend to fuss with my hair so I can walk my fingers around the spot he was staring at. I don't feel a break in the skin. I press down hard. There. And there. Nothing hurts. No blood on my hand. Thank God.

A moment later, the guy turns back to me. His wound has vanished. No blood anywhere. How can that be? A blond girl catches me staring at the oozing red slashes on her wrists. She snarls and flips me off. My face flushes hot and cold. I sneak another look. Her cuts are gone. A freckled, red-haired mouse of a girl in a lime-green hoodie huddles at the base of the barrier, trembling like a pile of feathers. She nibbles her raw cuticles and stares out at nothing, like she's trying to un-see something horrible. Her singed bangs and eyebrows smell of smoke and rotten eggs. An instant later, she's not singed and doesn't stink.

What's with this on-and-off house of horrors? What are all these people waiting for? What is this place? Looks like a bus stop for dead kids. Maybe I'm dead. I pat my body all over. Nope. I'm fine. It's just a dream. Still, scary as hell and way too real. What does Iz call hyper-real dreams? *Lucid* dreams. Right, that's what this is. Relax. You can't die in a dream. Good. Settled. Not dead. But why do I feel like an empty paper bag?

More kids pop onto the platform out of nowhere, one at a time, in quick succession—POP. POP. POP. With each one the same annoying buzzer sounds. Forget Mr. Sunshine. That's a wake-up call for the dead. I'm *not* dead!

A skinny bald girl with sunken eyes clings to herself like she's freezing. A kid squirms on the floor, gasping for air like he's drowning. He's soaking wet, but there's no water here. I offer my hand to pull him to his feet. He knocks my arm away and yells for someone named Danny. If Danny is here, he doesn't let on. What is wrong with this kid? What's wrong with all of them? I cover my ears, but the drowning kid's cries grow louder and more pathetic. Suddenly quiet, he stands and breathes normally, his hair and clothes perfectly dry.

Oh. Now I remember. The party. *Kyle plays City of Stars on his electric keyboard.*

He recorded himself and gave it to me for my ringtone.

I sing, "There's so much that I can't see . . ." Some people listen and sway to the music. Kyle smiles at me dreamily, the way he always does when I sing. I smile back and pretend not to watch Cassie and Alex making out against the wall. Their bodies merge like puzzle pieces as if they were one person, like that stupid name they made up for themselves: Calex. It kills me to see them, but I can't stop looking. Someone hands me a cup of beer. I chug most of it in one gulp.

There must have been something in the beer. I'm tripping. That's what this is. Rule #1: Never befriend a girl whose friends are druggies. Rule #2: Don't fall for her boyfriend. If she doesn't get back at you, her friends will. This stuff better wear off soon. I seriously need to wake up.

I lightly slap my cheeks, rapid fire. Nothing changes. An

old woman in a ridiculous neon purple vest, long white shirt and matching leggings, stands tiptoe, her back to a see-through sliding door. She studies me as if I'm a lost sock that turned up in the fridge. My heart revs like I'm in big trouble for something I did, only I can't remember what. I pretend to check my reflection in the glassy barrier, but I can't find my-self. The surface is blank. No reflections of any of us. I pound the barrier with both fists. Wake up! Crap. I'm still here.

I don't want to talk to Grandma Purple Vest, but I've got to find out what's going on. I elbow my way to her, blocking out everything around me as best as I can.

"Excuse me." I don't recognize the squeak that seems to be my voice. "Could you please step on my foot? Really hard?"

She chuckles softly. "No need for that, sweetie." To every-one else she booms, "Please prepare for departure."

Depart for where? Prepare how?

A sonic boom shreds the air. The herd spooks, frantically searching for a way out. Only one exit. No getting past Grandma. There must be fifty of us now, girls and guys, many are crying.

"Don't worry," I tell them. "We'll get out of here."

The crowd contracts around me until we are crammed to-gether so tightly there is no breathing room. I am seriously going to kill Cassie. Then Calex will just be Alex, and he and I will finally be together.

The vibration under my feet snaps me back to the plat-form. We rise quickly, gaining speed, until a sci-fi wormhole of swirling energy appears overhead. As if in warp drive, we rocket through the portal and enter a sea of stars from distant galaxies. Up ahead a towering cloud, gorgeous and terrifying, drifts in space like a cosmic ghost. I've seen this before. It's a nebula. Did I fall asleep again watching Nova? I can almost hear Tom Hanks's voice: *"Dust and gas thrown from the explo-sion of a dying star become the birthplace of new stars."*

I don't know if the space cloud is real, but it's so amazing I can't look away. Why isn't anyone else watching this? Be-cause the masses are asses. Isn't that what Cassie says?

As we speed through the cosmos, the stars spread farther apart. Endless night presses in like a cold weight, stomping out all hope. With no galactic lightshow to distract me, I slip toward Crazytown. I don't know where I am. Neither does anyone else who cares about me. I've got nothing to hold on to, but I'm holding on anyway, trying my hardest not to let go.

Without warning, we emerge into the amber half-light of a distant sun. Woozy, I grab the arm of a short guy. He whips around, eyes locked on my chest as if he can see my boobs through my top. He smiles hungrily, like he's eyeing a pizza with extra cheese. My neck heats with outrage. I want to shove him, shame him. Instead, I cross my arms tightly over my chest and try to turn away, but there is no room to turn. A large girl with golden-brown skin steps forward and bumps the guy off balance with her hip. Shorty finds a crack in the crowd and scrambles away like the bug he is.

She nods at me as if to say, "That's how to send a message."

Point taken.

An angry, ugly-looking bruise the size of a small water balloon, appears in the middle of her forehead. I gag. My legs give way. Golden Girl catches me under the arms. I force myself to look at her. Bruise gone. She's beautiful again.

Brain, quit messing with me.

"Prepare for arrival at Substation Thirteen," Grandma Vestie says, her voice loud and cheery.

The platform breaks through a layer of clouds. A vast, green, sunlit meadow spreads below us. It's filled with people, old and young, all barefoot and wearing flowing white shirts over white leggings. Purple Vesties wander among them. Everyone looks radiantly healthy. The platform hovers, slowly descends, and stops. The door slides open.

"Substation Thirteen."

I have no clue what Substation Thirteen is or why we're here, but some of the others must know. One by one, at least thirty kids step off the platform onto a moving walkway that noiselessly carries them into fog so dense they're swallowed whole. I want nothing to do with whatever is happening inside that monster fog. Golden Girl and I frown at each other in silent agreement. Not getting off here.

The door closes. "Prepare for departure. Next stop, Substation Fourteen."

The platform accelerates so quickly I stumble against a guy wearing a red basketball jersey. He throws up his hands, his ears turning redder than his shirt. I want to tell him that he did nothing wrong, but there's no time.

"Prepare for arrival."

We descend. Another lovely meadow with more healthy-looking kids, adults, and Purple Vesties comes into view.

"Substation Fourteen."

A breeze fragrant with ginger, cinnamon, and honey pushes through the open door. Dad's peach cobbler. Something tells me this is my stop.

I head toward the door. Mousy shuffles up beside me, sucking her fingers and smelling of smoke again. She grips my wrist with a soggy hand as her sad eyes search my face. I pretend to be confused, but I know exactly what she wants. I shake her loose and feel mean and ashamed. She looks away and takes her place on the moving walkway. Mousy and Basketball Guy and . . . two, four, six, eight, ten others . . . slide through a wall of mist.

I nudge Golden Girl. "Are you getting off here?"

She shakes her head.

Hmm. Maybe I should stay too. A weird impulse tugs at my brain. I step forward, but Grandma Vestie raises a bony finger in my direction. My shoes stick to the platform. I struggle but get nowhere.

"Hey, what are you doing? I have to get off here."

Grandma smiles kindly. "Not this time, dearie. Prepare for departure."

As we rise above the substation, the smell of peaches fades along with all expectations of a quick end to this insanity. Grandma Vestie flicks her finger and unsticks my feet.

"Please take me back to Fourteen."

We continue to ascend.

"You're making a mistake." I'm shouting now.

The other kids eye me like I'm some kind of psycho. I don't care what they think. I rush the door, but Substation Fourteen is already far below us. A wave of dizziness forces me back from the edge. No way am I jumping down there.

"Where are we going?"

"Don't worry. Everything is going to be fine. You'll get to where you belong." Grandma Vestie smiles reassuringly.

I'm not reassured.

Of the three kids left, I could definitely do without two of them. Shorty waggles his tongue in my direction. Jerk. Blondie flips me off with both hands. Golden Girl presses her arms to her sides, rhythmically blowing air between her lips like she's trying to keep herself from losing it.

"Prepare for arrival at Substation Fifteen."

The cloud cover parts and we land so softly it takes a moment to realize we've stopped.

"Substation Fifteen. Everybody out."

"No. I belong on Fourteen."

What am I talking about? I belong at home, in Veraz, California.

Blondie storms off the platform. Shorty pauses to adjust his crotch. He must think he's invisible. He's not invisible until the walkway drags him into the fog. An eerie brick red light pierces the mist. Whatever that light is, it can't be good.

Golden Girl raises a questioning eyebrow. I shake my head. She shrugs, waves goodbye, and steps onto the walkway. My throat tightens as she vanishes with the rest of them.

Iz waves from the car window. I sulk over our lost summer plans. I won't teach her to play the guitar she got for her birthday but hasn't yet touched. We won't do our first solo, full moon campout. We won't finish making her movie, Beyond Normal.

When she first told me her family was going to Thailand, we talked about the tsunami that swept away 227,000 people in fourteen countries. She said that could happen again but she wasn't worried because she had performed her special protection ritual using extra black salt, and Yolanda, her spirit guide, assured her that she wouldn't die in a flood. I was relieved, but only for a minute.

"Did she say how you would die?" I ask.

"In a public restroom."

I laugh nervously. "Yeah, right."

Iz shrugs. "It's okay that you don't believe. Even though you know that Yolanda's never wrong."

I stop laughing. It's true. Yolanda told m e I'd have good luck if I tried out for Our Town. *She was right. She also predicted my falling out with Cassie. I'm not a hundred percent with any of Iz's witchy stuff. Maybe it doesn't matter since she's one thousand percent into it. Still, thinking about Iz dying freaks me out.*

"Do you have to go? You could stay at my house."

"Don't worry, Nic. I swear to the Goddess Eternal that I won't use any public restrooms in Thailand. And if I drink too much tea, I'll hold it in until I get back to the hotel."

A wordless song filters through the fog like the wind chime outside my bedroom window. The silvery bells make me smile. That's *my* wind chime buried in this druggie dream. Just follow the sound and I'll wake up in bed. Go!

"It's time to go, Nicole," Grandma Vestie says softly. "Learn and progress."

How does she know my name?

Isabel

T HE FIRST MATCH sparks and dies. The head of the second snaps off and drops on the rug, also dead. I strike a third. A steady flame. Thank Goddess. Now, which candle should I light? Black or red? Black releases negative energy. Also good for healing. Nic and I definitely need that. Red protects, strengthens, provides courage. We need that too. Red or black? Black or red? Ow! I fling what's left of the match into my offering bowl. It doesn't belong there, but I leave it. Trying to ignore my burned finger, I strike another match and quickly light both candles.

Sitting cross-legged before my altar, I reach for the rose quartz crystal at the end of my necklace, press it to my heart.

"Goddess Eternal, I need your help. Open the channel."

I balance the Ouija board on my knees and center the planchette.

"I welcome all benevolent spirits to my space. The portal is open. My channel is open. My heart is open. I need your guidance. Speak, benevolent spirits. I am listening."

Suddenly my heart smacks against my ribs like a ball against a wall. What's this? Cardiac arrest? Sixteen-year-olds don't typically have heart attacks, but it's not impossible. I force myself to inhale slowly through my nose, exhale slowly through my mouth, again and again, while the wild thumping in my chest rages on. After twelve breathing cycles, my heart rate returns to normal. Thank Goddess. Not a heart attack. Just stress. I hope.

I place my fingertips on the planchette. A jolt of electricity races up my arms, across my shoulders to the back of my neck, where it grabs me, like a collar of icy pinpricks. Now what? Am I having a stroke? Strokes are even rarer in teens than heart attacks. But what else could it be? I lift my hands off the planchette. The prickling stops. Thank Goddess. It's not a stroke.

Then it must be a sign.

I've read about witches who receive signs right before a troubled spirit comes through the portal. Headaches. Cold teeth. Pulsing sensations on the tip of the tongue. I hope that's not what's happening because troubled spirits can cause lots of problems. I'm not sure I'd know what to do. I don't know anything about them. Yolanda isn't troubled, though she can be annoying at times. Her energy often vibrates at sloth levels and she drags the planchette around the board so slowly it can take thirty seconds to get from one letter to the next. If I figure out what she's trying to spell and say the word before she's done, she leaves and refuses to return until I apologize. Which I always do, because I love Yolanda. She's my spirit guide, always kind and helpful.

Nic says she doesn't believe in spirits. Sometimes she jokes about it. Like that time we were walking on Drake Boulevard and passed the shop called *Psychic Readings by Diana.*

Nic pointed to the Out of Business sign in the window and said, "I wonder if Diana saw that coming?"

Then she laughed so hard at her own joke she hyperventilated. Next came one of her hiccupping fits.

I told her it wasn't funny, but it kinda was.

Even though Nic insists she doesn't believe in spirits, she's turned to Yolanda plenty of times to ask about her future with

Alex. But last week Yolanda let her have it.

"*Why should I help you, Nicole?*" Yolanda zipped through the spelling, her anger surging under my fingertips. "*You called the talking board a toy. You called the planchette a ghost phone.*"

Nic's mouth fell open and for a long moment she just stared at the board. Then she cracked up.

"Good one, Iz. Impressive speed spelling."

"What? You think that was me?"

"Uh, huh. But you can still tell Yolanda I'm sorry."

"Tell her yourself."

Nic bent over the board and cupped her hands around her mouth. "Sorry, Yolanda."

The planchette spelled out "O K."

I smiled. Nic smiled. I sensed Yolanda smiling too.

So Nic says she doesn't believe in spirits, but she obviously believes in *magik* because she asks me to do spells for her. I know that spirits and spells are essentially the same thing. Of course, everyone's on their own path and Nic's my best friend, so I will always try to help her. Even if she doesn't think that's what I'm doing.

But maybe on some level Nic really does believe in all of it. Why else would she have surprised me on my birthday by bringing over her guitar and singing that song she wrote for me?

> Goddess Eternal, who gives so much
> With loving heart and loving trust
> Guide our lives in the Light
> Golden sun by day
> Silver moon by night
> May we love all beings, in all seasons
> Trust in the truth without seeking reasons

"Oh, Nic, thank you. I love your melody. Haunting and powerful. But how'd you know the words?"

"The other day when I came over and you were in the bathroom? I snooped in your Book of Spells. I hope you don't mind."

"No. It's fine. I'm happy to show you any of my spells, any time.

But there are so many. How'd you know that one was my favorite?"

"Easy. I went to the page with the most wax drippings."

Now that was funny. And true.

I touch the planchette again. It vibrates a bit and the prickling intensifies. Whoever this is, it's not Yolanda. I've never talked to anyone else from the Other Side except once. A spirit named Cookie came through, venting about her daughter and son-in-law who had poisoned her and dumped her body off a rental boat in Miami. She said if I didn't call the police, those two would get away with murder and take all her money. I called right away and left an anonymous tip, but I never found out if the murderers were caught. I felt bad about not being able to help Cookie. I performed a powerful forgiveness ritual, but I never heard from her again.

The planchette is rocking violently and the back of my neck feels like a party for fire ants. I need to rub the spot but I don't want to lift my fingers and break the connection. I breathe deeply and hang on.

"Greetings, whoever you are. Welcome. How can I help you?"

I've never asked to help a spirit before, but I need some good Karma after the fight with Nic. She must still be mad because she's not answering my texts.

The planchette zips back and forth across the board, bouncing between two letters.

I-Z-I-Z-I-Z-I-Z-I-Z-I-Z-I-Z-I-Z-I-Z

Iz? Nic is the only one who calls me that. My stomach seizes, and a wave of nausea rolls up and hangs behind my heart chakra like a time bomb. I release the planchette. Where's my phone? I shake out everything from my backpack. Pens, tarot cards, my charm bag. THUD. My phone. My hands shake and it's hard to type . . .

Hey, Nic. Are you OK?

I press SEND, willing the dots to pop up right away. They don't.

I text again.

Nic, I'm really sorry.
Please talk to me.

Nothing.

"Hey, Siri, call Nic." It goes to voice mail immediately. "Nic. You're scaring me. Where are you?"

An other-worldly howl from out in the hallway makes me drop the phone. The pitiful wail sounds like a dog locked out in a storm.

Or a ghost.

There's only one thing I know for certain at this moment. We don't have a dog.

I put my ear against the door. The howling becomes a moan. It's a spirit. A very troubled one. I should help it. No! I should not open the door. What am I thinking? Spirits can pass *through* doors. Maybe if I cast a protection spell, I can block it. I run to the shelf and grab my Book of Spells. I'm flipping pages, but I'm freaking out and it's hard to read.

From out in the hallway a familiar voice cries, "Isabel!"

It's Mom. Is the spirit hurting her? I yank open the door. Mom sits alone on the floor, slumped against the banister. My stomach free-falls.

"Mom, are you okay?"

She looks up, her face twisted in agony. She reaches for me. Her hand cold and sweaty. As she pulls me down beside her, she squeezes my fingers so hard it hurts.

"Mom, what's wrong?"

She looks away. After a moment, she inhales sharply, turns back and gently rests a hand on the side of my face.

"Sweetheart, I have some very sad news."

I know what it is. Don't tell me. I don't want to hear it. I *can't* hear it.

She swallows hard, eyes streaming. "Nicole is dead."

She wraps her arms around me and pulls in close, holding on like she'll never let go.

Nicole

GOLDEN GIRL SLIDES into the lightless tunnel, right behind Blondie and Shorty. I strain to hear what's going on inside. Silence. At least they're not being hurt, otherwise they'd scream. Not necessarily. Maybe they've been killed instantly. Ohmygod, I'm next!

I turn and run as fast as I can against the flow of the walkway. I swear I won't let this treadmill from hell feed me to that death trap. Maybe I can climb over the handrail.

As if the walkway senses my plan, it kicks into higher gear, jerks me to my knees, and speed-drags me backward into the tunnel.

"No!"

It's so dark I feel like I've disappeared. The pulse in my ears pounds as loudly as a Pacific storm hammering our roof, threatening to punch a hole in it or rip it off completely. How do I get out of here?

Follow the sound of the wind chime and you'll wake up in bed.

I don't hear chimes.

The palest shade of arctic blue light flashes around me. Hot air from below carries the faint smell of chlorine.

I am sitting in the bleachers between Cassie and Kyle, watching Alex warm up for his swim meet. It's muggy inside the pool building, and I'm sweating.

"Hey, Alex!" Cassie calls down to him in her sexy voice. Alex grins and waves. To all of us or just her?

Cassie was in a good mood at that point. A half hour earlier, when I rang her apartment bell, her mom was screaming at her on the other side of the door. I seriously considered ducking down the hall and waiting outside, but there wasn't time. Grim-faced, Cassie slipped out of the apartment. Neither of us said a word.

Iz always told me whenever she and her mom, Mandy, had a fight. It was usually about Mandy snooping through Iz's stuff, but if it was something bigger and she wouldn't tell me exactly what went down, I'd bug her until she did. Iz performed spells to help me, and I gave her advice on how to handle her parents. Cassie and I weren't that kind of friends. She never asked about my mom, and I didn't ask about hers. Most of the time, that made Cassie easier to be with than other people I met in high school.

Cassie yanks off my hood. My hair poofs out. "Quit it!" I pull up my hood and press my hands against so she can't do it again.

"You said you were sweating," Cassie says, like she did me a favor.

"I am, but now my hair is total frizz."

"No, it's not," Kyle's voice is gentle. "You look nice."

I had forgotten he was next to me. The look in his eyes makes me feel a little bit better about myself—and a little worse.

Cassie shrugs. "What's the big deal? Your hair always looks like that."

"Thanks a lot."

Thank God, Alex is at the other end of the pool.

"Stop!" I yell into the darkness.

The walkway stops dead. Whoa. It's smart, like Siri. When I get out of here, *if* I get out of here, I'm going to have an amazing drug trip story to tell.

A high-pitched CHEE, CHEE, ZING triggers a slight tingling at the top of my head and spreads down through my arms and legs.

"Cut it out!" The tingling stops. "Take me back to the platform."

As if mocking me, the walkway starts up again, continuing in the same direction as before, only faster this time. Hmm. Maybe it's too smart. I emerge from the tunnel, squinting, preparing to be blasted by light, but oddly, my eyes immediately adjust to the brightness. Golden Girl rides in front, alongside Shorty and Blondie. I hurry to catch up and tap Golden Girl's arm. "How weird was that?" I ask.

She barely acknowledges me. Shorty turns and we briefly make eye contact. I dare him to look at my chest. Lucky for him, he doesn't. Even Blondie isn't sneering or flipping me off. They all seem vacant, like they've been turned into zombies. I'm barefoot like the rest of them. All of us wear the same flowing white shirts over white leggings. The fabric, cool and soft against my skin, shimmers like sunlight on dragonfly wings. My thick, crazy hair that always sticks out in all directions, no matter how much product I slather on, miraculously hangs along the sides of my face like a flawless silk curtain. Finally, a perfect hair day, only Alex isn't here to see me. No one I know is. There aren't even any mirrors. Everything is white. White walkway, white windowless buildings, a glowing white domed ceiling, and an endless expanse of flat, white, empty space. Whose idea of décor is this? What is this place supposed to be? A germaphobe's idea of heaven? *Heaven*. My stomach sinks like a rock in a swimming pool. Are these kids really dead? Is that why they're acting like zombies? What am I doing here? I don't feel like a zombie. Maybe I'm *less* dead. Is that even a thing?

My thoughts blur like egg yolks in a mixer. I stare at my hand. My fingers shrink to the size of stubs. Underneath the skin a vein rises, blue and thick. The head of a snake breaks through and lunges at my face, jaws snapping angrily.

This can't be real. I shut my eyes. I hear murmuring in languages I can't understand. It all sounds like people pleading for . . . something. Their lives? Should I be pleading too? Is that the way out of here? My heart pounds so fiercely I can't breathe. This drug trip is going to kill me. See? That proves I'm not dead *yet*. Someone would tell me if I was.

Not necessarily.

I scream, long and loud.

No one reacts. I'm cracking up. I can't feel my pulse. Did my heart stop?

I scream again.

My throat burns. I stop. What's the point?

"Everything's going to be fine," Grandma Vestie said.

Why should I believe her? Why believe anyone here? Which is . . . who the hell knows where?

I can't be dead. This can't be happening. But what if it is?

A tidal wave of terror wipes me out, pulls me under, and drags me down. I sink to the floor, flattened by an invisible slab of concrete on my chest. I can't breathe. I can't move. If this is death, I can't do it. Not alone.

But no one here cares about me. They're so out of it they don't even care about themselves. There's got to be someone, somewhere, who can help me. Boy, was I wrong about all that witchy spiritual stuff. It's real. Iz was right and she knows all about it. She can help me. She may be the only one who can. All I have to do is reach her. Maybe she's thinking about me right this minute. Maybe she can hear me.

"Iz, please help me. I need you."

Nicole

"HELLO, NEWEST ARRIVALS, welcome to Substation Fifteen." A programmed fairy godmother voice fills the space where the walkway dumped us into a dimly lit room. Blondie, Shorty, Golden Girl, and I stand shoulder to shoulder with a few dozen other kids who must have come up on platforms before and after ours. People look around and whisper nervously to each other. I don't like being this close to a bunch of strangers, and I'm in no mood for socializing, but it's starting to feel like I don't get choices around here. In front of the room is a projection of a 3-D map.

"You are here," the gentle voice continues.

On the map, a small, forest green light pulses beside a model of a round white building. It's the first bit of color I've seen since I got here, not counting the flashing blue light in the tunnel and the revolting purple vests. God, I miss colors. It's like my eyes have been on a sensory deprivation diet of white on white. How long have I been here? I don't know. Breakfast is the last thing I remember.

I slice into my stack of blueberry pancakes, releasing a squirt of indigo juice into a puddle of amber syrup.

Dad and I made those pancakes together. Then we ate. Nothing special about that. But it feels like something big happened *after* breakfast and right before I found myself on that flying platform. *Think.* I left the house. To go where? We are still on Winter Break, so I wasn't on my way to school. It couldn't have been that long ago. I feel like an idiot, not remembering. Give it a rest. Sometimes a memory comes back if I focus on something else. Pay attention to the talking map.

The soothing voice drones on. "We trust your journey has been a comfortable one."

Depends on how you define comfortable.

"During your stay here at Substation Fifteen, you'll prepare for The Evaluation, which you must pass before moving on to your next destination."

I step closer to the map. "Are you saying we're all here to take a test?" It feels very weird talking to a projection, because, obviously, the voice is programmed, but there's no one else to talk to except these other newbies who seem to be sleepwalking.

"Is there a test on Substation Fourteen?" I want to know. "I was supposed to get off there, not here." Without warning my knees fold and I sit on the white-white floor. "How did you do that?"

"No questions, Nicole."

Ooh. Fairy godmother just turned into a bitch. And how does everyone know my name? That can't be programmed.

"Pay attention, Nicole."

What's she talking about? I'm the only one around here who *is* paying attention. Everyone else is zombied out.

I get back on my feet as the map expands to fill the entire front of the room. Whoa! There, on the projection. Blondie, Shorty, Golden Girl and me are exiting the tunnel. They recorded us. How creepy is that? They're probably still doing it.

I scan the ceiling. Nothing looks like a camera, but obviously there's something I can't see that sees *me!*

"Now where was I?" Fairy godmother is back. "Oh yes. Since you've all passed through the decompression tunnel and completed your transition, you are ready to learn and progress. Substation Fifteen's top priority is to provide comfort as you process your ordeal."

What ordeal?

"Throughout your stay at Substation Fifteen we will give you all the love, support, and encouragement you need. We will also equip you with whatever tools and resources your process requires. We hope you take full advantage of this special opportunity. At the conclusion of this brief orientation each of you will meet your personally assigned Mentor and receive your customized handbook. Actually, the only customized part is the first page. All the other pages apply to all of you. We encourage you to utilize your Mentor and handbook well. Both will be invaluable in helping you prepare for your Evaluation which will take place in thirty days."

I've heard enough. I rush to the door. It's the same kind of slider they had on the platform. No handle or anything. I push against it. Nothing.

"Nicole, stay in your place."

"No!"

A few newbies shift uncomfortably. I guess they are awake. One clears his throat, but mostly it's just zombie crickets. They act like they don't see or hear me, but I know they do. Golden Girl tosses me a worried look. It's sweet that she cares, but I've got this.

"I'm not sure I belong here," I whisper to the guy on my right. "Are you?"

He nods. "Oh yeah. Definitely."

"I'm not sure I belong here either." A girl on the other side of the room shouts to me.

"Okay," I stand a little taller. "I'm not the only one. Someone made a mistake. Open the door. I want to talk to the person in charge."

"That's enough," snaps the map voice.

The same unseen force Grandma Vestie used to nail me to the platform now sticks me to the floor. These guys must know they screwed up, otherwise they wouldn't be trying so hard to intimidate me.

"Fine." I pretend this latest trap is no biggie. "You're

stronger than I am, but you can't shut me up." I raise my voice. "I don't . . ." My jaw locks. Shit. They *can* shut me up. Not only that, I'm back in my place, in front of the map. How did that happen?

"Substation Fifteen has several unique sectors. Let's get familiar with each of them."

A cluster of sky-blue lights flash in the southeast sector of the map. I can't turn my head. They're making me watch this.

"Dormitories for new arrivals are here. Yours is Building Two, where you will find all the comforts of home."

Yeah. Right.

Sage-green lights ring a small area near the dorms. "This is the starting point for all dream tours."

Sounds like Star Tours in Disneyland. That could be cool.

Lemon-yellow lights illuminate a larger area. "This is the simulation center devoted to viewing memory projections."

We'd better get YouTube and Netflix or I'm definitely leaving.

"This is the meeting area." Pinpoints of indigo surround a section in the eastern sector of the map. "Five hundred of you are currently working on your higher education, but don't worry, there will always be a private space for you and your Mentor to sit and talk. Whenever you have a need, come to this area and your Mentor will join you shortly."

Sunrise-orange lights mark a portion in the northwest sector of the map.

"This is the library where you'll find many resources to aid your research. In addition to histories dedicated to the world's spiritual traditions, the library contains hundreds of tutorials for enhancing your skills. Ultimately, you must take responsibility for your own progress as you prepare for The Evaluation, but we are here to help in every way we can."

I want to tell her I'm not going to talk to any Mentor, but psychic glue seals my lips so all I can do is *think* very loudly: Screw your help.

A band of flashing magenta lights rim the entire map. "Finally, we come to the outer limits of Substation Fifteen. You are free to move about as you prepare for your Evaluation.

Please understand, though, that all of you require some level of supervision, otherwise you wouldn't be here. Some require more than others."

Why do I need supervision?

"Especially those who haven't yet accepted their current situation."

Is she talking to me?

The magenta lights blink out, and the map returns to the way it was when we entered the room.

"And now, new arrivals, it's time for each of you to meet your Mentor so you can learn and progress. Good luck."

Good luck?

Nicole

THE MOVING WALKWAY carries us out of the map room and back under the glowing white dome. The ride is almost over. As each kid reaches the front of the line, a Vestie steps up and takes them away.

I don't want a Vestie or a Mentor, or whatever they're called. I want to get out of here. Where's the exit? Who am I kidding? I can't walk out. Every kid has a minder tagging along with them. Oh, not everyone. Those kids over there are on their own. Maybe they don't need supervision. I don't. At least I didn't until I opened my big mouth. Now I'll bet they stick me with a Vestie. Oh, wait, those kids aren't actually alone. A tiny brick-red light hovers directly above each one, like a spying eye in the sky that follows every step they take. That's the same light I saw through the mist. That's how they recorded us coming out of the tunnel. Shoot. This place is like a prison.

Scratch *like*.

Do those kids know they're being tracked? I should tell them. No. I should keep my head down. Try not to get noticed and find the right moment to slip away.

"Hi, Nicole." A tiny and very enthusiastic Vestie grins at me as I step off the walkway. At least I think she's grinning. One corner of her mouth is almost hiked up to her nostril. The other corner won't commit. She's so petite I can't guess her age. She could be twelve, except the sorrow in her eyes makes her look at least a hundred.

"I'm Grace, your Mentor. But you probably already guessed that. Not my name. I just chose a new one today. And a new look. Just for you. But the Mentor part? I'll bet you figured that out. Purple vest. Can't miss us. Not my best color, but you could totally pull it off. Oh, yeah, you could. I like green. How about you? Hey, don't you love how we're already past the awkward part and talking about our favorite colors? What's yours? No, let me guess . . ."

She talks as fast as Iz, and she doesn't seem to stop for air. Her expressions change by the second. She'd be a great actress except for the fact that watching her is exhausting. The only thing more exhausting is waiting for her to shut up long enough for me to get a word in.

She keeps yakking and I'm tired of waiting, so I just say it. "I don't belong here."

She shuts up, and spins away from the walkway. "Come with me."

She expects me to follow. That's not happening. I'm not taking another step in this place. This is not how I'm going to spend the rest of my life or whatever comes next.

Grace pops up two inches from my face. Green flecks rim her brown eyes.

I did not see her move. How'd she get back here so fast?

The happy corner of her mouth droops as she focuses on me with the same intensity as Grandma Vestie. My eyeballs feel frosty, like I've stood too long in front of the open freezer trying to decide if I'm up for a toasted bagel or an English muffin. Grace clamps her fingers onto my head. She is way stronger than she looks, and I can't move out of her grip.

"What are you doing?" I brace myself for who knows what.

"Please be quiet, Nicole, and hold still. I'm attempting to view your memories."

"What? You can't just dig around in my personal—"

Grace's fingers stretch wider across my scalp. I get a whiff of rusty metal.

"Hmm ... vibrating in between frequencies. So rare for Substation Fifteen. That could explain the confusion and defiance."

After a moment, she releases me and continues muttering to herself. "Is the memory blockage causing the abnormal frequency? Or are the frequency variances causing the blockage? Perhaps something completely different is triggering both conditions. This is a problem."

"Do you have a headache?" She's talking to me again.

"Uh, no. Well, maybe a little. What's going on?"

Her concerned look scares the crap out of me.

"Is something wrong?" I ask like I really don't want to know because I don't.

Her eyebrows scrunch together. "You can't remember." She says it like that explains everything.

"Remember what?"

She presses her lips together tightly. She's not going to tell me, though her expression, a mix of confusion and pity, seems to say that she'd like to. It's weird. Grace expects me to remember something, but how am I supposed to know what it is if I can't remember? The right side of my head throbs. It's the same spot the kid on the platform stared at. Maybe there's a connection between that spot and the thing I've forgotten. Maybe it's a sign. Listen to me. I sound like Iz and that time she did a psychic reading on my mom's tweezers, which, for some reason, Dad never threw out, even though it's been fourteen years. Iz gently cupped her hands around the tweezers like she was holding a grasshopper, closed her eyes, and told me stuff about my mom that I didn't know. Of course, I don't remember Mom, since I wasn't even two when she died. Iz could have been making it up, but she didn't have to. Iz just knows stuff. Afterwards I checked with Dad, and everything Iz said about Mom was true. No surprise.

This thing that Grace expects me to remember suddenly seems super important, like life or death. Ooh. Not a happy thought.

A small white table and two white stools appear out of nowhere. Pairs of kids and Vesties sit and chat at nearby tables. This must be the meeting area. There's Golden Girl. I try to catch her eye, but she's not looking this way. Grace sits on one stool and gestures for me to sit on the other. I don't want to, but the next thing I know, I *am* sitting with absolutely no memory of doing it. It's like Grace has an invisible remote that controls me. Maybe all this white-on-white has made me unable to resist her will. Maybe it's also deleted my memory, not only making me forget what happened after breakfast, but also what I just did a second ago. If I've lost this much of my mind in the short time I've been here, what will happen if I stay longer? I'll be completely reprogrammable. That's what the Vesties want. Ohmygod, they're evil. I've got to get out of here.

I try to stand. My knees lock so I can't get up. I grab the edge of the table, trying to push up to a standing position, but my hands are too numb to grip.

"Re-laaax." Grace's voice floats me down a peaceful river to a place where I don't care about anything. "This will be easier if you calm down."

Don't listen. She's trying to turn me into a zombie. "Easier for who?"

"Nicole, I have to tell you something. And I want you to listen very carefully." She folds her hands on the table and looks at me with those sorrowful eyes. "You are a no body."

The words make no sense. I swallow. My spit is sand.

"You are dead." She live-streams kindness.

Her mouth keeps moving, but the roar in my ears makes it impossible to hear. Doesn't matter. I've heard enough.

You are dead. She said it. That makes it official. The words wrap my brain like a toxic vine, infecting me with poisonous thoughts.

Dead

Deceased

Departed
Defunct
Deleted
Expired
Extinct
Finished
Game over

An animal, hiding somewhere nearby, howls in agony, as if its leg were caught in a steel trap. I look around. No one seems to care. The animal is shrieking. My heart is breaking. Why isn't anyone helping the poor thing? The screaming intensifies. Grace touches me. I see her hand on my arm but I don't feel it. I don't feel anything. Just a burning in my throat. There is no animal. I'm the one screaming.

Grace encircles me. I collapse against her, my head on her chest. She strokes my hair.

Mom rocks me, stroking my hair and singing softly . . . "Once I had a little dog, his color it was brown."

Once I had a warm body, and a home, and a dad who loved me. I had a best friend who understood me better than I understood myself. I had a boy who I adored. I had my guitar and my music. I could do things and make things happen. And now . . .

One of Dad's non-negotiable truths is: *Everything is negotiable.* I want more time with the people who understand exactly who I am and how I see the world without having to ask. I want more time to know people I didn't get to know because I haven't met them yet. I want more time for writing songs and performing and more time to fall in and out of love and sing about that. I want my full share of laughter and successes and surprises, and opportunities, but not just the fun stuff everyone wishes for, I want the confusing parts and the disappointments, too. I want challenging new ideas that come with quiet, thoughtful conversations, and yes, I want to experience raging conflicts, because being alive means caring enough to fight about what's not right so you can make it better. I want more of Life's ever-shifting shades of color, and no more of the flat white nothingness of Substation Fifteen.

Dad is wrong. No re-negotiating this one. Dead is dead. I am an insignificant pebble lying at the water's edge on an empty beach. A wave crashes over me and pulls me back into the sea. I tumble aimlessly in the dark. I have no thoughts, no feelings. No dreams. A thousand years pass. I am ground into sand.

After who knows how long, I open my eyes. I am still a prisoner in this white world without a hint of color to cheer me up or to distract me from . . . everything.

"I'm very sorry for your loss." Grace sounds like she means it, but it doesn't help. Nothing can.

"I understand how hard this is. Life is a wonderful gift, but, trust me, you will get used to this. Of course, your memory malfunction makes everything more challenging. We will work through this together. I promise. That's why I'm here and why Substation Fifteen has provided you with this avatar to represent the last body you had. Very accurate, isn't it?"

What did she just say?

"This is an avatar? Do you hear how crazy that sounds? And you're wrong, Grace. It's not *accurate*. I didn't have this kind of hair."

"Oh, that was my idea." She's blushing. "Straight hair was your only FWF I could actually grant. That's a Frequently Wished For. I thought this hairstyle would cheer you up a little."

"Wrong again."

"I'm sorry you don't like it, Nicole. I'll give you back the hair you had."

"Go ahead. Who cares?"

She raises a finger and my scalp prickles. My hands fly to my hair which feels even more chaotic than on my worst hair days. "No. I changed my mind. Make it straight again. Quick. Before anyone sees me like this."

Grace looks at me as if I were a bit of broccoli stuck between her teeth. "Sorry, too late."

"What do you mean?"

"They only give me one wish to grant, and I've just used two."

"Who're *they?*"

The lower corner of her mouth twitches. She looks as if she's about to answer the question, but shuts it down.

"Fine. Don't bother telling me anything. I'm just a 'no body.' Isn't that what you just said? So what's the point of giving me an avatar?"

She smiles brightly as if she's relieved to be back on script again. "Think of it as a placeholder. To make communication easier. This way you can ask me *anything,* and I will answer to the best of my ability. What else would you like to know?"

She rests a hand on my shoulder. I shrug her off. She looks hurt. I don't care. We stare at each other. Hurt vs. pissed. This is pointless.

"Okay, Grace. Here are some questions for you: What was with the kids on the platform? Some of them were bleeding. I smelled smoke and burnt hair. A guy was drowning right in front of my eyes. Everyone was seriously messed up, except me. But people stared like *I* was messed up, too. How come I felt so sure that Substation Fourteen was my stop? Why wouldn't the platform Vestie let me get off at Fourteen? And these other no bodies? Why do they walk around like they're dead? Well, I guess we're *all* dead, I get that, but how come I'm the only one who seems to be awake? What am I doing here? And how long do I have to stay?"

She nervously scans the airspace. Is she looking for a red eye? Do they spy on Vesties, too? Is everyone a prisoner? What happens next? Or is this it forever?

I'm shaking with cold. I take a steadying breath. It doesn't work. "Grace, tell me the truth. Is this hell?"

She covers her mouth and glances skyward again. I lower my voice. "Am I allowed to say that word?"

Her mouth forms a tight little U, and I'm not sure if she's going to spit or blow me a kiss.

"Say whatever the hell you like. This is a free speech zone." She swats the air between us like she's clearing flies. "FYI, Nicole, there is no hell, no fiery furnace. No pitchfork-wielding demons in red onesies. Hell is a social construct created centuries ago by the most corrupt and cynical elites."

She's shouting now, but not at me. It's like she's fighting with someone who's not here. "All lies. And what have they been for? Nothing except to frighten the masses and keep them ignorant and submissive. The deception continues in service to the ruling class's obsessive need to maintain wealth and control!"

A red eye swoops in and hovers five feet overhead. We spot it at the same moment. Grace reaches across the table, pulls me toward her, and lowers her voice. "Delete all that." Then she flashes that crooked smile and giggles.

O-kay. Now I get it. Substation Fifteen is for lunatics, and Grace is one of them. I've never been in a situation like this. Last thing I want to do is set her off again, so I pat her hand and try to sound as calm as possible. "The thing is, Grace . . . I really don't belong here. Someone must have made a mistake. No hard feelings. I'm sure it wasn't intentional, but if I could just talk to . . ."

"We don't make mistakes. Let's go. I want to show you something."

And we're off.

We enter Dorm #2 and walk down an empty corridor lined with mostly closed doors. "Every no body gets their own room with all their personalized comforts from home." With the outstretched arm and cheery tone, she could be a rental agent. I'm not sold.

"Which one's mine?"

"This way."

I follow her down the hallway, passing an open door. Shorty is inside, talking to something in a big terrarium. I guess the rest of his home comforts include a mattress on the floor, an Xbox, and a bunch of video games. If I had to guess, I would have bet his walls would be covered with posters of girls whose boobs were falling out of their tops, but no, all Shorty's got is a really big poster about reptiles. And now he's lifting an enormous snake out of the terrarium. It coils around his arm as he strokes the fire-orange blotches on its back. O-kay.

I wonder what Blondie's idea of fun is. Maybe she's

secretly into Disney princesses. I doubt it, but as Dad says, "Life is full of surprises." Apparently, so is death.

"Here we are." Grace opens the last door on the left and walks into a room which is just like my room at home. I mean, *exactly*. It's freakin' amazing.

"Why did you do this?"

"Because we want you to feel comfortable while you're here." Grace smooths away the wrinkles on my fuchsia and white striped comforter. "I love your colors, Nicole. So cheerful."

She's right. One wall is plum raisin, and the other three are Italian straw, just the way Dad and I painted them last summer. He lobbied for purple passage and pale daffodil, but just because he's a professional house painter didn't mean he got to choose my colors.

I ask how they put these rooms together. She says maintaining a highly customized environment, like a bedroom, requires a lot of energy, but they do it because it helps the no bodies feel at home.

"We want you to learn and progress. We got everything right, didn't we?"

I want to check so I slide the bed out from the wall and peek behind it. My two signatures are exactly where I painted them! A plum "Nicole" painted on the straw wall. A straw "Nicole" painted on plum. I remember telling myself, "I'm going to use that graphic for my first album cover." The thought excited me at the time. Now the sight of my names makes me sick. I shove the bed back and try to forget about it. Trying to forget is even harder than trying to remember.

Nothing in this room is real, but it's real enough to hurt. Blinking back tears, I catch myself. Why not dive into the fantasy? I've got nothing else to do. I rush to open the window. It sticks mid-way, like always. I curse under my breath, like always, then give up trying, lean into the gap and catch a cool breeze pouring in. The smell of grass and a hint of lemon from our magnolia tree is just right. So is the angle of the sun glinting through the branches like a rising jewel. The wind chime swings gently from the hook under the eaves. There's Dad's

"Benson Painting—For All Your Home Decorating Needs" van parked in our driveway, with the two ladders strapped to the roof rack with red and blue bungees. On the other side of the fence, the usual pileup of balls, racquets, bikes, and scooters are scattered across the Greenberg's backyard like a coughing fit. I pull back from the window. This is my house. They got every detail right. It's all here. Oh, they forgot my guitar. But that's okay, it's not like I'll be sitting around . . . It's here! Behind the closet door. I pick it up. Resting my arm in its curve feels like hugging an old friend. My songbook lies on the floor, open to the last one I wrote.

Chances

I bring you my heart in my hand

Don't know if you'll be a loving man

or a thief to cause me grief

Beg me to stay

Turn me away

But I'll take my chances

I'll take my chances

Not my best lyrics. I'm glad Alex never heard it. But things might have been different if I'd had the guts to sing it to him.

I strum the opening chords, A–D–A–G, and sing, "I bring you my heart . . .

"Nice."

I forgot Grace was here. Damn. Forgot where I was.

"Thanks." I put down the guitar. "But who cares? They're not going to ask me to sing for The Evaluation. They'll just ask what happened, and I can't remember. What am I going to do?"

Her hand on mine is warm. I let it stay. She asks if I'm all right. I nod, but I'm not. It's easier to lie if you keep your mouth shut. That's a non-negotiable truth Dad never mentioned.

"Look, Nicole, even if you could remember everything, individual memories can't always be counted on as true. You need to know the truth for The Evaluation. But you don't have to remember all of it right this minute." She taps the side of my head. That same spot. It doesn't hurt but it gets my attention. "There must be someone, besides you, who has a piece of the puzzle." Her eyes dart left and right like she's reading the air. "What about your friends? Family? Teachers? You knew lots of people, Nicole. The others might help fill in the blanks."

She points to the space right above my desk, and a small spherical cloud appears, hovering in mid-air. "We don't normally give these out, but you have special challenges that require an out-of-the-box approach."

"What is that thing?"

"It's called a Life-Streamer. It allows you to view the people you left behind as they go on living life. You can't talk to them, of course, but observing them might help you remember what happened."

That sounds amazing. Before I have a chance to tell Grace to show me how it works, a small leather book with badly worn corners appears out of nowhere, and lands on my desk with a no-nonsense THUD. The title stands out on the cover in raised black letters on a red background.

The New Arrivals' Handbook to Substation Fifteen

With no help from Grace, the book inches toward me. Spooky! Iz would love this. I step back.

"It's all right." Grace murmurs. "The book will help you. Pick it up."

I cross my arms and glare at her. "I'm not touching that thing."

She flicks a finger in my direction, my arms unfold themselves, my palms turn up and come together like a bowl. The old book appears in my hands. Surprisingly, it weighs no more than a small bird. The cover is soft, like velvet and smells of cinnamon. With no help from me, the book opens. My hands shake so badly I drop it.

Grace catches it in mid-air. "Nicole, you have to read this."

I have to get out of here.

I run into the hallway, now crowded with no bodies and Vesties. Grace blocks my path. How does she move without being seen? Who cares? She's in my way. In spite of her size she looks dangerous. But I'm already dead, right?

"Move!" I scream.

She closes the distance between us and reaches for me. Everyone stops talking and stares. There's Golden Girl. She's watching, too. Her eyes shine with admiration like she's counting on me to be strong. I'm not strong. I'm too terrified to think. I take a deep breath, but instead of letting it out, I turn and run like hell.

Nicole

THE FLAWLESS WHITE surface springs under my feet, giving me a bounce. For once my boobs don't hurt when I run. I'm moving through an empty landscape that doesn't change. It's impossible to tell if I'm getting anywhere, but something is guiding me. Maybe I'm heading to Fourteen. Maybe some part of me knows how to get there from here. Who am I kidding? I have no idea where I'll end up. I only know that Fifteen isn't where I belong. That might be enough. Dead people don't need a plan.

I race past no bodies and Vesties walking and talking like they're all BFFs. Not Grace and me. We're both misfits. Why should I listen to her? Why should I study *The Handbook for Spooks*? So I can be like, "Yay! I made it to heaven."? Only this sure as hell isn't heaven. I ought to stand at the end of the walkway and greet every newbie. "Hey, dead girl. How's it going, dead guy? Welcome to Substation Fifteen where they spy on you 24/7. Oh, and by the way, just so you know, you are stuck here for thirty days until your personal Evaluation, which they're not telling you anything about. After that? Who knows where you'll go next? Good luck. Learn and progress."

Why'd I have to die so young? Maybe I did something really bad. Maybe that's why I'm here. I'm only sixteen. I didn't get the chance to do anything really good or really bad . . . I don't think. Why can't I remember how I died? Someone must know. God does! Since when do I believe in God? I don't know, but talking to her can't hurt. If God exists, she's probably around here somewhere. If she's not too busy, maybe we can chat. It's possible that dead people get priority. I don't know if God hangs out behind that white dome or under the floor. I don't want to guess wrong and turn my back to God. That would not be cool.

To play it safe I lie down on my side. OW! My neck hurts. I can't get comfortable. Maybe you're not supposed to be comfortable when you talk to God. I have no idea how to do this. My mouth is dry, and my palms are clammy. I feel like I'm about to go onstage not even knowing the first word of my first line.

I clear my throat as politely as I can. And swallow. And clear again. I still don't know what to say. Just say anything.

"Uh, hi, God. How's it going?" My voice sounds like its being pushed through a strainer. "I'm not doing so great because, well, you've probably heard . . . I died. I was hoping you could help. It's weird enough being dead, but not having a clue about what happened? It's *godawful.* Oh. Excuse me. I'm so sorry. I shouldn't have said that. My mom was the religious one in the family, but she died when I was eighteen months old, so I missed out on religious training and having a mom. Not that I'm complaining about how I was raised. My dad is the best. I love him so much. He's a wonderful human being. He's also very funny. He's got a list of life's non-negotiable truths. Like 'Everything is better with chocolate.' And 'When in doubt, take a nap.' Stuff like that. Yeah, he's awesome. Except, he's probably not doing all that great right now."

I picture Dad, slumped at the kitchen table, talking to my empty chair as if I'm sitting there or blaming God because I'm not. I wish my imagination were as lousy as my memory, then I wouldn't spontaneously see any of this stuff on my mental movie screen. I know Dad is sad, but how sad? I can't know what he's really going through. I've never lost a child. I've never had a child. Never will. Sad can mean lots of things. His reality is probably a thousand times worse than whatever I can imagine. A million times. I don't even want to think about this. I can't think about this. Think about something nicer.

I hug my knees to my chin and rock back and forth. I'm a rocking chair. I'm a rocking horse. I'm a swing.

up crisscrosses over the top of the pancakes and drizzles down the edge of the stack.

I stop rocking.

"God, please help my dad, Michael Benson. I don't expect you to bring me back to life, that'd be way too weird, and it could cause some serious mental glitches, especially with Iz. She's already kinda woo-woo. My dad might have a heart attack. He's got borderline high cholesterol, as you probably know. So . . . no. Don't bring me back to life. But how about if I just went back in time, *before* whatever happened? It would be like two seconds had passed, and no one would know that I died. I once saw a movie like that. What do you say? You could do it right now. I'm ready."

I sit up. I have no idea what time travel feels like, but it'll be so awesome to be home again in my own *real* room. I close my eyes and clasp my hands together tightly, just to give me something to hold on to.

Nothing changes. I'm still sitting alone in this all-white nowhere land. Maybe nothing will ever change again.

I've got to quit feeling sorry for myself.

Standing up helps, though I still don't know which direction to look. If God actually hears me, it doesn't matter. I straighten my back and look ahead.

"Okay, God, no do-overs. I get it. I haven't been good enough to deserve a second chance. Not that I was really bad. I'm sure I wasn't, but I must have messed up. A little. I can't remember specifics, but everyone makes mistakes, right? Look. If you don't want to give me a second chance, don't do this for me. Do it for my dad. He helps people all the time, even people he doesn't know, like that woman who was being harassed at Northgate Mall. My dad asked her if she knew the guy who was bothering her, and if she was comfortable with what was going on. She said, 'No.' And 'No.' My dad told the guy that the woman wasn't interested, and he needed to leave her alone. When the guy wouldn't quit, my dad had the woman walk away with us. In case you forgot, that guy followed us for a while before he finally gave up.

"Who knows what would have happened if Dad hadn't stepped in? Oh. You do. It would have been terrible, right? But now that I'm dead, my dad is probably too depressed to help anyone. If you take care of this, I guarantee he will keep on being the great guy that he is, and I promise that I'll be super kind for the rest of my life. So instead of losing one helpful person, you'll gain one. What do you say?"

No answer.

"I know you're super-busy, God, but could you give me a sign to let me know that you'll think about it and get back to me soon?"

I wait. Nothing. I feel like an idiot. Am I really expecting God to tell me how I died or take me back in time? This is just stupid. I better keep moving before Grace sends a red eye after me.

I run in the direction I'm being pulled. I haven't seen a Vestie or a no body in a long time. Actually, I don't know how long it's been. Does time even exist here? Probably not. I mean, aren't we all here because we ran out of time?

I keep running because I don't know what else to do. It's quiet in the outer limits. I wish my mind were this quiet and I could stop thinking about being dead and trying to remember what happened. I wish I could rest in peace.

"Make a wish," Iz says from behind the camera.

"What kind of wish?" I ask.

"Whatever you want. Just make something up."

"What? Like improvise? I can't do that. I need a script."

Kyle's microphone boom drifts close to my face. I swat at it and he yanks it up. He was eavesdropping. I don't care. I haven't said anything incriminating. If he knows what I'm thinking, I can't help that. If he wishes I were wishing for something else, I'm sorry, but we don't always get what we wish for.

"Does my wish come true?" I ask Iz.

She shrugs. "I don't know. I haven't written that part of the movie yet. But sure, why not?"

I knew she was talking about Lucy, my character, but I loved the idea that she could actually get *me* whatever I wanted just by writing it into her movie. I remember thinking what a great friend she is.

I need to talk to her. We had a conversation. Maybe recently? I feel like it was important. Something about Alex? Iz never trusted him. Were we texting or was she actually with me when I died? Ohmygod! Did Iz die, too? Some freak accident that killed us both? If she's dead, maybe she's here. That would be convenient. I could talk to her and she could help me remember . . . No. If she died when I did, she would have been on the platform with me.

I'm glad she's not dead, but I still need to talk to her. But how? I could ask God for a phone. Not funny. I'm totally alone. Iz, too. Does she still think of me as her best friend or am I a "was" as in, "Nicole was my best friend"? Best friends have to be available, otherwise what's the point? That leaves me out. So who will be her friend now? Who will go to her ritual tree with her? Who will turn her on to great Broadway musicals like *West Side Story*, and *Grease*, and *Hairspray*, and *Little Shop of Horrors*, and *Into the Woods*? She might never have discovered the classics if I hadn't loved them first because Dad and I watched them together. Who will star in her movies now? Who will shop with her at Goodwill for props and costume pieces? And what about me? I never dreamed dead people needed friends. But we do. I do. If I keep running, maybe I'll run out of needs and wishes and memories, and I'll be like the other zombies. That would be so much easier.

A big ugly cry surges up from my gut. I thought I was done feeling sorry for myself. Guess not. It's an old habit. I should have kicked it while I was alive, when I had so many other things to think about. Now there's nothing else to think about but myself and how messed up everything is.

I sink to the ground, a helpless, sobbing lump choking on mucous, gasping for breath. I wait for the self-pity to pass. It doesn't. Intense pain stabs the back of my eyes. I think I'm getting a migraine. I've never had one, but this is probably what it feels like. Maybe it's the abnormal frequency thing Grace was talking about.

I smell peaches and nutmeg. Ahhh. The throbbing lets up. I hurry forward with the same joy I felt when the platform stopped at Fourteen. I must be close to Fourteen. What's that thick fog up ahead?

DING. DING. DING.

The sharp sound pierces the mist. I flop onto my belly and crawl forward, slowly, blindly feeling my way across the flat surface. After a minute or two, my fingertips touch a ledge. I stop cold. I'm on a cliff!

I scream as my heart punches its way out of my chest and the concrete races up to meet me.

I've seen this split-second clip before. In a movie? No. This is much more real. I'm sweating. Look at my hands. Trembling so badly my fingers blur. This is *my* memory. It's a flashback of the last moment of my life! I *fell* and landed on concrete, on my head, on *that* spot. That's how I died. A sob erupts without warning.

Grace is wrong. I will never get used to this.

I scoot back from the edge. The fog clears, revealing a sheer twenty-foot drop and a packed waiting room below. People wait beside a sleek desk where a Vestie smiles and shakes the hand of the first person in line. At the tail end of the line a small, skinny redhead nibbles her fingers. *Mousy!* Maybe she can help me. I wave to her. She doesn't notice.

DING. DING.

The people inch forward as a drone-like thing scans every person. Another pleasant looking Vestie calls out a name. A thunder-faced woman jumps up from one of the long couches and strides toward him.

I stand, waving both arms overhead. Mousy spots me, her eyes bug out briefly. She steps out of line, quickly exits the waiting room, and turns left. I follow on the rim above, always keeping her in sight. When she's finally alone down there, she looks up at me. "Hi. You were on the platform. I'm Sofia, with an 'f.' What's your name?"

"Nicole. Why are those people waiting in line?"

"I guess some want to complain about their accidents. I just want to find out how the fire started."

"They tell you that stuff?"

"Yeah, you just have to ask."

"Move over, Sofia. I'm jumping down."

Jittery, I step closer to the edge. Instantly, black clouds fill the sky. The air closes in around me, heavy with humidity. Lightning splits the darkness followed by thunder so loud I cover my ears. A wall of rain hits me like a water cannon, knocks me on my butt then shuts off. A tiny red light pierces the gloom. *A spying eye!* The Mentors don't want me jumping down to Fourteen. I don't care. I've got so many questions. How did I fall? Where did I fall from? What was I doing in a place so far off the ground? Was I alone? Fourteen is the only place to get answers.

"Screw you, Fifteen!" I rush forward. Inches before the edge my feet lock in place. The Mentors again. Damn! Getting out of this place is harder than finding a bra that fits.

The drop-off is at least forty feet now. My head swims. Even if they weren't messing with me, I'm too scared to jump. I sit and hang my head between my knees. The spinning doesn't stop. I'm such a wimp.

"It's okay." Sofia calls up to me. "We can still talk."

She's kind. I try to smile, but I'm too disgusted with myself. I wouldn't talk to me if I were Sofia. Her mouth drops open like a mailbox as she stares at something behind me. I whip around.

It's Grace.

Crap.

CASSIE

LOLA SNIFFS AT dog poop piled up by the fence at the top of the Alderney Stairs. Some dogs eat deer poop. Horse poop. Even other dogs' poop! I don't let Lola do that, but she can sniff all she wants.

Shoot, it's been three hours. Why hasn't Alex texted back? I text again.

Nothing.

Fat gray clouds hang over the top of Mt. Tam, the Sleeping Princess. Soon rain is going to drench the part of the mountain that's supposed to be her head. How long has she been asleep waiting for some prince to kiss her? Wake yourself up, girlfriend, he's not coming.

The corn chips in my pocket are stale. Lola doesn't care. She gives me the big eyes. I flip her a chip. She snags it in midair.

Kyle must know where Alex is. I text him.

Kyle>

Hey Kyle. Where's
Alex?

Home.

> Why isn't he texting
> me back?

The dots blink on and off for what feels like forever. One, two, three, one, two, three. They disappear. What the . . . ?

> What's going on?

The dots start up again. Finally, Kyle's text comes through.

Nicole is dead.

"WHAT?" I shout. Lola yelps and lies down, head between her paws.

> If you are messing with
> me, I swear I'll kill you.

No joke.

I lean against a eucalyptus and slide my back down the trunk until I'm sitting at the base of the tree with layers of stripped bark all around me. I press my fingers into the corners of my eyes as hard as I can. I hold back the tears, but I can't hold back the rain. A drop hits my head. Two more fall on the back of my hand. It's coming down faster. My forehead, knees, and high-tops get wet. I don't move. I zip up Alex's gray hoodie, *my* hoodie because he gave it to me. It smells faintly of hair gel and sweat. My finger pokes through a perfect circle the size of a quarter that's obviously been cut out of the back of the hoodie. Who did that? Is this why he gave it to me? Wearing his hoodie always felt like his arms were around me, but now it feels like I'm wearing a ripped-up piece of secondhand crap. If it weren't raining . . .

Lola rests her head on my thigh. Her ears are soft between my fingers. She licks my wrist, and the tears come too fast to press away.

Nicole dead? That makes no sense.

She was funny and talented and smart. She was much nicer than my other friends. *I was nicer when I was with her,* and I sang a whole lot better. She made me believe I could actually become a real singer with ten million TikTok followers. Talking to Nicole about the future was so much better than listening to Buzz-Kill. We could have gotten past her thing for Alex and stayed friends. I could have made her understand she was wasting her time.

Was she?

The rain quits, just like that. That's life. It's stupid to expect anything else. Everything seems cool, then a second later, whatever ride you're on stops and you get booted. I pull the hoodie off. I stick four fingers in the hole and rip it apart. Then I toss the whole thing into the trash with the dog poop.

Sitting at the top step of the Alderney Stairs, I swipe through selfies of Alex and me and Nicole and Kyle. Something clicks in my brain and it's not good, like when my key clicks in the front door and Buzz-Kill starts screaming at me before I'm even inside. In every photo Kyle and me are on either side of Nicole and Alex. The two of them squished together, laughing. Are their heads touching in this photo? They definitely are in that one. Alex's hand is on my shoulder, but where's his other hand?

I zoom in on the two of them so no one else is in the picture. They totally look like a couple. How did I not see that? Because Alex was my boyfriend and I believed he loved me. I didn't see it because Nicole was nice. She was my friend and I trusted her. How stupid was that? Why did I keep inviting her to hang out with us? She was always trying to steal Alex. I see it now.

DING.

Alex? No. Damn.

Mariah>

Did you hear about
Nicole?

Yeah.

I can't believe that
Alex found her body.
Eww.

Alex found her body? Geez! What else don't I know?

Yeah. He texted me
right away. Poor baby!
We're both super
upset. We've been
texting nonstop.

I heard that her head
was crushed. Totally
caved in.

I picture Nicole lying dead, her eyes open, but blank. Large bloody chunks of brain ooze out of her cracked open head. I squeeze my phone so hard my hand hurts. I'm breathing fast, like I've been running. I want to run, but I can't move, just like Nicole. Lola snuggles closer. It doesn't help.

Gotta go. Alex wants
me.

How does Mariah know all about it? Did Alex tell her? Why didn't he tell me first? Why isn't he texting me back? Why am I waiting around for him like a pathetic loser girl? Forget this. I've gotta go to work.

I head down the Alderney Stairs, two at a time. It's raining again, but I don't care. A fat guy and his fat black Labrador retriever enter the alley below, filling the whole space. I yell at him to move. Lola barks at the lab. The guy pulls his dog in close and presses against the wall.

At Drake Boulevard I wait for the light to change. Nicole is dead. It's my fault. No! None of this is my fault. I didn't know Alex had been with her until Kyle showed up and said she was waiting for Alex to come back. I didn't force Alex to come to the park. I didn't force him to stay there with me. Alex is my boyfriend. I wasn't trying to hurt Nicole, but she was try-ing to hurt me.

Lola tugs at the leash. I look down. She's wagging her whole body as two little girls kneel beside her on the side-walk, petting her all over. I scoop up Lola in my arms. "Hey! You need to ask before you touch someone's dog."

The girls exchange nervous looks and stuff their hands in their jacket pockets. "Sorry," the older girl whispers. "We thought she was a nice dog."

"She is. But you didn't know that before you stuck your fin-gers in her face. If you go petting every dog that seems nice, you'll get bitten."

Nicole

GRACE DRAGS ME to the meeting area. "Sit!" She's exasperated and doing a lousy job of hiding it.

An instant later I'm sitting on a white stool, again with absolutely no memory of doing it. I'm beyond exasperated, if anyone is keeping score. "Why did you block me from jumping to Fourteen?"

"Because Substation Fourteen is for accidental deaths."

So that's how this works. They put us in substations based on how we died. The sorting hat messed up big time with me.

"My death *was* accidental. I fell. So why am I here? What is Fifteen for?"

Every no body and every Vestie within ten feet turns and stares as if we're all inside a Starbucks, and I'm standing on a table screaming, "Where is the nearest Starbucks?"

Grace lowers her voice and talks through clenched teeth. "Let's continue this conversation in private."

Before she gets a chance to stand, a broad-shouldered Vestie storms over to our table. Her helmet of tight gray curls makes her look like a poodle. "Mentor Grace, why hasn't Nicole read her handbook yet?"

"Uh, we had a slight delay." Grace flashes her crooked smile. "But don't worry. We're on it."

Poodle snorts. "You assured us that you could handle her."

"I *can*. I mean, I *will*. I mean I *am* handling her." She clamps her hand onto my wrist and pulls me to my feet. "Come on, Nicole."

"I don't need handling." I fight against her tightening grip, but she's not letting go.

Grace leads me to a place not far from the meeting area. This must be the simulation center. Why are we here?

Her palm presses against the side of my head. The white world of Substation Fifteen dissolves and a lake surrounded by trees appears. Silver lupines, the color of amethysts, grow in clumps among tall grasses. A bird calls from high in a nearby pine. Another bird, farther away, answers. Turtles sun themselves on a floating log. Gentle waves lap the smooth stones a few feet from a wooden bench where I have to sit because I'm overwhelmed by the color, the light, the sounds. But it's more than that. I know this place!

Dad and I sit on the wooden bench close to the lake shore and count turtles. Thirteen red-eared sliders and only one western pond turtle. Damn red-ear invaders! The pondies have virtually disappeared.

Dad's SF Giants' cap lies low on his forehead, but his nose sticks out and it's turning red. I grab the sunscreen tube and squeeze too hard.

"Oops!" I frown at the white goo in my hand.

Dad chuckles. "Girl meets one of life's non-negotiable truths: It's way easier to squeeze stuff out than push it back in."

What's the lake called? Nix's Lake? No. Forest Lake? Wrong. I know! Phoenix Lake. A fifteen-minute drive from our house. Hazy memories trip over each other and throw themselves into sharp focus on my mental movie screen.

The storm overflow slides down the spillway like a mini-Niagara. Dad and I toss fat sticks into the water and watch the current whisk them away. Spring wildflowers crowd the hillside. We quiz each other on their names. Sun Cups. Sky Lupines. Shooting Stars.

Both of us always blank out on Houndstongue, and we always swear that next time we'll remember. We never do.

Dad and I loved hiking here. This wooden bench was our midpoint stop for snacking on his homemade salty peanut, dried cranberry, chocolate chip trail mix. He used to say, "Nothing wakes up your mouth like a combo of salty, tart, and sweet." Another non-negotiable truth coming from the man who added chopped bacon and sweet potatoes to his spinach lasagna recipe. Sounds weird, but it tasted great.

On the way home from Phoenix Lake we always stopped at Mimi's Doughnuts because Dad insisted we do research for the day when we got our own deep fryer to make doughnuts at home. That day will never come. I smile at the turtles through my tears, or am I crying through my smile?

Grace shifts beside me. What is *she* doing here?

One turtle pushes another off the log. The second guy hits the water with a GLUNK and disappears. The turtles in the sun seem to be laughing at the one that went under. I watch the spot where I saw him last, but he doesn't come back up again. Gone forever. Like me.

I pick up a rock. I feel like throwing it at Grace, but instead I throw it into the water as far as I can. "This isn't Phoenix Lake, is it?"

"No. I pulled it from your memory and projected it. Such a lovely place. So peaceful. I thought being here would calm you down."

Not if it isn't real.

The rock's after-splash pushes out wave after circular wave, each one growing and spreading until what started as a BLIP way out there ends up moving toward the shore, until the cold water laps at my toes. The next moment, we're back in the meeting place. *The Handbook* lies on the white table between us.

"Ready to read your book now?" She glances skyward then throws me an encouraging smile.

I don't want to open the book but what other options do I have?

None.

"Fine. Let's see what else you guys screwed up on."

The Handbook

This official record belongs to No Body #:	3949454893300-1CF
Most recently deceased identity:	Nicole Sondra Benson
Date of latest demise:	January 4, 2024
Cause of latest demise:	Suicide

Suicide? The word pulses on the page, mocking me, daring me to deny it.

"Is that what Substation Fifteen is for?"

Grace nods slightly, her eyes glisten with compassion for me as if someone I loved just died. Okay, someone did. I shift on my stool, unable to get comfortable. I squint at the word *Suicide* and will the seven letters to morph into the word *Accident*. I stare so hard my eyes water. *Suicide* shimmers and shudders but the word stays on the page daring me to do something about it. It's not true. I didn't kill myself. I've got to fix this. But how?

Help me, Iz! Do you have a spell to undo lies? She can't hear me. She can't help me. I'm on my own.

I shove the book aside. "Depressed people kill themselves. I wasn't depressed. I don't even remember being unhappy. Dad and I made pancakes for breakfast. I poured on way too much syrup. We laughed. Does that sound depressed?" My throat closes up. I sniffle. My tough girl act falls apart. "Why did you write this about me?"

Grace flinches. "I didn't. I had nothing to do with what's in there. The highest-level Mentors compiled your personal data based on our records. If they wrote 'suicide' in your handbook, that can only mean—"

"—they're dead wrong. I didn't kill myself!" My voice pitches higher with each word. I sound like a screechy little kid who is flipping out!

"I . . . I remember falling." I try to sound sane, though I don't feel it. "But I swear I don't remember anything else. Is that normal?"

Grace shakes her head. "New arrivals typically remember all the details of their death, especially their last moments."

Not normal. I knew it. That proves they made a mistake. Grace is no help. I'm going to complain to the Mentors and they'll reassign me to Fourteen. Then I'll stand in line in that waiting room until I find out exactly how the accident happened.

How do they handle complaints around here? Maybe there's a Help section in this book. I flip a few pages and find this:

Like every other substation, Substation Fifteen is a training ground between your last life and what comes next, a place for you to pause, reflect, and work hard to gain perspective on the choices you've made, especially those that intentionally caused harm to others and yourself. Your path forward depends on your efforts to uncover the truth, and take responsibility. Your results will be assessed during your Evaluation. In these pages, you will find guidelines to help you learn and progress.

Time until The Evaluation: 30 Earth days.

FAQ

During this initial phase of your post-transition you may have questions. The following are our answers to the most frequently asked questions we have received from new arrivals. If you have additional unanswered questions, comments, or concerns, please do not hesitate to turn to your Mentor for help and guidance.

Question 1:   Why do I need a Mentor?
Answer: Because you were troubled enough to take your own life, you need to be closely monitored.

"I didn't take my own life, but if I *had*, what would be the point of monitoring me *now?* That's nuts. Who's running this place anyway? They must be a bunch of idiots."

Grace nervously glances to her left. A few yards away, a steely-eyed, shaved-head Vestie built like a refrigerator watches us intently. Grace lowers her voice. "You have to stop saying things like that."

"Who is that big guy and why is he staring at us?"

"Not us, *me.* Well, actually he might be watching you, too. That's Quinn, my supervisor. I got into a little trouble a while back, and he's observing me. If you ever need to talk to me and I don't show up at the meeting area, go immediately to the place where you got off the platform. Okay?"

"What do you mean? Why wouldn't you be here? Never mind. And what's the point of talking to you anyway? You don't listen to me. Nobody does."

A low growl rumbles from the back of Quinn's throat. Grace sits up as if she's been poked with an electric prod. That guy is a bully. I wish I could help her. I wish she could help *me.* Forget wishes!

Grace clasps her hands tightly. "Nicole, we're here to treat any underlying malfunctions in your mental processing that led you to commit suicide..." She sounds like a recording. This speech isn't for my benefit. "... and to help you process life in healthier ways so you can move on to wherever you need to go next. That's my goal for you and the goal of The Evaluation." She grabs my hand too quickly for me to pull away. "We care about you, Nicole." She's off-script now. "I care about you. But Substation Fifteen never wants to see you here again."

She's dead serious. It scares me, but I laugh. That's *why* I laugh. I hope I don't hiccup. Actually, it's not that funny.

"How could you possibly see me again? I'd have to live

again and die again to get back here. Wait! Do I get another life?"

My mind spins out on possibilities, like I've just been given an unlimited Amazon gift card.

"This is so awesome! Okay, so listen and please take notes. In my next life I want a mom who doesn't die while I'm still a kid. I want to fall for a guy who doesn't have a girlfriend and who will love me as much as I love him. Of course, I'll need a new body! I want straight hair. Any color is fine, though I'm thinking sable with streaks of burgundy would be killer. I'll need stronger fingernails for picking and strumming, because of course I'll be playing guitar again. Oh, and, smaller breasts. Not too small, but smaller than these and . . ."

"Stop!" Grace sticks her hand in my face.

I back up. Not because of her little hand, but the fire in her eyes. I shut my mouth. She continues. "We don't take requests, Nicole. And I will not talk to you about future incarnations."

Fine. I never get what I want anyway. Every dream dies. Death is so unfair. So I guess I'm stuck here. No. If I can believe Grace, it sounds like I'll get to *move on*, whatever that means, *if* I pass The Evaluation, which is . . . what? What does the book say?

> Question 4:   What is The Evaluation?
>
> Answer: An interactive learning experience designed to help you take responsibility for your performance in your most recent incarnation.

"Performance? Awesome! I can do that. I've got a great voice and . . ."

Grace mutters under her breath. "Everyone always gets stuck on that word. I've suggested an edit so many times, but do they ever listen?" To me she says, "Performance means *behavior*. Specifically, the actions you took, or failed to take, with the intent to hurt someone."

"I never did anything like that."

Did she just roll her eyes? She points to the only other sentence on the page.

> Successful completion of the program is based on how much of the truth you uncover and how effectively you make amends for your hurtful actions.

Successful completion. A chill freeze-dries the edges of my heart and pumps me full of dread much worse than the fear of screwing up my lines or embarrassing myself in front of Alex.

"What happens if I fail The Evaluation? Do I stay here until I pass? Nah. There'd be more of us here if it worked that way. They must send the flunkees somewhere else. Right?"

The sad corner of her mouth twitches.

"There *is* another place! I knew it! It's probably not Thirteen or Fourteen, either. Everyone looked too happy there. Is there a Substation Hadestown?"

Grace's eyes flick skyward and back to me again. She giggles nervously. "Nicole, where do you get these ideas?"

"I'm right! You guys like numbers. I'll bet flunkees go to Sixteen. What happens there?" I don't really want to know, but Grace can't lie. If it's a truly awful place she'll tell me not to worry about it.

"Don't worry about it."

It is truly awful!

I need to get out of here, but not in the direction I tried before. They'll be on me in a minute. The substations are stacked, like doughnuts, so I should be able to get to Fourteen from any direction. All I have to do is get to the edge of Fifteen, any edge, and jump down to Fourteen before they stop me. Then I'll be safe.

I slide off the stool, all casual, like I'm just stretching my legs. Vesties close in immediately. It's like my presence makes them swarm. Grace pulls me back into my seat. "You don't have to run. Thirty days is plenty of time. Trust me."

"Exactly how long is thirty days around here? How do you keep track of time?"

"Like this." Grace turns over my right hand so my palm faces up, then she separates my second and third fingers, revealing what looks like a countdown clock embedded under the skin along the inside of my middle finger. The clock reads 29:08:47:10. I can't take my eyes off of it as :10 counts down to :00 then resets to 29:08:46:59.

Ohmygod! They turned me into a timer app. No, I'm a *time bomb* set to detonate in twenty-nine days, eight hours, forty-six minutes no . . . forty-five minutes and fifty-nine seconds!

"*Handy? Right?*" Grace grins.

Her first joke. I'm not amused. Always knowing how much longer until my destruction isn't *handy*, it's nerve-wracking. I rub my finger to cancel the timer. I claw the spot until it hurts. The Countdown to Destruction continues.

"Take this thing off me." I thrust my middle finger in her face. I don't mean it in *that* way, but I kinda do.

She pushes my hand away. "Oh, I understand. You think you're being unfairly singled out. I promise you're not. Every no body on all the substations has a countdown timer."

"That doesn't make me feel better." I pretend not to see her shoulders slump. "I don't need this thing. Even if I had thirty years, I couldn't possibly remember everything I've ever done."

She perks up. "But you don't have to remember everything. Only what's relevant to your situation."

"You make it seem so simple, but this Evaluation sounds like a huge deal. I used to have a great memory. Not anymore. All the recent relevant stuff, which should be right at the top of the pile, is buried. It's all a blank, kinda like this place."

I know I'm whining and blaming her because my memory sucks, but I can't help it. "What if I can't remember anything? Or if I can only remember stuff the way I *think* it happened and that turns out to be wrong? The Mighty Mentors are going to know the difference, won't they?"

"Of course. They'll compare your memories to the Akashic records. Oh, you're not familiar? Those are multi-dimensional, multi-track recordings of everything that ever happened to you. To all of us."

"*Everything?* No. No. That can't be true. You're joking again, right?"

She shakes her head. My brain is on serious overload. I stare at Grace like I'm stuck in freeze-frame. I catch a glimpse of my handy countdown clock telling me that time is still a real thing whether I like it or not. 29:08:44:32.

"If you've got an Akashic record of everything, then why don't you just check it so I can find out what happened to me?"

"I can't. I don't have that level of security clearance. But don't worry. I promise you'll remember everything when you need to."

"You keep saying that, but why can't I remember it now?"

She shakes her head. "I'm really not sure. Maybe it has something to do with the circumstances leading up to your death."

Circumstances that I can't remember.

My gut fills with rocks. Not the pretty polished ones with inspirational inscriptions like Love. Hope. Peace. *Learn and Progress.* No, my rocks are dirty and cracked. They say things like: Lost. Doomed. Dead.

I feel like the drowning kid on the platform. Grace puts a hand on my shoulder. I let it be there, but it doesn't help.

"I'm trying to help you, Nicole. We've never made a mistake bringing someone here before, but maybe you're the first. Something is wrong. I've never seen a new arrival who was such . . .

". . . a pain in the ass?"

"I wasn't going to say that."

"Yeah, but you thought it."

She chuckles. And there's that cute lopsided grin that I'm actually starting to like. I want to trust her, but she's one of them. Or is she?

"You are a uniquely determined spirit." If that's supposed to make me feel better it's not working. I look away. With a gentle but determined hand under my chin she turns my head towards her. "Now look into my eyes, Nicole, and pretend we're having a moment."

What's she up to? I hold my breath.

"If you're absolutely sure you didn't commit suicide . . ."

Her mouth's not moving, but I hear her voice clearly.

". . . then get the evidence and prove it, and I promise I will back you up."

Are you really talking to me, Grace? I don't say a word, I only *think* the question, but she nods like she heard me! Did she really? I don't want to ask outright in case I imagined it, so I ask another question with my eyes, like an actress playing a scene, in close-up. *If I can prove that I didn't kill myself, will you help me?*

She nods.

She heard my thoughts. I can hear hers. She's on my side. I exhale and open my arms wide to Grace. But before we connect, Quinn appears and barks, "Come with me, Mentor Grace. We need to talk."

As Grace turns to follow him, she catches my eye, and I catch her message: *Go to the dorm. I'll meet you there.*

Nicole

BACK IN MY dorm room, I sit on the floor, leaning against my bed. I try to guess what Quinn's talking to Grace about. Probably me. What if they fire her as my Mentor and stick me with Quinn? I swear that would be the worst thing. I'll fail The Evaluation for sure. Then I'll . . . Oh, I'm doing it again. Cut it out, Nicole. It's not always about *you*. Think of Grace for a change. Right. What will happen to her? And *me?* How will I prove I didn't commit suicide now?

This is too depressing.

I pull my guitar onto my lap and strum a few random chords. Em–Dm–Am–Em–Fm–Am–Dm–Em. Hmm. I never used to write in minor keys. This sounds like someone trudging up a hill, in a storm, with rocks in her shoes, and a fifty-pound pack on her back. Maybe I could write a new song called *The Ballad of Dead Girl*. That would cheer me up for sure.

I stash my guitar under the bed. I feel like throwing rocks through windows, but there aren't any rocks in my room and this window definitely wouldn't break. I try to conjure Phoenix Lake. The image pops up for a second then goes wherever my memory clips go when they're not trying to convince me that I'm somewhere else instead of here. Maybe death wouldn't be so bad if I could download select memories on demand, binge-watch the best ones, and lose myself.

The small cloud that is the Life-Streamer hovers over my desk, cycling through colors so fantastic they have no names. As if sensing my interest, it plays a synth-pop tune like nothing I've ever heard before and, at the same time, as familiar as the sound of my name. It's one of those melodies that slips inside your head and makes you fall in love with it instantly. I'd give anything to write songs like that.

A puff of cool air brushes against my hand as I push it into the cloud. A hologram appears, split into four parts. Cassie, Dad, Iz, and Alex move around in their own windows. Alive!

Who should I choose? Does it even matter? Grace said all I get to do is watch. What's the point of that? What's the point of live streaming for dead kids? I don't need a reminder of where I am and where they are. My throat tightens. My eyes burn. I look away. The reflected colors dance on the walls. The music won't let go. Okay. Fine. I've got nothing else to do.

Within her section of the Life-Streamer, Cassie is walking her dog in the park. Boring. Don't need to watch that.

Dad leans heavily against the kitchen counter like he can't stand up on his own. He clutches the coffee mug I gave him, rubbing his thumb over #1 Dad, like he's Aladdin. I know what he's wishing for. Same thing I'm wishing for. It's the only thing I want, but neither of us is going to get it. It hurts to see him hurting like this. It hurts even more knowing that I'm to blame. I look away.

Iz crouches inside the hollow tree where she performs her witchiest rituals. She's burning something in her copper offering bowl. I wonder what she's wishing for.

Alex drinks soda from a can and wipes his mouth with the back of his hand. I blush to the roots of my hair. Spying on him like this is sexy.

"Welcome to Life-Streamer." The cloud talks! "Select your desired channel."

With a quick poke, I select Alex because, why not? Dad, Iz, and Cassie vanish and Alex fills the entire cloud. I whisper his name, though I'm pretty sure he can't hear me. This isn't FaceTime. We can't talk, but with some things you don't need to.

Ooh. That's an interesting thought.

I zoom in closer until I'm holding Alex's face between my hands. His sleepy green eyes and wet mouth are sexier than I remember. I move in for a kiss.

"What are you doing?" Grace stands beside me, her bottom lip sticks out like an angry shelf.

"Excuse me! Can't a girl have some privacy?"

"You're here to learn and progress, not waste time fantasizing."

"Give me a break. I wasn't wasting time. I was trying to figure out how to use this thing so I *can* learn and progress. It's helping me to see all of them again. But it's so hard, especially with no audio. I wish I could get inside their heads. How do I turn up the volume?"

Grace doesn't answer.

"Is there a volume control?"

"Huh?" She barely glances at me.

"Are you okay? What happened with Quinn?"

She shakes her head, then nods. "I'm fine. No. There's no audio. You just get to watch from here. But I can teach you how to go and visit them."

"Visit?" I want to make sure that I heard her right, before I get too excited. "You mean I can actually go back to Earth to see them?"

"Yes. Eventually. But for now, there are other ways to connect with the living. Come with me."

Connect with the living? If she means haunting, I don't want to scare anybody. But I also don't want to cause more trouble for Grace or myself by refusing to do what she says. So I walk with her, following close behind, and try to ignore the rapid-fire pinging inside my head like a GPS warning me that I'm about to crash.

I ESCAPE TO the woods, but there's no escaping the feeling that all of my energy, my whole being, is out of balance. It's been twenty-seven hours since Nic died. I haven't touched my talking board. I'm still processing how I could have known she was dead before Mom told me. *Nic told me herself.* That's the truth. I shouldn't be shocked, but I must admit, for all the ways my intuitive sense connects me to the natural and spiritual worlds, Friday's energy surge blew me away.

I haven't eaten a thing. Mom keeps pushing, but I'm not hungry. I haven't slept either, and I'm not going to. Whenever I close my eyes, I see Nic falling, I hear her screaming, and I feel like throwing up.

I tap into the universal life force, to be one with the birds, the trees, the dirt, the earthworms, but I'm outside of this world looking in. I don't deserve to be happy because of what I did.

I sweep every leaf and twig from the floor of my ritual tree, to prepare the space. I draw a circle of protection on the ground with my *athame*, sit in the center, breathing in and out twelve times. A persistent breeze out of nowhere spins like an evil whirlwind, pushing dead leaves back into the circle and throwing dust in my eyes. It hurts to open them. It hurts to keep them closed. I press my fingers against the lids and rub. Augh! I shouldn't have done that! Did I just scratch my cornea? I blink again and again. Ow. Okay. That's better. I think.

What was that about? Wind is a messenger. Dust is the message. It's a sign. Of what? My own blindness! That's it. I have to *see clearly* before I can make amends with Nic and complete this quest. I have to see the truth of what I did and understand why I did it.

I open my Book of Spells, clicking my pen as I think about what to write. I've never done that before. Pen-clicking was a Nic-thing. She did it when she was nervous. I always told her how annoying it was and she should take re-centering breaths instead. Now here I am, clicking away. I put the pen down and take twelve slow deep breaths.

Ahhh. Better. Now I write from my heart.

Goddess Eternal, please, Release me
Lighten my burden of guilt, give me the Key
Transform the effects of Negative deeds
Into the healing energy I Need.
Open my eyes so that I might see
The unseen truths that will set me free
In all ways, as you see best,
Guide Nic's eternal spirit to peaceful Rest.

Reading out loud, my voice sounds like it's coming from under a frozen pond where I'm trapped and drowning. I tear the page from the book, nearly ripping it in half. Calm down or this won't work.

I carefully fold the paper toward me and zip down the

crease. I rotate the paper ninety degrees, and fold, zip, and rotate again. Six times. Every fold is an act of centering, balancing my energy, forcing me to focus.

I drop the tight square into my copper bowl and light a match to one corner. The paper unfolds as it burns, undoing all my work. I hold my breath and wait. For what? An easing of guilt? A surge of forgiveness? Terrifying thoughts stomp around my brain, crashing into one another. What if Nic doesn't forgive me? What if this shame and regret stay with me for the rest of my life? What if Nic finds her own ways to punish me for what I did? What if she tries to steal my life force?

A feather of smoke rises from the bowl. A tiny spark sails through the opening at the top of the tree. The spot at the back of my neck tingles, like water boiling under my skin. It's a sign. Of what? Nic. She's watching me.

I clutch my crystal. "Goddess Eternal, protect me from harm."

The bubbling slows to a simmer, but I know this isn't over. Not a chance. I'm starting to wonder . . . no. Not wonder. I know what this is. Nic's not who she was. Her positive energy has been reshaped and distorted by what I did. Goddess Eternal can't protect me from my own evil doings. My own Karma. Nothing will ever be right again until I tell Nic the truth and make amends. For her sake and mine.

Nicole

"IT'S SAFE TO enter someone's dream, right?" I hope Grace doesn't pick up on the panic in my voice. But of course, she does.

"Don't worry. I'll be there with you. Whatever happens, remember: dreams are not real. No direct physical harm can come to a dreamer or a no body. Of course, this won't be an ordinary dream. Your presence changes that. When the dreamer sees you, he or she instantly realizes they are having a very special, hyper-real dream. They will respond to you with their conscious, waking mind, but they will remain asleep."

"Lucid dreaming! Iz is into that."

"It's lucid dreaming for the dreamer. For us it's *dream touring*, an essential investigatory tool for your research."

"Are you saying that anytime I dreamed about someone who died . . . like, my mom, she was actually doing research?"

"It's very possible. When a no body shows up in the dream of someone she had a connection with, the no body can talk to the dreamer and uncover lost memories or gain insights and perspective on the life she lived."

"Awesome. So, who is my dreamer? Iz? Cassie?"

Please make it Alex.

Don't even think his name! Otherwise Grace will know I want to go into his dream and refuse to take me.

"No one you know."

My face falls before I can catch it.

"I'm sorry to disappoint you, Nicole, but dreamers you know can block the connection, especially if they are having trouble accepting your death. Later on, when you learn how to push through those blocks, you can dream tour anyone you like. But first, you've got to learn the basics, and that's easier with no emotional history. That's why we're starting with a stranger."

Grace pulls a smaller, compact version of my Life-Streamer out of her shirt pocket and activates the thing. As it hovers just above her palm, an image of a darkened room appears. "Good. Dolores is asleep."

Dolores? Isn't that Spanish for *sadness* or *sorrow*? Or maybe it simply means: *Stay out of my dream unless you want to be stuck in a nightmare.*

Either way, not good. I check out potential escape routes all the while trying to appear casually bored. Grace isn't buying it. I suck at improv.

"Re-laax," she coos, tracing gentle circles on my back. "You'll be fine in Dolores's dream. I promise. This will be like learning to swim in the shallow end of the pool."

"Once a kid cannonballed into the shallow end and landed on my head. I almost drowned."

"Almost doesn't count up here." She offers her hand. "Ready?" I shake my head, but I take her hand and hold tight.

A strange sound covered in a thousand years' worth of dust floats in waves from the back of her throat: "Ahhhhooooouuuummmm. Ahhhhoooouuummmm. Ahhhhooooouu-ummmm." The sound reverberates within my chest, filling me with calm, washing over every worry I've ever had or ever will have. I've never believed in magic, but something is definitely happening. I feel . . . *purified.* I've never used that word in a sentence, but it's true! Compared to whatever Grace is doing, Iz's chants seem like *Twinkle, Twinkle, Little Star.*

I don't want to break the spell, but they've told me a hundred times that I'm here to learn and progress. "I want to learn how you make that sound. Will you teach me?"

Grace stops, mid–*Ahhh* and cracks an eye open. "Not now. But I'll tell you what I'm doing and why. I'm widening the channel so you can come into Dolores's dream with me. Later, when you dream tour on your own, you can simply think of the person you want to be with and go."

She resumes chanting, and I slip back into the Land of No Worries where I want to stay forever, except now I know that forever isn't as long as it used to be.

When Grace's last guttural "mmm" fades into nothingness, she tugs my hand and we're in a whole other place where the sound of running water and the scent of lemon dish soap fills the air. I effortlessly glide forward into a room with a bright overhead light. A lumpy, box-shaped, white-haired woman sings *Ob-La-Di, Ob-La-Da* as she washes dishes in the bubble-filled sink by the window. That must be Dolores. There's no one else here except a gray and black striped cat that's napping on the windowsill, its tail twitching.

A cat dreaming inside a dream?

Outside, light snow covers a garden where dry cornstalks rattle in the wind. It all looks solid and real, except for the razor-thin light shimmering around the edges of everything, even the corn.

"Dreams are not real."

The woman waves a soapy hand in our direction. "How nice to see you again, Grace. And who are you?" She turns her bright smile on me.

The distance from my mind to my lips feels like miles.

Grace whispers, "Tell Dolores your name."

"I'm trying!"

How come I can talk to Grace but not to Dolores? How come Grace hears me but Dolores doesn't? Maybe avatars don't use words to communicate with each other.

My mouth won't move, and my lower jaw aches as I try

forcing it open.

Damn! The shallow end is too deep for me.

If I can't even say hi to a nice old lady, how will I get any information from my friends? I won't. I'm going to fail The Evaluation.

A strangled moan rises in the back of my throat.

Grace presses the spot directly over my heart, warmth radiates from under her hand and pushes away the panic.

I give it another shot. "Niiii . . ." I manage to say, my mouth stuck in a stupid smile.

"Nee! What a lovely name . . . Wait! Are you little *Nini Benson*? Is your mother Michelle?"

My mom's name was Michelle Benson and she used to call me Nini. I remembered! But how could Dolores know that? Did Grace know the connection? I look over at Grace. She shrugs. Guess not.

Smiling and shaking her head in amazement, Dolores continues, "You look just like your mother. Except for the hair. Hers was straight and silky, like Mary in Peter Paul and Mary. And yours is . . . so different. And cute. You know she used to bring you to church every Sunday when you were a toddler. You sat on my lap while your mom played guitar for the congregation. Such a lovely woman and what a voice. You were too young to notice, but sometimes your mom's singing moved people to tears. Why that had to have been at least fifteen years ago, because I've been up here in Crescent City since . . . I don't remember. How is your mother, dear?"

I can't tell her Mom is dead. That might kill Dolores in her sleep. And if I tell her that I'm dead, too? Double heart attack.

"No physical harm can come to the dreamer."

Yeah, maybe that's true. Maybe not. I don't want to risk it.

Because I haven't said anything, Dolores asks again. This time a little louder. "Is your mother well?" All I can manage is a string of grunts.

Obviously worried, about my mom and me, she turns to Grace and lowers her voice, "Is this girl okay?"

Grace nods too quickly, and grins while somehow looking like she just swallowed a yellow jacket. "Oh yes. Nini's fine.

She doesn't talk much, but give her something to do. She loves to help." Grace plucks the dish brush from the counter. "Me, too. I'll just finish washing these dishes, Dolores."

"Oh, thank you. How kind. My guests will be here soon, and I still have to plate the cookies. Nini, would you please dry the cups and saucers? You can use that towel over there."

She points to a flowered towel hanging on the refrigerator door handle. Relieved to be off the hot seat, I shuffle across the checkered linoleum like a glitchy robot. My fingers don't work right either. I reach for the towel, my hand passes through the fabric, and three of my fingers vaporize. Frantic, I wave what's left of my hand in Grace's face.

"What's happening?"

"Your avatar is breaking up. We keep it solid for you at Substation Fifteen, but you're in Dolores's reality now."

My right hand vanishes completely. A moment later my left is gone.

"What happens if I disappear completely?"

"Calm down, Nicole. Breathe."

"Breathe. Breathe. Iz's mom, always says that. But it never worked for me when I had a body. Why should it work now?"

"It works if you do it correctly. Breathing re-balances emotions and turns off extraneous thoughts that interfere with . . . never mind. Just breathe and focus on what's left of your avatar and imagine making your avatar whole again."

I breathe in and out too quickly. Light-headed, I lean against the refrigerator, and force myself to slow down. Breathe in. Breathe out. Okay. Less dizzy. Less panicky. This might actually be working. I imagine my missing body-parts, like puzzle pieces, on my mental movie screen. Then I picture them reattaching to my avatar. It's not easy, but gradually I manage to dial my hands and fingers back in. I'm so relieved to be in one piece again, I hug myself.

Dolores doesn't seem to have noticed my disappearing and reappearing act. She smiles patiently and talks to me as if I'm a three-year-old. "We can't set the table with wet dishes, Nini, can we?"

Her tone is annoying and insulting, but hey, this is only a

dream. It's stupid to get pissed off. I'm here to learn something. Maybe I'm supposed to figure out how to pick things up. Patrick Swayze learned to do it in *Ghost* and it was the key to everything in the movie. Okay, I'm going to pick up that dishtowel without losing any fingers this time.

I breathe and focus everything I've got on the towel. I imagine the feel of its rough texture and folds. I imagine grabbing one end of it, pulling it off the door handle, holding it firmly, and carrying it to the sink, where I will use it to dry teacups.

I reach for the towel.

Got it!

Someone pounds on the front door.

"They're here." Dolores sings the words. "Nini, please let our guests in."

Okay. I can do that.

I step into the hallway. I'm walking like a normal person again. I make my way through a small living room made smaller by an oversize table set with grandma dishes, white-rimmed with a blue lace pattern, color-coordinated to the last detail by a blue glass centerpiece filled with white roses.

The knocking grows louder and more insistent. I quickly reach for the glass knob. My hand passes through it. Damn.

"Open up, Dolores! It's freezing out here."

I grab the knob again, and again my hand passes through it. I'm about to call for Grace when I stop myself. I can do this.

I take a slow, deep steadying breath and imagine my fingers gripping the cool surface of the knob. I reach for the doorknob and pull the door open. Yes!

A blast of icy air slaps me across the face so hard I gasp. A crowd of Dolores's friends push past me into the house.

Grace and I step out on the front porch. She pats my back, like a proud coach, or a mom. "Shut the door, Nicole."

I reach behind, and close the door. When I release the knob and step off the front porch, we're in my dorm room and everything looks the same. I flop on the bed and fall back against my pillow. "How about that? I did okay, didn't I? So, now I get to dream tour my friends, right?"

Grace shakes her head. "Not yet. You'll need at least one other practice session with me before you go solo."

"How come?"

"While you cannot physically harm the dreamer, if you're not patient and compassionate, you can harm them emotionally. You lost it a few times back there. So, tomorrow we will practice . . ."

"No. Let's do another one right now." I hold up my countdown finger. "I don't want to waste time."

The happy corner of her mouth droops slightly, so do her shoulders. She looks like she needs a nap, but how can that be?

"Are you okay, Grace?"

She nods more side to side than up and down. "Widening the channel enough for two is always a little . . . Never mind. If you're ready to go again, so am I. Next, we'll meet one of my favorite shallow-end dreamers. Bernard owns a doughnut shop in a small town in Minnesota. Guess what he dreams about?"

I salivate at the mention of doughnuts. I don't want to dream tour any more strangers, but I can't stop wondering if a dream doughnut tastes like anything real. While I'm here, I might as well find out. I also wonder, if I pass The Evaluation, will I ever again sink my teeth into an actual glazed pillow of sugary perfection. How does Grace know I love doughnuts? What else does she know? What about that guy Quinn? He seems to know everything about Grace, so he must know everything about me, too. He probably knows all the stuff that I can't remember. Ooh. Maybe it's time to be a good little nobody and start following the rules.

CASSIE

I'M EMBARRASSED HOW weak and pathetically girly I feel, staring at my phone and hoping Alex texts me. When am I going to learn that hope is for losers? I should know better since every single thing I've ever hoped for didn't happen or, if it did, someone destroyed it or messed it up before I got to enjoy it long enough.

I shove the phone into my back pocket. I'm not texting him again today, unless he texts me first. If he doesn't text before Monday, I still won't text him. I'm not even going to talk to him. Going back to school is going to suck for so many reasons.

Buzz-Kill pounds on my bedroom door. She hasn't said anything yet, but who else would it be? The Nobel Peace Prize committee? At least she's finally learned not to barge in here. "Cassie, *Days of Our Lives* is on." She says it like this is the best news ever.

"Why should I care?"

"Because you like the show. Come watch with me."

"No. *Days* sucks. Lemme alone."

Tap. Tap. Tap. Tap. I select every selfie of me and Nicole

and Alex, and all photos with the three of us plus Kyle. I'm tapping so fast my fingertip goes numb. I delete 679 photos. Out of my phone. Out of my head. Oh. Missed one. When did we take that? Who cares? Don't look. Just delete it. But I zoom in. The three of us eat fish tacos at the Siren Café in Stinson Beach. I look at Nicole's face for too long. My eyes water and my nose runs. I blink hard. Not hard enough.

"Damn!"

Lola lays her head on my knee. Her brown eyes shine with worry.

"What? I'm fine. Let's go for a walk."

Lola's leash always hangs on the hook on the left wall, inside my closet. Everything is where it's supposed to be. People would be surprised that I'm this neat, but when all you've got are one and a half dresser drawers and half of a tiny closet that you share with your sister, you'd better be neat unless you like wasting time looking for stuff. I like seeing my sister Jasmine's clothes and art stuff in here with everything that's important to me. Our room and our closet are home.

I don't have one tenth of what rich kids have, but thanks to my awesome sister, who gives me money whenever she's got extra, the stuff I've got is cool. Like my green high-tops. People say they're not cool. I say the masses are asses and rules are for fools.

Buzz-Kill snores through *Days of Our Lives*, stretched out on the couch, her mouth hangs open like she's catching flies. I tiptoe to the front door and quietly open it. She yells at my back, "Jasmine, get me something to eat before you leave!"

"I'm Cassie." I turn around to prove it.

"That's what I said."

"No, you called me Jas—"

"Shut up. I know the difference between my own daughters. Now heat up the rest of the chili and bring it here."

Whenever I hear the knife-edge in her voice, I watch her hands for any little flick in my direction or Jasmine's. Her hands move fast, and if I look away, she nails me with a swift punch. My left arm is her favorite spot. Or she grabs my wrist and sinks her nails into my skin. Most of the time, I duck in time. Or run. I haven't had the guts to hit her back, yet . . . but it won't be much longer. Before I can tell her I'm in a hurry and she should get off her fat ass and heat up her own chili, she reads my mind, like the witch that she is.

"Don't even think about telling me you don't have time. My hip is killing me." She moans to make sure I feel sorry for her. I don't.

I microwave the chili for a long, long, time, just so it will burn her mouth, but by the time I bring over the bowl, she's asleep again. It'll be cold by the time she wakes up, and she'll bitch about that, and the fact that I didn't give her a fork, because I don't give a fork. Lucky for me, I won't be here.

As I walk down the front steps of our building, Jasmine climbs up carrying a bag of groceries in one arm, her art portfolio under the other. She sets down her stuff and pulls me into a hug. I know she loves me, but she knows I'm not into PDAs.

"What's that for?"

"Why didn't you tell me about Nicole?"

I avoid her eyes.

She gently pushes the hair out of my face. "How are you feeling, little sister?"

If I knew, I'd tell her. Then I might feel less of it.

"I'm okay. FYI, Buzz-Kill's out cold. Also, there's no more chili. C'mon, Lola. Let's go see the kids."

Even though it's Saturday, the Child Caring Center is open. Every day is a workday for some kid's parent. I could have called Mr. Robert and made up an excuse for not coming to work today. But I'd only be thinking about Nicole and waiting for Alex to text, and what's the point of any that? Besides, it's my turn to set up the afternoon art project. We're making macaroni necklaces. Wouldn't want to miss the fun.

I need twenty-one cups of macaroni, twenty-one sheets of paper, twenty-one brushes, ten containers of glue, and four tubs each of red, blue, yellow, green, and orange paint. I pull stuff off the supply closet shelves and put them on the cart, but I keep losing count. As soon as everything's on the long table by the window, Angel and Lucas start fighting. Just what I need.

"Sit next to me, Miss Cassie." Angel pats the empty chair beside her, giving me her cutest four-year-old smile.

"No, next to *me*." Four-year-old Lucas hugs the empty chair next to him.

What's the big deal? I could solve this problem for them in two seconds, but the director, Mr. Robert, wants us to encourage the kids to solve their own problems. Like that's always going to be easy.

"Why don't you guys figure out a way for me to sit next to *both* of you at the same time?"

Angel kicks the empty chair beside her so hard it crashes to the floor. Her eyes get big. Lucas giggles like he can't wait for me to yell at her. I don't. Angel sets the chair right and whispers something to Lucas that I can't hear. A smile lights his face. He slides over to the empty chair beside him.

Angel points to the empty chair now between her and Lucas. "You can sit right here, Miss Cassie! That way we both get to sit next to you."

"Good job, you guys," I high-five each of them. It's cool they figured it out.

"We did copper-*ation*," Lucas says proudly.

Angel turns smug. "You mean CO-operation, stupid head."

Lucas's mouth starts to twitch, just like Buzz-Kill, and he balls up his fist like he's going to punch Angel. I cover his entire little fist with my hand. He looks up, surprised, then leans against me. Angel smushes in on the other side. The two of them are like Lola, only in stereo. "You're so nice, Miss Cassie." Angel slips her hand inside of mine. I let it stay there.

No way would I be hanging out with little kids if I hadn't gotten community service for shoplifting a stupid paintbrush because I didn't have the money to buy a good present for Jasmine, so, of course, I don't get paid for working here, otherwise I'd have the money I need to buy stuff.

"But the job is not without benefits," Mr. Robert says during my first interview, which must also be his lunch break because a big sandwich sits on a paper plate on his desk. He sips coffee from a

cup. It steams his glasses and makes his eyes disappear. When they reappear, he bends over and pets Lola. "You can bring your dog to work. I see that she's gentle. Same breed as my Sandy who used to nap right over there in her dog bed. I still have the bed. Lola can use it. Aside from pet privileges, breakfast and lunch are included. We offer a selection of the finest bananas, oranges, carrots, graham crackers, string cheese, and peanut butter for snack all day long. Oh, and juices. Sometimes apple. Sometimes orange. And occasionally, get ready for this, a surprisingly tasty pear-grape combo."

I wanted to laugh. He wasn't funny, but his voice made me feel good in a way I never felt before. I thought, just maybe, I had finally met an adult who wasn't out to get me. I caught myself before I smiled because I figured it had to be an act, and I'd be a fool to trust him. I downloaded my bitch face and said nothing.

Mr. Robert's lunch looks better than a Subway TV commercial. I can smell the bread and the salami. I love salami.

My mouth waters and I swallow fast before I drool. "Where'd you get that sandwich?"

"I made it myself. Would you like half?"

I shake my head. I don't want him to think I am one of those kids who don't have good food at home. Even though I am one of those kids.

"You sure? It's a big sandwich and it's already cut in two. Besides, I'm not that hungry today. I might not even finish one half. If you don't help me out, Miss Cassie, I'll have to wrap it up and take it home. But that would be a waste because fresh bread is never the same the next day."

It smells amazing and I didn't have breakfast.

"Okay sure. Why not? Just so it doesn't go to waste."

He hands me half the sandwich. It's the best sandwich I ever ate.

That was two months ago. I don't hide behind my bitch face around here anymore. Mr. Robert really is a good guy, and he always seems to know when something's going on with me, so what's the point of hiding? Still, some things have to stay hidden.

All the parents have picked up their kids. I'm not ready to go home so Lola and I sit in Mr. Robert's office. Part of me feels like talking to him, but I don't know what to say or how to say it. Mr. Robert offers Lola a biscuit from the box he keeps on the shelf for her. She takes it from his hand, and eats it without taking her eyes off me.

"You don't seem well today, Miss Cassie. How can I be of service?"

I ignore his question. He pretends not to notice. He opens the small fridge, pulls out an apple juice box and hands it to me. As I take it, my sleeve rides up, showing the bruise on my wrist. I cover it before he can see.

"Thanks." I stare at the box. I'm thirsty, but somehow poking the straw through the top suddenly feels like too much work. I count six coffee cups crowding the right side of his desk, each one is half-full or more.

"Hey, Mr. Robert, how come you never finish your coffee?"

"Good observation. Well, the truth is I only enjoy scalding hot coffee. My coffee maker provides exactly what I require. Several times a day I pour myself a cup. And that first sip . . . Ahhhh. Heaven! But no sooner do I get to the halfway point that a child or a teacher or a parent needs my assistance. By the time I get back to my coffee, it's cold. So, I am forced to pour a new cup."

"If you don't drink cold coffee, why don't you dump it?"

He looks at me, like maybe he's stalling so he can make up some BS.

"It's not prudent to throw things away, Miss Cassie. Someday, a teacher might come in here and say, 'Mr. Robert, we're doing a science lesson and we need a cup of three-day-old coffee. Would you happen to have one?' At which point I will respond in the affirmative and *presto!* My coffee will find a purpose. Everything and everyone has one."

Total BS.

He picks up the closest cup, sips, makes a face and puts it back on the desk. "Cold."

He leans on his elbow. "I'd like to talk to you about Angel and Lucas. I'm sure you've noticed how sometimes they're happy and affectionate, and the next minute they can turn meaner than you thought was possible for a four-year-old."

I nod.

"Maybe you've wondered why they do that."

I have wondered but something about these kids reminds me of myself at that age, and I don't want to get into it. I shake my head. "Nope. Haven't thought about it."

He gives me a kind, no-pressure look, but I know he knows I'm lying. That's the cool thing about Mr. Robert. He doesn't buy my BS, never has, but he doesn't make a big deal about it. Guess it's his way of encouraging me to solve my own problems.

He spears the juice box with the straw and gives it back to me. "I strongly believe their erratic behavior here comes from their not feeling safe at home. In both situations, neither of their parents have been able to provide a consistently loving environment. This is a very sad thing for children. It is a tragedy when a child cannot trust the adult who cares for her. And when that trust is missing, children find it hard to trust anyone. That's why those two are skittish around some of our staff. Interestingly, they trust me to be kind and respectful to them. They don't know you well, but they trust you too. Have you ever wondered why?"

I shrug.

He raises an eyebrow. "Ah. The game. I ask a question and you pretend you don't know what I'm talking about. Very well. I'll answer the question myself. Those little ones have special radar. You've got a soft side, Miss Cassie. A loving, caring side and those children sense it. You try to hide your soft side because you believe kindness shows weakness. But you're wrong about that. Vulnerability is true strength."

How can weakness be strength? I don't know what he's talking about, but I don't say anything, because if I do, he'll explain it in a way that might make me cry, and that would not be cool.

I stand. Lola stands. "We should get going."

Mr. Robert hoists himself out of his chair, walks over to the coffee maker, and pours himself a cup. "Ahh. Now that's hot coffee."

Before I can stop myself, I say, "A girl I know killed herself, and I'm pretty sure I had something to do with it."

I regret it instantly. I hold my breath, waiting, watching him. But he just sips his coffee. His glasses fog up. Maybe he can't see me. Maybe he didn't hear me, either. Maybe that would be a good thing.

Nicole

"WHAT ARE YOU doing out in the hallway, Nicole?" Quinn must have sneaked up behind me.

I give him double stink eye for trying to intimidate me and for knowing my name, but I drop it quickly, for Grace's sake, and I slap on my good girl smile. It makes my face itch, like a wool mask, but the show must go on.

"Nothing. I'm just passing through. I just finished a second dream tour session with Grace, who, by the way, is an awesome Mentor. You're so lucky to have her on the team. I'm progressing so quickly, which is why I'm giving her five stars on Yelp. Now I'm heading back to my cozy little dorm room to enjoy all the comforts of home while I process everything I've learned so far to make room for more learning and progressing."

I'm not lying, but he looks at me like he thinks I am. What's the point of telling the truth when no one believes me?

I hurry toward my room, looking over my shoulder and pretending I can't get away from him fast enough, just to mess with his head and get him wondering what I'm up to. I wish I were up to something. My countdown clock says I've almost used up two days and all I've learned is how to pick up a dream dishtowel and bite a doughnut that tastes like nothing. Less than nothing. How's any of that going to help me pass The Evaluation?

I peek in on Shorty. He doesn't seem to be worrying about anything. He's playing with his snake. I'm trying not to judge anyone else's idea of fun, but it's not easy.

Back in my room, I pull up a chair and activate the Life-Streamer. An instant later I'm zooming in on Cassie deleting photos of me on her phone. She stops at one of Calex and me at Stinson Beach. They're wearing matching *Aren't we a cute couple?* grins. Being that close to Alex, even for a minute, always made me hot. Look at my fake smile, like I'm working overtime to convince Calex that being their third wheel is such a blast.

Cassie's face crumbles as she stares at the photo. Huh. I thought she'd be happy I'm out of the picture forever. She's almost as hard to figure out as Calex. I never understood how they stayed a couple. Of course, I never said anything to Cassie, but Iz and I had plenty of conversations on that topic.

"Do you think he's into her because she's a bad girl? It definitely makes her seem cool. Even though Alex transferred to Veraz, he's still totally Chesterfield Academy. And honor roll, and an athlete, and kinda artsy, too. He'll probably go to Stanford. Could he be any less Cassie's type? So, why's she with him?"

Iz flips a page in her Book of Spells. "You don't care why she's with him. You just want to know why he's with her and not you."

It amazed me how Iz always saw right through my BS. I hated her for it. I loved her for it too.

I ignore her comment. "Cassie's got to be like a habit or something he's got no control over. Kyle went to Brookside Elementary with both of them. He said Alex and Cassie liked each other in fifth grade! Then his parents put him in Chesterfield for middle school. Now that they're in the school together again I guess the old spark got rekindled. Of course, it may not last, but even if they break up,

I should forget about him, right? I mean if he's into a girl like Cassie, he'd never be into me, right?"

"*Probably not.*"

"*But he might. Hey, Iz, I've got an idea.*"

The Attraction Spell had just started working. It might have totally worked if we'd had more time. Actually, no. Why am I lying to myself? Who cares if Calex's relationship made no sense? Cassie was always going to be in the way of Alex and me. But the most baffling part was why a nice guy like Alex wouldn't want a nice girlfriend like me instead of Cassie, the one-woman nuclear arsenal. Not that she targeted me much, but still. The song I wrote about her nailed it.

She sneers and jeers,
Celebrating people's tears,
Scoring points on their late-night fears
But no one dares to call out hers.

I was okay at snarky lyrics. Too bad I sucked at actual confrontations.

"*I should break up with Cassie,*" Alex gives me *his* typical I-really-want-to-kiss-you look.

Whenever Cassie wasn't around, I got the look, never the kiss. He'd come in close and pull away. It always killed me. Funny how many times you can get killed without dying.

Dad's all-time favorite non-negotiable truth is: *You've gotta poop or get off the pot.* That one was so perfect for Alex. I wish I'd had the guts to come right out and ask him, "Why don't you just break up with her instead of talking about it? Why don't you just kiss me already? Why don't you just do *something?*" But I didn't want to face the truth that a) I was in love with a total wimp and b) Calex would last forever. Either I had to accept it or risk making a move that would piss off Cassie and lose whatever "just friends" thing Alex and I had. So, he never got off the pot and neither did I. Or did I? I kinda feel like I did. Maybe. Crap. I wish I could remember what happened.

I check on Dad on Life-Streamer. He's asleep. Since I aced the doughnut dream, now is my chance to swim solo in the deep end. Grace doesn't need to know.

Thousands of towering, glowing, crisscrossing silver strands of... I don't know what, sprout from Dad's head, weaving and waving like tall grass, each one ending in a pinpoint of light. Brain waves? I zoom in and think about Dad. As soon as I do, my room vanishes, and I'm standing in what looks like a forest of seaweed. The silvery strands stretch far above my head, like a living curtain. I feel very small, but safe. The way I always did when I was with Dad.

His voice is muffled and panicky. I can't make out the words. I pull back the curtain. Every place I touch sprouts a bumpy node, and from each one, a new silver strand grows. I step through the opening. I can already tell that my being here has changed things, but I don't know if that's good or bad.

The softly lit clearing up ahead feels like the center of everything. As I walk forward the strands shrink away, revealing Dad frantically knocking on doors in a hallway that looks just like my high school. Room 8. Room 9. Room 10. He jiggles each door handle. They're all locked. He pounds on the door of Room 11.

"Nikki, are you in there?"

"I'm right beside you, Dad."

He turns, looks through me like I'm not even there, and moves to the next door. Why can't he see me? Even when I couldn't talk to Dolores, she saw me.

"Dreamers who knew you well can block the connection, especially if they are having trouble accepting your death."

That's why he's locking me out.

He knocks at Room 12. The number morphs into words: *No Admittance*. He rams his shoulder against the door setting off an alarm. Teachers pour into the hall, shouting and threatening to call the police.

"Dad, let's get out of here."

We run together but he has no clue that I'm with him.

The school transforms into a mall. If Dad notices the scene shift, he doesn't show it. I'm beside him when he jumps onto an up-escalator packed with shoppers, his eyes on a girl who's several steps above us. The back of her head looks familiar. Oh, wow. That's *me*. Only younger. That's my 13-year-old-self, but she's so confident. Look how she's rocking that turquoise tank top. Her boobs are big but she's owning them. She's owning this whole mall. How could she be me? I always covered up my chest. Hyper-sensitive about my looks. And about everything anybody said. I obsessed over every conversation, every text. I cried over the stupidest little things. Always thinking about Alex. Wondering if he was The One. And if he wasn't, would I ever find The One? Geez. How pathetic and annoying was I? How did Dad stand me? How did Iz? No matter what I was ranting about, she always listened and tried to help.

My 13-year-old-self doesn't look like she worries about anything. I never looked or acted like her. I never *was* her. So why is Dad dreaming of this unreal version of me? Huh. Must be the way he saw me.

And he saw me that way because he loved me.

I want to reach out to Dad but my arms won't move. They're weighed down. It's like I'm encased in cement, or maybe it's the reality of knowing that no one will ever love me like that again.

Two guys, who look to be around sixteen, ride on the escalator, one step below my thirteen-year-old-self. One puts a hand on her shoulder. The other whispers in her ear. She stiffens and tries to move away, but she's blocked by the crowd.

Dad's mouth twists in rage "Hey. Leave her alone!" He pushes hard against the wall of people. No one budges. My heart thunders. What if those guys . . . ?

Hold on. It's only a dream. No real danger.

Flushed and breathing heavily, Dad leans on the handrail. He never takes his eyes off my thirteen-year-old-self, who elbows her way upward through the shoppers. She jumps off the escalator and runs into the crowd, the creepy guys follow close behind.

Dad is sweating when he reaches the top step, hand clutching his chest. He could have a heart attack in his sleep.

He pauses for a second, catches his breath, then takes off after them.

He turns a corner. I follow. He's caught up with 13-year-old-me. The guys are gone. I need to talk to him but all his attention is on her. Maybe if I become her, he'll see me. How would that work when she's so perfect and I'm so . . . dead? Wait! She's just a memory. Is that any better than being a ghost? Neither of us is real so it's possible merging with her won't be that hard. I could pretend to be her. Everyone said I was great in *Our Town*. That I *became* Emily onstage. Weird thing about acting, the better you lie, the more the audience loves you for it.

But I don't want to pretend to be Dad's memory of who he thought I was back then. I just want to be me so we can talk. That's the only way I'm going to find out what I need to know. Dad may not think he's ready to accept my death, but when he sees me here, he'll be ready.

I ease into the body of my thirteen-year-old-self. The space is cramped, like a blanket tucked too tightly all around. I stretch my neck, my arms and legs. With each move, the memory shell stretches with me. The avatar of the body I had on my Last Day, replaces her body. My long white shirt and leggings replace her tank top and jeans.

"Dad." I reach out to hug him.

The veil lifts from his eyes. He sees me. His face crumbles.

"No." His voice cracks. He turns and stumbles away.

The dream vanishes and I am back in my dorm room on Substation Fifteen.

I shouldn't have forced it. He's not ready.

Isabel

MOM MADE ME promise to blow out all the candles on my altar table every night before I go to sleep. I'd rather let them burn to light Nic's path between worlds, but I'm trying to do a better job keeping promises. When these candles are completely gone, I'll light new ones. I promise to continue the ritual for at least one complete cycle around the sun so Nic will always feel the white light energy I'm sending to her. Maybe that will make up for what I did.

Sick waves slosh inside my stomach, like fishbowl water that needs changing.

Uhn.

I light a stick of incense.

"Magik bend. Incense burn.

Sickness end. Good health return."

The sloshing subsides.

"Thank you, Goddess."

Nic's photo flickers in the light of the candles, fading in and out behind curls of sweet smoke rising from the incense. Her teeth flash behind her lips. Her smile widens. Now she's laughing, snorting like a pig. I laugh with her and *at* her. Now she's hiccupping, like she always did when she got carried away.

Carried away.

I snap back to the dark silence, stunned at how easily the light and shadow trap me in the past, like a Dark Arts trick, like memory and movie-making, trying to convince me Nic is still alive.

I count the squares on my wall calendar backwards from today, Sunday, January 6 to Friday, January 4, the day she died. Time is a lie, so why do I hang these pages on my wall? Our days don't line up in neat, numbered boxes. Goddess Eternal teaches us that every moment was, is, and will be part of *now.*

It is 6:45 am. Only forty-two minutes until sunrise. Beyond my balcony door the starless sky shows no signs of light. Someone said the darkest hour is right before the dawn of a new day. Today won't be any brighter after the sun comes up. If I don't make amends with Nic, I will fall into darkness and never know the light again.

I swallow. My throat burns. The truth hurts.

I search through my Book of Spells for sigils I've drawn for good health, good luck, protection. Focusing on each one in turn, I try to catch a spark of the special power I need right now. Double crescent moons? No spark. A star with the diamond center? No. A crowned heart? Wrong. This loss, this guilt, this torment requires a new sigil.

The nothingness of the blank paper quiets my mind. My calligraphy pen strengthens my connection to the Goddess. My higher self will guide my hand.

Name the goal. What do I want? What am I aiming for? I don't know. I stare at the paper until my eyes go dry. No answer. It hurts to blink. Is yesterday's dust still blinding me? I have to clear it out, or the goal won't reveal itself.

Two drops of my special infusion of eyebright herb, goldenseal root, and chamomile soothe and hydrate my eyes. Instantly the answer comes: I want to apologize to Nic for what I did to her and clean up the terrible mess I made.

That's too many words for a sigil goal. Keep it simple.

I want Nicole's forgiveness.

Positive energy sparks behind my heart. I write the four words on the paper, exactly three inches high, no spaces in between. I slash through each vowel and repeated consonant with a single neat line always moving from upper right to lower left. I write what's left on a clean sheet of paper.

W N T C L S F R G V

Good. Now for the magik. The ten letters don't look like anything yet, but I can rearrange them to form a powerful symbol that will connect me with Nic and create the space for forgiveness.

I rearrange the letters at least twenty different ways, turning them on their sides, flipping them over, stacking them, and nesting them so close to each other that they share lines and spaces, like best friends.

When the symbol finally reveals itself, hope rises within me like sweet incense. I carefully redraw the forgiveness sigil in my Book of Spells on its own, special page.

When the ink dries, I trace the curves, peaks, and angles with my left index finger. Courage and strength flow into my heart.

I pull my talking board out from under the bed, the feel of it calms my spirit. I'm excited to talk to Nic. I miss her. I will ask for forgiveness, and she will forgive me. I know it. We love each other. Harmony and balance will be restored.

I set the planchette directly over the Goddess's eye and count twelve inhalations and exhalations.

"Goddess Eternal, please lighten my soul.

Open the portal. Bring in Nicole.

Let the love in my heart light a path straight and clear.

Let our undying friendship guide her spirit here."

My mind drifts and my thoughts weave between the ribbons of sandalwood smoke. I wonder if she believes in spirits now.

Nic shows me a small circle of gray fabric.

"What's this?" I ask.

"A piece of Alex's hoodie. You said you needed something of his for the ritual. He gave it to Cassie."

"What did you tell her you wanted it for?"

"I didn't. She leaves it in her locker, so her mom won't know they're dating. I know her combination so I just took it and cut this tiny piece out of the back. She'll never notice. And if she does, she'll think Alex accidentally ripped it."

She tries to give me the fabric, but I hold up my hand. "You stole it from Cassie! Forget it. I'm not touching that thing. It's not ethical to perform a ritual with stolen items. Unintended consequences will follow."

Nic grins and pushes the fabric at me. "It's okay. I'll take my chances."

"I dunno . . ."

"C'mon, Iz. Please. It'll be fine."

I knew it wouldn't. None of this would have happened if I'd listened to my knowingness. I know that with even more certainty now. But in that moment, my heart ached for her and with her. I felt how much she yearned for Alex's love. Nic was suffering and helpless. I love her, and I knew I could help, so I told her to write her name and Alex's on that stolen circle of fabric.

"Are you sure this will work?"

"Pretty sure."

I fold the circle north to south, east to west and stuff it into the amulet I place around her neck.

"Press this to your heart. Focus on the red candle and repeat after me: To win thy heart and bring you in, I wear this cloth that touched your skin."

Eyes shining, she repeats the words and hugs me. We hold each other close. Her heart chakra relaxes. She is calmer. Happier. I am too.

"Thank you, Iz. I'll never forget you for this."

A bird screeches somewhere over the hill behind my house and yanks me back into this world where my best friend is dead, and it's my fault.

The planchette jerks in fits and starts under my clammy fingers, like someone learning to drive a stick shift. I hold on, but it's not easy.

"Is that you, Nic?" I whisper to the space above my head.

Both altar candles snuff out at the same moment. Their smoke plumes form two winding fingers, pointing to the ceiling. My room dips into a darkness deeper than before I lit the candles, as if I'm traveling backward in time, instead of forward toward the sunrise. The planchette careens off the board and flips onto its side, like a car in a ditch. An icy ocean swells from the back of my neck, roaring over the top of my head. A wave of nausea pulls me under. I close my eyes, waiting for the sick feeling to pass. It gets worse.

I stagger to the door, but before I can turn the knob, the hinges squeak and the door yawns open. Rumpled and sniffling loudly, Mom steps into my room. "Awww, sweetie. You can't sleep either?" She brushes the hair out of my face. I want to hug her but my arms are weak and the thought of raising them is too much. I steady myself with a hand on the altar.

Dad slouches against the doorframe. His glasses low on his nose.

"Mike is putting together a memory board for the funeral," he says, his voice cracking. "He asked us for old photos of Nicole and you."

Mom smiles sadly. "We're walking over to his house after breakfast."

I relight the candles as calmly as I can. "Have a good walk," I say, fighting the urge to vomit.

Dad pushes up his glasses and clears his throat. "We want you to come with us, kiddo."

"The fresh air will make you feel better." Mom sounds like she doesn't believe it for a second.

I imagine Mike and my parents and me sitting in Nic's kitchen that's not hers anymore, looking through photos of birthday parties, Halloweens, family barbecues, and vacations we spent together in our cabin in Mt. Shasta City.

A foul-tasting burp unloads in the back of my throat. I cover my mouth and mumble into my hand. "I . . . I don't feel like going anywhere."

"I understand, sweetheart." Mom reaches out to me. I duck. She pretends not to notice. "It's okay. We'll just tell Mike that you're . . ."

"No," Dad gently wraps his arm around Mom's shoulders. "She needs to come with us."

Mom nods and straightens up. They stand together, blocking my doorway, so confident that they know what I need without ever asking me. My mouth fills with putrid saliva. I push past them and race to the bathroom.

Isabel

I rarely talk to Gabby beyond the occasional "Hey," but here she comes with open arms and a pity-smile just for me. The Goddess teaches us to be kind to others and to appreciate all manifestations of love, but what about fake kindness? Am I going to get this from people all day? I should have stayed home. I told Mom my stomach isn't right and my throat is sore. She would have let me skip school if Dad hadn't butted in.

"Mandy, she's manipulating you again because you let her. Like every time she wants to buy more of her witchcraft supplies."

"That's a lie. I don't let her manipulate me."

I hate the negative energy between them. Besides, I never manipulate Mom. She says she supports my beliefs and always hands over her credit card when I ask for it. But I know she wishes I was normal. She cares more about what Dad thinks than my health. Just to prove him wrong she sent me to school today even though I am sick.

"We'd better not hug." I tell Gabby, holding up my hands like a shield. "I've got a cold."

And a hug would make me lose it, and I'd be a mess for the rest of the day. I'm already a mess, physically, emotionally, spiritually, and none of my spells are helping. Not that I'd tell that to Gabby or anyone else.

She nods, understandingly and steps back. "So, so awful. When did you first find out about Nicole? And how did you find out?"

Gabby asks questions like a journalist, always gathering information just in case it should come in handy someday. I try to decipher her question. It sounds like she wants to know if my news source is better than hers. Telling her the top-level truth, "Nicole told me herself, through my talking board," is out of the question.

I go with the second level truth. "Her dad called my mom Friday."

Gabby looks intrigued, like she's thinking of a follow-up question. I turn to the box of markers sitting on the pavement, pretending to search through the colors. Black would fit the mood, but the only one here is out of ink.

People walk by without noticing me. They're talking about Nicole and a party some kids had at the beach. The weather has been weirdly summer-like. A few people call it *June-uary*. The forecast says today's high will be 84 degrees. Even so, I'm shivering in my wool cloak, with the hood up. I touch my neck. My glands are sore and as big as golf balls. This could be the flu. Or something much worse. I cover my mouth and pretend to clear my throat while I chant quietly into my hand:

"Goddess Eternal, please help me align
All healing energy, so that I feel fine.
Goddess Eternal, do hurry, please
Banish all microbes, discomfort, disease."

The angel Gabby is drawing on Nic's memorial banner has frizzy hair, big boobs, and a guitar. Nic would hate it, though she'd be thrilled that they taped the banner on the parking lot wall, right in front of the school, so no one could miss it. She'd definitely be pleased with this pile of stuffed animals, even though she always said stuffies were a totally useless gift unless you're a two-year-old. I can hear her bragging about how many hand-written messages there are already, and first period bell hasn't even rung.

"Thoughts and prayers!"

"We'll never forget you, Nicole."

"Heaven has a new angel."

None of this means anything. It could have been written to any dead girl, in any place, at any time. I need to write an honest, totally personal message to counteract these empty words. Something that will spark joy in Nic, in case she stops by.

I pick out a purple marker. The tip is way too fat to draw anything beautiful. Gabby watches me like a security guard at the mall. My stress and anxiety levels rise. It feels weird to be spied on. Most of the people at school treat me like I'm invisible, which is fine because filmmakers are supposed to be invisible. How else can you observe people at their most real? Other people call me a loser for making movies that they say no one will ever watch. They're just jealous because they lack passion for anything except gossip. They also mock me for being a witch. That's pure ignorance. I don't care what they say. They can't stop me and they can't hurt me. I am protected by the Goddess.

A flowery cross says: "Home with God." Whoever drew it definitely didn't know Nic. Nobody knew her like I did.

Gabby keeps watching me. I should write an in-joke message that only Nic would understand. Gabby will take a photo of whatever I write and post it with a comment with *her* interpretation. She's not mean, but that's how other people will take it. She'll end up apologizing to me, but she won't understand how things got out of hand because she thought she was being nice. It's impossible to predict what's going to help people and what will set them off. Someone might believe they're being a wonderful, caring, and compassionate friend, but the other person ends up hating what was done and hating their friend for doing it.

Forget about the in-joke. Instead, I draw a clunky, critique-proof purple candle with an orange flame. With my own calligraphy pen I write "NICOLE" in graceful letters that stretch skyward from the flame, like a spirit rising. Gabby will probably say it's awesome.

CLICK

Gabby grins behind her phone. "You're an awesome artist."

You don't have to be psychic when someone is that predictable.

The spot in the back of my neck feels normal. Thank Goddess. But I psychically scan north, south, east, and west just to make sure. I don't sense Nic. If I died while I was still in high school, I wouldn't come back either. Of course, if Nic came here, she'd be truly invisible, not just ignored, like me.

The bell rings. I hurry inside and join the river of students flooding the halls, showing off their new jackets and phones and the other stuff they got for Christmas and Hanukkah. Wiccans don't celebrate either. I insist on doing our family gift exchange on December 21, Winter Solstice. Mom is fine with that. I know Dad thinks it's all ridiculous, but he doesn't object, which is nice of him. The holidays seem so long ago I don't remember one thing that I got.

I turn down the hall to the math wing. Cassie stands in front of her open locker, whispering to Mariah. As Alex approaches from the other direction, Mariah slaps a book out of Cassie's hand. Cassie acts like she's shocked, but the timing is too perfect for it not to have been planned. The book falls inches from Alex's shoe. He steps over it and hurries to catch up to Kyle. Cassie kicks the book, sending it flying into Mariah's shin. Mariah winces but says nothing as she picks up the book and offers it to Cassie with a sympathetic shrug. Cassie rips the book out of her hand, and slams her locker shut.

Half-way down the hall, I watch Alex touch Kyle's shoulder and say something I can't hear. Kyle elbow-jabs him. Stunned, Alex watches his best friend storm off. I'm stunned, too. I've never seen Kyle attack anything other than a piano keyboard.

Alex pulls off his cap and shoves it into the side pocket of his backpack. He got a haircut. Too short. It makes his nose look huge. It's not Wiccan to be judgmental, but if he looked like that a year ago when he transferred from Chesterfield, Nic probably wouldn't have liked him and everything would have been different.

Nic and I are standing outside Ms. Moreno's room and I'm pointing to the announcement tacked on the bulletin board.

"Let's both audition for Our Town."

"Great idea. Except I can't act."

"What are you talking about? You've starred in my five movies."

"That's not like being on stage."

"You were great in the talent show."

"I sang a duet with Cassie. I had my eyes closed the whole the time. You can't do that in a play. I'm sure I could memorize lines and all that, but real acting means you've got to convince an entire audience that you are a completely different person. No thanks. I have enough trouble being myself."

Of course, she changed her mind when Alex signed up. She denied it, loudly, but he was the only reason she auditioned. When I got the part of Mrs. Webb and she got Emily, I was super excited. Mother and daughter! I thought we'd have fun rehearsing our scenes and shopping for costumes and props. That didn't happen.

When we started high school, things changed between us. Nic was all about starting a new social chapter in her life. Mom said not to worry about it, and since we had totally different class schedules and still hung out outside of school, I didn't really notice until the talent show. She became obsessed with Cassie and how awesome their voices sounded together. When Nic found out that Alex was Cassie's boyfriend, she wanted to hang with them all the time. I pretended I was fine with that, and she pretended she believed me. But we both knew the truth. That's why she gave me sad eyes when no one was looking. She wanted me to think she was sorry for hurting me. She wanted me to feel sorry for *her* and the tough choices she had to make. Like what was lost between us wasn't her fault. But whose fault was it? No one forced her to choose them over me. And what did she gain? Alex? I warned her not to trust him because that's what best friends do. I also tried to get her to understand that whatever energy you put out in the world will come back to you three-fold. What did I get for trying?

SCREEEECH

I plug my ears. Nic detested PA feedback. She said the sound was almost as obnoxious as crows. She was wrong about that. Crows are beautiful, cunning, acutely aware of impending danger. Crows are awesome.

SCREEEECH

"Good morning, Veraz Vikings." Mrs. Moss's mouth must be touching the microphone.

SCREEEECH

"Happy New Year and welcome back." I guess she's backed way up because now her voice sounds like it's coming from under a pile of laundry. "Dr. Campbell and I, and all of your teachers, hope you had a restful winter break and that you are ready to resume your studies."

Mrs. Moss pauses and sniffles into the mike. I know what's next.

"Unfortunately, we are returning to school on a very sad note."

Here it comes. The pressure in my chest pushes against my lungs, and I have to stop and lean against the wall. Don't lose it. Don't lose it.

"For those of you haven't yet heard the news, we lost a valuable member of our Veraz High School community to a sudden, tragic death." Her voice cracks. "Nicole Benson passed away last Friday."

I shut my eyes and squeeze them as tight as I'm squeezing my crystal. *Goddess Eternal, make me invisible.*

"Dr. Campbell wants you to know that we appreciate the memorial banner on the parking lot wall, and the gestures of remembrance some of you have left there and in front of Nicole's locker. Your tokens will remain until after the funeral service, when they will be collected. If any of you would like to talk to the school counselor, Ms. Goldman, she will be available for private conversations. You can slot yourself in on her shared calendar. You'll find the link at the bottom of the faculty page at VerazVikings.com. Also, if you'd like to share any personal written memories of Nicole, please bring those to Ms. Moreno, as she will be sending them to Mr. Benson, along with all the adorable stuffed animals. A funeral service for Nicole will be held tomorrow afternoon at 4 pm at Vintage Oaks Community Center. All afterschool clubs and team practices will be suspended to accommodate those who wish to attend."

The sound of shuffling papers crackles the airwaves.

"Oh, yes. One more thing, the following students will report to Dr. Campbell's office for a brief meeting this morning. Please arrive promptly at the following times . . . Alexander Traynor, 9:30; Cassandra Church, 10:30; Kyle Jackson, 11:15; Isabel Waterman, 11:40. The rest of you, have a good day."

My swollen glands throb. People who've never looked at me suddenly stare and snigger. I slide my fingers along the length of my crystal and look straight ahead, as if it's no big deal that I've just been called to the principal's office for the first time in my life.

Mariah squeals. "Not even first period and you're in trouble already. Way to go, Cass." She holds up her hand to high five her friend.

Cassie slaps it. "New record."

Their hands drop. As soon as Mariah looks away, Cassie's mouth ties itself into a knot. She's worried about talking to Dr. Campbell. I've never seen Cassie worried. I pull out my camera to record this moment. When I point it at her, Cassie's sneer fills the frame. She's staring, glaring, daring me to record.

Forget the moment.

I shove the camera into my backpack, and hurry away, clutching my crystal and whispering into my fist.

"Goddess Eternal, bind Cassie's power

From this moment from this hour

Freeze the fire of her wrath

Guide my steps far from her path."

When I get home I'll write Cassie's name on a piece of paper, put it in cup of water and stick it in the freezer.

In the meantime, I'm trying not to worry about what Dr. Campbell might ask me and what I'm going to say.

CASSIE

"DO YOU KNOW why I wanted to talk to you, Cassandra?" Dr. Miriam G. Campbell, PhD, says without bothering to look up from her computer.

Hmm. So many possibilities. She might want to talk about vandalism, cutting class, lying about vandalism and cutting class, but since Mrs. Moss announced my name along with Alex, Kyle, and Isabel, it can only be one thing.

"Honor society?" I ask.

Dr. Campbell eyes me over the top of her laptop like I am a roach infestation, or worse. "I want to ask you a few questions about Nicole."

Surprise!

"Cassandra, do you have any idea why she would have taken her own life?"

Dr. Campbell must have majored in dumb-ass questions in college.

"Funny you should ask, Dr. Campbell, because I've been wondering the same thing. All I can come up with is that she must have been insane. Isn't that what the psychology books say? Sane people never kill themselves, right?"

She raises an eyebrow, types, and keeps talking without looking at me. "Do you think Nicole might have been the victim of bullying? You two were friends. I assume you would have known if she was being harassed by someone at school or online."

I knew she'd ask something like that. As if bullying is the only reason a kid might want to check out of life.

"Wow, I never thought about that," I say, trying to look impressed. Adults, especially teachers, love it when kids treat them like geniuses. Dr. Campbell seems to be eating it up so I pour on extra sauce. "But, yeah, now that you mention it. It's possible she might have said something about that . . ."

Dr. Campbell leans forward, eyeing me intently. I've got her now. I pause, chew my bottom lip, bunch up my eyebrows. She nods encouragingly like that's going to help me think.

After a minute I frown and shake my head. "Nope. I'm sure she never said anything to me about bullying. But you know how secretive we teenagers can be."

Dr. Campbell sits back in her chair, ignoring my sarcasm or missing it completely, which feels like a total waste of a really good line. She grabs the red rubber ball off her desk and squeezes again and again like she's trying to jerk it off. She does this during all of our little chats.

She quickly finishes with the ball, drops it back in its little nest, and returns to her keyboard. "Do you have any idea what might have been bothering Nicole?"

"I don't like to speculate on other people's motives," I say, just for the fun of watching her face because I'm pretty sure she doesn't think I know the meanings of *speculate* and *motive*. "But since you asked, I'd vote for jealousy."

She forgets all about typing. I've really got her now.

"What about jealousy?"

"Jealousy makes people crazy. If someone wants what you have, they can get pretty nasty and sneaky while they're trying to steal it. Of course, some things can't be stolen, like my winning personality and outstanding academic record. Lots of people are jealous of those, but what's mine is mine."

I flash her a smile. She doesn't smile back. I figure we're done so I get up and head for the door.

"One more thing, Cassandra. The police want to talk to you Friday here in my office at 10:30 . . . during your free period. We'll see you then."

The cops? Crap!

Isabel

DECADES' WORTH OF student anxiety wore down the center of this bench outside Dr. Campbell's office door. I sense all of what every kid felt way before Mrs. Moss motions me to sit. As soon as I do, a headache drums behind my eyes. Without thinking, I touch the underside of the bench and bump against a mountain range of dried gum and who knows what else. Ew!

An inch-thick layer of deadly microorganisms clings to my fingers. I fumble in my backpack for my homemade hand sanitizer, contaminating everything I am touching, but this is an emergency. I pull out my spray bottle. Empty! I press my palms against the sides of the glass, but whatever remains of the aloe's protective energy is too faint to do any good, and I can feel the microbes multiplying by the minute.

"Excuse me, Mrs. Moss. Do you have any hand sanitizer?"

"No. Sorry, Isabel. It's on the supply list. Would you like a piece of candy, dear?" She holds out a ceramic bowl filled with sugar-coated almonds. How many people have touched those?

"No, thank you. I've got nut allergies."

Mrs. Moss pops an almond into her mouth and licks her fingers, the same fingers that held the office phone used by all the school secretaries who ever sat at that desk.

New research has revealed that the average desk contains 400 times more germs than a toilet seat, and office phones are dirtier than desks!

My stomach winds itself into sloshy loops as Dr. Campbell's door opens. Kyle steps out and quickly closes the door behind him.

"Hey, Kyle," I say, with a short wave.

He's about to reply but looks down instead and hurries out of the office.

That's odd. Kyle's one of the few people who's always been nice to me.

Mrs. Moss's phone buzzes. She picks it up and rests the mouthpiece against her chin. I can't look. "Yes, she's right here. I'll send her in."

I've worn my hood up all morning. I don't touch it as I enter, even though Dr. Campbell's office is too warm. So is her smile, which flashes for an instant then curls downward. She's attempting empathy. That's kind, though I'm not feeling it. I wonder how many heart-to-heart connections she misses because her excessive facial expressions get in the way.

Dr. Campbell's messy desk surprises me. Balled-up tissues, herbal cough drop wrappers, a dirty coffee mug with a picture of a wooden ruler that says Educators RULE, and a red stress ball sitting in a little nest made of glued twigs. The whole office is much smaller than I imagined. All the furniture doesn't help. Above the uncomfortable-looking couch hangs a framed poster with a yellow smiley face and the words, "Think positive, and positive things will happen."

"How are you doing, Isabel?" she asks, her voice quavering.

Think positive. "I'm fine."

"I'm glad to hear it." She sounds slightly disappointed. "But if you find yourself feeling anxious or depressed in the coming days or weeks, that would be completely normal. Nicole's death is a shocking blow for all of us. As one of her oldest and closest friends, I imagine this must be extremely challenging for you."

Without moving or taking her sorrowful eyes off me, Dr. Campbell waits. I'm not sure what for. My lower abdomen cramps.

"May I sit down?"

"Of course!" She leans forward and we lock eyes. "Isabel, we Vikings are a very strong community. We will help each other through our collective grief. If you ever want to talk to me or to Ms. Goldman, don't hesitate. We're here for you. Yes! We. Are. Here. For you."

"Your kind words mean a lot." Not a lie. Kindness in any form is meaningful. Thankfully, though, I've got the Goddess, so I don't need anyone else.

Dr. Campbell continues pity-smiling as if she's stuck in freeze frame. Watching her makes my cheek muscles ache, but looking away seems rude. She seems to need me to need her. Sigh. I slip my hand into my cloak and touch my crystal.

Goddess Eternal, give her something else to do so she'll stop staring.

Dr. Campbell's phone dings. She picks it up, glances down, frowning while she texts.

Thank Goddess!

After a moment, Dr Campbell's radar turns on me again. She's trying to keep her face neutral, but her right eyelid is twitching. I wonder why.

"Just to let you know, Isabel, there's going to be a police investigation into Nicole's death."

"A police investigation?"

Am I a person of interest? What do they want to ask me? What will I say? I shove my shaky hands into my pockets. Something jabs my left index finger. Ow! What's that? Am I bleeding? I want to check, but it makes more sense to keep eye contact with Dr. Campbell and nod so she thinks my question was solely motivated by intellectual curiosity

"It's routine in the case of suspected suicide, especially when the victim is a young person with no history or prior indications of mental health issues. It's important that we learn as much as possible about what happened to Nicole so we can do our best to prevent other tragedies. As you know, tomorrow is the funeral service. No afterschool activities. Wednesday is a regular day, though Thursday is staff development, so no classes . . ."

I try to stop imagining my pocket filling up with blood. I can't.

Dr. Campbell is still talking. ". . . detective is coming to school Friday to talk to you and Nicole's other close friends. Please let your parents know, so they can be here, if they wish. Not that there's anything for you to be concerned about. The detective is just trying to piece together what happened. But moral support in unfamiliar situations is always a good thing. We've scheduled your interview during your free period."

"That's good." I force a small smile. "I wouldn't want to miss class." Not a lie. Though if it were a choice between casting a forgiveness spell at my ritual tree and missing class, I'd miss class.

"That's the attitude that keeps you on honor roll, young lady. You may go now." She returns to her phone.

I should return to Geometry class, but it's almost the end of the period and my stomach hurts. It doesn't feel like gas. Maybe I've got an ulcer from all this stress. Or stomach cancer! Not likely. But still . . .

I hesitate in front of the Girls room. Yolanda's pre-Thailand trip warning echoes in my head. *"You will die in a public bathroom."*

I touch the door and quiet my mind. Granted, it's been a terrible day so far, but I don't sense danger. Besides, Yolanda's prediction couldn't have included school bathrooms because, technically speaking, they are not public bathrooms. Yes, this is a public school, but members of the general public cannot walk in off the street and use this bathroom. I'm pretty sure it's safe to go in.

The door swings toward me so fast it almost hits me in the face.

"Sorry!" Gabby shrieks. "I didn't see you!"

"It's okay." I step in front of her while she holds the door open and follows me back inside.

"So what did Dr. Campbell want to talk to you about?"

"My independent study project." Not an actual lie, since my current independent study project is focused on getting Nic to forgive me, and Dr. Campbell mentioned Nic four times in our conversation.

Gabby watches me make a big show of taking my change purse out of my backpack, feeding a couple of quarters into the tampon machine, and pretending to decide which product to buy. She finally gets the hint and leaves. I press CANCEL. My quarters clatter into the change shoot. Now what? After Geometry I've got study hall and nothing to study. Thankfully the bathroom is empty. I can stay in here as long as I want.

I turn my jacket pocket inside out searching for whatever stuck me. I can't find anything, but that's definitely a tiny bit of blood right under my index fingernail. Only a small puncture, but big enough for the Anxiety Bench microbes to enter my bloodstream.

Fingernails are twice as dirty as hands and fingers. Bacteria gets stuck under the nails and can so easily be transferred into your mouth causing infections of the gums and throat. Luckily, I always carry a nail brush. I fish it out of my backpack, I lather up at the sink and scrub my nails, fingers, and in between my fingers while I slowly count to thirty. I'm feeling light-headed. And hot. Ooh, it hurts to swallow! Cold water on my face does not help. Have the microbes gotten me already? I slip into the last stall, slide the lock, and lean my forehead against the cold metal door. My eyes burn behind my lids. An army of bad bacteria battles the healthy bacteria in my gut. The bad guys are winning. I hold my crystal against my throat.

"Goddess Eternal, with all creatures in your domain, please heal my body, relieve my pain."

I swallow slowly. That's better. Thank Goddess.

I open my eyes. The graffiti scribbled on the door is all about sex, love, and revenge. That's all it's ever about.

CASSIE

SOMEONE DREW FIVE stars inside the bathroom stall and colored four of them red. The same person probably wrote: "I'd pee here again and recommend it to friends!"

Someone else, different handwriting, wrote this list on the wall:

Things I hate:
1. *Vandalism*
2. *Lists*
3. *Irony*
4. *Lists*
5. *Repetition*
6. *Lies*

"*. . . the police want to interview you on Friday.*"

Making out with your own boyfriend isn't a crime, but if Buzz-Kill finds out I'm in trouble with the cops again . . .

"Cassie?" Someone in the next stall is talking to me.

"Who's there?"

"Isabel."

"How'd you know it was me?"

"You're the only one in school who wears green high-tops. Can we talk?"

I flush the toilet, reach for the latch, and pause. If I open the door, I'll have to look at Isabel's moony face. She probably wants to talk about Nicole. She'll stare at me with her weird grey eyes like she's some kind of witchy mind reader.

I don't unlock the door. "What do you want?"

"Wednesday, after the funeral, I'm going to try to make contact with Nicole's spirit."

Of course, she believes in spooks, just like Buzz-Kill.

"Oh yeah? How're you going do that?" Not that I care because it's all BS.

"Through my talking board."

"Your what?"

"My talking board. Uh, Ouija Board? It's a portal to the other side."

"Yeah. Sure, it is. Okay. Let me give you a tip, Isabel. Everybody already thinks you're weird, with that witchy routine and sneaking around, stalking people with your camera. Now you're talking to spooks. Look, I don't give a shit if no one likes you, but why are you making things so hard on yourself?"

Isabel peeks under the stall door, her weird eyes look up at me.

"What the . . ."

"So do you want to come to my house after the funeral and talk to Nicole?"

"Did you hear what I just said? No! I don't want to come to your house. Why would you even ask me?"

"Because we're metafriends."

"What the hell is that?"

"Both of us were Nicole's friend, so you and I are metas. That's why I thought you'd want to come over and talk to her."

"Well, I don't." I swing open the stall door and she stands up so fast, she almost falls over. "And for the record, Nicole wasn't my friend. If she was, she never would have . . . never mind. I don't want to talk about her, and I don't want to talk to her. Not on a Ouija Board or anywhere. I don't want to talk to you either. Now get out of my way."

I'm already stepping into the hallway when she shouts, "Cassie, you forgot to wash your hands!"

So effin' weird.

Nicole

THE LIFE-STREAMER zooms in on Iz's bed, with its wrought iron bedframe and delicate intertwining vines. Way too fussy for me, but it's so *her*. And there she is! Wearing her favorite Wiccan dress, a pale green fitted top that flows into a layered skirt of deep greens over indigo blue and the most gorgeous shade of amethyst purple. It's so good to see her. And not a white object in sight! I soak in the color like a paper towel on a spill.

I zoom out to take in the whole scene: Mandy is holding up a short black skirt and jacket ensemble on a hanger, store tags still dangling from the sleeve. Iz shoves the outfit aside and, turning her back on her mom, sits in front of her altar and stares at the lighted black candle. Mandy's angry. She shouts something. So annoying not to have audio. Whatever she said makes Iz sit up straighter and clutch her crystal necklace. Her mouth is moving. She's probably chanting to herself. Mandy sinks onto the edge of the bed, cradling the black outfit and crying.

This has to be about more than just clothes.

I feel like a snoop, spying on them, unseen like this, but I can't look away.

Greg lumbers in. He's tilted to the left, like all the air on one side of his body has been sucked out. He gathers up Mandy and Iz in his arms and the three of them cling to each other like a little island of misery. The black outfit. The black candle. The tilt. The tears. What's going on?

My funeral! Of course. Why haven't I even thought about that?

"IZ!"

Neither Mandy nor Greg move, but Iz jerks her head up and searches the ceiling. She heard me!

A massive sob moves through her like an earth tremor, transforming her face into one of those Greek masks of Tragedy, only this is no mask. This is all-out misery. The same wave of hopelessness and despair surging through me, setting my heart trembling like a piñata reeling from the last hit and dreading the next. Iz's parents surround her with love. She buries her face in her father's shirt. I zoom in closer yearning to feel my dad's arms . . . anyone's arms around me. But I can't get close enough to be inside this embrace. I am an island of one. No one comforts a no body.

My Life-Streamer blacks out. Grace stands at my shoulder, not even faking a half-smile.

"Hey! Why'd you do that?"

"Nicole, you are temporarily locked out of Life-Streaming because you exceeded your daily watching limit."

She never said a word about a limit. She insists she did. I insist that watching makes me feel better, and isn't that a good thing?

"Your assignment isn't to make yourself feel better. You're here to uncover the truth."

"I'm trying! I was just talking to Iz. She heard me!"

"She didn't hear you. I've already explained, there's no audio in the Life-Streamer. Iz is a very sensitive being. Likely, she sensed your presence. Anyway, you can't get to the truth through this." Grace flicks a finger at the Life-Streamer. Gone.

"No! Okay, I made a mistake. Whatever the daily limit is, I won't exceed it again. I swear to God. Can I say that? Just give it back. Please."

"Yes, you can say that and no, I can't give it back." She sounds like she's the boss, but her eyes flicker with uncertainty. "I'm sorry, Nicole."

She *is* sorry. It's all over her face. No point bugging her. Grace isn't the enemy, the Mighty Mentors are. They're after both of us.

I run my hand through my hair, scrunching and unscrunching fistfuls. For the first time I appreciate my crazy hair and the way it matches how all over the place I'm feeling. It's not a bad thing to have your outsides match your insides. It's also not a bad thing to let people know that you messed up, and because of it, other people are paying the price.

"I'm really sorry, Grace. You were in big trouble before I got here, and I've only made things worse for you. But if I pass The Evaluation, that would be good for both of us, right? The thing is, without my Life-Streamer I just don't think I can uncover the truth of what happened to me in thirty days."

"Two weeks."

"Huh?"

She nervously scans the room, I don't see anything, but still, she lowers her voice. "They cut your prep time in half. Your Evaluation has been moved up to the eighteenth."

My finger countdown timer reads 10:10:15:32.

"Ten days left? No way! That's not even close to enough time. Why are they doing this to me?" I'm screeching and I don't care.

"You really want to know why? Ok. You make the top-level Mentors uncomfortable. They want you to move on as soon as possible."

"But two weeks! Grace! I don't think I can. You've got to help me."

Her shoulders droop. Her sea-green eyes shift to a shade of yellow-brown flaxen that I've only seen in dead leaves. A tear slides down the side of her face. Whoa! I've never seen her cry. Funny, since I've cried so much in front of her. She always supports me, and now she needs my support, but I don't know how to help. Everything I do seems to make things worse. If I don't pass The Evaluation they'll send me to Sixteen, but who knows what they'll do to her?

I put my arm around Grace's shoulders for the first time and give her a side-hug. She seems impossibly tiny and fragile. I expect her to pull away, because she's a Mentor and I'm just a no body, but she leans against me. I encircle her and pull her closer.

"Don't worry, Grace. I'll pass The Evaluation without a Life-Streamer. And those high-up guys will be so impressed with you, they'll give you The Mentor of the Year award. I've already figured it out. I'll do live research at my funeral. I think it's happening soon."

"Wednesday at four."

How does she know that? Does she have a Life-Streamer with audio?

"Okay, then. Wednesday. I'm going."

She inhales sharply. "It's been a very *very* long time since you've been to a funeral. Your own is not the best place to get reoriented. You have no idea how the emotions of all the people will affect you."

What's she talking about? I don't remember ever going to a funeral. But she's wrong. I'm going to love this. Not everyone gets to hear the wonderful things people say about you after you're dead. I'm assuming people will say nice things, but they probably will. Iz might screen one of our movies. They'll play my favorite music. For sure they'll play a recording of me singing one of my own songs. It will be like a concert. Oh! And Alex will be all dressed up looking so hot. I've got to see that.

Grace is still talking ". . . the first time I went to one of my funerals I was not prepared."

What? She said *funerals*. Plural. She's lived and died more than once? I knew that's the way it works! I try to picture Grace as Grace, but different, of course, throughout all her lifetimes. Different faces, different bodies, different historic settings, but always the same Grace. It's so crazy to imagine, my train of thought runs off the tracks. I've got a zillion ques-tions. Most of them start with *In my next life* . . . but that didn't go over well last time I tried to bring it up, so I play it cool. "You know, Grace, when I first met you, I thought all Vesties, I mean *Mentors*, were mini-gods, you know, immortals."

She brushes off the thought with a snort. "No, we were just humans with special training. And you're going to need some before Wednesday. Go to the library and work on the tutorials for astral travel and aura reading."

It sounds like school. "Couldn't we just do private lessons? That would go a whole lot faster."

No answer. Grace vanished.

Nicole

I DIDN'T SPEND a whole lot of time hanging out in libraries when I was alive. I'm not a fan of forced silence or sitting still. I like getting on to the next thing. If Grace hadn't left so quickly, I would have told her that.

There must be a million books here. The shelves tower so high above me it's impossible to see where they end, *if* they end. Iz would be impressed. I can't wait to tell her about the levitating Vesties zipping from shelf to shelf, retrieving books for dead kids. Thinking about going back to Earth gives me the whirlies, that tickly, swishy feeling that comes when something great is going to happen very soon. It's almost as intoxicating as my best Alex fantasies.

I hate talking to Vesties, but how am I supposed to find what I'm looking for if I don't ask? Grace said I needed a tutorial about astral travel. That sounds like air travel. I get motion sick so I'll skip that one. She'll never know. She also mentioned aura reading. I've heard of that. Iz showed me a poster of rainbow colors radiating around a woman who was meditating in a lotus position. Iz said the colors represented her aura. I thought it was just a pretty drawing, but Iz swore auras were real. She said mine was yellow.

There are loads of different yellows. "What shade?" I wanted to know.

"Bright yellow."

Iz doesn't really pay attention to color, otherwise she'd know bright yellow isn't a shade. There's cadmium, canary, sunrise, and so many others. I wonder which was mine? Anyway, if Grace says there's a tutorial about auras, I guess they're real and Iz was right. Again. I'll check it out.

What else?

If I'm going to Earth to find out what happened to me, what else should I do to prepare? I'll have to learn how to talk so people can hear me. It would probably also be useful to know how to pick stuff up. Oh! And it would be awesome if I could make myself visible. Not so everyone sees me, just a select few... like Dad and Iz and... Alex! What's it called when a ghost shows herself? *Materialization!* I wonder why Grace didn't mention that? Maybe it's a really hard skill to master. Even Patrick Swayze couldn't do it until the very end of the movie, otherwise he totally would have shown up way earlier to let Demi Moore know he was with her. Of course, that was a movie and this is real death. I honestly don't know what's possible for a no body, but there must be a reason some people swear they've seen a ghost. Materialization must be real, and I want to learn how to do it. But maybe I should start with the easy stuff.

Where do they keep the tutorials?

I follow a stringy-haired no body, his arms weighed down by a load of old leather-bound books. I can't see the titles, but I'm pretty sure they're not best-sellers. He climbs inside a cubby big enough for his long legs and all his books. Identical cubbies fill the entire wall. Most are occupied by no bodies reading on their own. A few no bodies and Mentors read together. Unlike the meeting area, there isn't a lot of conversation here. Everyone seems to be studying hard. That's what I should be doing. I hope the tutorials are on video because I don't have time for reading a bunch of old books.

Back in the stacks, I'm about to cave and ask a Vestie to help me, when I notice the word *Tutorials* written on a door leading to a dimly lit side room. I let myself in, proud that I found the place on my own.

Clusters of no bodies sit on the floor in circles. Their faces glow in the light of the talking head holograms they're watching. So many different circles. So many different talking heads. Where do I start?

The round-faced tutor in *that* hologram announces the name of the session: Auras—The Body's Energy Field. Perfect! I hang out at the edge of the circle and listen in.

"An aura consists of seven different interrelated layers that form one cohesive body or electro-magnetic field." As the tutor speaks, bands of brilliantly colored light pulse and shimmer surround his body. Actual auras! I see them. "These colored layers are sourced from the body. Auric energies are linked to colors much like colors are linked to the chakra centers."

I have no clue what he's talking about, but the colors are so beautiful I can't look away.

"You might be more comfortable if you sat down." The gravelly voice behind me makes me jump. It belongs to a pot-bellied Vestie who looks like Nick Fury in *The Avengers*, minus the eye patch. He tilts his head to one side and studies me like I'm an extinct species he's only read about.

"What do you need to learn?"

"Uh, not this. I already know all about auras and most of this stuff. But I'm a little fuzzy on the details of my death, which is so annoying. I'm going back to Earth for my funeral and to talk to my friends about what happened to me so I need to learn to materialize. Which circle do I go to for that?"

"We don't *have* tutorials for that." Fury flairs his nostrils so wide his nose hairs stick out.

I swallow hard and try to un-see what's going on up his nose.

"No problem," I tell him. "Then how about the tutorial for . . ." I can't remember the word I was just thinking of. "Uh, it starts with an *n*. I mean a *k!* It has to do with moving objects without touching them."

"Telekinesis." Fury directs me to an empty spot in a tutorial circle where a dark-haired girl pops into view in a hologram, a pencil and a piece of paper on the table top in front of her. Her bangs and oversized glasses make her look like an engineering student, or maybe she's in law school, unless she's dead. Yeah, probably that.

"Welcome to session one of *Telekinesis*." Engineer Girl looks right at me. "To move a solid object, focus on the object's molecular structure and the electrical charges it emits. In other words, connect with the object's energy force."

"Hey, Iz. Remind me again what we're trying to do."

She inhales and exhales and holds her crystal. "We're not trying to do anything, Nic. In fact, we're trying to do nothing. We're just being with Nature, connecting with the positive energy that's all around to remind us of our true place and purpose. It would be easy if you weren't being so . . ."

"What?"

She steps into the hollowed-out base of what was once a redwood tree, sits on the ground, and opens her backpack.

"I don't mean to be judgmental, Nic, but your negative energy is blocking the connection with the cosmos. You have to clear away your assumptions about what is and is not possible. C'mon in."

I step inside the tree. Iz pulls out her ritual dagger.

Did she call that thing an anthem? No, that's a patriotic song. Whatever it's called I couldn't believe she wasted fifty bucks on something made of plastic with dried flower petals and a few red berries glued inside. Holding it high over her head, she looked like she was ready to fight a garden gnome. I had to bite the inside of my cheek to keep from laughing.

"I'm not being negative! But if we're trying to connect with positive energy, maybe we shouldn't be hanging out inside what's left of a dead tree that was struck by lightning! I mean, isn't that kinda negative?"

"Not at all. When lightning hit this tree, it released seeds that made more trees." She lowers her voice to her woo-woo whisper. "Being inside a hollowed redwood is a sacred honor. We are surrounded by tree spirit. Don't you feel it?"

My neck aches from bending over in this narrow place. I've got a cramp in my calf muscle and the smell of charred wood tickles my nose. If I feel anything else I don't know what it is.

We'd already been in the tree for an hour. I wanted to leave after ten minutes, but I felt like I owed her for the attraction spell, so I promised I'd try to be one with the universe. I did not mention that I was supposed to meet up with Calex and Kyle in half an hour.

"It's getting late, Iz. My dad wants to take me out to dinner."

"Oh! The energy is surging. Do you feel that?"

I didn't feel anything, but Iz's eyes are so hopeful I say, "Yeah. Wow! That's amazing!"

She beams at me. "I knew you'd feel the energy if you opened yourself to it."

Now here I am, listening to Engineer Girl go on about connecting with the energy. Props to you, Iz. You were right again.

Without missing a beat, the tutor adjusts her glasses and picks up the pencil. "Since you are no longer tied to an organic structure that is constantly emitting its own electrical charges, this shouldn't be too difficult. Remember, though, your success in telekinesis depends on aim and precision. Don't attempt to move anything before you intuit what the object is made of and how much it weighs. That's the first step and the only way to know how much force you'll need. Watch me."

She puts the pencil down and dramatically passes her hand over it, back and forth, as if she were performing a really bad magic act. The only thing missing is some *Abracadabra* action. No surprise, the pencil doesn't budge.

"I hope no one thinks they saw the pencil move." She chuckles. "Because I have not moved it yet."

Huh. I was sure she'd try to tell us that it *had* moved, and if we couldn't see that it was our fault.

"Before you move an object telekinetically you have to clear away all thoughts and assumptions about what is and is not possible as well as what you believe you can and can't do. Just rid yourself of those thoughts. Like this." She swirls the air above her head, as if she's clearing cobwebs.

"Once you've cleared the path of any obstacles between you and the object, use your mind to pull the object toward you."

Yeah, right.

Engineer Girl flicks her bangs out of her eyes and stares down the pencil. Immediately it wobbles, and rolls across the table into her palm where it stops.

Whoa! That's cool.

"Next, we write." She pinches the air above the pencil. It levitates! Then she uses her finger as if she were writing in the air. The pencil copies her hand motions and writes on the paper. With a final hand motion, the pencil lays down on the table and she holds up the paper. The words "Your turn" are written on it. Nice handwriting, too.

Okay. That looked pretty easy.

I pass my hand back and forth over my pencil. What is it made of? Hmm. Yellow paint. Wood. Graphite. Metal. Rubber.

All around the tutorial circle, pencils roll toward kids while I stare mine down. It doesn't budge. I suck at this. One kid spins his finger above his pencil and it twirls. The girls next to me got theirs to write on the paper. They're all having a great time. First real smiles I've seen on Substation Fifteen and all it took was moving a pencil. How depressing is that? Not as depressing as being stuck inside a failure loop.

I close my eyes so I don't have to see the rest of the kids congratulating themselves. Two ugly fuzz balls, grosser than the crap under our kitchen stove, appear on my mental movie screen. What are those things? Who cares? This is hopeless. As soon as I think it, a new gray ball appears in my mind's eye. I'll never be able to do this. Another fuzzy ball appears.

"Clear away all your negative thoughts and assumptions about what you can and can't do."

Are those fuzz balls my own negative thoughts? Maybe so. Well, there are only four of them. I can probably shoo them away with a positive thought.

I give myself a silent pep talk. "I will pass The Evaluation and move on!"

One fuzz ball vanishes. Ha! I guess I *can* do something right. That positive thought deleted another fuzz ball. But those two were just the top of a mountain made of thousands of my own negative thoughts. Undoing them one at a time would be like picking up a truckload of spilled popcorn with tweezers. That would frustrate the hell out of me. More negative thoughts! I need to lose all these in one sweep.

I imagine a psychic dust-buster sucking up the fuzz balls. The top ones vanish in a flash, revealing layers of others. Luckily, this dust-buster doesn't need recharging. My mental movie screen clears, the chatter inside my head stops, and I sink into the calm. Ahhh. But I still have to move the pencil so I can pass The Evaluation.

I focus all my powers of concentration on the pencil.

"Pencil, come to Mama."

As if it heard me, the pencil wobbles then rolls steadily toward me until it bumps against my fingertips. *Yes!*

I pretend to write in the air, so my pencil will get the idea of what I want it to do, but it doesn't move.

Crap!

If it's this hard to move a simulated pencil, how am I going to pick up anything on Earth?

A hand presses my shoulder.

"You need more practice," Fury says.

No, thanks. I've had enough, but I don't tell him that. I nod and wait for him to move along and harass someone else.

Maybe I don't need this telekinesis tutorial. I've seen *Ghost* six times, so that should help. Not that I took notes. I was too busy watching Patrick Swayze doing his thing, with shirt on and off. He was so hot. I can't believe he died in 2009. I wonder where he is now. It'd be really cool to see him.

Forget Patrick Swayze. His ghost was strong, and it took him forever to move a penny. Forget about telekinesis. I just need to talk to my friends.

I switch to a different tutorial. *Communicating with the Living* seems pretty straightforward and much easier than moving a pencil, until the onscreen talent warns about talking to skeptics, which, honestly, is probably everybody I know except Iz. I skip out on that one and sit in on *Astral Travel Part I*. About five minutes into it, my brain starts to itch. I need a break.

When I step out of the library, Grace is in my face, the lower corner of her mouth twitching wildly. "Time for your funeral."

"Already? But I thought . . ."

"Get going. I'll meet you there."

Nicole

"DON'T LOOK DOWN," Grace warns me. She doesn't have to. Heights still make me dizzy. On top of that, I'm motion sick from the trip. It would have been nice if right at the beginning of the *Astral Travel* tutorial they'd mentioned that even without actual ears or semi-circular canals, a no body can still feel like throwing up. It would have been nicer if Grace had brought me with her, instantly, so I could have skipped the turbulence. She said she could have, but she wanted me to figure out how to get here on my own so I can do it by myself next time. Thanks.

It took several frustrating attempts to figure out how to use some kind of soul-memory GPS or was it GGS (Ghost Guidance System)? It wasn't that hard once I realized that all I had to do was focus on Dad, but in a different way than simply thinking about him. When you spend years living with someone, you know them, on a deep level, and tapping into their essence—their core being . . . *Listen to me! I sound more woo-woo than Iz!*

Now that I'm actually here, at my own funeral, it's not all that great. It's hot and stuffy up here on the ceiling. What's wrong with the AC? Ew! That light's covered in cobwebs. And something stinks worse than air freshener. Plus they're looping Sarah McLachlan's "Angel." Who picked that song? I never liked it.

A heartsick sob pierces the muffled conversations and the downer music.

Who's crying?

A mass of dark fog hangs over the room making it impossible to tell who's who.

"Why does everything look so weird?"

Grace scans the room. "Individuals grieve in their own way, but with this many people in one space, emotions mix together. It's hard to read anything unless you focus in on one person at a time. See that bright violet light down there? To the left?"

I follow her finger, not a hint of violet anywhere. "Uh, no."

She clicks her tongue. "You said you completed the aura tutorial."

"You heard wrong. I said I completed *some* of it."

"Why do you make things harder for yourself, Nicole?"

I have no answer for that one.

Grace switches on her I've-Got-This-Memorized mode. "Auras are energy fields that radiate out from all living things and reflect an individual's personality, intentions, changing emotions, state of health, and mind. Auras are another form of reality expressing itself."

"Where's my dad?"

"Over there. Close your eyes."

"How am I supposed to see him with my eyes closed?"

"We sense auras psychically. Imagine that you are an *emotion* detector. Read the room with your eyes closed. Where are the strongest emotions coming from?"

I swivel right and left, slowly, like a sprinkler head. Something closes in around me, as if I've been stuffed inside an airless sack. A sharp pain erupts between my shoulder blades, like a nail in my back.

"OWOWOW! Something's killing me!"

"Not even close. Look at me, Nicole. This isn't physical

pain, and it's not yours. It is emotional pain expressing itself through someone's aura."

"I don't care what it is or whose it is. It feels like acid's eating away at my heart. Make it stop!"

"Only you can do that, by creating distance. Be the reader. Read the aura."

"I don't know how."

"Turn toward the aura."

"No. I don't want to."

"It doesn't matter what you want, Nicole. This is what you need to do to pass The Evaluation. Face the aura, only this time ignore any uncomfortable sensations and focus on the information the aura provides."

I glare at her so she knows how much I hate it when she plays The Evaluation card. She glares back. Whatever. I take a breath, squint my eyes into tiny slits and face the direction that hurts most. And like before, every part of me stings and burns. I scream and try to turn away, but Grace guides my head back toward the pain. How can this be what I *need*?

She presses her hand between my shoulder blades and relief radiates from that place, cooling the fire enough so I can follow her directions. Suddenly, the darkness clears enough for me to see faint violet light and other undulating colors. And Dad!

"I see my dad!"

"Read his aura. What does it tell you?"

Somehow the bands of color radiating off of Dad's body start to make sense. "He's trying to conceal a deeply buried poison." I have never before used the phrase "buried poison," but now, the words feel absolutely right.

"Dad can't forgive himself. He's battling despair and losing the will to live."

Sensing what's going on in Dad's heart feels like deciphering code. It also feels like pressing spiked bricks into my own heart.

I open my eyes. Gray and black light stream from Dad like toxic smoke. His auric waves rise up and engulf me. I want to decipher more, so I can help him. I focus on the densest section of the aura. My hands and arms start fading! This is exactly what happened in Dolores's dream. How did Grace explain it?

Substation Fifteen keeps our avatars solid for us while we're up there, otherwise, we have to generate our own power to exist.

I guess I had enough power before I started reading Dad's aura. This is wiping me out. I can't imagine how much more juice I'll need to materialize.

Dad whispers my name, again and again. His voice turns me inside out and bleeds me dry. A tear hangs onto the edge of his jaw like the last leaf of winter desperately clinging to a tree. Black auric waves crash over him. He is sinking. I am sinking.

"Nicole?" Grace's voice comes from far away. "It's not helpful to get sucked into your father's emotions."

Dad breathes heavily through his mouth, his face turning grayish-blue.

"What if he dies because of me?"

"It is a beautiful thing to care about others, Nicole. You are learning and progressing. But your father has his own journey, and you have to—"

"Can I at least let him know I'm here? That might make him feel better."

She shakes her head.

"C'mon, Grace. Show me how to give him a sign."

"No."

"Screw you!"

I descend toward Dad. Grace pulls me back. I whip around and clip her in the chin. Eyes flashing, she grabs my wrists and holds on so tightly I cry out.

Instantly, she lets go of me, her face flushed. "I'm so sorry, Nicole. Please forgive me."

I don't know what to say. I feel embarrassed and so ashamed. Watching Dad suffer made me crazy enough to hit Grace without even thinking about it! On top of that, I'm scared that I just got her and me into more trouble. I can imagine Quinn popping in and dragging us both away. "I need some air. I'm going outside."

Large metal letters cover the front wall of the building—Vintage Oaks Community Center.

A repetitive *knock, knock, knock* cuts through the motionless air. I hover above the massive live oak near the parking lot. A girl mercilessly whacks the tree trunk with a hefty branch. A pale-yellow aura shimmers around her body.

Fear of losing control.

The girl seems familiar, but I can't get a good look at her from up here. It doesn't help that her long brown ponytail whips her face with each swing.

I hover closer.

Cassie!

Cassie sings in the spotlight. I stand in the wings waiting for my turn to audition.

Ricochet, you take your aim

Fire away, fire away

She's armed and dangerous and she's killing my audition song. My version sounds whiny and pathetic in comparison. I'd give anything to sing like that.

WHACK!

Cassie smacks the tree again and again. With each blow her aura sparks, releasing waves of red, tan, murky green, magenta—*anger and frustration, resentment, regret, loneliness.* The next hit shatters the branch. She tosses away the piece of wood left in her hand then leans against the tree, crying quietly.

Cassie crying. Now I've seen it all. She is nothing like titanium. More like the cheap aluminum foil they wrap around take-out burritos.

What's going on here? What did I miss?

She stands, wipes her nose with the back of her hand and tucks in her shirt.

Her aura shifts to pink.

She's tough. Determined. Holds people to high standards and is quick to judge those who don't measure up.

She gives her sagging ponytail a quick tug and stomps up the hill. Something in me toughens up, too.

Up on the stage, a large photo of me rests on an easel. I'm holding my guitar, and smiling shyly at the camera. I remember that day.

I'm sitting on the floor, leaning against my closet door. I'm clicking my pen like crazy while I work out the lyrics of a new song. Then an idea comes to me, and I scribble in my notebook. I drop the pen and pick up my guitar.

We sold each otheR alibis

We digitized a compRomise

I itemized and faNtasized

But NeveR tRuly scRutiNized

I stop, scratch out two chords on the page and replace them with three others. Then I sing the lines again, drawing out the rhyming syllables, getting off on the raw power of my voice. I don't notice Dad in the doorway until he says, "That sounds awesome, Nikki."

I blush. I know the song is only okay, but he's smiling at me with so much love and pride I have to smile back, and he takes my picture.

Dad gazes at the photo. He's remembering that moment too. He smiles through tears. It's barely a smile, but it's enough to lighten a bit of his aura with splashes of bright blue.

Loyalty. Deep love of family.

I pop into the space in front of him and give him a hug. I don't think he senses my presence, but something changes. His shoulders relax. I wish he'd hug me back. Dad gives great hugs.

He covers his face as another wave of sadness pulls me down with him. Grace taps my shoulder. I don't want to move away from Dad, but I need to.

Grace and I drift around the room together. Nice-sized crowd. Lots of kids from school. Lots of teachers. Some adults

I don't know. It's easier now to see people through their auras when I'm not thinking or feeling too much. A murky indigo-blue column rises from the back of the room. For some reason I can't see the person at its center, but this aura's code is easy to decipher: Detached. Alone. Empty. Troublemaker.

I catch a whiff of something sickly sweet. "What stinks?"

"Lilies," Grace mutters. "Not my favorite flower either. Overpowering. Why not a lighter fragrance for a change? Like lilacs or gardenias."

Peach-colored lilies fill two silver vases that guard both ends of a polished white casket. *My casket.* A low roar thrums in my ears. A tidal wave of tears builds in my chest, trapped, with no way out, just like the girl in the white box.

From a tight, dark place I hear myself say, "I'm locked in there."

"No, you're not." Grace squeezes my arm. "The only thing in that box is an empty body that you don't need anymore. You are eternal, Nicole. Don't let emotions or thoughts mess with you. They are just vibrations. Random, constantly changing, fleeting and meaningless vibrations."

Alex steps into the center aisle. Though he's sweating in that white shirt, dark pants, and blazer, his hair plastered to his forehead, he looks so freakin' *hot.* Ohmygod! I'm a mess of super-speed vibrations and I feel *amazing.* What's he carrying? Pink roses. Just like the roses George brought to Emily's grave in *Our Town.* That's super sweet.

Cassie slips through a side door and watches Alex place the flowers on my casket and stands there, head bowed. His mouth turns downward, but in my mind's eye he holds a large plastic cup and smiles at me from the edge of the food court in the mall.

"Hey, Nicole. You here alone?"

"No. Iz and I are making a movie."

He points to the Spiderman poster on the wall. "This looks cool. Want to go Saturday?"

My heart stops. For a second, I think he's asking me out, and my mind plays a mental movie starring me and Alex making out in a dark movie theatre.

Before I grab him, I snap back to reality. Don't be an idiot, he's not asking me out!

"Sounds great," I say, with too much enthusiasm. "You and Cassie and me and Kyle could . . ."

"Kyle's already seen it, and Cassie's going to her sister's art show. I was thinking just you and me."

"Joke, right?"

He shrugs and gives me the look. I don't know what to do with my face. I don't know where this is going. He touches my hair. The tiny part of my brain that's still functioning wonders what will happen next. His hand grazes the side of my face with an electric caress, then something yanks my ear lobe.

"Ow! What are you doing?"

"My sleeve's caught on your earring!"

He tries to unhook us but he can't, and my neck pinches from tilting my head.

"Let go. I'll do it."

A moment later we are freed from each other, and maybe wishing we weren't. At least I am.

He holds up a strand of tinsel he plucked from my head.

"Trying to pass as a Christmas tree?"

I snatch the tinsel. Our fingers touch. We look at each other. We're barely breathing.

I didn't want that to happen. Yeah, right. Of course, I did. I wanted much more than that. But I wasn't cool enough to make it happen at that moment. Maybe everything would have been different if I had.

Cassie slides into the seat next to her sister. I slide into the space between Alex and my casket. I wrap my arms around him, holding him so close I hear his heartbeat. No. I *feel* his heartbeat, warming every part of me, even the parts I don't have anymore. Especially those. Grace says emotions are only vibrations, they're not real. I don't care. Whatever this is, it's more than real enough for me.

Alex looks through me, probably imagining what's in the white box.

"Don't think about my corpse. Not now. Not ever." I press against him, closer than the air. "Alex, feel me. I'm right here."

He turns and walks back to his seat. With every step he takes away from me, the heat and vibrations fade. I'm in love alone. Cassie looks the way I feel. I don't know what happened to Calex since I've been gone but it's obviously over for Alex. Obviously not for Cassie. But she's got plenty of time to find a new boyfriend. Plenty of time for everything. I've got no time. I've got nothing.

I hug myself to stop shivering, but it doesn't help. Grace touches my arm. I bat her away. "Do you know how bad this sucks?"

"Yes, I do." Her tone is dry and hollow.

We drift back up to our corner of the ceiling. A crow swoops past the wall of windows. Iz told me crows are a sign of something. I forget what.

"Try connecting with Iz. She's gifted, that one."

I scan the room and immediately spot Iz's first auric level. It's bright purple. Ha! She could be a Vestie without a vest! I'm about to share the joke with Grace, but she's focused elsewhere.

Okay. What can I figure out. Purple on first auric level. That means psychic. Eccentric. No surprises there. Ooh, and it also means conflicted. I wonder if that has to do with the fight between her and Mandy. Might as well ask. Maybe she'll hear me.

"Hey, Iz. Too bad your mom forced you to wear that black skirt. It's not that bad, but I agree, your green dress would have been so much better. Anyway, you are wearing your crazy yellow, green, and purple fingerless gloves. So, ha! Take that, Mandy!"

If Iz hears me, she's not showing it. She's fiddling with her crystal necklace and shifting in her seat like she's got to pee. She's probably just uncomfortable. Understandable. I'd hate being at *her* funeral.

Iz touches one of the tiny gold studs her grandmother gave her. Silver is the favored metal of Wiccans, but all of Iz's silver earrings have pentacles and dangling runes and things, so I guess she lost that battle, too. She pretends to scratch her earlobes while she secretly takes off the studs and stuffs them into her skirt pocket. The familiar searching look crosses her face. It has nothing to do with earrings. Iz senses something. Her eyes shoot upward toward my corner. The look intensifies. She senses *me!*

She inhales sharply, goes limp, and hangs her head between her knees.

Is she sick? Or is she hiding? Why isn't she happy that I'm here?

Iz's aura changes from violet to muddy blue. I read it like a warning on a pack of cigarettes: *Caution. Contents may contain fear of the future, fear of facing or speaking the truth.*

Mandy gently rubs the back of Iz's neck while her aura shifts to ghastly green. Shame. Deep regret. Guilt. About what? What did she do?

Ohmygod! Did Iz kill me?

Isabel

I PRESS MY crystal against my throat and focus all my powers on not barfing. Why didn't Mom and Dad believe me when I told them I was too sick to go to the funeral? The car window burns my forehead. When is it ever eighty degrees in January? In Miami, I guess. But here in the Bay Area? It's a sign. Of climate change, for sure. And what else? The heating of tensions caused by conflict and misunderstanding. Something stomps on my stomach. Ow! I try not to make noise. My head flops against the seat back. I feel my lifeforce draining away. Is Nic trying to kill me so we can finish this out on the astral plane? Ow. I hold one hand against my stomach and grab the handgrip above the window with the other.

Dad mutters about the traffic and how we are going to be late because we didn't leave on schedule.

"What's that look for?" Mom snaps. "You weren't waiting for *me*."

Dad nails me in the rearview mirror. "Well, *someone* was in the bathroom for over an hour."

Mom clenches her teeth. "Not now, Greg. Just get in the carpool lane and we'll be fine. What are you waiting for?

Get over."

"There is no northbound carpool lane after nine. How do you not know that?"

I picture Nicole's body lying inside her airless casket, under a blanket of flowers whose roots penetrate the coffin lid like a hungry vampire sucking whatever is left of her. Or maybe she's been cremated. That would be better for the environment. No wasted land. No wasted materials for a casket. Just an attractive ceramic jar filled with her ashes, mixed with bits of bone and toenails . . . with blue polish on them? No. That's crazy. Cremains are pulverized so nothing's left of the body but fine powder. I know that's true, but I can't rid my mind of blue toenails poking through the ashes. I swallow. My throat still kills. Dad shifts lanes, my stomach shifts, squirting a fresh warm yuck into the back of my mouth. I close my eyes, take twelve slow deep breaths, and mouth these words:

"Goddess Eternal, please help me be well.

Release all discomfort, 'cause I feel like hell."

Mom slides open the visor and checks her reflection. "I look awful! My eyes are so puffy." She slides the visor closed in disgust then turns to Dad. "Greg, can you *please* turn down the air? You're wasting energy. Never mind. I'll do it. You watch the road. Which button is it? Watch the road! Oh, never mind. Leave it on. What difference does it make? We've already messed up the planet beyond all hope."

Dad tries to explain how energy isn't wasted if it's hot enough to need AC.

Mom looks at her shoes and grunts. "Why did I wear these? They always give me blisters."

This doesn't sound like a question for general discussion. Maybe she's talking to herself or to her shoes. If Dad has anything on his mind other than driving, I can't tell.

Mom points to a blue car ahead in the next lane. "Oh, look! An Alaska license plate. Remember the lemonade we ordered at that seafood place in Anchorage? Turned out to be fish broth? And that snotty waiter thought we were being difficult until we told him to taste it." Her forced laugh sounds so insane I shove my fingers in my ears.

Dad rests his hand on Mom's knee. "Mandy, breathe."

Yes. Please. Time for some car yoga.

Mom pats his hand and inhales deeply through her nose. She sits up straighter and gently rocks her head from side to side. Her neck cracks. I wince.

"Ahhhh . . . Ohhhhh-----Ummmmm."

I inhale and exhale along with her. This is better. My lifeforce is restoring itself. I want Mom to breathe instead of talk. Better for her. Better for Dad. Better for me.

No such luck.

"I can't believe we're going to Nicole's f. . . funeral." Mom's voice catches in her throat. "I can't believe she's dead." Now she sounds like someone's strangling her. "Can you believe it? Our sweet Nicole? Such a smart and talented girl. So beautiful and loving, with such an amazing future ahead of her. Gone at sixteen? How can that be, for crissake? And *why*? I don't understand. I'll never understand."

Mom's words run together until they dissolve into soggy gulps. Dad grips the steering wheel like he's about to rip it off and throw it through the windshield.

I cover my mouth trying to block everything that wants to come out. My fingers are cold against my lips. It's freezing back here. If I ask Dad to turn down the air, they might start fighting again, but that would be better than listening to Mom cry, which only makes it harder for me not to.

She's sniffling, talking through her tears again. "If she really jumped, and I'm not saying she did . . . because we just don't know. We may never know. But if she did, she must have been desperately upset about something."

Mom turns around in her seat and looks directly at me. "Did she ever talk to you about being unhappy?"

Good witches don't lie. I squeeze my crystal.

Distract her, oh, Goddess right now, in this place

Turn her thoughts and attention away from my face.

A car cuts into our lane. Dad swerves. I'm slammed against the door. Mom gasps.

Dad curses the other driver. I rub my sore shoulder. Mom looks back at me. "Are you okay, sweetheart?"

I nod and silently thank the Goddess for the distraction.

But Mom's not done. "I know that some girls can be very emotional, worrying about their looks and popularity and all that. Obviously, Nicole was self-conscious about the size of her breasts . . ."

"Mo-om!"

". . . but she never seemed insecure. Not really. At least I never thought so. She was so talented. What a voice! And her portrayal of Emily was absolutely unforgettable. Performing takes tremendous self-confidence. All of that couldn't have been an act. It wasn't an act, Isabel, was it?"

When Mom gets wound up like this, she doesn't notice if I'm listening or not. And these questions? She doesn't really expect me to answer. Good thing because I want no part of this rant. I look out the window and let her talk. But now she shuts up.

"Isabel. Look at me."

I look.

She looks back, long and hard, like she's the prosecuting attorney and I'm under oath. Well, I am, but she doesn't know that. "Do you know what really happened on Friday? Did someone say or do something that upset Nicole?"

She knows that I know something, but she doesn't know what I know. Thank Goddess. If I don't answer the question directly then I won't be lying. I look down and think about how this black skirt will look and smell with vomit all over it. The thought of barfing is messing with my head and my stomach. I swallow hard, fighting the urge. The urge is winning.

Dad studies my reflection. "You look a little green around the gills, kiddo. Are you okay?"

I feel so miserable and pathetic I could easily tell him the truth. No. Not okay. On so many levels, not okay. but it's too much effort to talk. I clutch my crystal so hard the point jabs into my palm.

I look out the window, wishing I was in someone else's car, going somewhere else. Anywhere.

"I've read a lot about teen psychology." Mom says to no

one in particular. "Some kids internalize their pain so their parents won't worry. But people can't do that indefinitely. Eventually, troubled kids get to the point where they can't bottle it anymore, and they have to talk to someone. If Nicole got to that point and decided to end her life, maybe it was because she didn't think she could talk to anyone. Not even you, her best friend. Do you know what was going on with her?"

I look at my shoes and bite the inside of my cheek to keep from crying.

Mom reaches back and touches my knee. "Isabel, I'm talking to you."

Dad turns left and I tighten my grip on the door handle.

"I honestly don't know." I try to sound like I wish I knew. I hate myself for lying and for having a reason to lie.

I press my fist into my stomach to stop the sloshing. Mom faces forward again. We exit at Atherton Avenue, turn left, cross over the freeway. Dizziness forces me to shut my eyes as the car hangs a long left. It doesn't help. We stop at a light. I look out the window. A little girl in the next car sticks out her tongue at me. I look away.

Mom swallows a sob. "I'm sorry, sweetie. I shouldn't be asking you these questions. It's not helpful. I know how much you loved Nicole and how painful this must be." She wipes her nose. "Tell me, how can I help?"

"Please just leave me alone."

Her head droops. Her jagged sigh floats up from a deep, hollow place and hangs between us for a moment. On the steering wheel Dad taps out the rhythm of a song only he hears. The light turns green. We lurch forward. The roof of my mouth feels raw.

We turn into the parking lot of Vintage Oaks Community Center. A bearded guy under a green umbrella directs us down the center aisle past lots of parked cars.

"Find a spot out of the sun, Greg. I hate coming back to a broiling hot car."

"We don't have a lot of options."

"We only need one."

He parks and turns off the engine. I open the back door a crack. Demon heat rushes in. I slam the door and duck back inside. Too late. It's already impossible to breathe in here.

The AC is weak inside the community center. Sweat drips from my armpits and rolls down my sides.

"I'm getting a drink," I tell Mom.

"Want us to wait?"

I give Dad a look. He puts his hand on Mom's shoulder. "Let's go inside, Mandy. She'll find us."

Dead moths litter the inside of the light above the water fountain. Too many victims to count. The water is warm and tastes like metal, but I let the stream hit my mouth, pretending to drink. Water splashes on my shirt, but I don't move.

"If it isn't the stalker." The voice drips with venom.

I turn. Oh Goddess. It's Mariah. My stomach drops.

"Are you talking to me?" Pretending I don't know isn't a lie.

She rolls her eyes and slinks away like a cat that sprayed the couch and acts like it wasn't her.

How does she know what I did? Who else knows?

I feel sick. Maybe I'm dying. I walk into the bathroom. A public restroom! I leave quickly and follow a short hallway to a door that says Emergency Exit Only.

Is this an emergency? Not sure. Not yet. But everything's signaling it will be soon.

Mom texts. "They're about to start. Get in here NOW. We're in the second row, left side."

As I sit beside Mom she whispers, "Why is your shirt all wet? And do you really need to wear those ridiculous gloves in this heat?"

She reaches for my hands. I pull away. She leans closer. I shift. The backs of my thighs stick to the plastic seat, pinching my skin. I can't get away from Mom. Can't get away from my Karma. Can't get away from Nic. She's smiling at me from her photo on the stage while her body rots inside the coffin, right there. She wants me to look at her, but I can't.

I count chairs in the row in front of us. All twelve seats filled. Mike sits on the aisle. So much grief is radiating off of him it hurts to look, even from the back.

Through the big windows on the left wall, I watch the cars on San Marin Drive. A black car heads east. A gray car follows twelve seconds later. Are either of them on their way to a different funeral? No. This is probably it for today.

"Angel" plays over and over. I actually listen to the words for the first time. Angels comforting the dead. Sounds good, but what about me? Where can I find comfort?

I hold my crystal and whisper into my fist, "Goddess Eternal, I need you."

Dusty cobwebs drape the overhead lights. Dead flies dot the webs like raisins. I don't even want to think about the three hundred fifty-one different types of bacteria flies are known to carry. A dead fly could fall on any of us at any moment. Or fly poop! Someone needs to get on a ladder and do a thorough cleaning.

In one corner of the ceiling where there are no light fixtures or webs, a soft, amber light glows, then pulses. *What . . . ?* My crystal vibrates against my skin. Something up there moved. A shiver snakes between my shoulder blades, and the spot at the back of neck tingles. Ohmygoddess. Nic's here! I squint at the light and it breaks into tiny rainbows. Rainbows are a symbol of hope, connection, unity. A circle of warmth pulses in my heart chakra. Another sign. Of what? Nic wants my help. She wants . . . information. She doesn't know how she died. Sudden death can confuse and disorient spirits. These souls can only rest when they learn the whole truth; otherwise, they are lost for eternity. I can help by telling her what happened. But if I tell the truth, she may never forgive me. And without her forgiveness, *I'll* be lost.

Should I tell her?

A weight spreads across my back and pushes me all the way forward until my chest rests on my knees. My necklace falls out of my shirt and the crystal swings back and forth, like a pendulum, trying to answer my question. The crystal rotates counterclockwise. No. Don't tell her. It switches to clockwise, swinging wider and stronger. Yes. Tell her.

Okay. I'll tell her, and with the help of the Goddess, I will embrace the consequences. What about Cassie? I know what she did. Even though she doesn't know I know. She has to tell Nic her part, too, and ask for forgiveness. Where is Cassie? Right there. I wave. She's pretending to look out the window, but I know she saw me. I press my crystal against my chest. I inhale, thinking the word, *Goddess*. I exhale, thinking the word, *Eternal*. A dozen inhalations. A dozen exhalations.

Cassie, your resistance is going to cease
Telling truth to Nicole, you'll be released
I command you to listen to me
I command you to take responsibility
Together we will help our friend
And bring her questioning to an end.
We will do this, you and me
As I speak it, so must it be.

CASSIE

IF JASMINE WANTS to go to Nicole's funeral, it's okay with me. I'm not going. She ought to be okay with that, except she's not. She encourages me to do whatever I want, no pressure, as long as it's not "dangerous," and since I never tell her about any of that stuff, we're cool. So why is she being so pushy right now? She says I should pay my respects to Nicole. Nicole was a phony who used people, so screw respect. Jasmine says if I don't go to the funeral, I will regret it. That's not going to happen.

By some miracle, Buzz-Kill, who just walked in five minutes ago in her usual crap mood, takes my side. "That girl messed with you bad, trying to steal Alex and all. No way should you go. Neither of you should. Funerals attract evil spirits."

"There are no such things as evil spirits, Ma," Jasmine says.

Buzz-Kill kicks off her leopard stilettos and farts. Jasmine and I look at each other, but we know we'd better not laugh or mention the stink bomb. Buzz-Kill staggers up to Jasmine, breathing in her face. She wreaks of booze, but Jasmine doesn't flinch.

"Excuse me, Miss Jasmine-Smartest-Person-in-the-World, but you don't know nothing. I'm telling you, if Cassie goes to that girl's funeral, evil spirits will invade her dreams, and she'll scream all night long. Then how am I supposed to sleep?"

Same as always. Passed out drunk.

"Ma, people are coming together to support each other during a sad time. They'll probably get up and say nice things about Nicole."

Buzz-Kill's head is in the fridge, hunting for beer, so she's not listening to Jasmine. Surprise. She is. "Cassie's got nothing nice to say about that girl, so why should she bother going?"

"I'm not going," I say, though it feels weird to be on Buzz-Kill's side against Jasmine.

My sister hangs her arm over my shoulder. "I'll be right there with you, Cass. No one will force you to speak. I promise. Come with me. It's the right thing to do."

I want Jasmine to be proud of me. Come to think of it, if I don't go with her, what will I do? Alex and Kyle and Mariah will be there, and I'll be stuck here in this hot, smelly apartment waiting on Buzz-Kill and listening to her bitch about how effed up her life is. Come to think of it, even if we had AC, going to a funeral sounds like a sweeter deal.

Jasmine brushes my hair into a ponytail and braids it. I like when she does that, but I don't say anything. She gives me one of her black skirts to wear. It's too long and her white shirt is too tight in the shoulders and too baggy in the front because she's got way bigger boobs than me. But I wear what she gives anyway because I don't have anything that's either black or white. Jasmine also wears a white shirt and a black skirt, only hers fit. It's a nothing outfit, but she looks pretty no matter what she wears. We stand next to each other in front of the closet mirror. She says I look nice. Yeah, like an awkward nun on date night.

We tiptoe through the living room. Buzz-Kill is totally sucked into *Days of Our Lives*. We're careful not to talk because if we do, she'll scream at us to shut up because we're "ruining *Lives*." She should talk.

It's effin' hot outside. We run our asses off to catch the bus to Vintage Oaks Community Center.

It's hardly any cooler inside the building. Where's the AC? We follow the stream of people through the lobby toward the open double doors that lead into the main meeting room. That sappy "in the arms of the angel" song spills out of the main room. I peek inside. Lots of people are crying, so I guess it makes a good soundtrack. But, gimme a break. It's not like Nicole died of cancer after months of toughing out chemo and shit like that. She offed herself. Gotta admit that took balls. I'd never do it. Maybe her life sucked more than mine. Hard to imagine, but you never know. Anyway, she's gone now. Not my problem any more.

". . . may you find some comfort there . . ."

Yeah. I hope she finds comfort there. Wherever she is.

"I've gotta pee," Jasmine says. "Why don't you go in and get seats?"

"There are plenty of seats. I'll wait for you out here."

Jasmine disappears around the corner. People from school pass me on their way into the main room. I talk to Kyle for a couple of minutes. He doesn't blame me for what happened, but he's still pissed at Alex. I wish I were pissed at Alex. That would feel a whole lot better than this. Mariah asks me to sit with her and some of the other girls, but I blow her off because I want to sit with Jasmine, in case I embarrass myself.

A large poster board, right outside the door, is covered with a bunch of random photos, all starring Nicole. Her school photos, team photos, family photos. Nicole and Alex in the play. The ladder scene. Like I need to see that. Huh. There's me and Nicole at the talent show. Her dad must have taken it from the audience. We look good. I wish I could zoom in. Maybe I shouldn't have deleted every photo of her.

I sing in the practice room. Kyle accompanies me on piano. A girl with crazy wavy hair and big boobs walks in. She's in our grade, but I've never talked to her.

"Uh, Ms. Moreno thinks we should sing together for the talent show," she says, looking at Kyle's sheet music.

"A duet? That's a stupid idea. Who are we supposed to be, The Bellas? This is my solo. Tell Ms. Moreno you changed your mind about being in the show."

Instead of leaving, Nicole starts singing. Kyle backs her up, really getting into the music like he never does when he plays for me.

Her voice is higher than mine with zero belting power, and our styles couldn't have been more different, but her tone has such a cool airy quality, I wonder how it would sound with my rasp.

I start singing with her, doing runs I never thought of before and totally nailing them, first time through. She pretty much stays with the melody while I weave in and out. Kyle's fingers dance across the keys, wrapping it all together like a Christmas present.

"I'm bullet proof
Nothing to lose"

Our duet was killer.

My eyes sting. I turn from the wall, pull out my phone, and make like I'm reading a text. Someone touches my arm. I whirl around.

It's Jasmine.

"Ready?" she asks.

I shake my head. "You go in. I'll be there in a minute."

I hurry through the lobby and out the front door.

A line of ants weaves its way up the tree by the parking lot. They spend their whole lives following each other, nose to butt. Nothing ever shakes them up. Life must be nice when no one bitches at you and you've got no brain and no photos reminding you of stuff you don't want to think about.

I smack the tree with a long stick. Ants go flying. Others race around like they're on meth.

Alex walks up the hill from the parking lot. I stash the stick and step into the path. He's almost here. Don't say anything, just smile a little so he'll know if he talks to me, I won't be mad.

He walks by like I'm invisible.

I am not going to cry. I was stupid to think that what we did in the park Friday meant something to him. Obviously, not. What kind of a loser am I? He just ghosted me to my face, and I'm still hoping he'll turn around and come back.

I grab the branch and beat the tree like I'm trying to kill it, but the tree feels nothing. Not a bad way to be. The stick breaks. I toss it and start bawling. Cut it out, you pathetic idiot. Okay, I'm an idiot, but I'm *not* pathetic.

I sit with Jasmine in front of Ms. Moreno and some other teachers. The Rich Girls sit in front of us taking selfies. Posting to Instagram. Who was the hottest girl at the funeral? Who was most deeply moved by Nicole's tragic death? Whose eye makeup held up best? Who looks cuter than a raccoon?

Phony bitches.

My sister never fakes it. I once asked her why she cries so much. She shrugged.

"Guess I'm just wired to weep. It's not always the big stuff, or even because I'm sad. Sometimes life is just too much."

"Too much BS?"

"Too much for words."

Jasmine is an artist so she can say that stuff without sounding ridiculous. She's crying for real now. I wonder if she'd be that upset if I died. Yeah, of course she would, but not a whole lot of other people.

Buzz-Kill? Definitely not.

Alex places flowers on Nicole's casket. From the back he looks like an empty suit. I can't watch my ex-boyfriend stand there, broken-hearted, with everyone knowing that he's thinking about her, missing her, and maybe even wishing that I was dead and she was still here.

I get up, not sure where I'm going. Jasmine pulls me back into my seat.

"Stay right where you are, little sister, and hold your head up. You've got nothing to be ashamed of."

If you only knew.

I try to catch Alex's eye as he hurries back up the aisle. I want to tell him I'm sorry for everything he's blaming me for. I want to beg him to love me again. He looks straight ahead when he passes my row. My heart pounds, my nose runs.

I *am* pathetic.

I wipe my nose with the back of my hand, hoping no one's watching. Someone taps my shoulder.

"Would this help?"

I whip around to see Ms. Moreno, frown-smiling and offering me a tissue. I come *this close* to telling her to eff off. Instead I face front again and slump down in my seat.

Jasmine knows I'm about to lose it. She touches my knee, ready to say something comforting. If I let her, I'm gonna embarrass myself even more.

"Don't," I mumble.

She nods but leaves her hand where it is.

Isabel waves at me. Does she still think I'm coming to her house? She can believe whatever the hell her crazy mind wants to believe, not my problem. I pretend I don't see her. Why does she look guilty? Also not my problem. None of this is. Why throw a party for a dead girl? Stinky flowers. Sappy music. If this isn't all BS, what is? The only thing missing is a cake and the guest of honor. No, she's here, in that picture, smiling and soaking up all the attention, begging everyone to love her. I guess Alex does. Maybe he always did. They all love Nicole and feel sorry for her, except me. Why should I? She got everything she wanted. I've got nothing.

Nicole

GOING TO MY funeral was a catastrophic mistake. As if being a no body isn't enough to cope with, plus the stress of this stupid timer counting down on my finger constantly reminding me what's going to happen if—no, *when*—I fail The Evaluation. And let's not forget the ongoing frustration of being falsely accused of having killed myself when I know I didn't. But now I've also got to deal with the burden of knowing that I'm responsible for totally destroying any chance that Dad will ever be happy again, not to mention the possibility that my best friend might have murdered me. That sounds so crazy it makes my brain itch.

Whoever said "Dead is dead" obviously knew nothing.

At least Grace gave me back my Life-Streamer. For all the help that is. I need to talk to someone who can hear me. Someone who understands.

I step out of my dorm room into the hallway. A few doors are open. Don't know that guy. Or that girl. Directly across the hall, another open door. Inside the room, Golden Girl sits on her bed, deep in concentration, writing in a black notebook.

Seeing her again feels like the first good thing that's happened in a very long time.

Blue butterflies decorate her bedspread with some random orange ones for a pop of color. I've loved this bedspread every time I've passed this room, not knowing whose it was because Golden Girl was never in here before.

"Hey, hi," I say.

She looks up, not unhappy to see me, but not thrilled either. After stashing the notebook under a pillow, she eyes me nervously, which makes no sense.

I step into the room, not waiting to be invited. "Did you know we're across-the-hall neighbors?"

She nods.

On the wall behind her hangs a poster-sized photo of her at a women's march. She's holding a sign over her head: MY BODY! MY CHOICE! The camera caught her mid-shout. She looks incredibly powerful.

We introduce ourselves. She is Teeg. Cool name, but fearless Teeg in the photo seems nothing like the Teeg on the bed who now avoids all eye contact.

"So why didn't you come see me?" I ask.

She picks up a small green pillow and hugs it to her stomach like a shield to protect herself from . . . me?

"I . . . uh, thought about it." She bites the edge of her lip. "People say the Mentors are giving you a hard time because you did something bad. Is it true?"

My face must be going through changes because Teeg looks like she's trying to figure out what I'm thinking. Like Iz does. Always digging below the surface, trying to understand me better. I think Teeg and I could be friends. I want to tell her the truth, but I don't know where to start, so I just start.

"I didn't do anything at all, but yeah, they're pissed at me. Actually, you might get in trouble for talking to me. Maybe I should leave."

"Nah. Sit." She scoots over to make room.

I tell her I like the shades of blue in her bedspread—cornflower, electric, turquoise, and sapphire. She asks me how I know the difference.

"Easy. Electric blue, for example, contains between eighteen and twenty percent more white than turquoise."

She looks confused so I continue. "My dad is a house painter. We always had paint chips lying around. You know those long paper rainbow fans with every color and shade in the world? I actually learned to read from those."

She gives me a look like maybe she thinks that's very cool or very weird. Hard to tell, but if she trusts me enough to let me sit on her bed, I should trust her not to judge me for geeking out on colors. Maybe I can also trust her with other things.

"You know that time you saw me running away from the meeting place? I was trying to escape."

"Escape?"

"Yeah. I was trying to get to Substation Fourteen. That's where I belong. Not here. I've told the Mentors, but no one believes me."

I let the words hang in the air and fiddle with the bottom of my shirt, pretending I'm not worried she'll ask me questions I can't answer, like *How do you know you don't belong here?*

After a moment, she shifts her weight and the mattress creaks. "I believe you. I mean, you know where you belong better than anyone else."

I feel like hugging her, but I'm not sure how she'd take it, so I just smile to myself. "Thanks. It's weird but I've known it since the platform stopped at Fourteen. Remember how Grandma Vestie blocked me so I couldn't even walk? They're still blocking me."

"I don't get it. Why should they care if you go to Fourteen? What difference does it make?"

"I don't know. Maybe they're giving me a hard time because they can't admit they messed up for bringing me here. Fifteen is for suicides. I'm not one of *those* kids."

Teeg inhales sharply.

Uh, oh. *She's* one of those kids. That's why she's here. I'm such an idiot.

I reach for her arm. "I'm sorry, Teeg. That came out wrong."

She leaps off the bed and turns on me, eyes fierce, like the girl in the poster. "Don't judge what you don't understand."

I hold my hands up, so I don't get shot. "Teeg, I swear I wasn't judging you."

She glares at me, not convinced. Why should she be? I *was* judging her. I've been judging all of them since I read the word "suicide" in *The Handbook*. No. Way before that. I've always judged people who killed themselves. I'm still judging, right this minute, even while I'm swearing to her that I'm not.

The space between us turns to stone. My face flushes, but I force myself not to look away from her. She has every right to be pissed at me. What kind of a person am I?

A needy, insecure, self-centered, judgmental person.

I go to her.

"I'm so sorry, Teeg." I hope she believes me. She's the closest thing I've got to a friend here. Without her, I'm even less of a no body. After who knows how long, she exhales. Her eyes soften and she seems less scared. Of me? Maybe this isn't about me. Not everything is.

I wish I could hear her thoughts. I'd really like to know why a feisty, feminist golden girl would kill herself. I picture myself at The Evaluation, sweating under a spotlight while Poodle and Fury take turns shouting at me. "Why did you do it, Nicole? Tell us, why?"

I've got no answer. Maybe Teeg doesn't either. I put my arms around her. She stiffens, but she doesn't move away. We stand there, awkward as statues, but after a while she rests her head against mine.

"Thanks for not asking why," she whispers. "After the other times, that's all anyone wanted to know."

It takes a second to realize that she's talking about the other times she tried to kill herself. She must have had a rough life. If I were her, would I have done the same? Dammit. There I go again. I hate how my mind works. Every thought always comes back to me. I scan Teeg's room for something else to talk about. "You've got a ton of books."

"Not as many as my mom. She's a psychotherapist."

"My mom's dead."

Why'd I say that? To make her feel sorry for me.

Teeg's face falls. "I'm sorry."

"It's okay. It's not like I remember her." I shrug, pretending I don't want her to feel bad. Then I try to make her feel worse. "She died when I was a baby."

"Oh, Nicole." Her voice breaks.

What is wrong with me? I didn't want her to feel *that* bad. Or did I?

I want to stop doing this stuff. With everyone. But especially with Teeg. I've got to stop being such a needy, little . . .

Blondie blows into the room. I haven't seen her since we got here. Haven't missed her. "Well, look who's here." She's sneering.

I never heard her talk before. Vocal shocker. Blondie sounds more like a sweet six-year-old than the super bitch she is. She catches me staring. "What are you looking at, Big Boobs?"

I clench my fists. Girls like Blondie make me sick. Always in attack mode. Cassie's the same.

Teeg nudges me. "Don't take that crap from her."

Blondie laughs. "Who are you, Fat Ass, her life coach?"

Rage surges up my spine, through my shoulders, down my arms. Before I know it, I'm pointing my lapis blue painted fingernail at Blondie like a light-saber. "Do not ever disrespect me or my friend again. Her name is Teeg. I'm Nicole. You want to talk to either of us, use our names. Got that?"

Blondie, wide-eyed and shaken, nods. "Uh, huh."

I can't believe I just said all that and actually scared her. It didn't feel as good as I thought it would.

I lower my weapon and step back. "So, what's your name?"

She shifts uncomfortably, like she's waiting for me to come at her again. I don't. "Sam." Her expression is passive, her tone, harmless.

"Hey, Sam. Good to meet you. Look, you and Teeg and me might as well get along since we all live here."

"Dead kids don't live anywhere." She's trying to sound like a badass again, but her little girl voice cracks. She hides her face and hurries out of the door.

I look at Teeg, "She's nothing like what I thought."

"Maybe no one is."

I think of Iz. "Yeah. That might be true. You know, you were right when you said I didn't understand. I'd like to understand more. Especially about you and . . . how you got here."

She takes the notebook out from under the pillow. "If you're really interested, I could read you some parts of my journal."

A cold wave of dizziness washes over me. I reach for Teeg's arm to steady myself.

"Are you okay?"

"Yeah. I think so." I give her a quick hug. "Thanks so much, Teeg."

"What for?"

"For reminding me of something important that I'd totally forgotten. I've gotta go and check it out, but I'll be back, and if you're still willing to read me parts of your journal, I'd really like that. Also, maybe I could bring over my guitar and sing a couple of my songs. If you're interested."

"Yeah. That'd be great."

Back in my dorm room, where I only pretend to live, I tear the place apart looking for my own journal. I know I had one, and I've got to find it. There are answers in it.

One of Dad's non-negotiable truths states: *It's easier to find something if you know what you're looking for.* But I can't even remember what something that was once so important to me looks like. I try to picture the cover of my journal, but all I get are random, unrelated images. The nebula from the platform. Grace's half-smile. Stuffing my face with tasteless dream doughnuts. MiNik212274Zr9. What's that last one? Oh, my Insta password.

My brain is spongy. I can't think any more.

A small, three-ring binder pops onto my mental movie screen. Light blue threads hang from places where the cloth cover separated from the spine. My journal! That's what it looked like. The cube, the spiral, the abstract flowers with the swirly leaves I drew on the cover in red and black ink. My name in 3-D block letters. I remember exactly what it looks like now, but where is it? Dad isn't a snoop, like Mandy, but I would never have left my journal lying around. It wouldn't be under my pillow. Too obvious. Sorry, Teeg. Definitely not in this desk drawer. Too crammed with other stuff. I open the closet door. Total mess, exactly like home. I wouldn't have put my journal in there anyway. I must have hidden it in a small, uncluttered, out of the way place. But where? WHERE?

I don't know! My brain is useless. I flop onto the bed and hang my head and arms over the side. My fingers play with the lacey edges of the dust cover. Funny name, dust cover. It doesn't cover dust, it covers . . .

Wait! I drop onto the floor and scramble under the bed. I slip my hand into the dust cover through the special slit I'd made. I slide my fingers along the space between the bottom of the mattress and the wooden frame until I feel my journal. The whirlies boogie around inside me. I just have to read my journal and everything will come back to me. Then I'll pass The Evaluation, no problem.

I crawl out from under the bed, climb on top, lean against the pillows and open to page one.

> This journal is dedicated to truth-telling. I might as well be honest here since no one will read this until I'm dead. Haha!

Ohmygod. I wrote that two and half years ago, and all this time Death was waiting for me, laughing at my past self and my future self, knowing that someday I'd be a no body, reading those words.

It's a sign! I sound more and more like Iz all the time. Maybe if I try to *think* like her it would help me figure out what this could mean. What if I actually set up my death by writing those words? Is that possible? If it is, then maybe it's also possible that I set *other* things in motion by writing about them. What if I doomed other people?

I shove the journal back under the bed so I can't see it. I try to forget what it looks like so it will vanish from my dorm room.

Non-negotiable truth: *It's impossible to un-know what you know.*

A corner of the blue cover peeks out from under the edge of the dustcover.

This is stupid. I'm overreacting, like always. . . . *no one will read this until I'm dead* was a joke. People joke about death all the time. I used to say stuff like: *I'm dying to see you. I died of embarrassment. Death by chocolate.* I thought it was funny. Once. I must have lost my sense of humor when I lost my body. Whatever. I have to read the journal, otherwise I may not know the answers to some basic Evaluation questions and they'll send me to . . .

Stop thinking about that.

I breathe in deeply, and I pick up the journal. I flip past the first page without looking at it. The second page is blank. So are the third and the fourth pages. All the pages are blank! What happened to the rest of my journal? Did the Vesties delete everything to mess with me?

"This is so damn unfair!" I'm hyperventilating.

Teeg rushes into my room. "What's wrong?"

"This is my journal." I hand it to her. "But the first two sentences are all that's in it."

She flips through the blank pages and hands it back. "That's probably because you only remember the first two sentences."

Of course. Everything around here is a memory pull. I'm screwed by my lousy memory again. But what about her journal? She offered to read it to me.

"Teeg, is everything you wrote, from before, still in your journal?"

She nods. "All 208 pages."

"How could you possibly remember everything you wrote? Do you have a photographic memory?"

"Actually, my mom studied this and she says there's no scientific evidence for the existence of photographic memory. The reason I remember what I wrote is because I re-read every entry like a hundred times. I'm a little compulsive that way. You probably never re-read anything."

"I didn't. I just wrote whatever I felt at the time and forgot about it."

"Literally."

Another dead-end, except for the fact that this one leads straight to Substation Sixteen. "What am I going to do?"

"Have you dream toured yet?"

"Officially, twice, but not with anyone I know."

"How about unofficially?"

I squirm. What the hell? It's not like she's a Vestie. "I guess you could say I invaded my dad's dream. It didn't go well. He wasn't ready, but I think next time . . ."

"Okay. That's your solution. Tour your dad's dream again, and this time ask him to read your journal. Then go back the next night and he'll tell you what's in it."

I pull her into a hug. "Teeg, you're a genius!"

The Life-Streamer reveals Dad sitting in the kitchen. Other than the light above the stove, he's in the dark. Even so, I can see he looks awful. Like he hasn't slept in . . . how long has it been? He's sipping black coffee from the #1 Dad mug I got him for Father's Day three years ago. I zoom into the microwave clock. It's 3:28 am. If he's not sleeping, dream touring is out.

I switch to Iz. She's also sitting in the dark. She's hugging her stomach. It probably hurts. Poor Iz. The only light in her room shines from the altar candles. Her grandpa's photo sat there for a long time after he died. My photo has replaced his. I'm not Iz's best friend anymore, just someone she used to love who is dead and gone. That's half right. I'm dead, but not gone yet. I was nuts to think that she'd ever hurt me. Iz still loves me and the photo proves it. I'll just ask her to get my journal and read it and tell me everything.

Isabel

WHEN YOU'VE JUST been to your best friend's funeral and it's your fault that she's dead, it's impossible to think about anything else. I sensed another spirit up on the ceiling with Nic, maybe some kind of helper. She needs one. Because of me she is a lost soul who can't rest in peace.

I'm sick. I don't think I've got a fever, but it feels like a fork is scraping the inside of my throat. This is my Karma for shooting off my big mouth. Mom will kill me when she finds out. Dad will blame Mom and me. Nic will hate me forever, and I'll deserve it.

My heart beats dangerously fast, then seems to give up as if it suddenly forgot how to do its job. Maybe this time it is a heart attack. Either that or the throbbing ache in my left arm is a sign. I failed Nic when she needed me. I sense that we're both running out of time, and I've got to make this right, but how?

Breathing doesn't calm me down because the glands in my neck, swollen to what feels like the size of oranges, clog my airways. More bigmouth Karma. I drag myself to the balcony door, open it wide, and suck in the night air as best as I can. The smell of lemon and vanilla ride the breeze into my room. Nic's hair conditioner and de-frizzer!

Skittering footsteps cross the roof directly overhead. Is she up there?

I hurry onto the balcony, the damp deck is cold beneath my feet, but there's no time for slippers. I don't know how long she can stay, and I have to apologize.

I scramble up the ladder and hop onto the roof. "Nic? Are you here?"

HISSSS.

I scan the roof with my phone light. The shaky beam hits the base of the chimney.

GRRRR.

A raccoon that must weigh fifty pounds arches its back and stares at me through black marble eyes. It's a spirit guide. I reach for my crystal and summon the power of the Goddess. With a few deep breaths, calmness flows through me.

"Welcome, raccoon, creature of the night. I am Isabel, nature-lover. What is your message of peace and understanding?"

Fangs bared, the raccoon growls and lunges. I try not to scream as I fly down the steps, missing the last one and landing hard. I hobble into my room and slam the door behind me just as something smacks against the glass.

THUD.

Ohmygoddess! It's trying to get in.

I dare to peek over my shoulder. No raccoon. A motionless crow lies on the balcony, its lifeless eyes point at the sky, like it knew it would never fly again.

Poor thing flew into the glass.

Birds are messengers between heaven and Earth. They let the living know that a departed spirit is well. But crows aren't just any bird. They symbolize death, and Nic hated them.

A vicious raccoon and a dead crow. Could it be a message of revenge?

I carry a tall black candle out to the balcony, holding its protective light in front of me like a sword and a shield, protection against raccoons or anything else that might harm me. With every step serenity radiates from my heart chakra.

I dig a neat hole in the planter box and lay the crow to rest among the sage plants.

"I bid you goodbye, good rest, and good night. May your spirit find peace, may new wings give you flight."

What about Nic's spirit? She needs to find peace. She also needs to know how sorry I am before she does something terrible to me.

Back inside, I clap my hands toward the four corners of my room. I unroll my white silk cord to form a circle of protection on the floor. I pull my talking board out from under the bed. The planchette sits on the sun, not on GOODBYE. My heart jumps to my throat where there's no room to beat, so it drops into my stomach where it bounces against the walls. So many signs. None positive. I bring the black candle and talking board into the circle with me and place the planchette over the protective eye of the Goddess. I draw a pentacle on a scrap of paper for extra protection, but my drawing lacks strength. Can anything protect me now? Melting wax drips down the side of the candle and pools on the floor like black blood.

Nic lies in a pool of blood, her broken body a twisted heap.

Don't think about the body. Connect with her eternal spirit.

"The earth, the wind, the fire, the water, around, around, around, around.

Goddess Eternal, my heart is so heavy

Guide me, as I make the talking board ready

Open the channel, use this light, use this charm

To undo the hurt, and undo the harm.

May I speak from the heart so Nic can go free

Assure peaceful healing between her and me."

I inhale and exhale twelve times. My heart returns to my chest, calmer now. I lightly rest my fingers on the planchette, pinkies up, elbows out.

"My channel is open and my planchette is ready."

The planchette vibrates under my fingertips. I imagine myself as a satellite dish, smooth and curved, slowly revolving in all directions, ready to receive the positive energy about to enter through the portal.

I hope Nic can move the planchette. Hmm. You might have to be dead for a while before you can master telekinesis, and she's only been on the other side four days. If she can't speak through the board, maybe Yolanda can connect us.

"You wonder if I can move your *ghost phone?*" Nic laughs at her old joke so hard she hiccups. Is she actually speaking to me or am I imagining this?

"Is that you, Nic?"

The planchette zooms over the letters on the rim of the board and spells out YESYOUBITC . . .

Before it gets to "H" I fling the planchette out of the circle and race into the hall. At least I think I'm racing. Maybe I'm running in place, like in a nightmare. No. There's the stairwell. Hopefully the TV noise from downstairs drowns my footsteps. I silently close the bathroom door. The floor tilts. I slump onto the toilet. My stomach kills.

That couldn't have been Nic on the board. She never talked to me that way. She never had a reason before. Or maybe it was an evil spirit impersonating her. I'm sure I closed the portal last time. No evil spirit could enter. What if it wasn't Nic or an evil spirit? Maybe someone else is out to get me? Am I so messed up I moved the planchette without knowing it and called myself a bitch?

I wrap my entire body in a bath towel, head to ankles, like a cocoon, and lie on the floor. Nic and I are larva, in between lives, preparing to move into the next phase. When will that happen? The police want to talk to me Friday. Can they arrest me for breaking a promise and betraying a friend? What are the bathrooms in jail like? Will I be allowed to bring my silk cord so I can create a protective circle wherever I am?

The floor buckles. My mouth fills with a god-awful taste. I rinse my mouth, but the tap water tastes metallic. Stomach pain folds me in half. I heave up a gross-tasting string of spit. Headachy and weak, I face myself in the mirror.

Who is that girl? She looks like a ghost.

Staring into my own eyes, my face and body fade. My

runaway train of thought roars down the track.

If I hadn't told Nic to audition for the talent show, she wouldn't have become friends with Cassie. If Cassie hadn't been blind to Nic's feelings for Alex, she wouldn't have included her in everything Calex did. If I hadn't been so worried about losing Nic, I wouldn't have pushed her to audition for *Our Town* so we could be in the play together. If she hadn't gotten the part of Emily and Alex hadn't gotten George . . .

Stop. I'm filling myself with negative energy. Breathe. Ahhhhh.

I just want everything back to normal, but I'm afraid that normal is gone forever.

Back in my room, I slip under the covers, still weak from barfing too much, and thinking too much about things I can't change. My bed doesn't feel like my bed. My feet are icy and my crystal necklace pulls across my throat. I pull the chain over my head and slide it under my pillow. That's better. The crystal's healing power radiates through the non-allergenic foam. I sink into the softness. I just want . . . to . . . sleep.

I get out of bed and set up my talking board. My fingers perch motionless on the planchette.

"What is the spirit world like, Nic?" The question is barely out of my mouth before the planchette slides up to the alphabet and starts spelling.

H-A-R-P-I-S-H-A-R-D-E-R-T-O-L-E-A-R-N-T-H-A-N-G-U-I-T-A-R

I laugh out loud. Nic is testing my sense of humor. I guess I passed because she walks *through* my door without opening it. Her body radiates such positive energy I feel as if I am in the presence of The Goddess even though I know it's Nic and I know I'm dreaming. But it's more than a dream. Even more than a lucid dream. It's a *visitation*. Nic is really here. The tingle in the back of my neck confirms it.

Blessed be!

We rush to hug each other, and my heart chakra opens wider than ever with love and hope. Nic beams at me.

"Thank you for letting me into your dream, Iz. I'm so sorry for all the lame jokes I made about Wiccans. You guys are the best. Forgive me?"

She's asking *me* for forgiveness?

"Of course." I answer quickly, so that when I tell her what I did and ask for *her* forgiveness, she'll remember that I didn't hesitate. But she's talking again, so I don't get the chance.

Nic's eyes flick around the top of my head. Can she read auras? She must sense my conflict. Maybe she can read my thoughts, too. It'd be better if I just told her, so I could explain. But I'm too scared of what might happen. Telling her could be dangerous. It might mess with her energy and send her somewhere out of the astral plane. Then she'd have another reason to hate me.

She floats to the altar table and studies her photo. "It's nice to be remembered." she says, more to herself than to me.

Her loneliness weighs on my heart. I reach for my crystal. It's not around my neck. Panic rises in me like steam in the shower. I search the floor, my desk drawers. Then I remember that this is a dream. I turn back to the altar. She's still there.

"Let me tell you something, Iz. If you ever thought that all your problems will be over when you're dead, think again. There's this big test called The Evaluation. It's about what you remember, and you've got to pass it or else. I don't remember shit and I've got to take the test in ten days." She shows me her finger where a countdown clock ticks under her skin. "Nine days? Are you kidding me?"

She pounds the altar but her hand goes right through it.

"I can't even vent. What am I going to do, Iz?"

Poor Nic. She is a lost soul stuck in between the natural and spiritual worlds. She doesn't fit in anywhere. I rush to her side. "Let me help. Tell me what you need."

She exhales unsteadily and grins in a way that makes me feel like I am *her* angel.

"I've got so much on my mind I'm going nuts. The Vesties are out to get me. And you don't want to mess with them. They're in charge of everything on Substation Fifteen."

I really want to ask about the Vesties, but she's in constant motion and talking so fast I can't break in.

"The meanest one is Quinn. Even Grace is scared of him. They've got some history. But she won't talk about it.

Anyway, The Evaluation is a major deal, and I thought my dad could help me pass, so I toured his dream. But I freaked him out so bad he's not sleeping anymore. Also, he's kinda in denial about my death which makes talking to him impossible."

She hovers by the window, hugging herself and peering out at the stars. I had no idea being a spirit was so complicated.

"I can help your dad sleep. As for the denial stuff, no guarantees, but I've got an acceptance spell that might work."

She turns to me. "Thanks, Iz," she says, flashing a smile only to drop it an instant later. "Now tell me where I was on Friday."

Ooh. My stomach. It's a sign. I really need to tell her everything. But it's going to hurt her, and she'll hate me for eternity. I take a long deep breath and let it out.

"You were on top of the water tower above Sorich Park." There, I said it. I'm not ready to tell her the rest, but when I am, maybe it won't be so hard.

Her eyes widen with surprise and confusion. After a moment she nods to herself and laser-focuses on me. "I have to ask you something, Iz, and you've got to tell me the truth."

Uh-oh, she already knows. This is it. I reach for my crystal to give me the strength forgetting that I'm not wearing it. Oh, Goddess!

"Did you push me off the tower?"

A cloudburst of tears springs up from my heart chakra and surprises us both. "How could you think that, Nic? I would never hurt you. I love you and I hate that you're dead."

"Okay. Okay. I'm sorry. It was a crazy thought. You just looked . . . I dunno . . . kinda guilty at the funeral and I just had to ask. I'm sorry. I'm so messed up. I just can't remember anything. I don't think anyone pushed me. But the Vesties insist I killed myself. I don't think that's true. Could you do a psychic reading on me and find out if I actually jumped?"

"I'm not sure. I've never done a reading in a dream."

She smiles encouragingly. "You can do it, Iz. You're a super witch."

We sit on my bed, knees touching. I hold one of her hands in both of mine. She watches me intently, like she's reading *me* and would know if I were hiding anything.

I close my eyes. Whenever I've done this when I'm awake, mental images pour in along with body sensations and emotions. I'm getting nothing now. Maybe I can't read the dead. Hope sparks deep in my heart chakra. Then the image of a pink rose appears in my mind, each petal glowing. A snake coils around the rose and crushes the flower. The snake is jealousy, destroying hope. The snake swallows its own tail and ignites, a ring of fire fueled by shock and betrayal. The images are born from my intuitive mind, but the emotions are Nic's. Still, they are very powerful. I can't get carried away. Nic needs me to do the work.

I focus on the cool air coming in through my nostrils and filling my lungs. One. Two. Three. Four. I focus on the warm air flowing out of my mouth. Four. Three. Two. One. One. Two. Three. Four. Four. Three. Two. One. I am calm. I am clear. I have knowledge to share. I am here to help.

I am about to end the reading when I pick up one more emotion . . . *curiosity?* There is no image to go with it. I don't understand what it has to do with anything else I've just seen and sensed.

I open my eyes. Nic's gaze hasn't moved from my face.

"What did you see?" she asks as if her fate for all eternity depends on what I say.

So much pressure. The images and feelings just came to me. I don't know if anything I picked up was true.

"I didn't actually see you on the tower. It's hard to explain what I saw or sensed. I think I got your emotional state while you were up there. At first you felt intense love and happiness and hope, like you've never felt before. Something happened, though, and worry and doubt crept in along with a rush of anger, jealousy, and strong feelings of betrayal. Positive and negative energies battled inside you, pulling you in two directions at once. You couldn't keep your balance. Maybe you accidentally fell. I don't know, but I don't think you wanted to kill yourself, Nic. I didn't sense that at all."

"Thank you, Iz." She hugs me. I feel her light and her love. "I didn't kill myself. That's exactly what I've been telling everyone at Substation Fifteen since I arrived. The Mentors don't believe me. My friend Teeg does. I'm not sure about Grace. But I'm sure about you. That means a lot, because, well, Grace says you're gifted, and so if you say my death was an accident, the Vesties need to know that."

Does Nic honestly think I can communicate with the Vesties? Even if I could, I wouldn't invite them in through the portal. It sounds like their energy is very negative. I'm about to tell her that but she's already on to something else.

"I've got another favor to ask. Will you get my journal?"

I didn't know she kept a journal, but as soon as she says the word it appears in my mind's eye. A small, cloth-covered, three-ring binder with fraying blue threads hanging from the spine. I've never seen it before, but I know this is it. Red and green flames shoot out from the front cover. A jolt of fear erupts from my tailbone and lodges into the base of my skull.

"It's under my bed. I'll show you exactly where. I'm looking for answers and I'm sure I'll find them in there. Let's go to my house."

"You mean right now?"

"Yeah. Why not?"

The shifting mattress wakes me, but I don't open my eyes. Someone kisses my forehead.

"Sweet dreams," Mom whispers.

I pretend to be asleep. After she leaves, I get up quietly and perform the Acceptance Spell and the Good Night Sleep ritual for Mike. I hope this proves to Nic and to myself what a good friend I really am.

Nicole

THANKS TO IZ'S Good Night Sleep spell, Dad snores lightly on the couch. His arm hangs over the side like he's floating on a raft, his fingers drifting with the current. I enter his dream so easily, so I hope that means her Acceptance spell worked too. I don't know if that makes me feel better knowing that Dad has accepted my death or worse because it means he's letting me go.

Dad climbs the Gertrude-Ord Trail, high above Phoenix Lake. He lies on his back in a clearing of redwoods, watching a couple of turkey vultures career overhead. He chomps on an energy bar from Trader Joe's. No more homemade trail-mix. No crazy sweet and salty combos, no highs and lows, just the security of knowing exactly what to expect in every bite.

"Hi, Dad." I speak softly, careful not to startle him.

He sits up slowly and smiles, as if he knew I'd come because we had arranged to meet right here.

I sit beside him. He turns to me and looks into my eyes like I am a miracle that he'll never stop marveling at. He pulls me into a clover-scented Dial soap hug and fills me with longing.

Substation Fifteen isn't life after death. It's not life at all. I want to stay here with Dad and pretend I'm still alive.

"This is the first dream I've had about you since you died."

He must have forgotten the other one. "This is no ordinary dream, Dad."

"I know."

"How are you doing?"

"I'm okay."

He's lying. His face is a wall of crumbling stones. He shakes his head, like there's too much in it that makes no sense anymore, especially the non-negotiable truth that I am dead and will stay that way for the rest of his life.

This time I don't push.

"Dad, I want you to be happy again. Promise me that you'll try."

His eyes glisten as he tousles my hair like he did whenever I whined about my crazy hair. I used to hate when he did that because it messed my hair even more, but now I love it, and I don't want him to stop.

He stops and puts his hand in his pocket. "All my reasons for being happy are gone."

"Couldn't you find new reasons?"

He covers his face. Grief eats away at his heart like acid. There won't be any pieces left to put back together. This doesn't look like acceptance. I didn't come to watch this. I came to help him forgive himself.

I put my arms around his middle and rest my head against his heaving chest. "Dad, what happened wasn't your fault."

"You're only saying that because you forgive me, Nikki, and I love you for that, but I can't forgive myself. When you texted about your mother, I should have done everything I could to find out where you were."

"I texted you about Mom? That's so random. I don't remember texting you at all. What did I want to know?"

Sorrow and disbelief mix on his face, making a shade of miserable that I've never seen on a paint chip. He drags himself through a swamp of regret. I hold his hand, but he continues to sink, and I can't pull him back to safety. He lets go and sobs like I'm not here. I wish I wasn't because I'm useless.

After a while, he swallows enough tears to talk again. "A cop met me in our driveway when I got home. Said there'd been an accident. The girl in the hospital morgue didn't look like you. Her body bruised and broken, and her head smashed in so she didn't look like anyone. But she wasn't wearing your bracelet, so I thought, 'Thank God, it's not Nikki.' I was pissed at the cop for scaring the crap out of me for no reason. I remember thinking about the poor girl's dad. I felt for the guy, whoever he was, but I had to start dinner. I didn't want you coming home to an empty house."

Tears overwhelm him again. Even while his body is asleep on the couch and we are in his dream, his memory of last Friday is all too real. So is everything he feels. Too real for me, too.

As if he senses I want to leave, he takes my hand in both of his. "I wanted to get away from that awful place and pretend that I hadn't noticed the little bump on the top of your right ear."

I run my finger over the bump.

"Or the scar on your left knee from when you slipped on the rocks at Bridal Veil Falls."

The thickened skin always reminded me of an upside-down U. It's there. Fifteen got all the details right.

"I said to myself, and this is really crazy, 'If I pretend that I don't see the bump or the scar, then these things will vanish and none of this will be happening, and Nikki won't really be dead.'"

He bet on a miracle and lost. I want to give him hope, but I'm emptier than he is. He may only have a shadow life, but he still exists. I'll fade away forever if I don't fill myself up.

With what?

The truth.

"It didn't hurt, Dad. I don't even remember hitting the ground."

He nods. Maybe I've comforted him a little, or he just wants me to believe that I have.

"The police said they'd send me your phone records as soon as they're available. They think they'll have them Friday. Hopefully what they get off your phone will tell us what happened."

I've got to see that.

"Friday's also the day they're sending a detective to school to interview your friends."

Oh, that's good. I'll listen in on those conversations and save myself lots of time.

Dad goes on to say that people are wondering . . . *he* is wondering if I was depressed or in some kind of trouble. I don't remember any trouble.

"My one job was to take care of you, Nikki."

At the same moment, we both notice he's rubbing his thumb so forcefully across the top of his hand, his skin is stretching under the pressure. He stops abruptly and looks at me. "It was my fault that you jumped."

"I didn't jump, Dad. I swear I didn't."

Tears track down his face. He doesn't bother wiping them away. He doesn't bother blinking. He just stands there showing how much he needs to believe me. *I* need him to believe me. I ask if he does. He doesn't respond. His silence feels like a slap in the face.

"You don't believe me," I manage to say, my energy draining fast.

There's a stab of pressure between my eyes, like Quinn's meaty finger is prodding me, sending me a message from Fifteen, warning me to check my countdown clock. I stick my hands behind my back just as Dad reaches out to me, like he has a million times, but he's not sure I'll let him. I'm not sure I'll let him. For a long moment I don't move. Then I slip my hand into his.

"I've gotta go, Dad."

I lay on my dorm bed with no place to go. If I could sleep, and if I had dreams, would I remember any of what I've forgotten? If I can't remember what happened, then other people are going to have to remember it for me. Iz doesn't think I jumped, but she isn't positive. Maybe I did. Anything is possible. Maybe I wanted to kill myself. Why? And why did I want to talk about Mom?

Nicole

"**I** NEED YOUR help right away," I say, as soon as Grace appears on the stool across the table.

"I like this new sense of urgency. What do you need?"

"Two things. I want to talk to my mom. Can you check a database and find her?"

"I'm sorry, Nicole. I don't have clearance for that."

"Oh. It's got to be someone higher up, huh? Why don't you ask Quinn?" I know it's a dumb idea, but I can't think of anyone else.

She searches the area, trying not to be too obvious. Weird how she doesn't trust her own kind, but maybe not so weird.

No Vesties on the ground or in the air. She leans in and lowers her voice. "I can take a quick look for you."

She closes her eyes. The dusty chant rolls on the air. "Ahhhhooooouuummmm.   Ahhhhooooouuummmm. Ahhhhooooouuummmm." The rumbling sets my whirlies spinning into high gear. I'm going to see my mom!

The rumbling stops. Grace frowns. "Your mom is not in this realm."

"What? Oh. That makes sense. She died a long time ago. So she moved on?"

"Good possibility."

"She was a really good person. Went to church and everything. I'll bet God gave her another chance and another life. Whoa! That means my mom is younger than me." I grab Grace's shoulders. "Find out where she is. I want to tour her dream and talk to her."

"What makes you think I can do that? Besides, if your mom is currently living in a new incarnation, and that's a big *if*, she obviously is not your mom anymore. *She* could be a *he.* Either way, it's not likely this person who was your mother in a past life would remember you, Nicole."

I hadn't thought about that, but, yeah, why would she? I can't remember any past lives. I can't even remember what happened Friday.

"As for locating her, you'd have to do that yourself, but that won't be easy. You got to the funeral because your deep knowledge of your father guided you there. Memories of your mother are so limited, I honestly don't see how you'll locate her."

"This is so unfair. She dies when I'm a baby, and I don't even get to see her when I'm dead and I can go wherever I want."

Grace offers a half-smile. "I'm sorry."

"Save it." I stomp off.

"What was the other thing you wanted?"

I break into a run. Why get my hopes up asking her for anything? She's no help. But who else is there? Quinn? Yeah, right. Asking him for anything is so ludicrous it makes me laugh. I know that's just an expression, but I laugh. A lot. Then come the hiccups. Some things don't change.

When Grace pops up in my face, I stop short. So do the hiccups.

"Why were you laughing? What's funny?"

"In this place? Nothing."

She blinks once, but I know what she's thinking: *Nicole is a lost cause.*

Am I? Maybe not. I think I could pass The Evaluation if I stopped making things harder for myself and if she helped me.

"The police are talking to my friends on Friday. Of course, I'll lurk in the room and listen to everything, but I might also want to be able to talk to them. If I could be seen and heard I could get to the truth so much faster than by dream touring, but I need to talk to Iz first, while she's awake."

Grace blinks twice. I do my best to keep my avatar still so she won't know how mind-wracking this is. She probably knows. That's why she does it. Grace is kind, but she's not subtle.

"What are you saying?" she asks as if she knows exactly what I'm saying. For some reason that I don't understand, she looks like she hopes she's wrong.

"Grace, will you teach me to materialize?"

The corners of her mouth stretch farther apart than I've ever seen. This could mean yes *and* no. She might also be suppressing a laugh. She yanks me off the stool. Nope. She's definitely not amused.

The meeting area morphs into Phoenix Lake. Dark clouds huddle overhead. Deer tracks dot the muddy shore. Wind chops the water around the deserted turtle log. Even though we are alone on the bench in the middle of my memory, she scoots in closer and drops her voice. "We don't teach materialization here. It's not even appropriate to talk about it."

"Why not?"

She seals her lips as if she's trying to hold a tornado in her mouth and flicks her eyes skyward. Finally she lets loose. "It requires a level of personal responsibility that no bodies on Substation Fifteen haven't yet achieved."

"Because all of them committed suicide, and that's not very 'responsible.' Yeah, I get that, but you can teach *me*." I flash a smile of encouragement.

"No, I can't," she says it like that's the end of the conversation.

It's not.

"C'mon, Grace. I need this. You can trust me."

"That's just what Jane said."

"Who?"

"I shouldn't be talking about this." Sounds like she's arguing with herself. "Okay. Why not? Twenty years ago, I taught a no body how to materialize. I'll call her Jane. I knew I shouldn't have done it, because of the rules, but she said I could trust her, and she convinced me that she needed to show herself to someone who loved her desperately and needed to see Jane one last time. Jane materialized on Earth, but not as a gesture of love. Instead, she used the skill to haunt the person she blamed for her suicide. And that person became so distraught he murdered sixteen of his fellow students, then killed himself."

"Oh my God."

She nods. "That's why I'm on probation, and that's why I will not teach you or any no body to materialize ever again. Just so you understand. Oh, and you and I never had this conversation."

"Fine." I hop off the bench and slip in the mud, but that doesn't stop me. "I'll figure it out myself." Or Iz will help me.

"No. You won't." Her voice darkens with worry.

"Way to be encouraging!"

"Materialization is very difficult. It takes a tremendous amount of energy to maintain a body mock-up on Earth."

"Got it."

I home in on Iz. Phoenix Lake starts to fade and so do I.

"Nicole, wait!" Grace is at my side. I dial my avatar back in. "Let me give you a few tips."

Ha! I knew she wouldn't let me leave empty-handed, but I keep my face neutral. No sense rubbing it in.

Grace checks the sky again. Nothing. "They're always watching, even down there, so if you're having trouble, come back right away. I might be able to help you."

"Okay. Thanks. Is that all?"

"No." She says this like she's trying to convince herself that what she's about to do is okay, even though she knows it's not. "We are harmonically out of synch with the living. Our frequency is ten times higher than theirs. We have to slow down our vibrations to match theirs, otherwise . . .

A red eye appears out of nowhere, speeding straight toward Grace. I grab her to yank her out of the way. She shoves me aside.

"Go to Iz!" she barks, as everything drains into white. "Don't worry about me. I'm already dead."

Nicole

NO ASTRAL MOTION sickness when I pop into Iz's room, only a little wooziness, but that's nothing compared to my stress about Grace. What are they going to do to her? Should I have stayed to help her fight off the red eye? I don't think I could have done much, but there's always *something* we can do to help. Look at Iz. She's still trying to help me.

Iz sits cross-legged in front of her altar table where a black candle burns, and a perfectly ripe peach that wasn't there the other day rests beside a small wooden bowl filled with eucalyptus buttons. One of my guitar picks. The program from *Our Town* and a photo of Iz and me in costume on opening night, our faces pressed together, holding the flowers our parents gave us. Pieces of my life.

"This is so sweet, Iz."

Her head jerks up, and she sniffs the air. She senses me. Do I smell? She hurries to her bed and stuffs her phone under her pillow. Why is she hiding her phone?

"Nic, where are you?"

"Right here, Iz, next to the altar."

Still sniffing, she turns toward me. "Nic, say something."

"I'm here, Iz. Can you hear me?"

"I know you're here. Why aren't you talking?"

She can't hear me. Time to materialize. How? My avatar is visible on Substation Fifteen because they maintain it for me. In Dolores's dream, my avatar was useless, and worse, I started vanishing. But I was able to walk and talk and pick up things after I re-centered. It shouldn't be too hard to materialize, but I don't want to freak Iz out. Not like Jane did. I have to take it slow.

I breathe, deeply, in and out while I picture myself *as* myself standing here in front of Iz. A fuzzy outline of my outstretched hands, fainter than a shadow on a cloudy day, takes shape. And vanishes.

Huh. If I can't even mock up my hands for more than a second, how will I get Iz to see me?

I picture my whole body this time. I appear more solid, but so glitchy I can't hold my shape.

Iz extends her hands, gently patting the air three inches in front of my face. "I know you're trying to come through, Nic. Would incense help?"

Not sure. What if I suck at materialization even worse than telekinesis? Fuzz ball alert. Okay. Stop. I can do this. I *have* to, so I can take Iz to my journal.

Hmm. Grace said that no bodies vibrate ten times faster than the living. Maybe I can't materialize in front of Iz because our frequencies are out of synch. Listen to me. I almost sound like I know what I'm talking about, except I don't.

I picture my body again. It comes in faintly. I reach out to touch Iz, but my arm flops to my side and fades, along with the rest of me. Iz fades, too, along with everything around her.

I'm back in my dorm room, exhausted, lying on the floor, surrounded by all the comforts of home. Right. No comfort here. No connection to any of this stuff that used to be mine. No chance to connect with Iz. Learning to materialize will take forever. Good thing because that's how long I'll be at Substation Sixteen.

Fuzz balls!

I try Grace's weird dust-covered chant. "Ahhhhoooo-ouuuum." I sound ridiculous, but I feel better. Less hopeless. Is that even a thing?

"If you're having trouble, come right back. I may be able to help you."

I slide onto my stool at the meeting place. Grace always shows up immediately. Once she got there before I did. What's taking her so long? Is she in lockup for talking to me about materialization?

I wait, more anxious by the minute. At the next table Sam talks to her Vestie, nodding and listening politely. If I didn't know her, I'd think she was a nice girl. Maybe she is now. There's Shorty. His Vestie is a woman. He's looking into her eyes, not at her boobs. That's progress. So where is Grace already?

Quinn pops onto the stool on the other side of my table.

"Nicole." He says my name as if it's the answer to: What's another word for a pain-in-the-ass troublemaker?

What's he doing here? "Where's Grace?"

He stares, as if trying to figure out who's to blame for letting me out of my cage. "It has come to our attention that you are working with unauthorized parts of the curriculum."

If he thinks I'm going to confess, he's nuts.

I push away from the table and race through the meeting area, avoiding Vesties and bumping into every no body who's not quick enough to get out of my way. Where is Grace? Without her I've got no one on my side. I run past the dorms and the library. The moving walkway carries glassy-eyed new arrivals fresh from the tunnel. Every now and then I glance behind, expecting to see Quinn closing in. He's not there. He doesn't pop in to block my path either. No red eyes overhead. Hmm. This is way too easy. Something is definitely up or about to come down on me.

At the landing I peek out from behind the Substation Fifteen marker. A tight crowd of Vesties, Fury and Poodle among them, surround the platform where Grace stands like a prisoner, head down, hands folded in front,

"Prepare for departure," Grandma Vestie says.

Where are they taking her?

Grace manages to catch my eye without moving her head. She mouths the word "Go."

The platform rises. What's above Fifteen? A bomb explodes in my heart. Ohmygod! They're taking her to Sixteen. This is my fault. It's all over now. For both of us.

Quinn appears at my side. I watch his hands, like massive claws, reach for my shoulders, as if in slow motion. I don't care what happens next. Finally, I'm getting my wish. No more thoughts. No more memories. Rest in peace.

Grace's voice screams inside my head. "Fight!"

A fiery jolt electrifies me. Without thinking I grab Quinn's hand and bite down as hard as I can.

"OW!"

He staggers backward while the other Vesties turn as one, their faces pumped with rage, and surge toward me with the power of a tsunami.

With all my energy, I home in on Iz and in less than a breath, I'm on her balcony.

She's watering plants, talking to them. Her copper watering can glows in the late afternoon sun. That black hooded nightshirt with the long bell sleeves makes her look like a tall raven. She wasn't wearing that when I left. How long have I been gone? I check my time bomb counter. Only seven days, eleven hours, fourteen minutes, and thirty-two seconds left.

"Iz, I'm here."

She turns in my direction, and nods. I'm not sure if she can see me, but at least she hears me.

She walks inside, gesturing for me to follow. As if I need an invitation.

I sit beside her in front of the altar. She lights a black candle.

"Goddess Eternal, open the channel."

Sounds good, but how, exactly, do I harmonize our frequencies so she can see me? I can't bring her up to my level. Can I get down to hers? I touch her right arm. She yelps in pain like she touched fire. I pull my hand away. Grace was right. The difference in our frequencies is too much. Maybe I can try to slow myself to a level *below* hers. Then our frequencies might be close enough for her to see me. What vibrates more slowly than a human? Something inanimate!

I rest my palms on top of the altar. A super low vibration rumbles in my chest. Oh yeah, dead wood is definitely slower. Am I too slow now? Have I turned into a piece of furniture? Whoa! Look at my hands and arms, and my chest. I'm filling up and rounding out. I'm not an invisible empty paper bag any more. I look like me.

"Nic, I see you. You're beautiful."

I slowly raise my arm. She does the same. We move in cautiously for a high-five. I don't want to burn her again. Slowly, slowly, our palms meet and the space between us vibrates gently, warmly. We grin at each other, locked in the joy of the moment, two reflections, laughing with each other, daring to believe what's happening is actually happening. I'm afraid to talk. Don't want to break the spell, but I'm here for a reason.

"Iz, I need your help and I don't . . ."

She shushes me, lights two sticks of incense with the flame of the candle. Sweet, woodsy smoke curls drift toward the ceiling like a no body with all the time in the world. I don't have all the time in world. I don't know how long I can last at this energy level.

As the candle flickers, Iz's hands rest calmly on her knees. She breathes in and out for what seems like ten years. She calls this *grounding and centering*. I used to call it her woo-woo act. I'm done with put-downs, but my countdown timer may just have sped up.

I groan. "Iz, can we just . . ."

"Goddess Eternal, keep me open and brave

To help Nic find what she seeks, b'yond the grave.

I will help my friend any way that I can

My word is true as I raise my hand."

She raises her hand and smiles at me. "Talk to me."

Finally, it's my turn.

"Yeah. Sure. Okay. Show me our texts from Friday so I can remember what happened."

Her hand flies to her neck where her crystal necklace

always hangs except it's not there, and she seems to just remember that. Her hand fidgets around her throat as if she's thinking about strangling herself. She jumps to her feet and flings open her night table drawer, digging through stuff. She searches under every item on her desk. She looks behind each cannister on the shelves, opening every one, poking her fingers inside. Finally, she stands in the middle of the room, eyes closed, shaking.

"Iz? Are you okay?"

She nods. Barely.

"Good. Now show me our texts."

She hesitates a moment, then jumps up and snatches something off the altar, too quickly for me to see, and stuffs it into her pocket. She puts up the hood of her nightshirt and drags herself back toward the bed as if she's walking to her execution. I feel draggy myself, and weak, like I'm disappearing. Grace wasn't kidding.

Trembling, she pulls her phone out from under the pillow.

"Promise you won't be mad?"

"Sure."

She sighs, unlocks the phone, and finds our text thread. I read over her shoulder.

Nicole>

Thanks for nothing.

> Why are you mad at me? I'm your best friend.

You didn't have to send it.

She shuts off the phone.

"Wait. I wasn't done reading. What were we talking about? What did you send me? Show me the rest so I can remember."

She slides the phone into her desk drawer and pushes the chair against it. "Maybe you're not supposed to remember everything. It might cause you pain and unleash a lot of negative energy that could . . ."

My countdown timer buzzes. This thing has an alarm? Seven days left until The Evaluation. "Iz, show me the frickin' texts!"

She scrambles across her bed and barricades herself on the other side. I feel worse than I did when I yelled at Sam. "I'm so sorry. I didn't mean to scare you."

Breathing hard, she pulls her anthem knife out of her pocket and holds it an inch from my nose. "Go away, Nic. You don't have my permission to be here anymore."

I don't want to leave, but I'm fading fast. "I'm sorry. Okay? Forget the texts." I can barely hear my voice. "Just please go get my journal."

Isabel

I SCAN THE room, trying to pick up emissions. I don't sense her anywhere. Thank Goddess I'm glad she's gone, and I'm sorry, too. You can feel relief and regret at the same time.

She came to me for help. A Wiccan is always honored to serve. And I am. I'm not ready to show Nic the texts, but I *can* get her journal. And that will help her remember what happened. Unless she already remembers. Then why would she pretend she doesn't? To get back at me for what I did because she actually remembers everything that happened on Friday. Would she do that? I don't know. I don't know anything anymore. What do I do if she comes back to fight me? I have to prepare.

Queasy, I reach for my crystal. I keep forgetting it's gone. I've got to find it. When did I have it last? Where was I? Too many things to think about.

I bag up some sea salt and stick it under my pillow, along with two cloves of garlic to make sure she doesn't enter my dreams tonight. I search my Book of Spells for a way to protect myself. Here's one!

"Goddess Eternal, encircle me with your strong arms . . ."

What am I saying? I don't need protection from Nic. She isn't a dark spirit. She's a bright light. She loves me. I love her, too. She's got to know that. She was wrong to blame me in that text. But everyone makes mistakes. I wasn't the one who betrayed her. I was trying to help her. I'm going to tell her that next time. If there is a next time.

Warm air whooshes through the vent beside my bed, but I shiver as if I'm submerged in ice water.

"Isabel, dinner's ready," Mom calls through my door.

"I'll be there in two minutes."

When her footsteps fade down the stairs, I open my phone and re-read all of our texts from Friday. They sound like they were written by a heartless person and a terrible friend. I feel awful knowing that Nic had to read them. That's bad enough, but it's so much worse knowing that I sent them to her. I'm so ashamed of what I did. If I delete them all no one else will ever know. If I don't let Nic read the texts and she really doesn't remember what I said, then I won't be tempted to lie. That would be a good thing. Maybe better than telling truth. Easier, for sure.

After carefully cutting a slice of eggplant into twelve equal pieces, I cut each twelfth in half. My parents stare at me. I pretend I don't see. I can't stand it when they team up and look at me like they need me to be happy. It makes me feel responsible for the pain my unhappiness causes them.

"Isabel, you seem a little distracted," Mom says. "Would you like to talk?"

My glands might be a little less swollen. Thank Goddess. But a dull throbbing pain blooms above my right temple and seems to be spreading.

"We've all had a terrible shock," Dad says softly. "It's normal to feel out of sorts for a while."

"It's also totally normal to feel a little depressed," Mom

adds, studying me closely.

"I'm not distracted, or out of sorts, or depressed." I lift a strand of melted mozzarella cheese and twist it around my fork, stretching, stretching, until the strand is arm's length over my head. Mom and Dad watch, fascinated, as if I'm a celebrity chef on one of their cooking shows demonstrating a new way to cool cheese before serving it to guests. I reel all the cheese into my mouth.

"By the way," I say, talking around what feels like a tennis ball of cheese. "A police detective is coming to school Friday to talk to a few people." The light over the table flickers. Is Nic here? Did she just hear me mention the police?

"It's routine to talk to the victim's friends after a suicide," Dad says, checking his phone. "You don't need us there, do you? Because Friday is crazy for me."

I shake my head. Nope. Don't need. Don't want.

"I'll be there for you, sweetie," Mom pats my arm. My skin stings under her hand. The overhead light flickers again, goes out completely, and comes back on brighter than ever. No one notices. In thirty-nine hours, I'm going to be in the same room with the police, and my mom. I wonder if the lights will flicker then.

I race upstairs and lock the bathroom door. I sink onto the cool tiles and lie flat. Mom's voice rises through the floorboards. Mugs scrape and clink on the kitchen shelf. The kettle whines. Mom and Dad brew some What-Should-We-Do-About-Isabel tea. Every now and then the microwave whirrs and dings as they reheat their tea and let it get cold again.

WHAT A WASTE of a day off from school. Alex and I could be hanging out if he wasn't still ghosting me. Maybe I can get him to change his mind. I used to be really good at that. I text him.

Alex>

Hey, babe, I know
you're upset. Me, too!
It sucks that she's
dead. We should talk.

What does that even mean? Want to start an effin' support group?

DING

Mariah>

Hey!

Hey

What are you doing
today?

Hanging out with Alex.

Are you sure?

WTF is that supposed
to mean?

Nothing. GTG.

Screw Mariah. Screw Alex. I'm getting out of here.

I sort through my clothes. Oh. The jeans I wore on Friday. Dirty from lying on the ground with Alex. I'm never wearing them again.

I cut the legs into long strips, braid them together, knot both ends and dangle it over Lola's head.

"Hey, Lola, wanna chew toy?"

Lola leaps up and bites the end of the jean braid. I yank my end. Wagging her tail, she pulls harder. I let go and she runs down the hall with it, like she wants to get away but also wants me to chase her.

I'm done chasing.

I wander into the kitchen. Behind her door Buzz-Kill snores louder than a chorus of garbage trucks. Annoying as hell, but at least I don't have to talk to her.

Where's Jasmine? Oh, yeah. Thursday is Life-drawing class. 8 am–noon with no break. Geez. Sure, she loves it, but what's the point of loving anything that much? Nothing lasts.

Lola shows up without the jean braid. See? What did I say? Gone already.

Lola and I eat nachos. The floorboards in Buzz-Kill's room groan. She's getting up.

I duck into the bathroom and lock the door.

"Cassie, I gotta talk to you."

She remembers my name. Not completely wasted.

"Leave me alone so I can crap in peace."

"Why are you such a smart ass?"

"Why are you such a bitch?"

Buzz-Kill has had a lousy life. But why blame me for everything that ever happened and everything that's gonna happen 'til she dies? Which I hope is soon.

"The school called." Her voice shifts from attack dog to I've-got-dirt-on-you.

Great. She knows.

"Why do the cops want to talk to you about Nicole?"

"I dunno."

"Like you didn't know how that fancy paintbrush got into your pocket?"

"I told you a million times. It was for Jasmine, and I forgot to pay for it! What are we even talking about? You shoplift all the time."

"It's not shoplifting if you don't get caught. Haven't I taught you anything? You're as hopeless as your father."

"Do you even know which guy was my dad?"

She kicks the door while I take my time wiping, flushing, and washing my hands. A locked door between Buzz-Kill and me is like a trip to an effin' spa.

I can't find my toothbrush, so I squeeze toothpaste directly into my mouth, push it around with my tongue, and rinse. I drop the cap in my pocket. Buzz-Kill hates it when she can't find caps.

Lola yelps. I yank open the door. Buzz-Kill is squeezing the life out of Lola's paw.

"Let her go!"

Single-handed, Buzz-Kill hoists Lola over her head, out of my reach. I shove her against the wall and stomp on her bare foot. She screams and drops Lola who races into my room.

Jasmine opens the front door. "What's going on?"

Buzz-Kill fake-cries and holds up a limp hand. "The damn dog bit me!"

Jasmine looks at me, shocked.

"She's lying, Jasmine. I swear."

I grab Lola's leash, and coax her out from under my bed and fast-walk through the living room, pushing past Buzz-Kill. She grabs for my ponytail and misses by a mile, stumbles, and falls heavily on Jasmine's art bag. She clutches her knee, yelling like she's been shot or something. I know she's faking, and I wish I could leave, but maybe she's really hurt this time. I turn and offer her a hand up.

"Get away from me!" She screams and keeps screaming.

Jasmine shoos me away. "Just go, Cassie. I'll take care of her. Go."

As soon as I step away, Buzz-Kill lets go of her knee, smiles sweetly at Jasmine, and asks for a beer. I knew she was faking. I hate how she works her BS on Jasmine because she knows she can.

I scoop up Lola and get the hell out of there.

The perfect family lives two blocks from our building. Perfect Mom and Perfect Dad are so annoying. They always smile at each other and at their perfect kids. Happy to be home together. Or packing their mini-van, happy to go places together. Their car isn't in the driveway now. Wonder which happy place they're at.

Lola sniffs their front lawn, circles a few times, squats, and pushes out a long turd that looks like a question mark. Does it mean something? Like seeing Jesus in a grilled cheese sandwich? Maybe Lola is asking me a question: How come I was born a dog? Why are squirrels so effin' annoying?

It starts raining. I pull the toothpaste cap out of my pocket and pop it on the poop, like a mini-marshmallow on chocolate. I picture the perfect kids stepping in super-soft poop and tracking it all through their house. Their perfect mom won't like that.

Should I pick it up? Nah. Not my problem.

A minute later, my problem texts me.

(415) 555-0412>

Hey, Cassie. It's Isabel.

> How'd you get my number?

From Nicole.

> Why would she give you my number?

She didn't exactly.
I really need to talk to you.

> I told you I don't wanna be your spook board buddy.

It's not about that.

What then?

Can we talk in person?
I could come to your
house.
I know where you live.

You are such a stalker.
If you ever show up at
my house, you're
dead.

Okay. I won't. Just
meet me somewhere.
PLEASE.

Fine. Top of Alderney
Stairs. 20 minutes.

Isabel

THE PEACEFUL SLEEP Ritual didn't work on me. Surprising since it's always worked in the past. Bad sign. Did I mess up the ritual? Not say the words with the right clarity and conviction? I can't stop thinking about Nic. Worry causes stress. Stress causes sleep deprivation. Sleep deprivation causes more stress. So does not knowing where my crystal is.

My mouth is dry. Stress causes dehydration which causes more stress. I take a long drink from my water bottle. The band of dread tightens around my middle. That didn't work. Might as well do some homework. Maybe that will distract me.

I pull up my notes app. I already did everything except Ms. Moreno's assignment: "Write a letter or a poem to Nicole. Imagine you are communicating directly with her. To be shared with Nicole's dad."

Hmm. What could I write that isn't a lie and would be okay for Mike to read? The cursor flashes on and off, a tiny black line on a white screen, like a signal trying to break through from the other side. Blink. Blink. Blink. Blink. Blink. Blink.

She's using my computer to send me a message. What's she saying?

Is-a-bel. Living well?

My gut twists.

Is-a-bel. Go to hell.

Stop watching the cursor blink. Just type.

Dear Nicole,
I miss you. Nothing is
right without you . . .

That's true. Good, but why isn't anything right? *Because I killed you.* I can't write that. I shouldn't even think it. She probably hears my thoughts.

I delete the file and shut my laptop. My Spanish textbook lies on the floor: *Dos Mundos*. Two Worlds. *Sí, soy yo.* Yes, that's me. I'm divided in two. One part of me lives here with my parents, but it's not home anymore. Another part exists in a parallel universe where I'm still making movies with Nicole. That's not home either because every good memory turns into an endless looping video of me texting things I knew would hurt her and then watching her up on the tower, crying and falling and screaming and crashing. It kills me to watch, but I can't shut it off.

It still hurts to swallow. The glands in my neck are rock hard. Maybe it's cancer! Maybe it's already gone to my brain and I've been hallucinating. That might explain some things. Maybe I didn't really see Nicole at the funeral or in my dream or right here in my room because she wasn't here and she never demanded to see the rest of the texts.

My heart jumps around like a defective robot vacuum, banging into the wall, again and again. Too stupid to turn around. Too stupid to know the difference between a dead end and an open space. I used to be able to follow the rhythm of my pulse. Now there is none. Quick, quick, quick, slow. Quick. Slow, slow. Quick. Silence. What happened? Did my heart stop?

I have to calm down. Chamomile tea.

The chamomile canister only holds dust. The last few borage flowers huddle together in the corner of their canister. Fennel? Empty. It never helped with anxiety anyway. Lavender? I pry open the lid and stick my nose in it, breathing deeply. Inhale. Exhale. Ahhh.

"Thoughts cannot harm me or weaken my soul
My truth is my strength, I know what I know."

I don't have cancer, and I'm not crazy. Nicole *has* been here. I've seen her. We've talked. Maybe I'm not the only one. Who else would she go to? Alex? No, he betrayed her. Kyle? I can't ask him. He's pissed at me for some reason.

I text Cassie. Once when I was at Nic's house and she was in the bathroom, I casually went through her contacts. I would have told her that I snooped if she'd asked, because I never lied to her. But she never asked. I had an intuitive sense I should put Cassie's contact in my phone. I didn't know why at the time. Now I do.

Cassie doesn't like me so of course she gives me a hard time, but she finally agrees to meet me at the top of the Alderney Stairs.

Alderney Street ends in a steep narrow stairway, fifty-three concrete steps long, an alley between two wooden walls, connecting to the end of Cordone Street with its towering eucalyptus trees and view of Mt. Tam. Nicole and I always took this shortcut to Redhill Shopping Center and to the Ridge Trail. Way before that, we took it to Sunny Hills Elementary School. Every day, starting in third grade, we ran up these steps picking up eucalyptus buttons. Whoever got the most buttons got five points. Whoever got to the top step first got five points. Nicole was always faster, but I always had the most buttons. By fifth grade she said the game was too childish for us, so we stopped. I still thought it was fun, but I didn't want to play alone.

Cordone, the short street at the top of the Alderney Stairs, is usually quiet during the day, but beer bottles at the base of the trees remind me of how the place changes at night. Not that I'd ever come here after dark.

The long stairway is gray and wet, with a gloomy, closed-in feeling. Thick mist from above swirls down into the alley, making it hard to see what's ahead.

Halfway up the step I slip on a eucalyptus button and bang my shin. My jeans rip below my knee, and blood pours from the gash. I should go home right now and put antiseptic on this, but I have to talk to Cassie. After the way I begged her to meet me, she'd be so pissed if I didn't show up. Who knows what she'd do to me? Maybe she's not even coming. She might have been lying. What if some guys are up there drinking? Day off from school, why not? What if they harass me? I can't run faster than a bunch of guys, even drunk ones. Especially not with a soon-to-be infected knee.

Up at the top of the stairs a ghostly figure in an oversized black hoodie leans against a streetlight in the mist. A dog barks. My heart freezes. I back away. Something bumps the back of my leg. I jump and head for the steps, not daring to look behind. The ghost blocks my path.

"Scared of dogs?" the ghost asks.

I recognize Cassie's voice. I exhale.

"No."

"Oh, that's right," she says with a nasty laugh. "You only like black cats."

"Not true. I love all cats. Dogs as well."

The four-legged white mop at my feet wags its whole body, thumping its tail against my leg. I kneel and pet her. Cassie has a friendly dog? I never thought of her having a pet. If I had, I might have guessed a saltwater crocodile. According to udderlypettable.com that's the animal most likely to take down and eat a human without hesitation. I smile to myself at the thought of Cassie walking a crocodile. And Nic said I had no sense of humor.

Cassie pulls an open bag of chips out of her pocket, pops one in her mouth and tosses one to the dog.

"What'd you want to talk to me about?" Her words, a dare.

Without my crystal I don't feel so powerful, but I'm not afraid of Cassie.

"Nicole."

Her eyes narrow. "You said this wasn't about the spook board."

I meet her gaze. "It's not. I'm doing research. I want to know if you've had any dreams about her."

"Hmmm, let me think." She scrunches up her face, like she's trying to convince me that she's actually trying to remember, then drops the act because she knows I see right through it. "Nope. I only dream about hot guys, not dead girls. But if that's your thing . . ."

"Nicole is communicating with me."

She snorts.

"You don't believe in anything, do you, Cassie?"

She reaches down and scratches behind Lola's ears. "I believe you're feeling so guilty about something bad you did to Nicole that you had to text *me* for help. Which, I gotta say, makes you pretty ballsy considering we aren't friends and you're scared of me. What did you do to hurt her?"

She munches another chip and tosses one to Lola, who snags it, mid-air.

"I'm not scared of you, and I'm not guilty of anything." That came out louder than I expected, but it's not a lie. I didn't intentionally hurt Nic. "You and Alex are the ones who hurt her. She should have been mad at you guys that day, not me."

"She was mad at you? Why? Did you . . . ? You *did!*"

"What are you talking about?" I feel caught. I don't answer. I don't have to.

"Kyle said he saw you walking away from the woods with your camera. He figured you were making one of your little movies. I'll bet you stalked me and Alex and recorded us making out. You did, didn't you? Then you must have sent the video to Nicole while she was up on the tower. Way to stomp on a girl's heart while she's hanging by a thread. Wow. And I actually thought you were her friend."

"I was . . . I mean I am!"

She holds out her hand. "Lemme see the video."

"I deleted it."

She eyes me closely. "You're too stupid to lie. But deleting the video was not smart, Honor Roll girl. The police will get

Nicole's phone records, and they'll see the video. When they look at your phone on Friday, which of course they will, they'll know you destroyed evidence. This will not look good on your college apps, Isabel." She shakes her head with fake concern. "Unh, uh. Not good at all."

A hot knife of fear cuts into my gut.

The wind picks up as I hurry toward the stairs. An arctic blast whips through the alley, a shower of eucalyptus buttons rains down on me. I'm shivering so badly I can barely run without falling.

Dad's car isn't in the driveway. His coffee mug drains upside down on the kitchen sink. The ceiling boards creak as Mom walks around in their room. Panting, I tiptoe upstairs, carrying my shoes. Their bedroom door is closed, thank Goddess.

In my room, I peel off my cold wet clothes, slip on my bathrobe, grab a bar of black salt soap, and creep into the bathroom.

The shower pulses over my head and shoulders. The hot water hurts my cold hands and feet, but I don't move out of the way. The salt stings my skin, especially my cut knee, but I have to rub hard or the purification won't work.

"Goddess Eternal, may this salt soap bar
Protect me from evil, in realms near and far,
Help purify my space of negative energies
And make powerful all protective boundaries.
May the salt cleanse body and spirit as one
And return, down the drain, to the earth, when it's done."

I bump into Mom in the hall, her yoga mat tightly rolled under her arm. "Namaste, sweetheart. Why didn't you dry your hair? You look tired. Still not sleeping? Me neither." She clears her throat like she's about to say something, then shakes her head as if what's inside is too big for words.

"I was thinking," she unrolls and re-rolls her mat, even though it doesn't need it. "Since you're off today, maybe you'd like to come with me to yoga. This one is a silent restorative class."

I don't want to go with Mom, but I don't want to be here alone either. Enforced silence sounds like a healing remedy. I won't have to talk to anyone. Maybe I can silence my brain.

"Okay. I'll be ready in two minutes."

As I open my door, a shiver jackknifes between my eyes. Nic sits on my bed, holding my phone.

Isabel

IC APPEARS AS a faint form that no one except me would notice. She glares at me like I had just ripped out her heart.

"Why did you delete the texts? You knew I didn't read the whole thread. Those were going to be my study notes for The Evaluation!"

Through tears of rage and frustration, she goes on about the Vesties and how they've always been out to get her and how horrible and unfair it is that *I'm* making things impossible for her, too!

"No, I'm not. I'm trying to help you." I want to shout, but I have to keep my voice down so Mom doesn't barge in. "I deleted those texts because it would upset you to read them again. Besides, you said, 'No more texts.' Remember? I thought that meant you didn't care about them anymore."

"I don't care what you thought." She flies around the room like a fuming tornado. Suddenly she stops, dead still, in front of the altar and studies her photo in the candlelight. Her anger shrinks as if the energy of the candle and incense has calmed her. She must feel the love I put into the altar display. She must know that I would never intentionally hurt her.

I watch her breathing, trying to control herself. She turns to me.

"Okay. I don't need to read the texts, though it would have been really nice to get the truth, word for word. But since they're gone now, we'll just have to do the best we can. What do you remember?"

"I can't."

"You can't remember what you wrote?"

"No. I remember, but I can't tell you, because if I do, you'll hate me forever."

"No, I won't. I promise."

The air solidifies around our standoff. I can't decide whether to trust her. We never had to think about that before. Now we do.

Her hands fly at me, like talons. It takes all my courage not to run. Her fingers glom onto my head, probing my scalp forward and back, side to side, like a light-footed crab.

"What are you doing?"

"Shhh!" she hisses. After a moment her arms drop to her sides. "I was trying to do a memory pull, but I don't know how." Her voice is a ragged sigh. I touch her arm gently.

"Do you still want me to go and get your journal?"

"Yes!"

Nic's dad squints as if he's looking at me through haze, trying to figure out if I'm actually standing at his front door like I've done a thousand times or if it's a dream. Maybe he's thinking that if I am here, I must have come to see Nic, which would prove she is still alive. I want to tell him that I'm really here, and she's here with me, but not the way he wishes. I decide not to say anything.

Mike's eyes snap into focus, and his shoulders deflate. He forces a small smile, but it slips onto the porch and he doesn't bother picking it up. He hugs me awkwardly, as if it hurts to touch and be touched. He smells like bananas.

"Thank you for texting, Isabel. It's sweet of you to think of me. This must be so hard for you. How are you doing?"

"I'm okay."

The three of us know I'm lying. Maybe it's not a lie. Maybe we are okay. We're here, together, on this beautiful morning. The sun, infusing this moment with positive energy. Banishing all negativity.

"Come in." Mike, holds the door open. I step inside.

Being in Nic's house again, with the family photos, the cushy old couch where we ate Mike's trail mix and did homework and watched old movies, is like walking barefoot on sharp rocks. No matter how careful I am, every step hurts. And I don't have my crystal to clear the space.

I'm not okay.

I follow Mike into the kitchen. "You can come over anytime and sit in her room, if you'd like."

I don't think I'd like that, but I told him that's why I wanted to come.

"What are you baking?" I try to sound the same as I have every other time I've asked him that question.

"Banana chocolate chip muffins. Baking is the only thing I can focus on, so I'm baking. A lot."

He opens the freezer door revealing a wall of bulging plastic bags filled with frozen cookies and bread. A bag tumbles onto the floor. He picks it up, "Here, you like chocolate chip cookies. Take this home." Another bag escapes. He stuffs it back into the freezer, it jumps out again. After a couple of tries, he manages to close the door. "Maybe I should dial back on the baking."

Nic drifts over to the counter and examines a stack of sympathy cards. A business card sticks out of one.

Jorge P. Moreno, PhD
Grief Counseling — Group Support
Tuesdays 6–8 pm
San Rafael Community Church
Drop-ins welcome
415-555-8990

29200 N. San Pedro Road   San Rafael, CA

The oven timer buzzes.

Mike pulls two full muffin tins out of the oven. They look and smell heavenly, like they were baked with magik. "I need to pop these out and get them on a cooling rack," he says. "You can go upstairs to her room."

Nic hovers by the back door that leads from the kitchen into the yard, pressing her hands against Mike's brown jacket which is hanging next to a line of empty hooks. I don't know what she's doing, but it would look weird if I just stood here watching her.

I walk upstairs as slowly as I can while still moving forward. Oh Goddess, why did I agree to this? I haven't been thinking straight since I lost my crystal. I don't want to go into Nic's room and see all her stuff. I don't want to read her journal.

I stare at her closed bedroom door, trying to keep myself from running out of the house. Why am I so scared? It's just Nic's room. I've always loved her room. Not now.

I reach for the white ceramic doorknob, inhale, hold my breath, grip the knob, twist and push open, but that's as far as I go. Sunlight on her carpet welcomes me. I exhale. The little brass elephant I bought for her in Thailand sits on the window facing the yard, as if it's waiting for her to come back. I step inside. Her guitar calls to me. I lean over and trace the smooth curve along its side. So many unsung songs that no one will ever hear.

I sense Nic's impatience at my shoulder.

"You'll find the journal under the bed."

"I don't want to go under there."

"Go!"

My belly gurgles uncomfortably as I crawl among the dust bunnies, crumpled old tissues, and who knows what other microbes.

"It's inside that slit in the dust cover." Excitement rises in her voice.

I point my phone flashlight overhead at a six-inch-long tear in the gauzy fabric that's stapled to the underside of the bed. The opening looks like a hungry mouth. I don't want to stick my hand in there.

"What are you waiting for?"

I grab for my crystal. Why do I keep doing that? "Goddess Eternal, please keep me from harm . . ."

"Just do it!"

I carefully slip my fingertips into the gap, and run them along the length of the wooden boards. "I don't feel anything."

"What? That's impossible. Stick your hand in all the way."

I shudder. Not doing that. Instead, I pull down on the edge of the fabric and shine the light inside the opening. "Look for yourself, Nic. There's nothing in there."

She looks. "Where's my journal? What happened to it? What if we can't find it? What am I going to do?"

A chill wind swirls the dust bunnies around me. My nose tickles. My neck hurts. Out goes my phone light, turning the space under the bed into a flat dark cave. Something skitters over my hand.

I scoot backward as fast as I can. My foot bumps against something hard.

"Is this what you're looking for?"

Mike stands over me holding a small blue binder.

Nicole

MY JOURNAL LIES on the kitchen table, like a corpse in the morgue. Dad and Iz avoid looking at it. The living assume that no bodies take our secrets with us, but some of mine are right in there. Hmm. Maybe this isn't such a good idea.

Dad absently sips black coffee from his #1 Dad mug.

"At least put a little milk in it, Dad." I wish he could hear me. I'd tell him all that caffeine isn't good for his heart.

"I never knew she kept a journal," he says.

"Me neither," Iz glances in my direction, trying to make me feel guilty. I don't. She didn't tell me every little detail about her rituals. No, that's a lie. She *did*. I just didn't listen unless the spell was going to help me. Hmm. That doesn't sound great.

"So how did you know her journal was under the bed?"

"Don't tell him the truth, Iz. That could give him a heart attack."

"Uh, I had a dream."

"Nice recovery," I whisper.

She reaches for the necklace that she's still not wearing. She frowns briefly, puts her hand in her lap, and resets her face.

"I've been having dreams too," Dad says as he looks at my journal the same gut-wrenching way he looked at me in the dream. Having a dead daughter isn't good for his heart either.

"I looked through her songbooks, her desk drawers, her closet, dresser, just in case she left a note. I hated snooping through her stuff, and I know she'd be furious at me."

This is so unfair. I have no rights. Nothing is mine anymore. Anyone can just look at my journal, my laptop, my phone, my dead *body*!

"I'm sure she forgives you, Mike."

"Of course, I do, Dad."

"Thanks for saying that, Isabel. I was just looking for answers, because . . . not knowing what happened to her is driving me crazy."

Me, too, Dad. It'll also get me sent to Sixteen. Damn! I'm just thinking about myself again. No, I'm not. I'm thinking about Dad, too. It kills me seeing him so miserable. Okay, not *kills*, but hurts . . . a lot. But I'm also thinking about me. It's *my* journal.

My fingers are fading out. They're always the first to go. "Iz. I don't know how long I'm going to last. Can you move this along?"

She shoots me a look as if to say, "Show your dad some respect."

She's right. I need to chill.

Dad gestures to a plate piled high with perfect-looking muffins. Wish I could have one. Iz chooses the top muffin and carefully plucks the blue cupcake wrapper, like she's trying to peel off a Band-Aid without ripping the skin. A chunk of cake sticks to the paper, leaving a gap in the side of the cake. She pokes it back into place like she's patching a wall. It won't stay put. Some things can't be fixed.

Dad takes a muffin, puts it on his plate, then ignores it. "This morning I thought of her guitar case as a possible hiding place for a note. She sometimes kept it under the bed. When I looked, I noticed the rip in the dust cover."

His thumb lightly strokes the journal, like he sometimes stroked my hand when I was upset. Whatever was going on with me, Dad always tried to make me feel better. What can I do for him?

"At first I thought it might be another songbook, so I looked inside, but as soon as I realized it was her journal, I closed it. It felt like an intrusion, you know? I haven't read any of it. But maybe I should. Trouble is, her handwriting is so small, and I need new glasses, and..." He looks at his hands, they shake as he slides the book across the table and it stops in front of Iz. "Would you read it to me, please?"

She hops to her feet. "Uh, excuse me, I need to use the bathroom."

Behind the closed bathroom door Iz whispers, "I'm sensing very strong negative energy from your journal, Nic. I don't want to read it. I don't even want to touch it."

"Seriously? Look, I swear there's nothing negative in anything I wrote."

"Do you remember what you wrote?"

"Well, not exactly, but what could be bad? There's nothing sexy in it, if that's what you're worried about. I was a virgin. Just read it. Please."

Back in the kitchen Iz eyes the journal as if she's afraid it might attack her.

"C'mon, Iz. You promised the goddess you'd help me."

She inhales and opens the journal to the dedication page.

"Don't read him that page!"

She reads the page silently and quickly flips to the next one.

"What was that?" Dad asks.

"Just her name. Here's the first entry."

I lean over her shoulder.

September 4

Dad wanted to see what I'm wearing tomorrow. My first day of high school! I showed him my outfit, which I paid for with my own money, and (surprise) he went ballistic. He actually said, "If you wear that, you'll give boys ideas."

WTF? If some guy acts like a pig that's *my* fault because of what I'm wearing?!

He started pulling clothes out of my closet. "How about wearing this instead?"

Unbelievable! Like I'm supposed to take fashion tips from my dad? He needs to get a life and stop obsessing over mine. In less than four years I'll be in college. He won't know what to do with himself when I'm gone.

Dad covers his mouth, like he's blocking a scream. He grabs his jacket off the hook and explodes through the back door. I start after him, but Iz stops me.

"That's exactly what I meant by negative energy." She shuts the journal and shoves it so hard it falls off the table, hitting the floor with a sharp smack. "I knew I shouldn't have let you talk me into this."

I'm about to say, "You have fights with your mom about

clothes all the time. What I wrote wasn't that bad." But I stop myself. Maybe *he won't know what to do with himself when I'm gone,* wasn't that bad two years ago, but right now it sounds godawful.

"I'm sorry I pressured you, Iz. I swear I don't remember writing that. You have to tell him . . . I don't know what you should tell him, but just say *something* to make him feel better."

"Tell him yourself." She gathers up her stuff, refusing to look at me.

Dad sits on the bench under the magnolia tree, gazing at the garden, choked with winter weeds. Normally, on a clear January day like this he'd be on his knees in the dirt, happily pulling up weeds "hand over fist" and talking about the new variety of sugar snap peas he would plant come March. Now he seems like he couldn't care less about gardens or spring planting. Like he's given up on the weeds. Maybe he feels like he doesn't belong in his own backyard or anywhere. I know the feeling.

I hug him from behind. His heart beats sluggishly, maybe trying to decide if it's worth beating at all. His sadness seeps through me like ice water, draining my energy, but I can't let him go.

"I'm so sorry, Dad. I didn't mean to hurt you."

If I didn't mean to hurt someone and I didn't know that I'd done it, would it still count as a bad thing? Yeah. Probably. But at least I wouldn't feel like crap. Here I go again, just thinking about myself. Think about Dad. He's more miserable than before he heard what I wrote. And I'm more miserable, too. But if he'd read the journal on his own, when he first found it, who knows what he would have done? At least I'm here now, and I can try to make him feel better.

A large dry leaf lies on the bench like an abandoned rowboat. Dozens of pods bursting with cherry red magnolia seeds lay scattered on the ground. Dad and I used to play a game where we'd line up some seeds on the center crease of a leaf and take turns carrying that leaf to the garden gate, like passengers on a boat. The trick was not to let any of them fall overboard.

While he looks the other way, I manage to pry one beautiful smooth red seed from a pod and place it on the center crease of the leaf beside him. A moment later, he spots it. I hold my breath and hope he'll take it as a sign that I'm here and remember our game and the good times.

Angrily, he swipes the leaf off the bench and sends it flying. He gathers pods off the ground and hurls them, one after another, as far as he can. Some smack against the fence. Some sail into the Greenberg's yard.

Great. Your think-happy-thoughts trick made him feel even worse.

I hover close to his ear, wanting more than anything to get inside his head so he can hear and understand what I'm about to say. "Dad! Listen. I love you. Add that to the top of your non-negotiable truths. I love you. That never changes. And I want you to be happy again. Please, try."

I brush against the wind chime. Tiny stars fill my heart. If Dad hears anything, he doesn't show it.

The kitchen is empty. Iz and the journal are gone.

Damn.

Our car splutters to life in the driveway as Dad backs out, nearly running over one of the neighbor kids' bikes before whipping around and tearing down the hill.

Where is he going?

I slip through the roof and sit beside him. I don't need a seat belt. He drives through The Hub, where five roads meet, and turns left on Redhill Avenue. He always listened to 70s and 80s rock—in the car, in the garden, while he baked, while he painted. Now he drives in dead silence, his unblinking eyes fixed straight ahead. Does he even see the road?

When the car in front stops at a red light, Dad slams his brakes at the last second, inches before ramming the rear end.

"Dad! Watch it."

He goes through a red light on Lindaro, just missing a car turning from the other direction.

"Dad!"

On 2nd Street he abruptly changes lanes, cutting off a driver who blares his horn. Dad doesn't react.

Geez. This is crazy. Is he trying to kill himself?

I grab the wheel but I don't have enough strength to overpower his grip.

He merges onto the freeway, weaving between lanes. Thank God there's not much traffic. He exits at North San Pedro Road. We never come out here. Where's he going? Dad turns into the San Rafael Community Church parking lot and finds a spot in the darkest corner, farthest away from the building. Since when does Dad believe in God?

Oh wait! This is *that* church. He's going to the grief support group! I reach over and hug him. "I'm so proud of you, Dad. I know this will help you feel better."

Of course, he doesn't hear me. And he doesn't move. Did he almost kill himself in a car accident just to sit in a church parking lot?

The gray Tesla pulls in so close on our left it almost knocks off our side mirror. A tall woman in a Prussian blue jacket bolts out of the car as if she were ejected. She shoves her hands deep into her pockets and yanks open an unmarked door at the side of the church. Amber light spills into the gloom, illuminating her short, cool-looking white hair. Something drops from her pocket unseen. The church door closes behind her, leaving the parking lot darker than ever.

Dad studies the situation outside his window. No way can he open the door. He throws up his hands then starts the car. The engine coughs and stalls. Dad roars like a lion caught in a net. I imagine him mentally venting about cars that don't work, people who can't park, and most of all, how unfair life is when your daughter hugs you goodbye after breakfast and never comes home again. I hug him tightly and we roar together. I'm trying to make both of us feel better. It's not working.

The church door opens. Dad turns the key. The car sparks to life, but barely. He watches the same woman open the church door, retrieve her lost glove, and disappear inside again, taking the light with her. Slowly, so slowly, he backs out of the space.

Isabel

I WAVE A tight bundle of lighted sage into all corners of my room to protect against whatever negativity might still be in Nic's journal. Smoke rings rise and the aroma of minty earth infuses me with peace.

She wants me to read everything. The Evaluation is soon, and she's in a hurry. I'll take notes, so when she comes back, and I know she will, I can tell her what's in it.

I pull the journal into my lap. Now that I have more time to hold it and do a psychic reading, I sense Nic's state of mind and all the conflicting emotions she felt while she was writing. Frustration. Embarrassment. Dissatisfaction. Longing. Loneliness. Those feelings live on within this book, sending out tiny jolts of energy behind my heart. I also sense love, hope, excitement, wonder, and appreciation.

I open the book and skip the entry about Mike. I don't want to re-experience any of that negativity. My name jumps off the next page. Fear jolts my second chakra. It's a sign. The journal isn't safe. I should keep my distance. I miss my crystal. It hurts to remember losses. Maybe that's the real sign. Maybe I need to forge ahead on the path of peril without the

Goddess's protection. Maybe that's the only way to complete this quest.

September 6

I'll always love IZ, even though we've always been so different, but lately our differences are too big to pretend they don't matter and that we're still best friends. Even back when I loved dressing up and playing fairy games in the woods with her, I knew it wasn't pretend for her, it was real. It's still real! She talked to birds and deer, swearing that they talked to her, spirit to spirit. She still talks to every dog and cat she meets. She goes into a trance in that tree of hers. Sure, Harry Potter is cool, but believing that you're actually a witch? That's nuts.

But hey, I won't judge her, that's not who I am. I just wish she wasn't so woo-woo at school. She dresses like it's medieval times. And seriously, what's with the cape and why does she have to carry her Book of Spells everywhere? If she's got to have

it with her all the time, why not bury it
in her backpack instead of holding it so
everyone sees it? I guess I should be grateful that she doesn't bring her broom to
school. Not that the smelly herbs she
wears around her neck aren't embarrassing enough. Today she chanted in the hall
on the way to lunch. Not just whispering
so only I could hear, but full-on chanting,
asking the Goddess Eternal to bless the
building and all the kids for a safe and
joyous school year. People looked at her like
she was crazy, because she is.

She says *I'm* the one with the problem.
She wants to do a cleansing ritual to help
me accept others without judgment. I am
not a judgmental person! I respect her beliefs, as nutty as they are. But we're in
high school now and let's face it, Iz is a
weirdo.

People must think I'm a weirdo, too, because I hang out with her. I only do it because I feel sorry for her. She has no

otheR fRieNds aNd NeveR will. But if I keep
this up, it will RuiN high school foR me. I
doN't waNt to huRt heR feeliNgs, but I'm
goiNg to tell heR that staRtiNg tomoRRow,
I'm Not talkiNg to heR at school.

I sense Nic right next to me, leaning against the other pillow.

Outside of school it seemed like nothing had changed between us.

We shoot scenes for Beyond Normal.

We try on vintage clothing in a shop in The Haight.

We hike and picnic on Bolinas Ridge.

*We poke through boxes of old books at the Book Fair at Fort Ma-
son.*

We give the Berkeley Rep cast of School Girls a standing O.

But at school, I became invisible. Even out of school, she'd
sometimes lie about having to go somewhere and leave me
waiting for her, then later she'd try to make me believe that
we'd never finalized our plans. All of that imparts a bad taste
that won't rinse out, not even with a long gargle of lukewarm
chamomile tea.

I turn to her. "Why are you even here if I'm so weird? Why
did we keep texting and acting like friends if that's how you
really felt?"

"No. Listen, Iz, when I called you weird, I meant it in a *good*
way."

Always the master at turning things around. How many
times did I stand up for myself when she was unkind, and I
ended up apologizing because she said I'd hurt *her* feelings?
I've had enough.

"I always knew when you were lying, Nic. I still do."

She holds up her hands in surrender. "Okay. Okay. You're
right. When I wrote weird, I meant it in a *bad* way. I'm so
sorry. I was just venting, but that was two years ago. I was a

stupid self-centered freshman. All I cared about was being popular. I swear I didn't mean any of it."

If I let her go on she'll probably say I'm hurting her feelings. I'm not falling into that trap ever again.

"So you didn't mean it when you wrote: 'I'll always love Iz'?"

"No! I meant *that* part. But none of the bad stuff. You know I love you. Even though we stopped hanging out at school—my fault, I admit it—we still hung out a lot outside of school. Doesn't that prove anything?"

She cries and swears she loves me. She begs me to forgive her for what she wrote and for the way she treated me. Is it an act? Is she trying to manipulate my emotions so I'll let her read the rest of the journal over my shoulder? I don't think it's an act. Look how upset she is. She means what she's saying, and I want to forgive her. Forgiveness creates peace. But if I allowed myself to forgive her and love her again, I'll have to take responsibility for what I did and ask for *her* forgiveness. Right now, I don't feel like asking her for anything. That would give her power over me. If I just keep my mouth shut for a change that would give me time to think about this.

Flames of red and green negative energy spew from the cover of the journal.

"Nic, I'm burning your journal in a cleansing ritual tomorrow."

She sniffles and nods. "Good idea. I'll be there with you when you do it. But first we've got to read the whole thing, together. Okay? I'd do it myself, but the paper is too thin and I can't turn pages."

"No. I'm not reading any more of this. I'm not touching it. The journal has to be destroyed to release the negativity and pain you've caused to the people you wrote about, even if they never knew what you wrote. Since you've denounced the words, burning the journal will release you, too."

"You *can't* burn it. It belongs to me. I have rights!" She lunges and snarls like a dog barking at the garbage collector who's just doing their job.

"Goddess Eternal . . ."

I grab a fistful of salt from the bag from under my pillow and fling it in her face.

"With salt from the sea, I send thee from me."

She staggers backward, knocking against the edge of the altar. The photo of us slips onto the floor. The glass shatters.

"Go away, Nic. Don't come here again. Don't contact me. Don't enter my dreams. I'll program my deep consciousness to wake up the instant I see you."

Nicole

THAT SALT-BOMB really did me in, and I'm not sure how this is going to work. But it's Friday and she's getting ready for school. This is the day she washes her hair. That will give me the time I need.

I pass through the ceiling and enter her room. My journal lies on the floor open to the last entry. I try to turn pages so I can read more of it, but my fingers pass through the paper. Looks like what's open here is all I'm going to get.

January 1

Happy New Year! New Year's Resolution: No more waiting around for things to move to the next level with Alex. I'm going to steal him away from Cassie. I know I said that last year. I seriously worked at it. I got closer to Cassie so I could spend more time with Alex. I got to know Kyle just so I could find out what was going on between Alex and Cassie. I even pretended I liked Kyle the same way he likes me. (Not great, I know, but it worked and the four of us got to hang out together.) I give myself an A for effort, but only a C— for achievement.

This year, I'm getting an A+ by making Alex love me. Friday, the fourth, is going to change everything. I'm going to ask Alex to hang out with me on the water tower. Cassie is going to be at her cousin's in Sacramento until Sunday so I'm pretty sure he'll say yes. When the moment is perfect, I'm going to kiss him, and it will be so epic he'll break up with Cassie and I'll win.

Ohmygod! What a conniving poser I was. I can't believe how easily I used people. I hate myself. Did my friends hate me? The police interviews are today. I've got to hear what they say about me.

Iz is out of the bathroom. I'm out of here.

Dr. Campbell sits behind her desk, wiping the corners of her eyes, as she talks to the police detective seated in front of her. "As you can imagine, everyone is upset. The four students you'll be speaking to were Nicole's closest friends."

She checks her laptop. "Alex Traynor is first. He and Nicole co-starred as the young lovers in *Our Town*."

Dr. Campbell, the detective, and the entire office vanish as my favorite part of the play takes over my mental movie screen. My heart simultaneously swells and melts the way it did whenever Alex and I rehearsed.

Resting my elbow on the top of a short ladder, I gaze through an imaginary window at an imaginary sky. The stage lights are dim except for a blue, soft-glow spot overhead. Alex pretends to look through his window from the top of an identical ladder. Dressed as George Gibbs, he's wearing a light blue, collarless shirt rolled up to his elbows. Wide suspenders hold up his loose-fitting brown pants. My hair is pulled back behind my ears, and a long ponytail of soft curls falls over my left shoulder. I'm wearing my favorite Emily Webb costume, a light, white cotton blouse with a wide collar and tiny, cloth-covered buttons down the front. Dressed for 1901, I feel like a kinder, more thoughtful girl.

Turning my face to the blue spotlight, I tilt my head so my hair swings free. I sigh dreamily and talk about the moonlight. I feel him watching me and imagine him thinking how irresistible I look in that light.

The other scene I loved was right before the wedding. Emily freaks out, and George calms her down by saying that he loves her and needs her.

I look directly into his eyes and tell him that all I want is someone to love me.

We fall into each other's arms, just like the script says.

Emily and George became Nicole and Alex. I wanted the moment to last forever.

The officer's nametag reads: Detective V. Lee. She rests a hand on a black notebook and absently clicks her pen with the other. "Emily and George," she says.

"You know the play." Dr. Campbell seems surprised.

"I played the Stage Manager in ninth grade. Five-foot three Korean-American girl. Radical casting for 1982."

"I'd say. Anyway, I want to make sure you handle these interviews delicately. I don't want any of my students to feel like they're being accused of anything."

"Talking to students is a big part of my job." Irritation creeps into V. Lee's voice before she reins it in. "I appreciate your concern, but you don't need to worry."

Blah. Blah. Where's Alex?

Why does this waiting feel familiar? Why do I feel like he's not coming?

V. Lee is talking ". . . valuable evidence in these cases is often found on phones."

"Do you have Nicole's phone?"

"We do."

I want to see it!

"It was badly damaged in the fall. We're still working on retrieving its contents. If we can't, we've got other options."

The phone buzzes. Dr. Campbell grabs it. "Please send him in."

Alex shuffles in. My own personal heat wave flares up. Without his funeral blazer his shoulders look narrower and hunched forward, like the ceiling is pressing down on him. Scratches of angry red bumps line his forehead. The same rash covers the backs of his hands. Not the most attractive look, but those green eyes undo me. If I weren't already floating, I'd launch into orbit. When V. Lee introduces herself, Alex frowns. That mouth. I wish he didn't have this effect on me anymore because I can't do anything about it now.

Alex sits on the edge of the couch unconsciously rubbing the knee of his jeans. V. Lee repositions her chair to face him. I hover behind her so I'm facing him, too. She writes *Alex Traynor* at the top of a blank page in her notebook, along with 1/11 9:34 *am*. She holds the pen with her right hand, but her writing leans left like a lefty.

"Alex, when was the last time you saw Nicole?"

Alex mumbles and V. Lee asks him to speak up. "I said Friday. Around noon. We were up on the tower together."

We sit close, dangling our legs over the edge of the roof. His thigh lines up with mine. Fire and ice pulsate along the border of our bodies. He must feel it too because our eyes hold for a long moment, then, without realizing, mine slip down to his mouth and that full bottom lip. He leans toward me. I meet him halfway until there is barely any space between us. We hit pause at the same moment, savoring the anticipation of what comes next. I can't hold back any longer. I kiss him softly. He kisses me back. Our lips part, and our tongues explore the secret softness of our mouths, shyly at first, and then I completely lose my mind.

I blush at the lost memory, thrilled to have it back in my collection.

"What were you two doing up there?"

Alex shrugs. "Nothing much."

I can't believe he said that. We had our first real kiss. Or did we? Am I remembering it the way it happened or how I wanted it to happen? What if I never find out the truth?

"We sat there for a while," he says. "Watched the cars on the freeway. Talked. That's all."

Deep gold ripples muddy the rest of his aura as they push outward.

Confusion. Tension. Conflict.

Wait. That's not right. I'm sure we kissed, and it was epic. Why would he lie about it? Unless he's embarrassed that he kissed me. Or he thinks the truth will get him in trouble. Or maybe he just wants to cherish the memory and keep it private. Yeah. That's it. How romantic. I swoop in and rest my head on his shoulder. I sniff his shirt. *Oranges.* I trace the top of his ear with my finger, imagining how soft it feels and what he'd do if I were alive and we were alone again. He'd kiss me again, for sure. I'm getting hot.

"Alex, are you aware there's a No Trespassing sign at the bottom of the tower?" V. Lee wants to know.

"Kids go up there all the time."

"Have you climbed to the top before?"

"Yeah. With Cassie. But last Friday was the only time I went up there with Nicole. It was her idea, which is kinda weird because she was scared of heights."

Alex stands one step below me on the ladder. I hold tight to the handrail, his warm hands cover mine. He's so close behind me, I lean back against his chest as we take the steps together, one at a time, and I forget all about being scared of heights and of Cassie.

V. Lee clicks away on her pen. Iz was right. It's very annoying. "Thirty feet is very high. Any idea why she'd want to meet you there?"

"I dunno." Alex shrugs again. I never noticed how much he does that. It's more annoying than pen-clicking.

"I'll tell you why, V. Lee," I say, not that anyone hears me. "Cassie told me it was romantic to make out up there. I wanted Alex to feel the difference being there with *me*. Iz's attraction spell was working, and I knew if he kissed me, he'd break up with Cassie."

V. Lee nods encouragingly in Alex's direction. "Okay. So you and Nicole talked and looked down at the freeway. What happened next?"

"Cassie texted to come meet her at the park. I decided I was going to break up with her but I didn't want to do it over text, so I left."

"Just like that?"

"Yeah."

"Did you tell Nicole where you were going?"

"Oh, yeah. She was really happy."

I remember this part clearly. I was excited watching him climb down the ladder and get on his bike. He looked so sexy swinging his leg over the bar. I remember thinking about how amazing it was going to be when he got back and he wouldn't be Cassie's boyfriend any more, he'd be *mine*.

V. Lee clicks her pen and doesn't hide the contempt in her voice. "Why did you leave Nicole alone on the tower when she was afraid of heights?"

Dr. Campbell clears her throat in warning. V. Lee ignores her and studies Alex's face. He looks away and scratches the back of his neck. "She said she was fine waiting for me up there."

I remember saying that. I remember waiting for a long time. And I remember I was not fine. He promised he'd come right back, but he never did. He never even answered my texts. Now I can't stand being near him. I hover in front of the couch, watching his aura as closely as V. Lee watches his expressions. Does she notice how much he's sweating? She turns to a blank page in her notebook and clicks her pen. "Alex, how would you describe your relationship with Cassie?"

He squirms. Good.

"It's complicated." The words rush out like they're burning his mouth. "I really like Cassie. A *lot*. She's tough in a cool way that most girls aren't. She's not afraid of heights, that's for sure."

Ouch.

"Also, she's funny and smart, even though she doesn't give a sh... I mean she doesn't care about school. Most people don't know this, but she can be really sweet. The problem is... I don't know what the problem is. We just break up a lot."

"That wouldn't have happened with us if you came back like you promised." I shout in his face.

The detective writes in her book. "When Cassie texted, did you tell her you were with Nicole?"

"No. I didn't want to get her jealous. She already thought something was going on between me and Nicole because of the play. A lot of people thought that. But we were just friends. We were acting."

I feel like punching him. "You know it wasn't *all* acting."

V. Lee flips back a page and skims her notes. "I'm confused. If there was nothing between you and Nicole, and you liked your girlfriend *a lot*, why break up with her?"

Alex opens his mouth then quickly shuts it as a band of pink edges out the deep gold in his aura. Love. Hope. What's that about? Alex shrugs. Seriously? Another frickin' shrug?

"I liked them both. I dunno. Maybe I broke up with Cassie because I wanted a change."

"You're such a liar." I wish he could hear me. "You never broke up with her. What kind of change are you talking about? Someone different to make out with? Screw you, Alex. I'm so glad you were never my boyfriend."

V. Lee looks up from her notebook. "How did Cassie react when you broke up with her?"

Alex rubs the rash on his forehead and avoids her eyes. "She wasn't upset, if that's what you mean. She said she didn't care because she was going to break up with me anyway."

Another lie. Cassie never would have said that. How many lies is that? I've lost track. I can't even look at him.

"How long were you at the park?" V. Lee asks.

Alex attacks the rash on his right hand so hard the skin starts to ooze. Ew. Another good reason not to look.

"I dunno. Maybe five minutes, ten at most. Then I headed back to the tower, like I promised Nicole."

Not true.

V. Lee clicks her pen slowly at random times, which makes it more annoying. "You say Nicole was fine when you left her on the tower. I wonder what could have happened in such a short time to change her mood so drastically. Unless you were at the park longer than five or ten minutes."

Alex's aura darkens to muddy blue. Panic.

"Uh ... it might have been a little longer. Cassie and I played ball with her dog for a while before I headed back up the hill."

More lies. What a total waste of time. I float toward the ceiling, ready to pass through. V. Lee's voice stops me. "Let's talk about how you found Nicole's body."

Ohmygod! *Alex* found me? He saw my head smashed in? This is so embarrassing.

V. Lee flips to a different section of her notebook. "The police report describes how you were riding your bike up the switchback trail toward the water tower when you heard the sound of 'something heavy rolling downhill. I heard branches breaking.' Is that correct?"

Branches break inside my head. A sneaker wave of cold dread knocks me flat and drags me under.

Alex swallows so hard I hear it go down. Dr. Campbell hands him a paper cup filled with water. He takes it, but doesn't drink. "Yeah. The rolling stopped with a THUD lower down on the slope. Then everything was silent." He gulps the water and stares at the empty cup. "I knew something was wrong so I got off my bike and hurried toward the sound. Poison oak grows everywhere along the slopes. Not the easiest thing to identify without the leaves, which are gone this time of year. The bare vines are still deadly."

He holds out his hands to prove his point. V. Lee nods and recoils.

"I ran across the canyon and tripped and fell. That's when I spotted her blue top. She was lying against a tree. Her head was . . ."

Thank God I didn't feel any of that. I was already dead. The fall from the tower must have killed me instantly. Or did it? I heard branches break.

I lay at the bottom of the tower, teetering on the edge of the slope, unable to pull myself to safety. Something like an unseen magnet pulls on me. In spite of the piercing pain, throbbing pain, deep bone pain, I hold on to life with everything that's left in me, But I'm not strong enough. Never strong enough. I give up or give in. The pain releases. Instantly I hover six feet above my body and watch, horrified, as my body tumbles down the slope, plowing through sticker bushes and dead branches, rolling over rocks and broken bottles, picking up speed until my body crashes into a tree. What used to be Nicole Benson lies twisted and broken, hidden by deep shadows, her skull crushed, her mouth full of shattered teeth. She is lost.

Spooked and sick, I soar like a rocket, busting through the ceiling, levitating high above Veraz High School.

veraz, Spanish, adj. truthful.

Now that's funny.

Higher and higher I rise until Sorich Park comes into view, turning my face to the sun so I won't see the water tower and won't think about . . . Doesn't help. Maybe Iz was right. Maybe I'm not supposed to remember everything.

CASSIE

"DID MY MOM tell you I was here?" I ask the cop who walks toward me across the field, waving her badge in my face.

"No. She said you were in bed, sick with the flu."

Should I cover for Buzz-Kill? Nah. "She lied."

"Because she thought she was protecting you?"

I laugh so loud, Lola jumps. "Oh, yeah. That's her number one purpose in life."

Detective V. Lee looks at me like she knows who's lying now. I kneel and tighten my laces, even though they don't need it. "So how'd you know I was here?"

"I knew you had a dog, but I didn't hear barking when I rang the bell at your apartment, so I figured you might be at the park, since it's this close. How's your community service going at the childcare center?"

She knows that too? I'd better watch out.

"It's going."

"Glad to hear it. So, did you skip school today because you thought you were in trouble?"

"Nah. I don't do school on Fridays."

The cop chuckles. "Three-day weekends are nice."

A cop with a sense of humor? I wasn't expecting that. Didn't expect her to pay attention to Lola either, but she scratches the special spot behind her left ear. Lola wags her whole body.

"We don't have all the facts about Nicole's death, so we can't rule out anything yet." The cop gives Lola an extra pat before standing up again. "That's why we're talking to her friends."

Lola pulls me in the direction of the eucalyptus trees at the edge of the park. The cop follows along. "I can save you time. Nicole jumped. For attention, I'll bet. That's why she did everything."

I shouldn't have said that because the cop whips out her notebook and holds it so I can't see what she's writing.

"It's not like I'm happy Nicole's dead." I try to sound like I'm not just saying it, because I'm not. Lola noses around the strips of bark on the ground. "It sucks. But she wasn't exactly an angel."

"How so?"

The cop clicks her pen oh so casually, like she wants me to think that was a random question. I take my time answering because I want her to think it was just a random comment. I pick up a stick and hold it over Lola's head. She jumps for it, like I knew she would. I drop her leash and fling the stick toward the picnic tables, all empty because even in California, January is still January. Lola pounces on the stick, then drops it just as quickly and jumps up on one of the tables, staring at a spot above her head, twitching her tail the way she does when she sees a squirrel in a tree except there is no squirrel. There's not even a tree.

"What's up, Lo?"

Lola looks surprised as if she's wondering what's wrong with me that I can't see the thing she's looking at. *Dogs.*

The cop watches me, still waiting for me to tell why Nicole wasn't an angel. What am I waiting for? Why not just tell the truth? Who am I protecting?

"For starters, she dumped her best friend. Not that I give a crap about Isabel. That girl is weird. Did you talk to her yet? She thinks she's a witch. But where's the loyalty, you know? If you can't count on your friends, you're screwed. Nicole pretended to be my friend just to get close to Alex, but I was on to her from the beginning so she never suckered me in. She got Kyle, though. Poor jerk. I told him to watch out for her, but he didn't care. He was hopelessly in love with her. Still is."

"You weren't in *Our Town*, were you, Cassie?"

She knows I wasn't. She's trying to catch me in a lie. I should just say "no." But what fun would that be? "Do I look like the kind of girl who'd be in a school play?"

"Sure."

"Well, I'm not. But if I was, none of this would have happened."

"Why is that?"

"People kept telling me Nicole was flirting with Alex during rehearsals, so I snuck in to see what was going on. That first time, Ms. Moreno was explaining how actors do what she called a *stage kiss*, where one person tilts their head to one side and the other person tilts the opposite way, and kisses them right here, like two inches away from their mouth. The kiss is supposed to look real from the audience, but it's not real. Of course Nicole and Alex had to practice. A lot. Anyway, I just happened to be watching the rehearsal, though he didn't know I was in the audience. Gotta say, the kiss looked real, but when I talked to him about it, he said I had nothing to worry about, so I let it go. Still, I kept hearing that I should be worried, so I went to rehearsal another time. And I saw them up against the wall in a dark corner of the auditorium. She was pressing her ginormous boobs against him. He wasn't totally innocent. You know guys. He didn't touch her or anything, but from how he was standing I could tell he didn't mind what was going on. I didn't want to make a scene so I caught up with Nicole later and told her she'd better stay away from my boyfriend. That was the last time I talked to her."

The cop writes in her notebook. "May I have a look at your phone, Cassie?"

I unlock my phone and hand it over. "Knock yourself out. I've got nothing to hide. You can even look at the texts between me and Alex if you're into that kind of stuff. Oh, those are from Friday. G-rated. We were just talking about meeting up. You won't find anything between me and Nicole. Like I said, we stopped talking in the middle of December. I deleted all the earlier texts between us, before she started acting so obvious around Alex. I deleted all the selfies we took and the audio files of our duet rehearsals. I don't need those kinds of mind-wrackers."

The cop swipes through selfies of me and Alex. We look like we belong together, but maybe it was just like a stage kiss for the camera.

"How long were you and Alex together at the park last Friday?"

"I'm not sure. I lost track of time." I purposely sound vague so she'll ask what we were doing.

She's ready to write in her notebook. "What were you doing?"

"Making out."

Her eyebrows shoot up. *Gotcha!*

"Did you and Alex make out before or after he broke up with you?"

"Who told you he broke up with me?"

"Alex." She flips back a page in her notebook and reads. "'She wasn't upset when I broke up with her. She said she was going to break up with me anyway. We played ball with her dog for a few minutes, then I headed back up the hill.' That's what he told me a couple of hours ago."

"Well, he lied. Nobody broke up with anyone that day. Also, we did a whole lot more than play ball with Lola."

I smile, all coy. I want her to ask me more about that because I'd love to go into details just to prove my point. But she doesn't.

Instead, she says, "Why do you think he lied?"

I grab Lola's leash, give it a tug, and she jumps off the table. "How should I know?"

"Sounds like you're annoyed with him."

"Nope. We're done. I broke up with him on Sunday. Didn't know that, huh? Maybe you're not such a great detective."

She clicks her pen like crazy, as if she's going to nail me with the million-dollar question. "Did the breakup have anything to do with Nicole?"

"Nope. Alex was getting to be annoying."

The cop shuts her notebook and sticks it in her back pocket. "People react to death in different ways. You might want to cut him some slack."

Suddenly she sounds like she's my mom. Well, not *my* mom, but somebody's.

I download my bitch face.

Nicole

AFTER ALEX'S INTERVIEW with V. Lee, I was ready to quit my research because what's the point when people lie? Then my countdown timer buzzed. Only six days left. That got me thinking Substation Sixteen might possibly be worse than crash landing on concrete and rolling downhill over broken glass. I had to eavesdrop on Cassie in Sorich Park. Was she telling V. Lee the truth when she said Alex didn't break up with her? Or was *he* telling the truth when he said he did? So weird that Lola saw me. Cassie didn't know I was there, so she could have been telling the truth about making out with Alex. She didn't give details, so how come I saw them clearly on my mental movie screen having at it in the woods? Did they actually do it or was I remembering my own paranoid fantasy of what I was afraid they were doing in the park while I was waiting for him to come back? If he'd dumped me and then came back to the tower, I would have made out with him. I was that pathetic. But if he'd broken up with Cassie, like he said, she would have beaten the crap out of him. But she says he didn't break up with her and they made out. What am I supposed to think? Who's telling the truth? Cassie's aura is hard to read. Is she such a good liar she can control her aura? Is that even possible? I just don't know what to believe.

One thing is sure, what she said about me was harsh, but true. I wasn't an angel. I didn't care about Iz's feelings when I stopped talking to her at school. I didn't care about Cassie's feelings when I made my two-year-plan to steal Alex. I didn't even care about Alex's feelings when I came on to him again and again. Like that Beatles' song Dad likes, I was all about I, me, mine. I'm not proud of how I acted, but yeah. No angel. I did care about Kyle, though. We were friends. If I had known that he liked me as more than a friend, I wouldn't have constantly pumped him for information about Alex. Cut! Lie alert. I knew exactly how Kyle felt about me. I used him because I knew he'd let me. I hate how self-centered I was, and probably still am, but at least I'm not lying to myself about it anymore, for all the good it does at this point. Kyle never lied to me. He won't lie to V. Lee either. That's why I am back at school ready to hear what he says.

Kyle slumps on the edge of the bench in front of Mrs. Moss's desk, his headphones resting on the back of his neck. Whatever song he's swaying to must be in his head. Every minute or so, he stops to add a few more bars of music to what he's already written in his notebook. He's writing a new song. I wrote my songs by playing around with guitar chords and thinking of melodies that went with the chords, and lyrics that went with the melodies. I never wrote actual music on paper like Kyle, with key and time signatures, sharps and flats, measures, and all that. I learned about that stuff when I took piano lessons, and when you do it that way, anyone can play your songs, even after you're dead. My songbook is filled with lyrics and chords. That's all. So even though writing music for guitar is so much faster, no one will ever know how my songs are supposed to sound. That sucks because some of them are really good.

I wish I could hear Kyle's new song. Maybe it's about me. Not self-centered anymore? Yeah, right.

I stick my head through the closed office door. Dr. Campbell types like she's punishing the computer for bringing her bad news. Dad had a non-negotiable truth about that: *You can kill the messenger, but you can't kill the message.*

They're keeping Kyle waiting because V. Lee isn't back from the park yet. Of course not. She has to drive. I just had to *think* myself here.

V. Lee hurries into the office, past Kyle and through me. She smells faintly of eucalyptus and Lola. Mrs. Moss tells her that Dr. Campbell is waiting for her. A couple of minutes later, the desk phone buzzes, and Mrs. Moss tells Kyle to go in.

He settles uneasily under the Positive Thinking poster, and V. Lee gets down to business. *Kyle Jackson, 1/11 1:42* already heads a new page.

"Kyle, when was the last time you saw Nicole?"

He grips his headphone cord like a lifeline and mumbles into his hand. "Do you mean alive or dead?"

Ohmygod! He saw my body, too? Poor Kyle. Look at his face. I'm desperate to remember stuff, and he's dying to forget. Every time he thinks of me, *dead girl with smashed skull* will pop up on his mental movie screen. How sickening.

V. Lee clicks her pen about twenty times. "I don't understand, Kyle. Only Alex was mentioned in the police report. He called 911. He showed the officers where to find Nicole's body. When were you there?"

"Alex texted me right after he found her. I was at High Tech Burrito. I told him to call 911, then I rode my bike to the place and waited with him, but I left before the police came. I just couldn't be there anymore."

Kyle's voice catches. He's not crying, but close. Me too. His aura spins freely around him. He's telling the truth. He tilts his head, like he's listening to music or searching his mental playlist for something to wash away the horrible memory. V. Lee sits back in her chair and folds her hands in her lap, her voice gentler now.

"When was the last time you saw Nicole alive?"

"Uh, I'm not exactly sure. Friday. I talked to her at the water tower while she was waiting for Alex."

Great. Now everybody knows how delusional I was about Alex. Who am I kidding? Everyone always knew. This is almost as embarrassing as being caught dead.

V. Lee writes in her notebook. "Did Nicole ask you to meet her at the tower?"

"No. It was my idea. That morning Alex texted me that Nicole texted him to meet her there. He said yes because he thought Cassie was out of town. I don't think Nicole knew that part."

I knew. Mariah told me. I remember thinking, "Why is she giving me an update about Cassie? We aren't friends anymore." It never occurred to me that the whole thing might have been Cassie's idea to set me up while she was gone. And it was Mariah's job to keep an eye on Alex and me. I fell right into the trap. After I found out Cassie was away for the weekend, I texted Alex. It feels really sneaky now. Stealing someone's boyfriend is never okay. How come I was fine with it? How come Alex was okay with cheating on Cassie? Dad has another non-negotiable truth: *A guy who cheats on his girlfriend to be with you will cheat on you to be with the next girl.* I wish I'd thought of that at the time.

Kyle continues. "I didn't like the sound of Alex's plan. I knew Nicole would get hurt. So I went to the tower. Alex's bike wasn't there, so I knew he was gone. Before Nicole saw me, I took her photo. She looked like an angel up there."

He shows V. Lee the photo on his phone. I look too. He's right. I was an average-looking girl but in his photo, with the sun behind me, I look radiant. Even beautiful. They say average-looking girls are grateful for any attention we get. That's messed up. Average-looking is plenty good enough.

"Lovely picture." V. Lee hands back his phone.

"Turns out Cassie didn't go to Sacramento. She texted Alex while he was with Nicole and told him to come to the park. So he left Nicole to go break up with Cassie. At least that's what he told Nicole. Only she didn't believe he'd actually do it. When I got to the tower she was freaking out, convinced that he wouldn't come back. I tried to calm her down."

"Did you climb up the ladder and sit on the roof with her?"

"I wanted to, but she wouldn't let me. She wanted me to go to the park and get Alex to come back. I didn't want to leave her so upset, but she insisted. I should have stayed with her."

He rubs his eyes, like he's trying to wipe away something he sees. I think he blames himself for my death. I wish I could tell him it wasn't his fault. He starts to slip on his headphones like I've seen him do a hundred times whenever something's going on that he wants to tune out. V. Lee stops him by scooting her chair in closer and touching his arm.

"What happened when you got to the park, Kyle?"

He seals his lips and shakes his head. A moment of silence passes. V. Lee doesn't move. Then Kyle gets a spacey look and starts talking slowly and deliberately like he's watching something no one else can see. "Isabel was hurrying away from the woods at the south end of the park. She was holding her camera. Her head was down and she was muttering to herself. She didn't see me, and I almost called to her, but she was lost in her own thoughts."

What was Iz doing at the park? Must have been working on the movie. There was a scene where Lucy gets lost in the woods, but how could she record that without me?

". . . I had a feeling I'd find Alex in the woods. Cassie, too. When I saw Cassie's dog chewing on a stick, not far from the trailhead, I kept going. I didn't have to go far. They were making out under the trees."

I can see them, on my mental movie screen, like I was right there. How is that possible? And how is it possible that Cassie actually told the truth? She and Alex *did* make out after he promised he was going to break up with her. Was he planning on coming back and lying to me so I'd make out with him some more? What a skunk! So if Calex never broke up, then Cassie was just making out with her boyfriend. No crime in that. But if he broke up with her and told her about his feelings for me, and she made out with him after *that*, then they're both skunks.

Kyle keeps talking, all reluctance gone. "At first, I was embarrassed to catch them like that. More embarrassed than they were. Then I blew up at Alex for keeping Nicole waiting at the water tower. Cassie had no idea what I was talking about..."

Seriously? Huh. Then I wasn't setup by Cassie and Mariah. That makes Alex the only lying, cheating skunk in this story.

"... but she caught on quick and started in on him, too. He yelled at both of us and got on his bike. I didn't know where he went until I was at High Tech Burrito and he ..."

Kyle's voice breaks. The tears surprise him. Dr. Campbell places a box of tissues on his knees. I rest my hand on Kyle's shoulder. He seems to calm down. Maybe he feels my presence. He grabs a fistful of tissues, and wipes his eyes and nose. When he speaks again his voice is almost a whisper. "Why do girls fall for guys who treat them like crap and ignore the ones who really care about them?"

For a second I think he's talking to me. Wrong. He's looking at V. Lee. Her face softens.

"Not all girls, Kyle."

Only the delusional ones.

Isabel

FROM THE CORNER of my eye, I catch Mom's hand reaching out to me. I shift away. Too late. She squeezes my arm. Her touch triggers a swarm of killer bees in my solar plexus. Her stress compounds with mine. Doesn't she know that physical contact transmits the emotion you're feeling? Isn't it bad enough that we're sitting on the anxiety bench?

Mrs. Moss pops a candy in her mouth, licks her fingertips, and grins at Mom. "They should be ready for you soon."

Ready for *you*, as in you guys. Third-person plural. Exactly what the receptionist in the doctor's waiting room says while you sweat it out with your mom. Only your mom isn't getting a vaccination, you are. *You*, as in second-person singular. You, as in *me*. Why am I in so much trouble when Mom's the one who started it?

When I walk into the kitchen, Mom quickly closes her laptop and grins so hard her eyes disappear. "Welcome home, sweetie. How was school? Do you have a lot of homework? What can I get you to eat?"

Her words wash over me like a flash flood of cheer designed to distract. I pretend it worked, but I'm wondering why she shut her computer so quickly. Was she looking up an old boyfriend? Is she having an affair?

After Mom leaves for yoga, I open her laptop. Being unethical throws me off balance, but a stronger sense tells me there's something important I need to uncover. If she really wanted privacy, she'd change her password to something other than my birthday. I realize that's a justification, but it's also the truth.

I review her history and open the Facebook page she was looking at when I came home. It belongs to Michelle Barone. Never heard of her. Is she an old girlfriend of Dad's? A current girlfriend? Is she Mom's girlfriend? I don't get a positive read on any of those thoughts and Michelle Barone's photos offer no clues. None of these people look familiar.

Mom strides into the room, fuming. "What are you doing on my computer?" She reaches for the laptop, trying to snatch it away.

She's hiding something big.

I hold on.

"Isabel, why are you snooping?"

Anxiety and nausea block my second chakra. My brain broadcasts random justifications. Pick one.

"You snoop through my stuff all the time. I know your intentions are good, but still . . . Will you please stay out of my room when I'm not here, Mom? Okay? Will you?"

She sighs, grudgingly, then agrees. I trust her because she always tells the truth when I ask her a direct question. I point to Michelle Barone's profile picture. "Who is this?"

Mom looks like she's about to lie, but she can't. Something drags down her energy level so she's having trouble meeting my eyes. Her face cycles through a kaleidoscope of expressions: worry, embarrassment, shame, confusion. I picture her teetering on a high wire. I'm up there, too, without a net. I want to reach out to steady her, but I'm scared that I'll accidentally cause her to fall. I lower my voice, like I'm talking to a desperate person on a ledge. "You can trust me, Mom. Who is she?"

She absently twists her wedding band around her finger. Maybe she's making a wish. Finally, she confesses. "Michelle Barone is Nicole's mother."

I lose my footing and fall. My mind floods with questions, but I wait for her to explain what she just dumped into our shared space. The only explanation I come up with sounds impossible, but it's all I've got so I blurt it out. "Nicole's mom is alive?"

Her lips fold tightly onto each other and all she can do is nod.

A psychic earthquake rips through something I'd always believed was quake-proof. "You lied to me." I can barely say the words.

Her gaze wobbles but I hold on, refusing to let her look away because I need the truth, even if the truth is about lying. She stops spinning her ring but doesn't let it go.

"Yes. Dad and I lied to you, and Mike lied to Nicole. We did it to protect you both from the truth."

I'm not sure I'm ready to hear any more about whatever they thought we needed protection from, but Mom tells me anyway because now that she's started, she can't stop.

"Soon after Mike and Michelle got married, she met someone online. She never told me. Dad and I found out from Mike, the day after she walked out on him and Nicole."

Mom's face darkens. Is she thinking about Michelle and the guy she left her family for fourteen years ago? Is she thinking about Mike and what that was like for him? I'll bet I'm the only one thinking about Nic, who wasn't even two years old at the time and suddenly had no mom. How did that feel? What was it like to be engulfed in such profound sadness and confusion without the language to talk about it? How do you heal from a loss like that?

Before I notice how close I am to unraveling, Mom grounds me with a fierce hug, as much to comfort me as to show how a real mom is supposed to act. "What kind of mother leaves her child and never comes back, never calls, never even sends a birthday card? I'll never understand it. Mike made up the story that Michelle died of cancer so Nicole wouldn't feel unloved or abandoned. We all agreed to stick to it. She was so young we thought it was for the best. The truth is, by her own choice, Michelle was dead to Nicole, so the lie didn't seem like much of a stretch at the time."

"How long have you guys been Facebook friends?"

"A couple of days. Maybe she reached out to me thinking I'd help her reconnect with Nicole. If that's what she wants, it could be a good thing. Of course, I won't do anything without Mike's permission. I'll talk to him and he can decide how he wants to deal with this."

"Nic doesn't need a mom like that."

"I'm not surprised you feel that way. It's hard to forgive, but people can change."

She's right. Goddess Eternal helps people become more loving and accepting and forgiving. Maybe I can use my power to heal the relationship between Nic and her mom. It feels strange to think of Nic with a mom, but she's got one so how can I help? I guess I start by asking Nic what she remembers about her mom. Then I'll ask if she ever wished she could talk to her. Then I could . . .

As if suddenly telepathic, Mom says, "You'd better not be thinking about telling Nicole about this before I talk to Mike."

"But, I'm her best friend. She deserves to know the truth."

"Isabel, you have to promise not to tell Nicole. This isn't your news to deliver."

I promised.

Nicole

IZ STRUGGLES TO untie her backpack drawstring. The muddiness in her aura's yellow-brown band increases by the minute. Tight, busy mind. Working overtime. Straining to solve a problem. Yeah, she's got a problem, and it's got nothing to do with a stubborn knot.

I perch directly behind her on the back of the couch. "I'm right behind you, Iz, so you'd better tell the truth."

She scoots forward so quickly her phone slides off her lap onto the rug. Bending to pick it up, she sneaks a peek at the adults in the room. They're busy with other things. Dr. Campbell grumbles at her laptop. Mandy repositions her legs into a tight lotus, perfectly balanced on a folding chair. Despite her serene expression, her aura flashes dark red, light tan, and light blue. Frustration. Overlooking facts that don't fit her version of the truth. If she thought it was so important to be here with Iz, then why isn't she sitting next to her? There's plenty of room for yoga on the couch.

V. Lee flips to a new page in her notebook and writes *Isabel Waterman, 1/11 2:15 pm* at the top. "May I please see your phone, Isabel?"

"Don't you need a warrant for that?" Iz squeezes out the words.

"Yes. Or you or your mother could simply give me permission to have a look while we're all sitting here."

Mandy nods once. "It's fine with me."

Iz doesn't move. It's like she has become a living freeze-frame.

Mandy clears her throat. "Isabel?"

Crickets. Mandy reaches for the phone. Iz comes to life and hangs on. She and Mandy play tug o' war, only it's not a game. I always thought Mandy was the perfect mom. Seeing them mix it up in public is like watching an evil version of Marmee from *Little Women*. What's going on?

Mandy shoots Iz a cut-the-crap look. Iz exhales long and loud, lets go of the phone and watches, horrified, as her mom taps in her password and hands the phone to V. Lee. No way did Dad know my password, though he'll probably know everything about me after the police send him my phone records. Not great that he'll see everything, but I will too, and that's what I need. What day did he say that was happening? Friday. That's today.

"FYI, Iz," I say, "your plan totally failed. I'm going to be reading everything later, including your deleted texts."

She closes her eyes and murmurs under her breath so no one hears except me. She's asking the Goddess for forgiveness. Geez, those texts must be pretty bad.

V. Lee swipes through Iz's texts.

"Are you looking for anything in particular?" Mandy asks, her voice mid-way between casually interested and desperate to know.

"Any information that might help us determine Nicole's state of mind last Friday."

I read along.

RoshanaMoon>

> Hey Roshana. Just
> heard about this
> Winter Solstice

Gathering in Fairfield
Sunday. Want to go?

Oooo. That looks so
fun. But Sunday is my
little sister's birthday
party. Dang it!

How about a spell so
you can be in two
places at once?

Haha! I wish. It's a spa
theme. Can you
believe it? Wish it was
a witchy magik theme
instead.

Ravenwing>

Hey Isabel!

Ravenwing! We are
cosmically connected
to be sure! I swear I
was just thinking about
you and I was going to
text you. Whoa! Magik!

I want to show you my
new rune set.
It's made of redheart.
FaceTime me.

Kk.

Iz has friends. Weirdoes, but still. How come she never
told me about them?

Because she knew I'd call them weirdoes. No, I wouldn't. Yeah, I would. Damn. Okay, that's it. If I get another life, top priority: Quit being so judgmental. It's not a good look.

V. Lee keeps scrolling. "Lots of texts between you and Nicole, up through Thursday of last week, but nothing on the day she died. Did you two have a fight?"

Iz tries to keep her face calm but her aura ignites with a wild burst of gold.

Total and utter confusion. "No."

"Then why no texts?"

Mandy watches Iz like she's wondering the same thing. I whisper in Iz's ear, "Tell her what you did with our texts."

Iz flinches and hugs her stomach. Mandy unfolds and comes over to sit on the couch. She rubs Iz's back.

"Last Friday was our first Unplugged Day." Mandy says to V. Lee, as if everyone knows that.

"What is she talking about, Iz?"

Iz jerks her head in her mom's direction like she's wondering the same thing.

Mandy presses her palms together, smiles serenely at V. Lee and pours on a thick layer of Namaste syrup. "Our family just instituted a weekly technology break where we abstain from all texting and all media, social and otherwise, in order to be mindfully in the Now and with each other."

V. Lee hands the phone back to Iz. "How nice for you. But I'm guessing Nicole wasn't taking a tech break last Friday. I'm thinking she might have spent *too much* time on her phone that day. Harassment via text or social media is a serious problem for many young people. Rude or disturbing comments can eat away at self-esteem, cloud judgment, increase depression, and/or trigger suicidal thoughts."

She sounds like our Health and Wellness teacher. I'm bored, but Iz eats it up. Always the honor roll student. She'll probably raise her hand at the next question.

"Isabel, was Nicole the victim of online harassment?"

Iz doesn't raise her hand, but she jumps on it. "No."

That's true. If anything like that had happened, I would have gotten her to perform a protection spell for me.

"Can you think of anyone who might have said or done something to make Nicole feel threatened or betrayed?" The last word hooks onto a hazy memory that wriggles like a fish desperately fighting not to be reeled into the light of my mental movie screen.

Iz bites her lip. Her aura pulses wildly. Balancing the truth with the need to lie. She's struggling with a memory, too. Is it the same memory that's hiding from me? She looks away for a long moment. Too long. The adults watch her and wait. Me, too. The pulsing of her aura quickens. Suddenly she sits up like she's just found a missing puzzle piece.

"I saw Cassie and Alex messing around at the park on Friday."

"Kyle said he saw you there with your camera," I say. "Does this have something to do with what I'm trying to remember?"

Iz doesn't react, pretending she can't hear me, but we both know she can.

"Did you tell Nicole what you saw?" V. Lee asks.

"No." Iz's voice sounds like it's coming from inside a clogged drainpipe.

A hazy object flickers on my mental movie screen. Something is rolling around on the ground. What is that? The image clicks into focus. It's two *somethings* moving as one. My heart seizes up. A chill of dread surges through me. "Ohmygod, Iz! You sent me a video of Cassie and Alex making out. And now you wish you hadn't. That's why you deleted it. But wait. I'm remembering else. Something you sent me after the video. What was it?"

She leaps from the couch like the seat is on fire. Her muddy aura pushes outward, sprouting pulsing flares like tentacles. Shame. Regret. The bell rings in the hall. She grabs her backpack and heads for the door. Mandy stands. "If you're finished questioning my daughter, may she be dismissed?"

"*I'm* not finished," I say.

V. Lee nods to Dr. Campbell who turns to Iz. "Thank you, Isabel. You may leave."

Iz hurries out of the office without a word or a backward glance. Fine. Let her go. I've heard more than enough BS for one day and just enough facts to know I'm getting closer to the whole truth. Before I do anything else, I've got to see if the police sent Dad my phone data yet.

Nicole

DAD AND MANDY sit at Iz's kitchen table. As he opens his laptop, the slate-blue sky outside the window fades to charcoal gray. Greg stands in front of the open refrigerator door like he's forgotten why he went in. I hover on the counter between the toaster and the food processor. Everything is spotless, as always. The mint-green sponge, also clean, rests in the sparkling chrome holder on the sink. Mandy likes everything just right, but something isn't right. The corners of the room press inward, and an invisible layer of gloom encases everything and everyone. Dad grumbles at his laptop, checking his email every few seconds. Mandy holds her hands over her teacup, warming them in the rising steam like it's a campfire. She inhales so forcefully her nose whistles.

Where is Iz? I pop into her room. She sits inside her circle of protection, eyes closed, clutching her anthem knife.

"Neither of us can hide from the truth, Iz." I leave without waiting for her response.

Back in the kitchen, Dad refreshes the screen. "Finally." His voice a mix of anticipation and dread. I hover by his shoulder as he opens the email from the Veraz Police Department. Eagerly he clicks on the enclosed link that pops him to an official-looking website that prompts him for his phone number. He throws up his hands and snorts.

Greg looks at the computer screen. "They're going to text you a code to verify that it's you trying to access these confidential phone records. They're protecting the information, Mike."

Dad nods and enters his phone number. An instant later his phone dings as the text with the code comes in. He enters the code into the computer and a folder appears on the screen. He exhales like he's blowing out a candle that refuses to go out. I'm the candle, not the strongest flame at this point, but I'm hanging in there.

He clicks on the folder. It opens to a directory of three names and links. Alex. Isabel. Dad. He pulls his hands off the keyboard and looks down.

"You want me to open the files?" Greg offers.

"It's okay, Dad. Go ahead. We've got to find out the truth." I know he can't hear me, but he sits up straighter, shakes his head, and clicks on Alex's link. My outgoing texts appear on the screen.

"These texts are between Nicole and Alex," Dad says, his voice rusty, as if he hasn't used it in days. "All from last Friday."

I don't remember what I wrote, but I was pretty crazed at the time. I'm embarrassed already.

Greg pulls his chair to Dad's side of the table for a better view. For some reason, Mandy seems more interested in playing with the string of her soggy tea bag. Dad slowly reads from the screen like he's translating from another language.

"Actually, these were all sent by Nicole.

"11:30 I'm waiting ;)

"11:35 Let me know when you're on your way back.

"11:40 Where are you?

"11:42 What's taking so long??

"11:45 Did you break up with her yet?

"And here's the last one, about thirty minutes later.

"12:13 Alex, UR such a jerk!"

I remember the flirting and trying to sound casual, like we were already dating and I had the right to ask where he was and what he was doing, but under it all, I was freaking out. Was all of that really only a week ago? Geez.

"Sounds like she expected him to meet her and she didn't like waiting," Dad says. "She kept texting, but he never answered. The little shit."

"He was *busy*," I say. "It doesn't bother me now ... as much."

Dad closes Alex's link and clicks on Isabel's. Our texts appear on the screen. I move in closer. I'm finally going to see everything that Iz deleted from her phone.

"11:48 Isabel says, 'Look at this!'

"There's a video attached," Dad says.

Mandy looks up from her tea. "Isabel went to Sorich to shoot exteriors for her movie."

Dad presses PLAY and the video opens on the screen showing Alex and Cassie lying in the shade of the forest, their legs entwined, their mouths and bodies pressing together hungrily.

Greg looks away from the screen like he's embarrassed. "Uh, I don't think this is for her movie."

I've seen this video replay in my mind, and I've seen it on my phone. I don't want to watch again, but I can't look away. Something squeezes my throat so I can't breathe. I've felt this exact feeling before.

A chainsaw rips through my heart as my phone plays their make-out session. How could he? He was just here kissing me, but not like that! I thought he liked me. Is my butt too big? I'll bet it's my thighs. Why did he kiss me then? Was it just because I kissed him first? He swore he was done with Cassie. Look at them going at it. What an idiot I am.

I text him. Alex UR such a jerk! No answer. Of course, not. He's busy.

What am I going to do? Go to the park and confront him? What for? He's her boyfriend. If I show up all crazy jealous, she'll know something's up, and she and Mariah will come after me. No. Not going to the park. Not staying here waiting for Alex either. He's not coming back. But maybe he will, and he'll act like nothing happened because he won't know that I know. He may even want to make out with me. No way would I let him. Well, maybe I would, if first he admitted what he did and apologized and swore it would never happen again. No. Forget it. I'm going home.

The ground looks like it's a hundred feet away. The steps of the ladder are so narrow and the rusty handrail looks like it could fall off at any minute. How am I going to get down? If Kyle was really my friend, he would have stayed with me no matter what I said. He'd come back if I texted him. No, he's forgotten all about me. Probably left the park. And what about Iz? What kind of friend sends a video like that? She ruined everything.

I text Iz, angrily punching the keys. "Thanks for nothing!"

I shouldn't have been mad at her. She was just trying to help.

The progress meter on the bottom of the video window crawls ahead for a few more seconds and then Dad's computer goes dark, but my mind is on fire. Of course, the video crushed and depressed me the first time I watched it, but did I kill myself over it? That seems like an overreaction, even for me, but I don't know. I really don't.

"Geez," Greg says. "Why would Isabel send that video? She had to know it would upset Nicole."

Dad ignores him and continues to read the texts aloud. Maybe it's for Mandy, who isn't looking at the screen, or maybe he just wants to say my words to feel closer to me, though it's hard to imagine reading this stuff is any more comforting than reading my journal or listening to a loved one's 911 call right before they died.

"Nicole says, 'Thanks for nothing.'

"Isabel asks, 'Why are you mad at me? I'm your best friend.'

"Nicole says, 'You didn't have to send it.'

"Isabel responds. 'What was I supposed to do? I saw them!'

"There's a break of several minutes," Dad says. "Nicole's last text to Alex happened during that time. Then she returns to Isabel and says, 'You could have lied.'

"Isabel says, 'Why would I? So you could go on believing that he liked you more than he liked her? I couldn't let you do that.'

"Nicole says, 'I can believe whatever I want!'

"Isabel says, 'Fine. But don't ask me to lie. I won't. I never lie to you, not like some other people you think you can trust.'

"Nicole asks, 'What's that supposed to mean? Aside from Alex, who else has been lying to me?'

"Isabel says, 'Never mind.'

"Nicole says, 'Tell me!'

"Isabel says, 'I promised I wouldn't.'"

Mandy inhales so sharply we all look at her.

"What?" Greg says.

Mandy ignores him. "What does Isabel say next?" she asks Dad, her words stepping on each other as if they're being chased out of her mouth.

"She doesn't. Nicole sends the next one. She says, 'Promised who? If you're such a great friend, prove it. Tell me who else has been lying to me.' Then there is a four-minute delay before Isabel responds. 'Your dad and both of my parents have always lied to us about your mom. She's not dead. She walked out on you and your dad. Here she is on Facebook.'"

Mom not *dead?* What the hell? She *walked out* on Dad and me? What the bloody hell? Dad's been lying to me for my whole life? My mind flips inside out and explodes into a thousand pieces leaving bits of short-circuiting wires. The kitchen counter opens up and down I go, tumbling like Alice into an endless rabbit hole, passing by everything I ever believed about my mom, my dad, my life. I never belonged to the Dead Moms Club. Without knowing it, I was in the Your Mom Left You Because She Didn't Love You Club. They both totally suck. Mandy can be too much, but Iz never doubts that her mom loves her. That's something. A huge something that I thought Dad's fairy tales guaranteed forever. He told me more than once that when Mom was "dying," before the angels carried her into the sky, she had said to him, "Leaving Nini hurts much more than being sick. Promise me you'll keep on telling her that I love her always *in all ways.*" All ways of BS. Same as the lie he'd tell me in the spring, on clear nights, when we'd sit in the backyard and I'd point to Vega, the brightest star in the constellation Lyra. He'd say that Vega was actually Mom watching over me. I loved that part of the story best because Lyra represents the lyre, a string instrument, and Mom played the guitar, just like me.

How could I *not* remember this text? Obviously I read it on the tower and I clicked on the Facebook link. That's the reason I texted Dad asking about Mom! It wasn't at all random. But I completely blanked it out. I remembered the make-out video before seeing it again, but not this breaking news that Mom's alive, that she ditched us, and Dad's been lying about it for my whole life. Is this the reason I jumped off the tower?

Greg shakes his head at the screen like he's trying to decipher an uncrackable code. "How in the world did Isabel find out about Michelle?"

Mandy's fingers tighten around her teacup and whispers, "From me. Michelle reached out with a friend request early last week. I was on Facebook when Isabel walked into the room. I shut my laptop immediately, but she found the page in my history and asked who Michelle was. I told her."

Why would Mom reach out to Mandy? She must have wanted to get in touch with me! If I'd only known the Facebook link came from Mandy and not from Iz doing some random research, I wouldn't have killed myself. Not if there was a possibility Mom wanted to connect with me. I never stopped loving her or missing her. I just hid it from Dad because, even as a five-year-old, I knew it would make him sad if he thought he wasn't enough for me. All that time I wished for a mom, I actually had one, but she didn't want me. Then later, she did, but it was too late. This is so freakin' tragic I can't stand it.

Greg squints at Mandy as if suddenly the kitchen light is too dim for him to recognize his own wife. "You told her?"

"I had no choice. But I made her swear not to say a word to Nicole."

"And you seriously believed she wouldn't?"

"What was I supposed to do, Greg? She asked me, point-blank, 'Who is this?'"

"You should have lied," he says without hesitation. "Made up some BS. That would have been a whole lot smarter."

"I couldn't lie to our daughter."

"What are you talking about? We've been lying to her about Michelle for years. And by the way, you were fine hiding the fact that Michelle contacted you from me and Mike, which is the same as lying."

"No, it's not."

Mandy's and Greg's auras spark and crackle at each other like red lightening under clouds. Contempt. Resentment. Frustration. Dad's aura fans out in waves of black. Blocked grief. Unleashed rage. Revenge.

"You screwed up big time, Mandy," Dad says, his voice colder than I've ever heard it. "You made things so much worse. Greg's right. You should have kept your mouth shut and come to me right away. Then I could have told my daughter the truth about her mother."

Mandy snaps. "If you'd told her years ago, none of this would have happened."

Stop blaming him! It's not his fault or yours. It's not Alex's fault. Or Cassie's. Or Kyle's. Or Iz's. So just stop fighting!

Silence presses down on the room like a garbage compactor. Dad's hands rest motionless on the keyboard. Mandy and Greg slump in their seats. No one makes eye contact. No one moves. It's as if they've all reached their limits and can't stomach the possibility that there may be more facts to find. There are. The Dad link is still unopened on the screen. My text to him is in that file. I don't remember what I wrote, and I sure don't remember what he replied, but it's obvious from his miserable expression that he remembers everything.

Dad slowly slides the cursor over the link and clicks. The file opens. "The last texts are between Nicole and me." He reads from the screen, his voice breaking. "At 12:20 she texted me and said, 'Why did you lie about Mom?'"

Of course, I would ask him that. What did he answer?

"That completely threw me off. How was I supposed to answer a question like that in a text? I knew some day she'd probably find out, and I'd have to explain everything, but I wasn't prepared. I . . . I was working on the Gallagher's ceiling. Sue Gallagher was standing at the foot of the ladder, complaining about how long the job was taking when Nicole's text came in. I didn't care if Sue thought I was rude or whatever, I texted right back. I said, 'Where are you?' She didn't answer. I texted again. 'Nikki, tell me where you are, sweetheart. I'll come and meet you and we'll talk about this.' No answer. I called her. She didn't pick up, so I left voice mail, begging her to call me back, but she didn't."

I'm sorry I didn't call you back, Dad. I was too shocked and angry to talk on the phone. I thought you wouldn't tell me the truth and I didn't want to hear more lies.

"She must have been so upset with me," he says to no one in particular. The tears come. He doesn't bother to wipe them away. I cry with him and *for* him and for me. No. Enough. I don't have time for this. I need the truth.

Nicole

WHY DIDN'T DAD ever tell me what really happened? Did he think I couldn't handle it? What was the story behind Mom splitting? Why didn't she take me with her? Why didn't she ever come back to see me? The only way to talk to Dad is when he's asleep, so once again I push through the silver kelp forest of his dreaming mind.

He doesn't seem surprised to see me standing at the top of the curved wooden steps at the southwest end of Phoenix Lake as he makes his way up. Puffing, he nods, as if my being there were the most natural thing. We fall into step and hike along a high narrow trail, the still lake shines below, visible through the pines growing almost right to water's edge. I skip the intros. No need for "Hey, Dad. How's it going?" because I already know. It's a good thing dreams let you get right to the point.

"I understand that you made up the story about Mom to protect me when I was little, but why didn't you tell me truth when I was older?"

"I was scared you'd be mad at me for lying. So I kept putting it off because I was worried I wouldn't know how to comfort you without a fairy tale. You deserved to know the truth. That way you could have reached out to her if you wanted to. Nikki, I'm so sorry."

What's that sappy old movie about the dying girl who says, "Love is never having to say you're sorry"? Such complete and total BS. Dad loves me and I love him but that doesn't keep him from apologizing. He needs to say the words, for himself, and he knows that I need to hear them. I guess love is always saying you're sorry when you mess up, and especially when you've done something to hurt someone you love. They should do an updated remake of that movie. Dad's right, though. If he'd told me about Mom when I was alive, I would have been so mad that he lied to me. I'm still mad.

I sit on a tree stump and trace angry zigzags in the dirt with a pointy stick. Dad watches me closely, as if he's worried about what else I might do. The stick is long and sharp. I grip it tightly. He knows this is a dream, but he's probably thinking about the non-negotiable truth: *Lies come back to bite you.* Or poke you in the eye. Or stab you through the heart. But not all lies are created equal. There are lies meant to keep you in the dark so you'll trust the liar while he uses you. I'm talking about you, Alex the Skunk! Wait. I did the same thing to Cassie and Kyle. That makes me a skunk, too. But not Dad. He lied so I'd feel loved instead of feeling rejected. Nothing skunky about that. I look up at him. He holds out his arms like an open doorway. I drop the stick and step out of the darkness, into the sunlight. I bury my face in his shirt. I feel his heartbeat, strong, steady, reliable. I'm home where I belong. I know I can't stay forever, but I can stay for now.

"Did Mom know you told me that she was dead?"

He seems surprised by the question, but not all that surprised. Like when you notice the slime ring on the inside of the cottage cheese container but you convince yourself it will taste fine if you only avoid the edge. When you dip in your spoon and it tastes revolting, you're not really surprised.

"At the time she left I told her that was my plan. She didn't say anything one way or another, so I took that to mean that the lie was okay with her."

"I guess she was glad to be rid of me."

He shakes his head sadly. "I don't think so. She wanted to get rid of *me*. She fell in love with someone else. Of course, that's no excuse for turning her back on you. That was so . . . wrong."

"The guy she hooked up with, did he hate kids or something? Is that why she stayed away?"

He hesitates a moment and shakes his head. "I . . . I don't know."

"Where'd she meet him, anyway? On one of those sites for cheaters?"

"Nikki, your mother would never . . . "

"How could you defend her, Dad, after what she did to me? Do you still love her or something?" I'm shouting. He winces. I don't know why I never thought of this before, but it's obvious now. I wasn't Michelle's only casualty.

Poor Dad. All these years and he's still in love with someone who doesn't care. I know what that's like. That's why he never remarried. Never dated. I'm about to apologize for throwing his feelings for Mom in his face. No time. Dad's yelling now. "Why are you giving *me* a hard time? I'm the parent who stayed. Doesn't that mean anything?"

He reaches out to me, but I won't let him touch me now. Part of me wants to reassure him that I love him and appreciate everything he did for me. Another part of me wants him to stop defending her. She doesn't deserve it. Not for what she did. It's all so messed up and unfair. I'm pissed, but not at him.

I kiss his cheek. "I love you, Dad. That hasn't changed. It'll never change."

He nods. He gets it. That's all I can do here.

But I'm not done with Mom. I'm so pissed at *her* and so pissed that I can't tell her how pissed I am. This is useless. I'm done with this dream.

It's cold out here in the backyard under the magnolia tree. The stars, with no competition from the fingernail moon, put on an impressive show. I pick out Pisces, the two fish, tied together with a silver chord, swimming in opposite directions at the same time. Dad wanted me to know that one because of my birthday, March 17, and because he said I was like those fish, the way I would sometimes pull myself in two different directions, not sure which way I wanted to go.

The only light inside the house shines from my bedroom. I float up and peek in the window. Dad lies on my bed, staring at the ceiling, as much of a lost soul as I am. I wish I could help him. Thank God Iz burned my journal so he can't read any more of my rants. I'll stay out of his dreams from now on, too. I wish he could help me, but he can't answer my questions about Mom. I've got to go to the source.

Isabel

MOM AND DAD barely talk to each other or to me. The negativity in the house is so thick. Moving from room to room feels like walking through sludge into a strong wind, dragging a fifty-pound rock.

I need to fix this with my most powerful conflict resolution ritual. Which candle should I light? Ah. The gray one, the color of neutrality and balance, best for spells that neutralize negative energy. I place a few drops of bergamot oil mid-way up the candle. I focus on my clear intention as I rub the oil upward to the candle's rim, repeating the motion again and again. With my athame, I carve my initials, Mom's, and Dad's into the wax. This is necessary since we are all contributing to the negative energy flowing among us. Breathing in, I bring in peace. Breathing out, I let go of mistrust. I light the candle, gaze into the flame, and chant,

"Goddess Eternal, bring compassion, respect
To my family, so we may re-connect
With love, not anger. With love, not pain.
May resolution come. May harmony reign."

The last few days have been extremely unsettling. Saturday morning, Mike called and asked for Nic's journal. If I had burned it like I promised, I could have told him I didn't have it. That would not have been a lie. But I hadn't burned it yet, so I gave it back to him, and because I didn't destroy it, all the negativity Nic put into the journal still exists in the world.

Sunday night, Michelle posted to Nic's memorial page: "Nicole, my angel, I want you to know that I am eternally sorry for not reaching out to you directly when I had the chance. I can only imagine what a shock it must have been to hear about me from Isabel, bless her heart. But we are commanded, in Isaiah 43 verse 18 to 'Forget the former things. Do not dwell on the past. Now you are safe in the arms of Jesus.'"

I don't know if Mom saw the post. I hope not. Gabby definitely did. Monday morning, she rushed me in the library. My third chakra flared and I sensed bad intentions.

"Everyone knows," she says.

"Knows what?"

"Everything you did."

She was right. People I've barely made eye contact with in the past stopped me in the hall to say I am the worst friend in the world. That's not one hundred percent accurate, but there is truth in it. I have betrayed my Wiccan oath to spread joy, peace, and harmony. By Monday lunch, texts with the same negative energy flooded my phone. Tuesday was worse. People piled on, on Facebook and Instagram and TikTok.

Wednesday, I stayed home from school and told Mom I had stomach problems. Not a lie. I spent the morning in and out of the bathroom. I drank plenty of water because diarrhea will dehydrate you and dehydration leads to stress and I don't need more stress. I deleted all the texts, blocked all the numbers. I deleted my accounts, shut down my devices and kept them off.

I sit in front of my altar and cast a Tarot card reading for myself. Nothing remarkable turns up until I flip over the eighth card, my situation card. The VIII of Cups. A red-cloaked figure walks away from eight unevenly stacked cups in the foreground, toward a forbidding mountain. The card represents abandonment, loneliness, walking away from a bad situation. It can also mean searching for the truth.

Or telling the truth.

What feels like a tornado of iron nails spirals through my gut. Uhhhh. I pull the blanket off my bed and wrap it around me.

The Ninth card represents my hopes and fears. I flip it over. The Magician stands in front of his altar, his powerful tools spread before him. Do I let hope energize my tools to bring me closer to Nic's spirit? Or do I shut my gifts away forever because I am afraid to face her?

The tenth and final card I draw is the outcome card. The Moon. A full moon and a crescent within it. Twin towers. Two howling wolves separated by a stream. This card is so powerful, it vibrates in my hand. What does it represent? A time when things are not what they appear to be. Is it a full moon or a crescent? Are the wolves howling in unison or at each other? This card speaks of a misunderstanding that might be based on a truth that I can't admit to myself.

I carefully gather the deck, slide it back into its leather case and crawl into bed. I can't block out the truth of the cards. If Nic and I are the wolves and this is the expected outcome, where do we go from here?

I pretend to sleep while Mom and Dad have dinner. How can I use my gifts for good? How can I learn what I need to know if I stay in Veraz surrounded by memories of Nic? Where is she now? What is she going through? Will she ever forgive me?

The knock on the door interrupts my endless questions.

"Isabel?"

"May we come in?"

Mom and Dad. If I say nothing, they'll leave me alone. I don't want to be alone. "Okay."

They come in, Dad leading the way. He pulls out my desk chair. Mom sits on the edge of my bed, studying me the way she did when I was little and not feeling well. She used to press her lips against my forehead, like a kiss, only she'd stay there for a full minute. She said she didn't need a thermometer to tell whether I had a fever. She was always right. I thought it was magik. She doesn't kiss me now. Just rests her hand on my forehead. Her fingers are cold.

"No fever," she reports. "That's good."

She couldn't ever feel what's burning inside me.

Mom looks at Dad. They silently warn each to keep things calm for my benefit. "We need to have a family meeting," Dad says.

I feel like a hermit crab without a shell. I'd like to hide under the covers, but I remember my oath. You can't make positive change by doing nothing.

I drag myself into a sitting position. "What do you want to talk about?"

"You." Dad pulls the chair closer to the bed. "Aside from the upset stomach, what's going on?"

I want to tell them, but I can't take any more of their blame and judgment so I don't say anything. Dad has never been particularly intuitive, but he seems to sense why I'm hesitating and he doesn't push. Instead, he rests his warm hand on mine and leaves it there. He's never done it before. It's a Mom move. Hope sparks in my heart chakra.

"You can talk to us, kiddo."

Dad's eyes are kind. Mom's lips are pressed together, like she's holding her breath, sure that what I'm about to say will break her heart.

I count to twelve.

Goddess Eternal, oh wise one
Truth be told
The moment has come.
It's the only way.
Help me be strong.
By telling the truth
I can right the wrong.

"I . . . I sent a video to Nic . . . when she was up on the water tower." I stop and inhale, but I can't fill my lungs. It's like I'm standing at high altitude where the air is too thin to breathe.

"Yes. We know about that. From Nicole's phone records. Why did you send it?" Dad's voice is calm. He's not accusing me. He wants to understand me. I need understanding.

I hold on to his eyes and continue. "I felt like Nic needed to know the truth about Alex before she got hurt. But . . . I should have waited. I knew where she was. I knew that the video would upset her. But I didn't think she'd blame *me*. I was trying to help her. But she wouldn't listen. She accused me of being a bad friend and that just really hurt. I . . . wanted to hurt her back. So I sent her her mom's Facebook link."

Mom inhales sharply. I expect an explosion, but it doesn't come. "You knew about that too?"

Dad and Mom nod slowly, painfully. I see disappointment in their eyes. My parents are ashamed of me. My stomach hurts. I hug myself. Mom folds her hands in her lap and closes her eyes. Her aura is dark green. Dull orange. Sadness. Regret. Same as me. I can feel her trying to connect psychically. She's trying to take on my sadness, add it to her own, carry it for both of us. I won't let her. This is between me and Nic.

"Everyone knows what I did. It's all over social. They're calling me . . . a murderer." I choke on the word.

"What a heartless thing to say. You didn't murder anyone. Don't even think it. Nicole made a very bad decision. No one should blame you."

"But I am to blame."

Dad shakes his head. "No. You're not."

"I was a terrible friend. I wish I could take it all back, but it's too late."

"I understand," Mom says. "I called Mike, and I apologized for what I did and didn't do. We had a good talk. He doesn't blame me or you. But I still feel responsible."

Dad rests a hand on Mom's arm, "I'm sorry I turned on you, Mandy. That wasn't fair."

Mom takes his hand and mine. "Losing Nicole is so hard. For all of us."

I wish this conversation was over and we could just be here and feel close to each other. But I'm not finished. I have to tell them one more thing. I don't know if it will help, but I have to be honest. "Nicole is still upset with me."

"How do you know that?" Dad wants to know.

"I've talked to her. I've seen her. She's been here."

Mom and Dad glance at each other and back at me. They don't say anything but it's clear they think I'm losing it. I'm not. Am I?

"Sweetheart, Dad and I have been talking and we think it makes sense to temporarily move to the cabin in Mt. Shasta, just until this blows over. It's cold up there now, but they haven't had much snow so we can take hikes. It's always so lovely. Fortunately, Dad and I can work from anywhere and you can home-school for the remainder of the year. What do you think?"

I'm ready to leave Veraz. Mount Shasta, a dormant snow-capped volcano, the center of the Earth's root chakra and a natural center of pure, healing energy could ground me. Calm me. Quiet my mind. Maybe from there I could reconnect with Nic in a much more positive way.

"Let's do it," I say.

Mom and Dad flash smiles at each other. She looks like she's about to cry with joy. "We're so glad you like the idea. How soon can you get ready?"

Magikly speaking, it matters which day we move. If I'm moving to make a new start, I choose a day when the moon is new or waxing. If I want to get away from a negative situation, I move when the moon is full or waning. Since I want to make a new start *and* get away from negativity, it doesn't matter.

I tell them I can be packed by tomorrow night. "How about if we leave Friday?"

My stomach is more settled this morning. There is music in how Mom and Dad call to each other, "Should we take this?" "Do we need this?" "What do you think?" I quickly pack up my camera and all my tech but as I turn my heart to each element of my Wiccan world, I slow down. I carefully wrap each candle, along with my incense, incense holder, special matches, white sage smudge sticks, Book of Spells, calligraphy pens, ink, athame, tarot cards, carved carrier box, casting cloth and runes, pendulum and pendulum mat, ritual bowls, herb canisters. I haven't used my talking board since the last time Nic was here, and I'm not sure when I'll use it again, but of course I'm bringing it along with my beautiful planchette. My Wiccan treasures fill two large cardboard boxes. I pad the empty space between them with scarves so nothing jostles around during the move.

I put my books in the third box, clothing in the fourth. The fifth box is reserved for accessories. Hats, gloves, earrings, rings, bracelets, necklaces, amulets.

I write a description of each box's contents on the side with a purple marker. Purple represents calm nerves, self-esteem, life purpose, transformation, divine guidance. I need all of that.

I haven't found my crystal, but it's time to let it go and move on.

Dad said it was a good thing the Shasta house is furnished, so anything we need from home will fit in the car. My first chakra buzzes uncomfortably. The bed in the Shasta house emits an uncomfortable energy that I've never been able to dispel.

"I want to bring my own bed. And my bookshelves, and desk, and altar table, and my planter box, the one with the sage." I don't mention the dead crow.

Mom and Dad agree, in spite of the extra expense. They don't even try to convince me I should leave anything behind. It's nice how supportive they can be when they're being supportive.

The movers will drive with my stuff and the other large items Mom and Dad have just decided are also essential. I wish I could leave Nic behind, but Karma always follows.

CASSIE

I'VE BEEN PUTTING in triple shifts at Child Caring since it's the only place that takes my mind off Alex. He hasn't been in school since last Friday. Kyle said Alex's poison oak is so bad his eyes are swollen shut. It's even inside his ears and mouth. Ugh. Home alone, itching like crazy and popping special, high-dose steroid pills. Poor baby. I have to quit calling him that. He's not my baby anymore. I've stayed mad at him for longer than this, but he's never been mad at me for this long. And for what? Like he had nothing to do with it, and it's all *my* fault? I still think about *us* every minute at school. I keep my bitch face on and pretend I broke up with him, not that it matters. No one dares to mention his name around me.

No one talks about Nicole, either. They took away the banner and all the stuff around her locker. I don't think about her at school, but I can't stop the weird dreams. Like the one last night.

Nicole and I walk through the woods at Sorich. We stop under the cluster of pines where Alex and I made out. She points to the spot. "It was here, wasn't it?"

She doesn't sound mad or jealous so I nod.

The sun beams through the branches like a spotlight. I find Kyle's piano accompaniment of "Titanium" on my phone and pump up the volume. We step into the light and sing. We sound awesome enough to be a four-chair turn on The Voice.

A squirrel runs between us and dashes up the tree trunk. Nicole chases after it. Climbing with no hands! The two of them scamper higher, jumping from branch to branch. I stand at the base of the tree, looking up, and wonder out loud, "How is she doing that?"

The squirrel runs to the end of a narrow branch that sways under its weight. Nicole crawls out after him. I call to her, "Nicole, come down!"

She smiles and waves. The branch snaps. She falls. I scream.

I woke up panting so loudly Lola put her front paws on the edge of my bed and licked my wrist. It was too early to get up, but I got up anyway. I knew I was done sleeping, and if I just stayed in bed I'd keep seeing her fall.

Pre-school playground drama beats obsessing about ex-boyfriends and violent death. Huh. Gray clouds. Looks like rain. Good. Something else to think about.

Jade, a new girl wearing a pink jacket, sits on the ground holding the back of her leg and screaming. Angel sits on the climbing structure, watching Jade like she's a cartoon character that Angel hasn't decided is a good guy or a bad guy.

"What happened?" I ask Jade.

"She pinched me really hard." Jade sobs and points at Angel who looks at me as if she has no idea what the girl is talking about. Yeah, right. Angel's fingernails left impressive dents in Jade's leg. Luckily there's no blood.

I hug Jade and wipe her nose with a clean tissue from my pocket. "You're okay. Oh, look. There's an open swing. Want to grab it before it rains?"

The new girl races toward the swing but not before sticking her tongue out at Angel.

"I want to swing, too," Angel whines.

"I'm sure you do, but we need some Let's-Talk-About-It time. Help me bring the trikes and big wheels into the shed."

Angel climbs down from the structure as slowly as possible. She lets me know that she thinks swinging is more fun than putting away playground equipment. She seems surprised when I agree with her. She stops moping.

With one trike left on the playground, the rain starts. The other kids and staff hurry into the building, but Angel jumps on the trike, her legs flung out to the side like wings. "Zoom me, Miss Cassie."

I run, pushing the trike from behind. Angel shrieks with joy, like she's flying. I shriek with her, and for that one moment I don't think about anything else.

I close the shed door and let Angel click the lock shut. We head back inside. "Why did you hurt Jade? You know that's not okay."

Angel shrugs. "She was in my way."

"Not a good reason. You need to apologize to her."

With the official "I'm sorry" and "I forgive you" over and done with, both girls help me set up snacks. We set out hand-decorated place mats, napkins, apple juice boxes, and put four carrot sticks and four wheat crackers with peanut butter on each paper plate.

"Look, Miss Cassie," Angel says. "We're all co-operating."

The three of us high-five each other.

Still smiling, I call the other kids over to the table. Angel and Jade sit beside one another, and look inside each other's wide-open mouths, comparing chewed-up peanut butter and graham crackers. Gross, but cute.

At the end of my shift, I grab a stick of string cheese from Mr. Robert's fridge and clip Lola's leash onto her collar. Mr. Robert is on the phone, but I feel him wrapping up so I hang back and pretend to be having a hard time peeling off the plastic cheese wrapper.

He puts down the phone. "Hello, Miss Cassie. I hope you had a rewarding shift. How can I be of service to you?"

I must be getting used to this place because the way he talks doesn't seem weird anymore. It also seems normal that he always knows when I want to talk to him without me saying anything.

"Uh, my community service hours end this week, so I'm wondering if maybe I can keep on working here, for pay, like the regular part-time staff."

"Your time is up already? Hm." Mr. Robert says this like he's trying to get me to believe he doesn't know exactly when I started and when I'm supposed to be done. He takes off his glasses and carefully lays them on his desk, then opens the shiny black eyeglass case, takes out a soft gray cloth and unfolds it. He sprays something from a little plastic bottle onto the lenses and gently wipes them dry. Buzz-Kill wears glasses when she watches TV. She never cleans them. I didn't know it was a thing.

"We've all appreciated having you here, Miss Cassie. You have proven to be a great asset to our team."

He continues wiping his glasses, every now and then holding them up to the light. I guess he's making sure he's gotten rid of all the smudges because they would *not* be a great asset.

"So can I have a job?"

He slowly puts his glasses back on, folds the cloth, puts it inside the case, and shuts it with a snap. "I will consider your proposal."

"Oh. Okay. Thanks." Lola and I head for the door.

"How are things going otherwise, Miss Cassie? Outside of the center, I mean."

I turn, not sure if I should sit down again or what. "Okay, I guess."

Something tickles the back of my throat, like when I have a cold, but I don't. It's been happening whenever I think about Nicole. I clear my throat, but it's still there, like a guilty reminder or something. Isabel has plenty to be guilty about. I don't. He was *my* boyfriend until he broke up with me. Technically I made out with my ex. Nothing wrong with that. Neither of us was with anyone else. Except . . . he kinda was. He'd already asked Nicole out, and she said yes. As soon as he broke up with me, he was technically *her* boyfriend. Why didn't I think of that? I did. For a second. Then I stopped thinking about it. I made out with Nicole's boyfriend. I'm guilty.

Mr. Robert waits for me to say more. The tickle makes it hard to talk, even though I haven't tried yet. I clear my throat louder this time. It's not helping. He opens the fridge and takes out a pear/grape combo juice box and hands it to me. How does he know that's my favorite?

"It will soothe your throat."

I make a big deal of poking the straw through the top of the box so he won't notice that I'm freaking out. I drink the whole thing without looking at him, crush the box, and drop it into the trash where it hits the bottom with a quiet thud and lies there, all alone.

"Remember that girl I told you about? The one who killed herself?"

He nods slowly. The tickle is worse. This time it's harder to stop clearing my throat. Maybe I should stop talking. He hands me a bottle of water from the crate beside the coffee maker. I shake my head and manage to swallow.

"Well, the day she died, my boyfriend broke up with me to be with her. I lied to the police about that. I wasn't under oath or anything. But still."

I'm talking fast. Just want to get it over with. Don't stop for a breath. Don't let him ask me anything. Just keep talking.

"Right after he broke up with me, I came on to him and he . . . responded. She was waiting for him on the water tower, but I swear I didn't know that at the time. I'm not sure what I would have done if I had known, but I know for sure if I hadn't kissed him, we wouldn't have made out, and she wouldn't have jumped."

Mr. Robert sits on the edge of his desk facing me. I know what's coming. He's going to say he doesn't want someone like me working here. He's going to tell me to get out right now. I download my bitch face so when he says it, he'll think I don't care.

He folds his hands and looks down at them for a moment, then back at me.

"I appreciate your courage, Miss Cassie. It's not always easy to own up to what we've done, especially the things we're not particularly proud of. I respect you for that. However . . ."

Here it comes. My bitch face starts slipping so I look away.

"... I respectfully disagree with your assumption that you know for sure this girl wouldn't have taken her own life if you had acted differently. You *don't* know that. She made a choice and so did you. She doesn't get any more choices, but you do."

What choices do I have?

His phone rings. He glances at it. "Excuse me, Miss Cassie, I have to take this." He swipes his phone. "Hi, Britta. How are you? Yes, I have that information all ready for you. May I put you on hold for a moment, please?"

He looks at me through spotless lenses. His eyes shine. "I'd appreciate the chance to continue our conversation about your proposal. Would you and your sister like to join me and my wife for dinner this evening at our home?"

No one has ever invited me to eat at their house. If he was going to fire me, he wouldn't go to all that trouble. But he might. What the hell? Judging from his lunches, dinner will be a whole lot better than nachos.

"Okay."

"Excellent. I'll text you our address. Enjoy the rest of your afternoon."

He pats Lola and hands me a package of graham crackers and a couple of dog treats.

"Thanks," I say. The tickle is gone. I stick the goodies in my jacket pocket and Lola and I head for Sorich Park.

Nicole

ANY TIME SOMEONE would mention their mom, I'd zone out. Having a mom, with all the stuff that goes with it, had nothing to do with me. It's been so long since I've thought about her. Who knows if any of my random memories were real? But I've got to remember something that we actually did together. Maybe I could use that like a point on a map to help me locate her. Otherwise, I'll never learn the truth and I'm going to end up ... Stop. Focus. Maybe I could remember what it felt like to be with her. But I don't even remember what I called her. Mom? No. Not as two-year-old. Mommy? Possibly, but I don't think ... *Mama!* That's it. A long-buried memory fills my entire mental movie screen. It's solid and bright and so alive.

I sit on Mama's knees, facing her, as she pretends to sleep in the white rocking chair by the window. The breeze plays with the wind chime. Nervous and excited, I slowly reach out with one chubby little finger and touch her closed lips. Instantly her mouth flies open and she leans forward like she's going to bite me. I squeal with delight and pull my hand away as fast as I can. She flashes a smile. We laugh and laugh.

The space behind my heart tingles and my lips vibrate with a present time smile. The buzz spreads from my cheeks to my scalp. A warm wind swirls around me. The air smells of furniture polish and dried flowers. Light pours through tall narrow windows of colored glass, illuminating a galaxy of tiny dust particles. What am I doing in a church?

Dozens of short white candles flicker at the base of a hand-painted wooden statue of a mournful-looking woman wearing a blue shawl over a long white dress. I think she's supposed to be Jesus' mom. Virgin Mary? A sharp dry sound like the snap of fingers echoes off the walls. I spin around. A spikey-haired woman at a side table lights a candle and shakes out the match. She places her flickering candle among the others at Mary's feet. The candlelight illuminates the woman's face from below. It's Michelle. Looking older than her Facebook profile, but still. Her aura is murky, indigo blue. I saw the same color at the funeral in the back of the room. She was there! She never once showed up for any of my birthdays, but she didn't want to miss my funeral. How's that for balls?

Michelle sits in the front row, smooths the wrinkles from her denim miniskirt and absently touches her plastic hoop earring, a screaming shade of radioactive green. Soulful face upturned, she makes the sign of the cross as if she's posing for a religious work of art. She presses her palms together and closes her eyes. I hover beside her. She smells from cigarettes. I touch her shoulder. No reaction. Her frequency is higher than Iz's. Maybe that's because she's praying or something? I won't try to materialize, too hard and too much energy to sustain, but maybe I can talk to her by tapping into an audio-only frequency.

"Michelle."

She gasps, sitting bolt upright. She hears me.

She gazes at the ceiling, her eyes sweeping the overhead beams. "Is that you, Lord?" she whispers.

"No. It's *me*. Nicole."

She crosses herself again, and races out the back door of the church, down the stone steps and into the street, nearly colliding with a guy parking his motorcycle.

Wild-eyed, she speed-walks around the corner to a dirty red car with dented front and back bumpers. She fumbles with her keys, drops them, scoops them up and finally manages to unlock the door and slide inside. I pass through the roof and drift above the passenger seat. An overflowing ashtray sticks to the dashboard next to a little plastic Jesus. The air stinks. I wish she'd open the window. She shakily lights a cigarette and inhales deeply, blowing the smoke in my direction. Holding the cigarette between tight lips, she turns the key, squeezes the steering wheel, and peels away from the curb, tires screeching. No signal or anything. She darts into a strip mall parking lot and cuts a sharp left into the first open spot, overshooting the curb and hitting a trash can before slamming the brakes and cutting the engine.

If I weren't already dead, I'd never ride with her.

She takes several long drags on the cigarette and side-blows smoke in my face. The smell makes me sick. I could roll down the window, but that would freak her out. She bats down the sun visor and talks to her reflection in the mirror.

"Everything's okay. A bit too much religious devotion just then put me over the edge for a moment. But I'm fine now. Just fine."

"You're not fine, Michelle. You're the worst mother ever. If I cared enough to feel anything, I'd hate you."

Her yelp unleashes a string of sobs. I don't want to feel sorry for her, but I shouldn't have come on so strong. She was a terrible mom, but if I don't dial it down, she'll get defensive and probably answer every question with a lie.

"Oh Lord, please forgive me for I have sinned. My very worst sin has come back to hold me accountable in your eyes. I do not shy from any punishment you deem appropriate, but please know that I am repentant. Truly I am."

She's lying already. I'm so pissed I could strangle her, but I've gotta push my emotions aside and keep my mind clear or

I won't get anything helpful from her. And it's not like I've got any backups at this point.

I try the AhhhOhhhUmmm thing, silently. Not sure if it works that way, but after a minute I feel a little less homicidal. "I'll only be a couple of minutes, Michelle, then you can get back to your life. I just need the answer to a simple question. Why did you disappear after you left Dad? And why didn't you stay in touch with me?"

She snuffs out the cigarette in the ashtray, crowding out old butts, and releasing a shower of ash onto the dashboard. She leans in and whispers to plastic Jesus, "Lord, I know you want me to tell her the truth and to talk to her directly, as if she were sitting right here in the car with me. Okay. I will." She turns to the passenger seat and looks right through me. "You were my baby girl, Nini. I didn't want to leave you. I swear I didn't. But your father kicked me out of the house."

"No, he didn't."

"I swear to God, he did. And after that, he wouldn't let me see you."

She sounds like she means it. Her aura proves it. But maybe she's a really good liar, like Cassie. I don't know what to believe. "You were trolling websites for cheaters."

"That is a lie. I didn't meet Jeffrey online. We met at a café on an open mike night. He's also a musician. We fell in love. We got married."

"Are you still married to him?"

No answer. I guess that means no.

"I was wrong to break my wedding vows. I did a lot of praying about it. But your father should not have made up that ridiculous lie about me dying of cancer. Was he thinking you'd never find out the truth? The man's such an idiot."

"Leave Dad out of it, Michelle."

"Aw, honey, can't you, just once, call me Mom?"

"Why would I do that? Moms take care of their kids. You left. You didn't fight for me. You're my mother. That's just biology."

She sighs deeply and shakes her head. "I was eighteen and pregnant. Only two years older than you. I liked your dad, I might have even loved him, not that I really understood what that meant, but I wasn't ready to get married. Abortion wasn't an option for me. So we got married, and you were born. I always knew I wasn't cut out to be a mom. I was too self-centered. That didn't change. I loved you more than anything, but I couldn't stop thinking about everything I was missing out on. You were such a needy little thing. It's amazing I found any time for my own thoughts. I didn't have a minute to myself. I swear I felt like I was drowning. That's why I had to leave, otherwise I would have gone crazy. I knew your dad would take great care of you, all on his own. And he was a good dad, wasn't he?"

I nod because loss and longing clog my throat. Then I remember that she can only hear me, so I manage to whisper. "He was the best."

"There, you see? I was right. You were raised by the better parent. By leaving, I gave you what you needed, and I had the chance to pursue my dream of playing music in a serious way, not just playing Michael Row Your Boat Ashore at church once a week. Do you remember me playing guitar and singing to you?"

I wish I could lie, just to hurt her, but her singing is one of the few things I remember. "Yes."

"I know it's hard to forgive me for leaving you, but you've got to believe me when I say I wanted to stay in touch, and I would have if your father hadn't blocked me at every turn."

"Why would he do that?"

She doesn't hesitate. "He was hurt when I trashed the marriage and he wanted to punish me. I couldn't deny my infidelity, and I didn't have any money for a lawyer. I thought he'd get over it and let me see you. I prayed to Jesus to soften his heart. That never happened. I guess he wanted you to forget that you ever had a mom."

"No, he didn't. He made up beautiful stories about you. We baked a cake for you and sang to you every year on May 11th. See, I remember your birthday even though you never remembered mine."

"I'm so sorry, Nini. I mean Niki."

"Don't call me that. Only my dad gets to call me that. And I'm sure he wouldn't have kept you from seeing me without a really good reason. So, what was it?"

"I told you, he was hurt and I . . ." Her voice trails off.

"What aren't you telling me?"

DING.

A text comes in on Michelle's phone. She fishes it out of her purse.

Shelby>

Hey. It's 4:15. Where
are you Mom?

Knives press against the right side of my head and my world shrinks to three letters on a screen. Mom.

Nicole

I'M BACK IN my room but I can't stay long. I can't imagine they'll let me get away with biting a Vestie. I pace my dorm room floor expecting Quinn or some other creep will barge in at any moment and drag me to Substation Sixteen. I'm not going to wait around for that to happen, but I need a place to think about what I just remembered. I can barely keep myself from sticking my head out my imaginary window and howling. Michelle has *another* daughter! Something tells me I already knew that, but reading the text ripped away the bandage I must have slapped over this memory and blew a new hole in my brain, which has so many holes at this point it's amazing I can think at all. Still, I don't have the answer to the one remaining question: *Did I jump?*

I've got to go back to the tower to find out. Not the actual tower, but the tower in my memory. The tower as it was on that day, in those last moments.

Grace pulled my Phoenix Lake memories and projected them so I could *be* there. I never tried mocking up memories solid enough to walk into, but I bet I could do it. I can astral travel, dream tour, do telekinesis, even materialize . . . kinda.

Mocking up my memory of the water tower can't be harder than any of that.

It isn't. The tower barely starts coming into focus on my mental movie screen and I'm here. Just like that. I stomp on the roof a few times to make sure I won't fall through. The echo rumbles beneath my feet. Nice job on the obvious stuff. Let's see if I remembered little details of that day. The random shades of green paint cover the roof. Check. The freeway noises hum below. Check. Dogs bark in nearby neighborhoods. The breeze, minty with eucalyptus, sails in from the north. A crow slices the air, squawks loudly, and lands in the tree at the trailhead. Check. Check. Check.

A whole lot happened up here on my last day. Remembering the final moments isn't going to be fun, but my countdown timer says three hours left. Better get on with it.

I don't need to replay how I felt waiting for Alex, or what it was like watching the make-out video. I already know everything I need to about my fight with Iz. I could start with the newsflash that Michelle isn't dead and Dad lied. No. Been there. Fast-forward. I text Dad. He texts back. He calls. I ignore him. Not in the mood to start a long, emotional conversation without being home. Skip all that.

I might as well start by clicking on Michelle's FB link. The sick urge to swipe through her photos overwhelms me. The voice in my head says, "Don't." But I can't resist. I study a picture of a girl grinning at her massive birthday cake. The post is from June 24th. Michelle writes: "Happy 14th birthday, my beautiful Shelby. I am the luckiest mom in the world to have you as my daughter!"

Shelby was born on June 24, fourteen years ago. According to Dad's story, Mom "died" on November 20 the year before, which must have been the day she walked out on us. I count on my fingers. Skip November. Start with December. January. February. March. April. May. June. I count and recount, clinging to the insane idea that seven is not actually seven. Screw that. Michelle had an affair and got pregnant. That's why Dad kicked her out. That part of what she told me was true, but everything else was BS. How she didn't want to be a mom and wasn't cut out for it. Lies.

I sit on the roof of the water tower, hunched in a ball, trying to get small enough to fit somewhere, but there is no place for me. The world closes in, and I gulp air, never getting enough, like the oxygen has suddenly gone missing. I am a punctured balloon that will never fill up and float again. My mom left, and when she finally had the chance to own up to why she turned her back on me, she lied to my face. She said she loved me, but she had better things to do with her life than being a mom. Lies. She wanted to be a mom. Shelby's mom. Not mine.

I wish I could haunt her for what she did to me. Show up in nightmares so scary no amount of church candles would protect her. But if I did that, the Mentors would probably skip my Evaluation altogether and send me directly to Sixteen. Not worth the risk. Forgive and forget? I don't think so. I don't care about Alex anymore. He loves Cassie, not me. End of story. But I can't get over this.

The same obnoxious crow keeps squawking. Maybe it's laughing at me because I'm the best joke around. I'm about to scream at him to shut up, but he flies off before I get the chance. I guess he's got better things to do than waste time watching a loser.

Everyone's got better things to do. Except me. I crawl to the edge of the roof that's next to the top of the ladder. The world below wobbles out of focus. I turn and back up toward the ledge. Reaching behind me I clutch the handrail, the rusty bits scratch my palms. I lower my right leg, feeling for the top step with the toe of my shoe. There! I stand on the step with both feet, clutching the railing. I peek down the length of the ladder and inhale sharply as I shut my eyes. I'm such a very long way from the ground.

I lift my face to the sun and lean back. Too far. I sway. I shout, I grab for the handrails. Too late. I free-fall, screaming. The concrete rushes up to meet me.

Grace catches me. I cling to her like a drowning person. The moment passes. When I can breathe again, I say, "You're here! How'd you escape Sixteen?"

Grace shakes her head. "There is no Sixteen. I was in Time Out. No biggie."

I'm not sure I buy that, but she's clearly done talking about it. "I'm so glad you're here, Grace. As a witness. You saw what happened up there? My god, that was awful, but it proves I was right. I didn't jump. I fell."

"Are you sure?" she asks, like she's not. "Do it again and this time pay closer attention to your hands."

I am on the ladder once more, holding on to the railing with only my left hand. Every instinct screams at me to hold on with both hands, but I won't. I don't want to make it harder to let go.

"Why not just do it?" I say to myself. "My entire life is based on a lie, so what's the point of going on?"

I'm unraveling, with no power to stop. I release my pinky from its hold on the railing then, as if watching someone else's hand, I release my fourth finger. A moment later, I'm only holding on with my thumb and index finger, squeezing so tightly the sharp corners of the peeling paint jab my skin. I stare so hard at my fingers they look distorted and vaguely android. I press my body against the ladder.

I look at the sun, lean back and wonder what it would feel like to float away. I loosen my grip for an instant, less than an instant. I lose my balance.

"No!" I grab for the handrail, but all I catch is air. I tumble backward, head first, screaming. The concrete races up to meet me.

I hit the concrete and lie flat, pulling in ragged breaths, as I stare up at the ladder that seems to go on forever. Grace stands over me, offers her hand and pulls me to my feet.

I wipe my nose with the back of my hand, not because it's running, but because I need to feel my avatar again and give myself a minute to recover. "Do I have to do it again?"

"Depends on what you saw that time."

"I let go. I actually wanted to kill myself for a second, then I instantly changed my mind. It was suicide *and* an accident. That's why I don't fit in on Fifteen."

She nods.

"What happens now?" I ask.

Grace waves a finger. The tower vanishes, and she and I stand in my dorm room, beside my desk.

"Have a seat."

I sit.

"From the moment Alex left you alone on the tower you made certain choices that brought you here. But they weren't the only options available. Write."

A pencil and a blank piece of paper appear. My blank mind waits. How long will this take? My countdown timer says two hours! Dad's non-negotiable truth pops up on my mental movie screen, written in a fancy font:

THERE ARE ALWAYS OTHER OPTIONS.

Now that I'm not teetering on a ladder thirty feet above the ground, it's a lot easier to think. I pick up the pencil and fill the page quickly. My stupidity presses heavily on my heart. It's crazy and sad to think of all the things I could have done besides letting go, but it's also mind-blowing. Something shifts. I shake my head. I can't believe I ever thought I had no other choice.

"Show me what you've got," Grace says.

I show her.

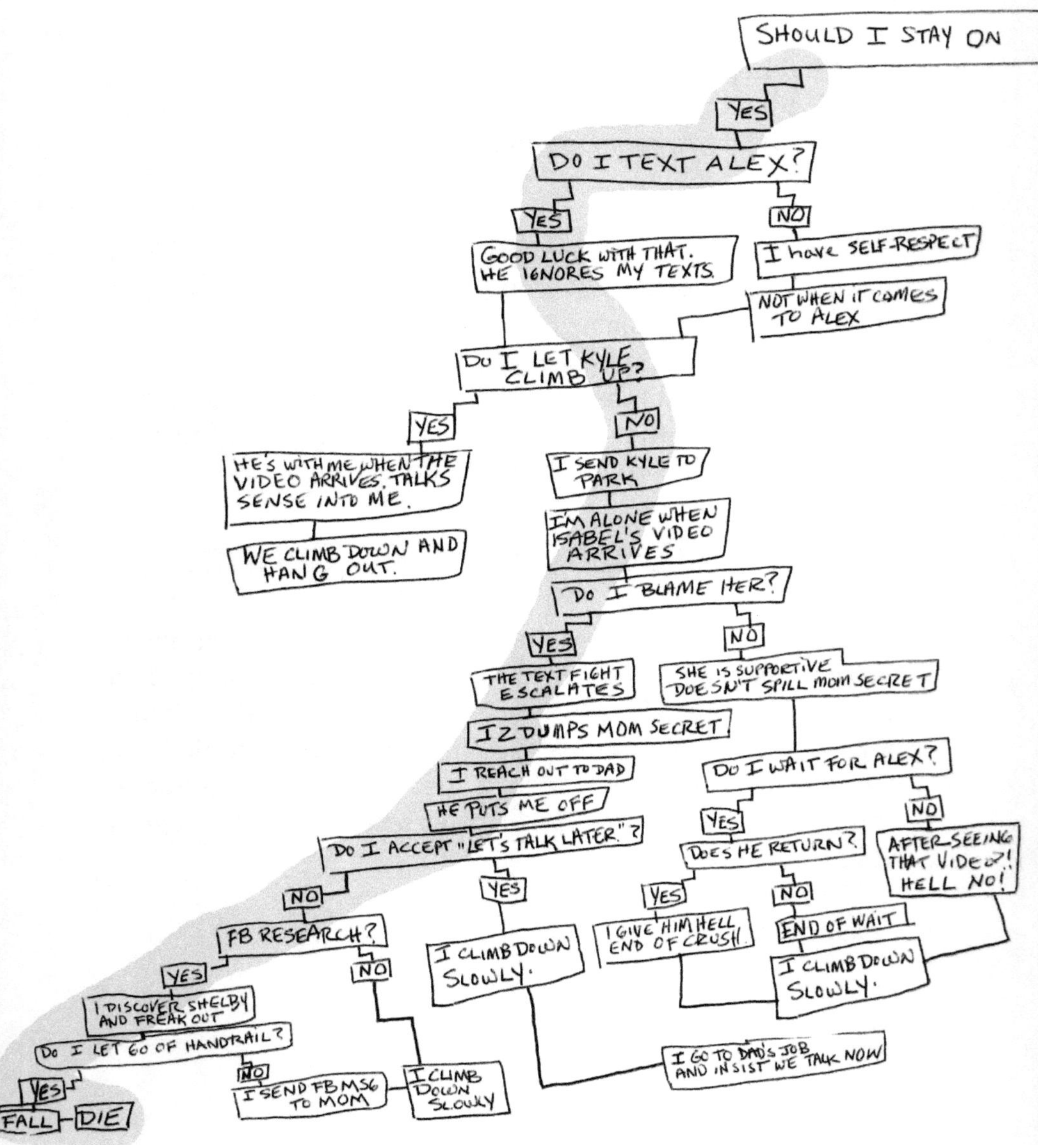
SHOULD I STAY ON
YES
DO I TEXT ALEX?
YES
NO
GOOD LUCK WITH THAT. HE IGNORES MY TEXTS.
I have SELF-RESPECT
NOT WHEN IT COMES TO ALEX
DO I LET KYLE CLIMB UP?
YES
NO
HE'S WITH ME WHEN THE VIDEO ARRIVES, TALKS SENSE INTO ME.
WE CLIMB DOWN AND HANG OUT.
I SEND KYLE TO PARK
I'M ALONE WHEN ISABEL'S VIDEO ARRIVES
DO I BLAME HER?
YES
NO
THE TEXT FIGHT ESCALATES
SHE IS SUPPORTIVE DOESN'T SPILL MOM SECRET
IZ DUMPS MOM SECRET
I REACH OUT TO DAD
DO I WAIT FOR ALEX?
YES
NO
HE PUTS ME OFF
DOES HE RETURN?
AFTER SEEING THAT VIDEO?! HELL NO!
DO I ACCEPT "LET'S TALK LATER."?
NO
YES
YES
NO
I CLIMB DOWN SLOWLY.
I GIVE HIM HELL END OF CRUSH!
END OF WAIT
FB RESEARCH?
YES
NO
I CLIMB DOWN SLOWLY.
I DISCOVER SHELBY AND FREAK OUT
DO I LET GO OF HANDRAIL?
NO
I CLIMB DOWN SLOWLY
I SEND FB MSG TO MOM
I GO TO DAD'S JOB AND INSIST WE TALK NOW
YES
FALL
DIE

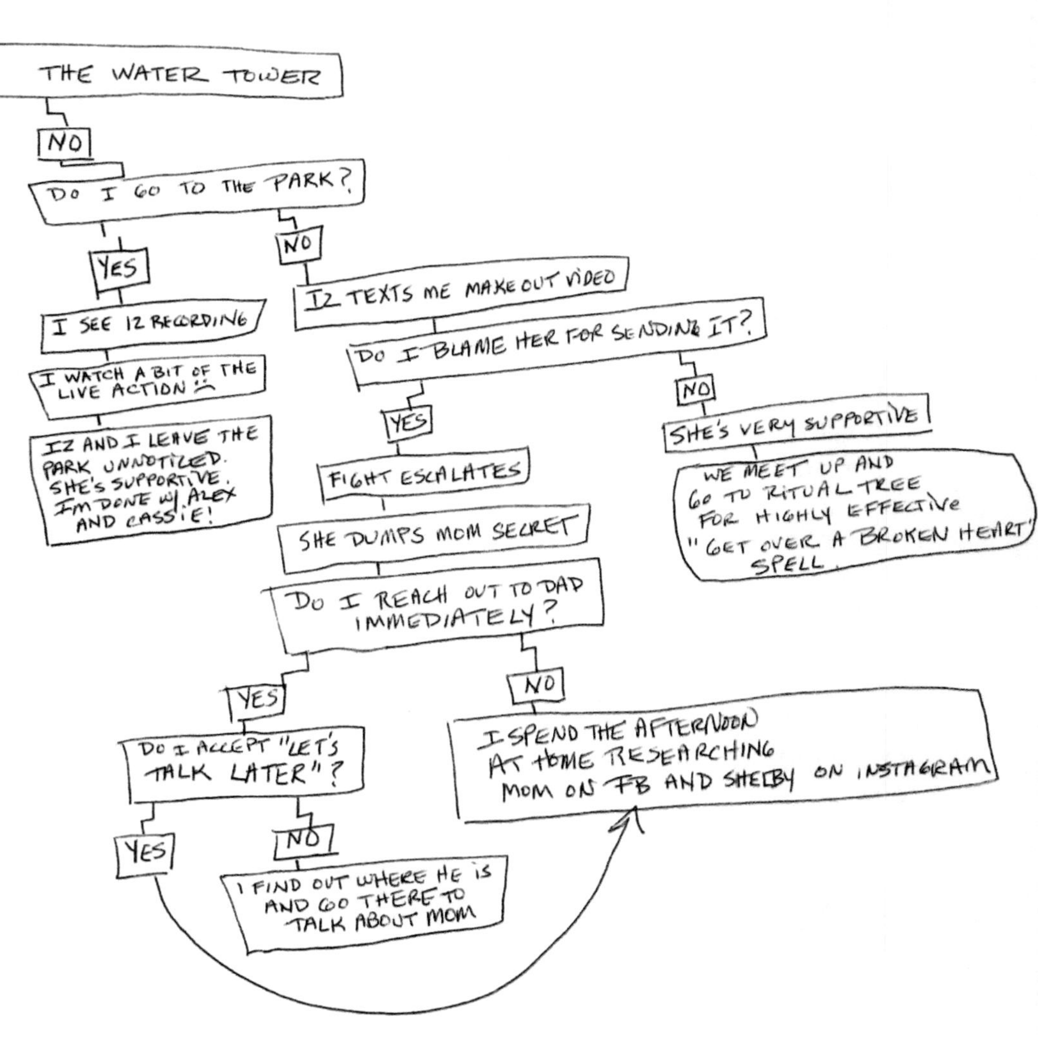
THE WATER TOWER
NO
DO I GO TO THE PARK?
YES
NO
I SEE IZ RECORDING
IZ TEXTS ME MAKE OUT VIDEO
I WATCH A BIT OF THE LIVE ACTION
DO I BLAME HER FOR SENDING IT?
IZ AND I LEAVE THE PARK UNNOTICED. SHE'S SUPPORTIVE. I'M DONE W/ ALEX AND CASSIE!
YES
NO
FIGHT ESCALATES
SHE'S VERY SUPPORTIVE
SHE DUMPS MOM SECRET
WE MEET UP AND GO TO RITUAL TREE FOR HIGHLY EFFECTIVE "GET OVER A BROKEN HEART" SPELL
DO I REACH OUT TO DAD IMMEDIATELY?
YES
NO
DO I ACCEPT "LET'S TALK LATER"?
I SPEND THE AFTERNOON AT HOME RESEARCHING MOM ON FB AND SHELBY ON INSTAGRAM
YES
NO
I FIND OUT WHERE HE IS AND GO THERE TO TALK ABOUT MOM

After a moment or two, she places the paper in my hands and watches me closely. A thick red line that I didn't draw now runs through every choice I made from the moment I decided to stay on the tower and wait for Alex until the moment I died.

I look up. The down-corner of Grace's mouth rises expectantly.

"Uh, do you want me to explain the whole thing?" I ask, hoping she doesn't.

"No time. Just tell me your top take-away."

"Doing X instead of Y creates other options."

She nods. "Good work."

I smile. "Thanks. Hm . . . So . . . ?"

"I want to show you something."

She points to a spot four feet off the floor and sweeps the air. A glowing white holographic line stretches across the length of my room, a green point on one end, a red point on the other.

"This line represents the last three years of your life as Nicole Benson. The red point marks the last few moments of your last day." As she talks, the white line begins to grow, extending past the red point. On this new stretch, more green points appear, each one sprouting its own array of purple points.

"What are all of those?"

"They represent possible futures that might have come to pass if you hadn't let go of the ladder. You can tap any one of them and have a look."

"You mean I can see what my life might have been like?"

"No guarantees any of them were destined to happen. They are just possibilities."

I randomly select one, then another. With each selection a brief hologram appears.

I'm seventeen, onstage at Veraz High, taking a curtain call. My dad and the rest of the people packed into the audience stand and cheer.

I'm seventeen and a half, driving with Cassie. Music's blaring as we sing along.

Nineteen. Drinking hot chocolate with Iz in front of the fireplace at the Mt. Shasta house. We're sharing stories about our lives at college.

Twenty. Road tripping with three girls who seem to know me well and like me a lot, even though I don't recognize them.

Twenty-one. Studying abroad in London.

Twenty-five. Working backstage at a theatre company in Portland.

Thirty-three. Directing a play in San Francisco.

Thirty-six. Rehearsing a play off-Broadway.

Thirty-nine. Clinking wine glasses with a smiling guy I've never seen, while Dad beams at us. He's with a woman I don't know, but her eyes are full of love, and she feels like family.

The array of possible futures fills my room in every direction. I am thrilled and breathless. I want to see it all and live it all. I select more and more points and the future expands.

"Nicole. Time to stop."

Her voice startles me. I had forgotten she was here, forgotten I was here and not somewhere on the timeline, living my life.

She waves a finger and the timeline vanishes.

"Wait!" I say, as if she were unplugging me from life support. "I want to see more."

"No. I shouldn't have done that. We're not supposed to show possible futures. I just thought it might help." Grace's eyes well up. "I'm sorry. I screwed up again."

I put my arm around her, like I'm the Mentor and she just stepped off the moving walkway.

"No. It's okay," I say, not just because I don't want her to feel bad, but also because it really is okay. "I needed to see some of what I missed. I thought by letting go of the handrail I could delete all the uncomfortable thoughts and feelings and memories. I wiped them out for a while, but they all came back anyway. Thing is, I never once thought about how much good stuff I might be wiping out, too. You didn't do anything wrong, Grace. I'm the one who screwed up."

Grace's face lights up like fireworks. Everything about her shines. "Congratulations, Nicole. You just passed The Evaluation."

"Really? That was it?"

The digits on my countdown timer have morphed into jaunty little stars that flash a couple of times, then they're gone. I look up expecting, I don't know, maybe a shower of confetti. It doesn't happen. Who cares? I passed!

"Thank you, Grace. Seriously. Thanks for all your help and for . . . everything. I know I wasn't the easiest no body to work with, but you were always so . . ."

I want to say much more, but the words won't come. Maybe there are no words. Sometimes you don't need them.

Grace flashes her lopsided smile. Like always, there's joy and sadness in that smile. I guess both are part of everything, all the time. She opens her arms wide. I'm right there, hugging her back. Why do I feel so small? Grace is taller than me! Much taller. When did that happen? She holds me. Warm. Strong. Soft but solid. I rest my head on her shoulder and close my eyes. I don't know for sure, but I think this is how a good mom hug feels.

"Goodbye, Nicole." Her tone is gentle. "And good luck."

She pulls away. I open my eyes. All the color is gone from the walls along with every bit of my dorm stuff. We're standing in a large, empty, white box.

I look around, stunned. "What just happened?"

"We need this room for the new arrival I'm about to meet at the walkway. It's time for you to move on."

Move on. Move over. Move along.

"Oh. Sure. No problem. Uh, just gimme a minute to pack up."

It's a lame joke, but Grace chuckles. She doesn't fool me. I don't fool her, either.

"Take your time." She steps back as I the look at the walls. No hint of Nicole Benson remains. This space could become anything. The possibilities are limitless. Kinda like my future. I close my eyes and breathe in. Breathe out.

"Okay. All packed." I turn to Grace, but she's gone. Already on to the next thing. Me too. I'm ready. Almost.

CASSIE

BEYOND THE FIRST bend in the switchback trail, eucalyptus trees fill the ravine and block the sun. The trail disappears into shadows. Lola pulls forward on the leash, hot to trot. I yank her back, harder than I mean to.

She looks at me, wondering why we're waiting when up ahead there's so much mud and eucalyptus bark and dog poop to sniff and pee on. Why am I waiting? Suddenly this hike doesn't seem like a great idea. What am I scared of? Nothing. I just haven't been up here since . . .

"Maybe we should walk around the shopping center instead. What do you say, Lo?"

I turn back toward the park. Lola won't move. She barks at me as if to say, "Don't be scared, Cassie, I'll protect you."

I have to laugh. She weighs, what, ten pounds?

"Okay. You win."

The trail isn't muddy enough to mess up my high-tops, but it will be muddy enough to piss off Buzz-Kill when we get home and I accidentally forget to clean off Lola's paws.

Jasmine and I used to hike up here, before we got Lola. It was always a great escape from Buzz-Kill. Jasmine taught me to watch out for poison oak. "Leaves of three, let it be. If it's hairy, it's a berry. If it's shiny, watch your hiney."

All the leaves are gone now and there are no berries, just tons of cinnamon-colored poison oak branches growing up and down the slopes. I duck under an overhanging vine. Even if you just brush against them, they will eff you up. Like they did to Alex. Don't think about him.

When the trail widens to a dirt fire road, I unhook Lola's leash and let her run free. Sometimes coyotes pick off little dogs up here, but I'm not worried. Lola loves me and stays close. I wish certain people felt that way.

As I round the last bend at the top, the water tower comes into view. It doesn't seem that tall until I get close. It hurts my neck to stand beside it and look up. I walk around to the rusty ladder on the other side. Forty-two steps. Should I climb up? I've done it before with Alex. Don't think about him.

Where's Lola? Oh, right over there, nosing around under a eucalyptus tree at the fork in the fire road. That's good. Okay, well, I can't climb up the ladder with her, and I'm not leaving her down here. I don't want to go up anyway. I don't need to see how far Nicole fell from the roof. That's not even counting how far she rolled into the ravine.

Her head was totally crushed.

I sink to the concrete, my back against the tower. The cold metal presses through my shirt. I have to swipe at my eyes with both hands. Good thing there's no one here. There's a rock or something under my butt, but I don't move.

"I'm really sorry, Nicole. I should have let him come right back."

Lola trots over to me and drops a stick at my feet. "Aw, thanks. Just what I need." She licks my nose. I hug her and bury my face in her neck. Suddenly she wriggles out of my arms, grabs the stick, and runs down the right fork of the fire road.

I whistle. "Lola, come!"

She runs away faster.

Damn.

I run after her.

Lola sits perfectly still in the middle of the dirt road, staring at a spot directly over her head.

I don't see what she's looking at, but I get that same creepy feeling I had when she jumped on the picnic table and stared into space.

"Come on, Lola. We're going home."

She doesn't move.

"Hey, Lola. Want the stick?" I bend over to pick it up but before I touch it, the stick moves by itself and writes the letter "S" in the dirt.

"Holy shit!"

I scoop up Lola and run down the switchback trail, back through the park. I run up the hill behind our building, around the front, and up the stairs. I don't stop running until I'm in the apartment, door locked behind me, sweaty and breathing hard and feeling like an idiot.

What just happened out there? It couldn't be what I'm thinking because that's impossible. But if Isabel isn't totally nutso and spirits are an actual thing, why would Nicole come after me? Well, she obviously saw the video, so there's that. But she got what she wanted. Well . . . half of it. She broke up Calex forever. But if she can pick stuff up, maybe she wants a fight. No, I think she was writing with the stick. Maybe she just wants to tell me something.

"Hey, Cass." Jasmine calls from the kitchen.

Her charcoals and pastels are spread out on the table. She carefully holds the top edge of a giant portrait of Lola. "What do you think?"

"Looks just like her." I reach for a piece of gray charcoal. "Uh, can I borrow this?"

"Sure." She clears space on the table and puts down a clean sheet of paper. "Want to sit down and work here?"

"No thanks." I take the paper and head for my room. I whistle for Lola and she follows me inside. I turn on the closet light, step inside and close the door.

Lola stares at the empty space above her head and whimpers.

"She's here, isn't she, Lo?" I sit on the floor. Lola sits beside me, her body trembles against my leg. I place the charcoal next to the paper. "Okay, Nicole. If you want to tell me something, fire away."

Nothing happens. Of course not. I stand and open the door, about to turn off the light, when Lola barks. On the floor behind me, charcoal scratches across paper.

I step back inside and shut the door. All by itself, the chalk finishes writing and drops onto the floor. The word "SORRY" fills the page.

I blink rapid-fire, but the effin' tears come anyway. Ohmygod. It's a double freakin' miracle, a million times cooler than a grilled cheese Jeez. I don't know which part is more amazing—that a ghost just wrote me a message or that Nicole is seriously sorry for messing things up between Alex and me.

The front door slams followed by stumbling footsteps in the kitchen. Buzz-Kill's voice is loud and slurred. "Look at you, Jasmine. Such a hard worker. Such a talented girl and such a *whore*. Gloria saw you with that boy."

"Ma, let go. It's for school."

Paper shreds in a single angry rip.

"Slut!"

I race into the kitchen just as Buzz-Kill nails my sister across the face. She raises her hand again, and I step in between them, my fist balled tight. Buzz-Kill's eyes burn with hate. She raises her hand, this time aiming at me. I'm ready for her. I'm so ready.

She looks away, lowers her arm, and steps back.

I turn to see if Jasmine's alright. Pain knocks me on the floor before I know what happened. Then I figure it out. Buzz-Kill kicked me in the back. The throbbing doesn't let up and my back twitches like crazy, but I keep my mouth shut because I don't want to scare Jasmine.

"Cassie, look out!"

I catch a glimpse of something rising over my head and roll out of the way just as Buzz-Kill screams and a frying pan clatters to the floor. Jasmine yanks me to my feet. Lola's teeth clamp onto Buzz-Kill's leg.

"Lola, leave it!" She lets go. I scoop her up and we run.

Across the street from our building, Jasmine and I stop and look back. No one comes out the front door. Still, we walk more quickly than usual. I put Lola down and gasp. My back is on fire.

"Are you okay, little sister?"

"Yeah. She doesn't kick hard when she's that wasted."

It's not much of a joke but it's enough. Jasmine smiles. That's good.

She gets a text. She raises her eyebrow. Maybe it's the cool guy from art school.

I bend over to clip on Lola's leash. Whoa. That hurts like hell, but I grin. "Looks like you're busy. I'm gonna take Lola to the park. I'll catch up with you later."

She takes my hand. "Thanks for standing up to her, Cass. That was brave. I'm the one who's supposed to take care of you."

"You did. You dragged my ass out of there before I beat the crap out of her."

Lola barks.

"And you helped, too, Lo."

We laugh, then Jasmine frowns. "You know we can't go back. Not tonight. Not ever."

She's right. But where will we go? I'm worried but I don't want her to know it. I nod. "We'll figure something out."

Jasmine takes out her phone.

Lola takes off down the street, away from the park.

Damn!

Leash in hand I follow as fast as I can, which is pathetically slow because each step kills. The pain in my back is shooting down through my legs now. When I get to the corner, I don't see Lola. I walk up the block, whistling and calling for her in every direction. Why doesn't she come? Maybe she's hurt. Maybe she was hit by a car. A sick, cold weight presses on my heart. What if I can't find her? I don't know which hurts worse, my back or the thought of losing her. Yeah, I know.

I spot her on a side street, sitting in the middle of the sidewalk, wagging her tail at nothing. "Lola!" I break into a jerky run.

"Hey, Cassie."

It's Alex. I turn. He's behind me looking so effin' cute, but I give him the stink eye because why does he have to know I still care?

"Oh, are you talking to me now?"

"Are you okay?"

"Yeah, why?"

"You're limping."

I don't want him feeling sorry for me.

"No, I'm not."

I bend down and clip on Lola's leash, and the pain in my back hurts so bad my hand flies to the spot, and I gasp.

He helps me straighten up. "You're hurt. What happened?"

I brush him off. "Nothing. Hey, did you hear? Buzz-Kill just won the Mother of the Year award . . ." The pain again. I can't hide it.

"Geez. Did she hit you?"

I should look away because if I don't I'll start believing it's possible to get what you wish for. But it's not possible. Not for me. Not with Alex. Not after . . . Too late. His arms are around me, but he's very gentle. It's like he knows exactly where it hurts and he doesn't want to make things worse for me. My back's still killing me but my heart feels great. For the first time in my life, I feel like I finally won something.

My phone dings. (415) 555-8739 appears on the screen with UNKNOWN caller. Who is that?

(415) 555-8739>

Hello, Miss Cassie. Mr.
Robert here. I hope
you are well. Our home
address is 11 Cordone
Street. My wife and I
look forward to seeing

you and Jasmine for
dinner tonight at 7.

Huh. He *looks forward* to seeing us. Does he really mean it?

Mr. Robert opens the front door with a big smile. "So nice to see you, Miss Cassie."

"Thanks." I step inside. My back still hurts but I feel better after Alex took me to Safeway and got me some ice to put on it. Still, being here in Mr. Robert's house is strange. Lola sniffs his slippers.

He bends down and scratches her butt. "Hello, Lola."

She wags her tail then walks right past him toward the kitchen, probably to find out what smells so amazing.

Mr. Robert and Jasmine grin at each other like this is some kind of family reunion. "So lovely to meet you, Miss Jasmine." He reaches for her hand.

"Nice to finally meet you, Mr. Robert."

She's so relaxed and polite. I'm proud she's my sister.

We're a little late because Jasmine insisted that we bring flowers, and it took a while to find a place. I told her it was a stupid idea, especially since I was probably getting fired. She gave me a funny look and said, "It's never stupid to be kind. Which ones should we buy?"

Jasmine hands Mr. Robert the flowers. "These are for you and your wife."

"Ranunculus. Beautiful flowers! How very kind."

We walk into the kitchen. Everything smells delicious. Mr. Robert's wife is a short woman zipping from stove to counter top, stirring stuff, and shaking something into a pot. Now she's holding a mother of a knife, quickly chopping a bundle of long green vegetables into tiny bits.

She pauses, looks up at us and waves. "Hi Cassie. Hi Jasmine. I'm Betty. So glad you could join us. I'd come right over and hug you two beautiful girls, but as you can see, I'm up to my elbows in garlic and chives."

Mr. Robert holds up the bouquet. "They brought us flowers."

"It was Cassie's idea," Jasmine adds.

I wish she hadn't said that. "I hope you're not allergic or something," I mumble.

"Allergic to flowers? Lord, no! I love 'em!" Betty gushes, and I know she means it. "Thank you, sweetheart. Now can you snip off the ends of those stems, fill that vase over there with water, just a third of the way, pop those lovelies in, and set them on the table?"

Taking orders from Betty feels nothing like taking orders from Buzz-Kill. It's weird, but I just want to make her happy.

When the doorbell rings. Mr. Robert and Betty hurry into the living room and swing open the front door. A tall, long-haired guy walks into the living room. Big hugs all around. His name is James, and it turns out he was one of Mr. Robert's foster kids, for like four years, before he turned 18, so this used to be his home. It also turns out Jasmine knows him from art school. They seem really happy to see each other. I'm okay with that. He seems cool.

Dinner is baked salmon with lemon and garlic butter and wild rice, which isn't actually rice, it's grass seed. Whatever. It's *good*. I try the roasted Brussels sprouts in something called a balsamic reduction. I didn't think I'd like them because they look like mini-cabbages and I hate cabbage, but they are okay. Betty made a little bowl of fish skin and brown rice for Lola. She eats that so fast. Later, when I look for her, she is curled up asleep under the table, like she lives here.

At the end of the meal, Betty serves something called Apple Brown Betty. The smell of apples and cinnamon makes my mouth water. I think it's funny she named a dessert after herself, but why not?

Mr. Robert says, "Before we partake in my talented wife's delectable dessert, I have an announcement to make." He stands and turns to me.

Here it comes. I hold my breath.

"Miss Cassie, you have completed your community service obligation at Children's Caring Center. I appreciate the time you spent with us. Thank you for that. Now that you are no longer mandated to serve the children . . ."

Get lost.

I find Jasmine's hand under the table and squeeze tight.

". . . I am offering you a permanent, part-time, salaried position as a teaching assistant at CCC."

He didn't fire me. I've got a job!

Wow. I won two things in one day. I'm so excited I almost knock over my water glass. But I grab it in time. Maybe I'm done messing up.

"Thank you, Mr. Robert. I accept your offer."

Betty claps. James gives me thumbs up. Jasmine hugs me. I wince. Mr. Robert looks concerned. He picks up a pillow from the living room couch, brings it around to my side of the table, and gently tucks the pillow behind my back. I lean into it. It feels good. Nothing could beat this moment. Then Betty brings out ice cream. Cherry vanilla. I'm not a fan of cherries and I only ever eat chocolate ice cream, but this stuff goes great with Brown Betty.

We all eat in happy silence until James says, "Mr. Robert, have you got anyone staying in my old room?"

"Not at the moment," says Betty, looking sideways at her husband.

Mr. Robert slowly folds his hands and looks across the table at me and Jasmine as he speaks. "As a matter of fact, my wife and I were just discussing the situation and we're both hoping that comfortable room will be occupied again very, very soon."

I'm wondering if he's thinking what I think he's thinking. I look over at Jasmine. She's nodding, and damn, she looks like she's about to cry.

Me too.

Isabel

THE ROOM IS cold and smells of fear. The bed offers no rest. Thank Goddess I brought my pillow and blanket from home. I set up a sleeping space on the floor under the window, where the bed's negative energy can't reach me, but my thoughts won't let me sleep. What can I do? I can't set up my altar table because it won't be here until tomorrow morning when the movers deliver all of my stuff. I wish I'd brought my magik boxes in the car. Dad said as long as we hired movers, we might as well let them take all the boxes so the car wouldn't be so loaded down and we'd get better mileage. It's good to conserve energy and protect the planet, but I don't have a candle or even a stick of incense to light.

I pull on a sweater and a pair of tights, extra socks, and my boots. I wrap my cape around me and tiptoe out the back door. The cold night air stings my face. Heaviness weighs on my heart chakra. I pull my cloak closer. No help. It's not the chill I need protection from. It is the consequences of my own thoughtless acts toward Nic.

Mount Shasta's energetic vibration reaches through darkness and lifts my spirit. I am grateful for the stars and for this moment of wondering about beings who inhabit distant worlds.

Back in my room, I lay on the bed, still wrapped in my cloak. I close my eyes and breathe. Tomorrow, after my things arrive, I'll take what I need and walk to Mt. Shasta City Park.

The movers arrive at 9:24 am. They bring my shrink-wrapped furniture, mattress, and headboard into my room, then continue unloading their truck. When I set up my space I will feel more at home, but I have to get to the park now. Saturday is the best day for rituals about Karma and communication. The number eleven represents increased sensitivity and spiritual insight. 11:11 am is a propitious time to start.

I lift my ritual bowl out of the box and place it in my backpack along with an empty potion bottle, a green candle, and matches. Something behind the plastic layers wrapped around my headboard catches my eye. I'm not sure what I'm looking at. I peel away the plastic to get a better look. My crystal necklace comes into focus! How in the world . . . ? That night I took it off, I stuck it under my pillow so . . . I must have pushed it off the edge of the bed in my sleep and it caught on one of the wrought-iron leaves. That's why I never found it under the bed.

I untangle the necklace as carefully as if I am freeing a butterfly caught in a net. I slip the necklace over my head and press the crystal against my heart. More than ever my spirit is dedicated to restoring trust with Nic.

At the entrance of the park, I touch earth to honor the spirits of the place. The sound of rushing water draws me in. A sign points the way to Big Springs Headwaters, but I don't need directions. I know where I'm going.

A woman meditates at the edge of a stream where clear water falls and foams and bubbles over flat stones. Her long blue coat hugs her pregnant belly. Her white-blond braid hangs below a black turban cap embroidered with a silver moon and stars so uniquely lovely it must be handmade.

Without opening her eyes, she speaks to me. "If you're wondering if the water is safe to drink, it's better than safe.

It's sacred. These are the headwaters of the Upper Sacramento River."

It seems perfectly normal in this place that she would sense me here and know what I was thinking.

"Thank you," I say, filling my potion bottle in the stream. I feel her watching me. I turn. She smiles, her deep brown eyes shine with an inner light. "Blessed be."

The same variety of miner's lettuce that flourishes in thick clumps not far from my ritual tree in Veraz pushes through the wet earth along the stream. I'm surprised to see it when it's not yet spring, but here it is. Carefully, so as not to damage the roots, I pick some young leaves. Delicate, refreshing, a taste of home. I cross a narrow wooden footbridge. From the stream under the bridge, I choose a small, smooth gray stone and put it in my pocket. I wander under the trees. Dew glistens on the moss-covered tree trunks. Morning sunlight filters through branches. The divine energy of the natural world surrounds me. I search for redwoods, but we are too far inland. Only pines grow here and none are tall enough to attract lightning, so no hollow trees of any kind.

What else can I use for a ritual space? I clutch my crystal. "Goddess Eternal, help me find what I need."

A few minutes' walk in the direction of the sun, I come across a tree stump. Maybe a foot and a half around and ten inches high, a perfect little table rooted in the ground. I unpack my ritual bowl and place it in the center of the stump. I fill the bowl with pinecones, pine needles, miner's lettuce, and the river rock. I sprinkle everything with sacred headwaters. I place the green candle beside the bowl and light it. I close my eyes and chant.

"Goddess Eternal, Healer of wounds and scars
With love and hope I call to you.
Like sacred waters shining in the sun
Let my spirit and Nic's shine together as one."

"Iz!"

I hear Nic's voice only an instant before she appears on the other side of the tree stump. Beaming at me, she reaches over and playfully flicks the ends of my hair. "Your hair is getting longer."

"Nic, I have to talk to you."

"Me, too. Let me go first because I don't know how long I can maintain my avatar. Look, I'm sorry for being a bad friend, for hurting you in little ways and big ways all along. And at the end I shouldn't have blamed you for the video. Thing is, when I let go of the ladder, I blamed everyone else for how I felt. Everyone but me."

I can't believe what I'm hearing. "You let go?"

She frowns, and nods. "I was curious. Just for an instant. No. Less than an instant. So I let go. I immediately changed my mind. But, yeah I let go."

I'm staring at her. I need to know why she'd do something so stupid, but I don't want to ask her. Don't have to. She hears me thinking.

"Why'd I do it? I thought ending my life would erase all the pain from Alex and from my mom. It didn't work because it doesn't work that way. Instead of letting go I should have held on and thought about my dad, and you, and my other options. Being dead is harder than living. They make you own your mistakes and clean up the hurt you caused. Don't get me wrong. That's a good thing. It changed me in a way that needed changing. That's why I had to come talk to you before it was too late. The hardest part of all of it is getting to this point where I don't have to blame anyone. Now I know the truth about what I did and what kind of person I was. Iz, you are the best friend I will ever have, and I'm sorry I ever doubted you. Please forgive me." Her voice cracks.

"Of course, I forgive you, Nic."

She doesn't pretend. Doesn't look away. Neither do I. My breath rises and falls with hers. I rest my hand over her heart. We are connected.

I continue, "I messed up, too. My intentions were not pure when I sent the video. I wanted to prove that I was right about not trusting Alex. That was self-serving. I should have waited until I had your best interests in mind. Waited to tell you until we were together, instead of dumping it on you when you were alone up there. I'm also sorry about telling you about your mom. I was trying to get back at you. You deserved to know the truth about her, but it shouldn't have come from me. Please forgive me."

"You got it, Iz. I love you."

"One more thing..."

"What?"

"I never burned your journal. Your dad asked for it back before I got the chance."

Her face clouds. "So he's got it?"

"Yes, but he said he realized you were just venting, and he didn't need to read any more of it. He just wants to keep it. He loves you, Nic. I love you, too"

She nods and puts her hand to her heart. "I know."

My eyes mist up. "I . . . miss you. No one loves me."

"What are you talking about? Your parents love you. Look where they brought you." She opens her arms to take in the forest. "They packed up their life because they want you to be happy. That's how much they love you. Everyone thinks the goal in life is to be popular and have lots of people love you. Wrong. The goal is learning to love other people."

She smiles. Beautiful, radiant, just for me. Something small inside shifts in the direction of hope.

"Will I have a good life?" I ask.

"You're seriously asking me that? Gimme a break, Iz. I'm dead, but I'm not psychic. I've got no idea what's on your timeline."

I nod. Of course, that makes sense. She can't tell me my future. But that's okay, as long as we can still talk like this and be together. Together. My heart lurches forward. "Am I going to see you again?"

She smiles sadly and shakes her head. "No. I'm moving on."

My throat tightens, like I'm about to cry, then I'm not. Suddenly it's okay that this is the end for us because I feel like I'm moving on too, in my own way.

We hug. There's nothing left to say.

"Have a good one, Iz."

"You, too, Nic."

She vanishes.

I take everything out of the ritual bowl and carefully arrange it on the tree stump. This is my place now, and I'll be back. I blow out the candle and pack it away with the bowl and potion bottle. I hoist my backpack onto my shoulders. A warm breeze plays with the ends of my hair. I smell spring.

Nicole

TEEG SITS CROSS-LEGGED on her bed, writing in her journal.

"Hey," I say from the doorway.

She looks up and smiles. "Hey. I thought you were gone."

"I wouldn't have left without saying goodbye."

"Get in here." She pats the bedspread and scoots over to make room.

I sit beside her. She rests her pen in the journal but she keeps it open. "So, while I've been studying my ass off, what's Nicole been up to?"

"Short answer, I've been trying to fix stuff that I broke."

"An apology tour? Love it. Learn and progress. So how'd it go?

"Uh . . . better than expected, I guess. And worse. I think I did my best."

"I'm sure you did." She nudges me playfully. "Hey, there are two sides to an apology. You can only do you."

"Yeah. That's the truth."

We fall into a slightly awkward silence.

"So what else is new?" she asks.

"Well . . . I passed The Evaluation."

"Seriously?"

I nod. She high fives me.

"I never thought I would."

"Oh, I knew you'd figure it out. So, how did you die? What's the truth?"

A sharp pain blooms on the right side of my head. "The truth . . . is complicated." I look down at her bedspread and start tracing the wings of one of the butterflies. Teeg touches my shoulder. Her eyes are kind. I take a breath. And another.

"It turns out the Mentors didn't make a mistake. I was in the right place the whole time because . . . I killed myself."

It feels weird to say it, but as soon as I do, the pain eases. I fold my arms tightly across my chest, hoping Teeg doesn't ask for details but expecting she will.

She doesn't.

"So, what happens next?" Her tone is gentle.

I shrug. "They haven't told me anything except that it's time to move on."

She frowns, but says nothing.

"What?" I ask.

"Are you scared?"

I'd been scared to fail. Scared of Sixteen. Scared of the truth. But right now, after all this, was I scared to move on? If I were, I'd know it. The jolt of dread that came with every doubt and worry throughout my entire life would certainly grab me now and not let go. But I don't feel it. Just to make sure, I ask myself the question again and let it echo through every corner of my mind. *Are. You. Scared?* I wait for the jolt. Nothing happens.

"Nope. Not scared." I laugh, because it's true. "Well, bye, Teeg. And good luck."

We hug, and I head for the door.

"See you around." We say it at the same time, though we both know that probably won't happen.

I walk into the hallway. It's dark except for a small circle of amber light illuminating the floor. I'm drawn to the spotlight, like an actor on a stage. Wait. I don't know my lines. I chuckle because I finally get that it doesn't matter. There is no script. Never was. It's all improvisation.

I step into the spotlight. Blue-white mist swirls around me. Suddenly, without moving, I'm moving—rocketing through space again, only this time without a platform or an avatar or anything that looks the way I once looked. I'm light and shadow. I'm wind and stillness. I'm nothing and everything. Moving fast. Faster. No idea where I'm going or who I will be when I get there. I'm not worried. I'll deal with whatever comes next and try not to hurt anyone. And that's the truth.

Isabel

WE'VE BEEN IN Shasta for almost two years and it doesn't look like we're moving back. That's fine with me. The only person I care about in Veraz is Mike. For the first six months after we moved, my parents would call him and I'd listen in. All the conversations were the same. Dad would say hi then Mom did all the talking. She was kind and encouraged Mike to talk about his feelings, but he wouldn't or couldn't. His energy was so heavy my stomach hurt. The only thing I remember from those conversations was when he told us the police had completed their investigation.

"They said there was no evidence of foul play. And without a note, they couldn't rule out suicide or an accident. So, you know what they came up with? The cause of death was traumatic brain injury and severe internal bleeding. I think we could have figured that out on our own."

After that he didn't pick up the phone any more. He wouldn't answer texts.

I sent him healing energy. I did several full lavender rituals to lift the weight of grief from his heart. I sensed that nothing was working until one night, as I lit the black candle for him and brought him into my space, I felt a shift, a weight lifted from his heart.

Mom's phone buzzes. It's Mike. He tells us he's been going to a grief support group led by Dr. Jorge Moreno who happens to be Ms. Moreno's uncle.

"I'm not a therapy kinda guy, but one day I found his business card in my jacket pocket."

Joy and relief spark within my heart chakra. Ohmygoddess! Nic must have put the card in there the day we looked for her journal.

"The first time I went was right after Nikki died, but I only got as far as the church parking lot. It was too soon. Two months ago, around her birthday, I was close to rock bottom, and I found the card again, so I went. I actually got myself inside the building that time."

Mom claps a hand on her chest. She's teary-eyed. "I'm so glad to hear this, Mike."

Dad thumbs-up the screen. "Yeah. Big step."

"A dozen or so of the saddest looking people in the world were sitting in a circle. I thought, 'How the hell is it going to help me to join this group?' I didn't even sit down. Then Jorge talked about his son, Tomás, who was seventeen when he committed suicide twenty years ago. For years, driving past the high school was impossible, so Jorge drove an extra seven miles out of his way to his office every day. Seeing parents with their teenagers, or kids of any age, was impossible. So was seeing anyone who was happy. That's when I thought, 'That's exactly how I feel.' But he didn't want to feel that way anymore. And he told us that he doesn't. So I figured, maybe there's hope for me.

"The group's been a good thing. I don't feel so alone or so hopeless. I actually met a woman there. She lives in Sonoma, but she works in Marin. We've been meeting up for coffee, and we're going to the de Young Museum next week. Bizarre coincidence, her daughter Teeg died the same day as Nikki."

Teeg? Nic's friend from Substation Fifteen! Blessed be.

I get up early the next morning. It's January 4th. The winter sun is surprisingly warm.

Behind the garden toolshed I draw a circle on the ground with my athame. I kiss my crystal. I'm so glad to have it back, I never take it off.

I place a rock on the North edge of the circle, a turkey feather (air) on the East. I place a candle (fire) on the South and a cup of water on the West. The four elements in all four directions.

I burn white sage and a dried bay leaf in my ritual bowl. I carve her initials, N B, into the black candle and rub it with my special blend of jojoba and apricot kernel oil.

I light the candle and chant.

"On this second anniversary

The Wheel of Life turns

The candle burns

Bring peace to Nic's spirit

May she walk the gardens of Summerland in serenity

Wherever she is, she is never far from my heart

May she know that I remember her always."

I place the hardened candle drippings and the burnt herbs into a black bag.

"Goddess Eternal, make me mindful of your hand in all things throughout the natural world."

MEOWWW

A smallish black cat paws the turkey feather.

I smile. "Hello, there. Welcome."

The cat tilts its head.

"Where do you live?"

The cat flicks its tail along the ground, the feather flips into the air, twirls and floats down, resting on my knee.

"That way?" I point eastward.

The cat nudges me with its head. "Okay. But where?"

Nextdoor.com lists lots of lost cats in the neighborhood. A large gray cat named Blue. Sebastian, gray and black stripes. A white cat with black markings named Tucker. None like this one.

"Maybe your owner doesn't know you're missing. I'll check again later. In the meantime, you can stay here with me."

The cat meows impatiently. I've never been able to communicate directly with animals, but I sense this cat wants me to refresh the screen. When I do, a new Lost Cat post appears from someone named Sabine Melcher, along with a photo of the black cat.

"Is your name Faeryn?"

MEOW

Faeryn means "of the faeries." She's got a Wiccan name. Hmm.

I take Faeryn's photo and message it to Sabine. She replies immediately and tells me to come over. Five minutes later, Faeryn leads me along a street with pine trees and no sidewalks. No surprise, we're heading east.

Sabine stands at the bottom of a garden path, beside a tiny one-room cottage. The top of the path leads to a single-story wooden house tucked among a stand of pines. Her bare feet stick out beneath a flowing green and blue skirt. Her white-yellow braid is intertwined with blue borage and she wears a black turban cap with hand-embroidered moon and stars. She's the woman from the Headwaters Spring! The little girl she balances on her hip locks eyes with me.

Faeryn rubs against Sabine's leg. She strokes the cat lovingly. "Welcome home, my little wanderer."

She gently places her daughter on the ground and extends her hand to me.

"Hello, Isabel. We meet again. Thank you for bringing Faeryn home."

Her hand is warm and strong, her voice, rich and round.

"You're welcome. But I don't think your cat was actually lost. She brought me right here."

The little girl rushes me and wraps her arms around my legs so suddenly I'm almost knocked off balance. Her mother's laugh is like a forest stream tumbling over stones.

"Isabel, this is Fiona."

"Does she do this to everyone?"

"Only people she knows."

"But she doesn't know me."

Again, she offers that wonderful laugh. "The Goddess works in mysterious ways, doesn't she?"

I blush with pleasure. "She does." I'm suddenly shy and excited at the same time.

Sabine picks up her cat. "I need to take Faeryn up to the house to feed her. Are you okay out here with Fiona for a bit?"

"Uh, I'm not very good with kids."

Fiona grabs my hand and leads me to the small one room cottage. "Looks like she wants you to see something in my studio."

Magical ink drawings take up most of the space along the cork wall over the desk. No. They're *magik*. A white wolf snuggles against a sleeping woman. Blackbirds nest in a young girl's hair. A winged cat flies above a flaming forest.

My stomach flutters, but in a good way. I feel weightless, like I'm flying with the cat in the drawing.

Ohmygoddess! Where's Fiona? I'm supposed to take care of her.

I spin around. Fiona stands in the corner, in front of an altar with candles and a ritual bowl, a long black and white feather, a casting cloth, and a pendulum. A talking board lies on floor nearby.

Fiona toddles over and hands me a carved wooden planchette. As I take it from her, the tingling I haven't felt for two years awakens at the back of my neck.

"Nic?"

Fiona giggles. Her laughter, like raindrops bouncing off small stones, grows and grows until the little girl, red in the face, hiccups loudly and we laugh together.

Suicide Prevention Lifeline

If you or someone you know, is having thoughts of suicide, call or text 988 to reach the 988 Suicide and Crisis Lifeline or go to SpeakingOfSuicide.com/resources for a list of additional resources.

The 988 Lifeline is a national (U.S.) network of local crisis centers that provides free and confidential emotional support to people in suicidal crisis or emotional distress 24 hours a day, 7 days a week in the United States.

If you need help and you're not in the U.S. here's a website that lists the suicide prevention helplines in every country around the world:

blog.opencounseling.com/suicide-hotlines

If you or someone you know needs help, please reach out.

Annie's Next Book

Leeta Simtar—A Life on Two Planets:
The Unauthorized Biography

"Fox knows how and when to surprise, and her warm and empathic way of writing Leeta's relatable arc through internal monologues feels personal yet universally urgent, examining her real-world struggles of marginalization, racism, and rigid hierarchies that enforce systemic exclusion." —*BookLife by Publishers Weekly (Editor's Pick)*

". . . Fox's novel tells a richly told story of going rogue. A rousing tale about a young woman coming to terms with an unresolved past." —*Kirkus Reviews*

For fans of Alechia Dow and Pittacus Lore comes *Leeta Simtar: A Life on Two Planets*—the latest book from young adult author Annie Fox about an interspecies hybrid looking to find herself on a new planet.

A coming-of-age story that explores the meaning of birth family and found family, *Leeta Simtar* shows readers how breaking out of the past can help us figure out where we're going next.

Leeta Simtar isn't the only interspecies hybrid on the planet Fure, though she is, without a doubt, noticeably different from all the others. Not only is she impossibly tall and wildly unpredictable, she leads with her feelings, in contrast to everyone else's steady calm and logical demeanor. When Leeta's offended, she rages and attacks. When something touches her deeply, she gushes and weeps. No wonder she has always believed something's wrong with her, because clearly, she doesn't belong on Fure.

When Leeta suddenly finds out that what she's believed about herself is a lie, she is more than ready to discover the truth. Since no one on Fure is talking, her only hope is to go rogue and find her own answers. She travels forty light years in search of others like herself—assuming there *are* others.

With just eight days to unearth her origin story, Leeta follows clues that lead her across time and space hoping to find where she truly belongs. Readers of young adult science fiction, speculative/what-if fiction, and coming-of-age stories will connect to Leeta's intergalactic adventure. They'll be rooting for her to get what she needs, whether that means returning to Fure armed with the truth, staying in a far away place with her new found family, or finding home within her own heart.

**Now available in ebook, KU, print,
or audiobook wherever you buy books.
Order now, anniefox.com/leeta**

ACKNOWLEDGEMENTS

THERE ARE ALWAYS at least two stories within every novel. The first is the actual story that finally comes to life on the page after countless months of wrestling with characters and dialogue, plot lines and turning points, plus the massive task of defining and describing the physical details of a totally imaginary world.

The second story surrounding a novel is the unwritten tale of the people within the writer's circle who supported her during her years of obsession. If this were a film, the second story might be called *The Making of "The Little Things That Kill."* Since no film crew recorded all the kindnesses I received, it's my honor to give a well-deserved shoutout and heart-felt thank you to my people.

I'm eternally grateful to . . .

Mark Maletesta, a truly good guy and exceptional author coach. He never stopped believing that I could do this.

Rachel Abrams, my first editor, who provided needed encouragement and an essential roadmap forward when I was lost in an impenetrable fog.

Janna Balthasar, my second editor, who *got* and loved this story on a whole other level. She brought a unique, dramatic perspective to her review of the manuscript, which I incorporated to make the story so much stronger.

Liz Amini-Holmes, my sister-of-another mother and resource for all things Wiccan. Whenever I needed someone to hear a new chapter, she was always right there listening with an open and discerning mind.

Maria Marquis, our audiobook narrator, whose uncanny voice talent infused my fictional characters with all the emotional nuance of the living (and the dead).

Mark Wasserman, who sent me a NYT article a decade ago that served as the seed for this book and later was my first reader of the completed manuscript. Much later, he served as my eagle-eyed copy editor who knows more about comma placement than I ever will.

Phillipe Bosher, who I met in Germany at devcom. He wasn't just being polite when he said he'd love to read the manuscript, he actually meant it! His positive "review" was so heartfelt and appreciated.

Special thanks to my amazing, creative, funny, and oh so loving family. Each of you knows better than most, what it's like to live with a writer . . .

Fayette Fox, my daughter, whose novel *The Deception Artist*, began on NaNoWriMo, and showed me it could be done.

Ezra Fox, my son, whose novel *Unwrap My Heart* also began on NaNoWriMo.

Both of my kids challenged me to "Go for it Mom!" and I thank them for that, and so much more. (Oh no, I'm weeping.)

David Fox, my husband and partner in publishing and in life, who, for years, patiently listened to my reading aloud story revisions, always catching plot holes and whatever else needed catching. His attention to detail on page, website, video, audio, social media is unsurpassed. David has always done what he can to help me be my best. (Damn, weeping again!)

And to every person I've spoken with (over coffee, at conferences, while traveling), who asked me "What are you working on?" Then on hearing the brief synopsis of this quirky story, encouraged me with their positive responses. I thank you all.

ABOUT THE AUTHOR

WITH 30+ YEARS as an online teen adviser, Annie Fox has helped countless teens with their friendship and relationship challenges. She has written books for kids and adults, but now she writes for teens. *The Little Things That Kill: A Teen Friendship Afterlife Apology Tour* was her debut novel and *Leeta Simtar: A Life on Two Planets* is her latest.

Annie lives in the San Francisco Bay Area with her husband, David, and Gracie the Dog. When she's not hiking with them or baking killer sourdough bread and chocolate cakes, she continues to validate the experience of young people through Q&A, and writing YA fiction with the power to open hearts and minds.

Thanks for reading *The Little Things That Kill*. If you enjoyed this book, please consider leaving an honest review on the site where you bought the book or your favorite review website.

Sign up for Annie's newsletter at subscribe.anniefox.com
- Follow Annie on TikTok: @anniefoxauthor
- Follow Annie on Instagram: @annielfox
- Follow Annie on Facebook: @anniefox.author
- Follow Annie on BlueSky: @anniefox.com

www.ingramcontent.com/pod-product-compliance
Lightning Source LLC
Chambersburg PA
CBHW051245210726
48287CB00002B/359